The Sixth Hour

Holy Land Mysteries

Book I

S. E. Thomas

The Sixth Hour
Holy Land Mysteries Book I

A Novel

Published by The Dramatic Pen Press, L.L.C.

Lolo, Montana

ISBN-10: 0692366040
ISBN-13: 978-0692366042

To my son,
Dakota Aaron Thomas.
You are a delight to my heart and
you pour love and acceptance
on everyone around you.
Thank you for your desire
to be who God made you to be
and for inspiring this series.

Table of Contents

Map of First Century Jerusalem

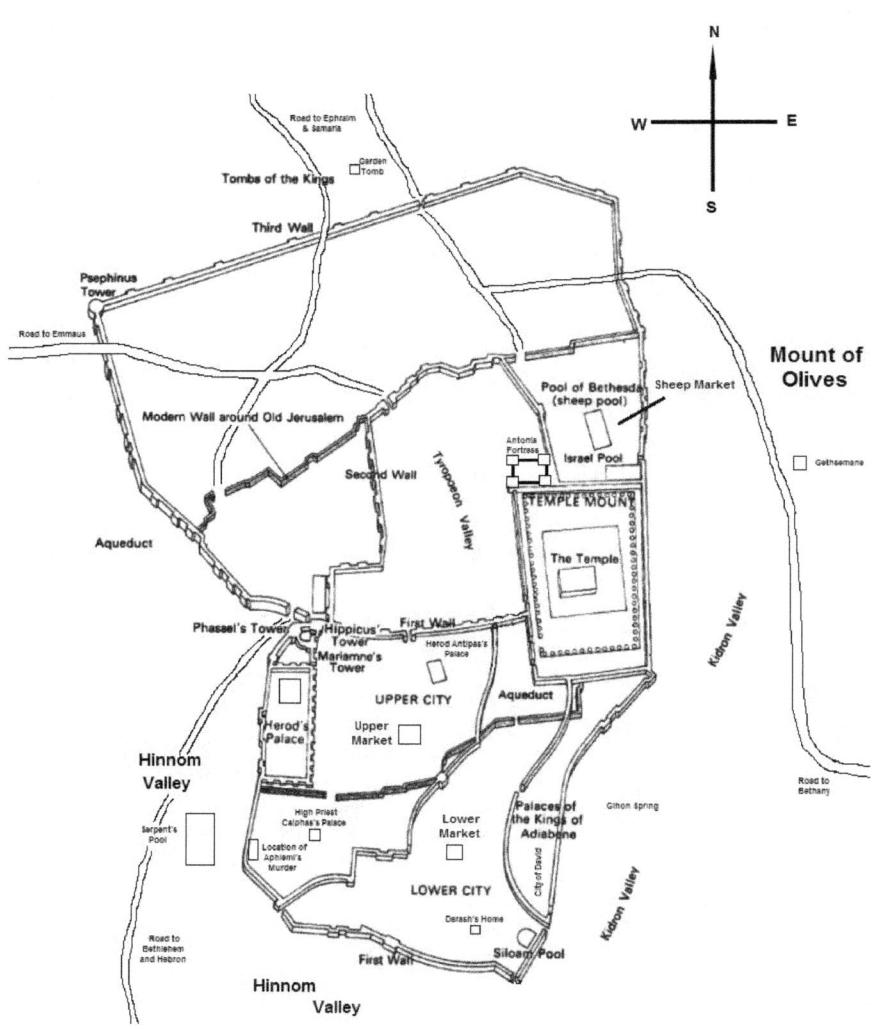

This illustration is an adaptation of an image
from the public domain.

Darash's Home

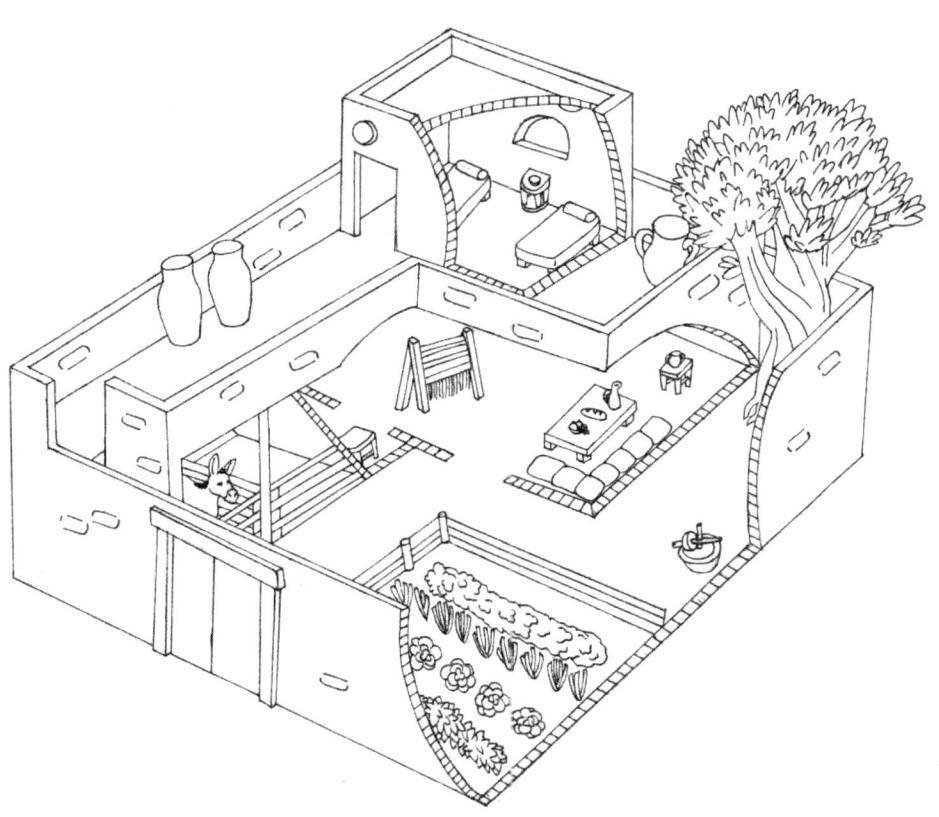

*It was now about the sixth hour,
and darkness came over the whole land
until the ninth hour,
for the sun stopped shining.*

~ Luke the Physician

Chapter One

In Darkest Hours

She waited in deep shadow beneath the city wall, as instructed. A young moon cast only the dimmest light, and Jerusalem lay sleeping. Her breath formed small, ghostly clouds in the cool night air. She pulled her cloak tighter.

Where is he?

She took three steps along the wall, keeping in shadow, but going far enough to look around the side of the nearest home toward the streets. No one. She turned, pacing in nervousness down the narrow alley between the wall and a row of homes. A few, slow steps later, she startled at the sound of a voice behind her.

"I told you to stay out of sight," he growled and pulled her back into deeper darkness.

"I feared you would not come," she said.

"Be quiet!" came his hoarse whisper, "and stay out of sight! You know my coming here could ruin me!"

He was angry, but she approached and took hold of his cloak at the shoulders. She drew her body closer to him, willing him to have patience with her—to remember the precious moments they had shared.

"But you came anyway... as you always do." She felt one arm slip around her and smiled even as tears stung her eyes. Surely he would find a way to make their impossible situation better. She sighed and snuggled closer. "What are we going to do?"

He said nothing.

"How are we going to tell them about us?" she persisted. "How will we tell them I am going to have your child?"

"We cannot."

"But your betrothal is not even confirmed yet."

"It was legalized this afternoon."

"What?" She glanced up, panic seizing her. "But surely, it is not too late?"

The thin light illuminated only the outline of his features. They were hard, unyielding. He seemed different... emotionless. His right arm, though encircling her, felt rigid and pitiless. The other hung at his side. Had he given up? Had he decided to distance himself from her—let her face this disgrace on her own?

"Tell me, my love," she said, her heart aching, "what shall we do? Should we simply slip away?" She felt her desire turn to desperation. "What are you going to do about this?"

She felt him stiffen. His arm gripped her in an embrace so tight and restricting, it caused pain.

"I am going to take care of the problem," he whispered in a voice not his own.

Terror and bewilderment gripped her. She tried to pull away but he held her fast. In the dim moonlight she watched his other arm rise above her head. He was holding something. A rock! She fought him, clawed at his neck and felt her fingers catch on something.

A crunching blow to the right side of her head sent a burst of light and pain through her body, trapping the scream in her throat. She collapsed and slid from his arms to the frozen ground. The last images she saw were two feet disappearing into the darkness, through wisps of steam rising from a gathering pool of blood.

סֶ לָ ה

He is going to destroy me.

Darash kept his eyes on the larger boy. Elias circled, looking for an opening—a weakness. It did not take long for Elias to find one. He charged, staff raised, and brought it down full force toward Darash's skull. Darash raised his staff in self-defense, stopping the other boy's assault, but staggered back as he did so. Elias did not relent in his attack. As Darash retreated, Elias advanced, swinging his staff again and again, clashing against Darash's raised stick and sending shock waves along its length. The smaller boy just tried to hold on.

Darash felt himself losing ground, pushed farther and farther from the center of the square toward a line of teenaged spectators. A few moved to avoid the onslaught. Others pushed him forward into the fray. He moved to the right, away from the crowd, defending his left side. But he was too late. Elias landed a swift blow against his unprotected right side, doubling him over in pain and shock. Darash dropped his right arm over the spot. Then, in a surprising display of speed and strength, Elias swung again, crying out as he did so. His staff landed in its heaviest blow yet against Darash's stick—now held aloft with only the left hand.

Darash lost his balance and dropped his weapon. Elias had him on his back in the dust. The smaller teenager gazed up at the butt of a staff now hovering directly before his eyes. Elias's lips turned up in a sneer. Though the spectators cheered and laughed, it was hardly a victory worth celebration. Elias moved his staff away from Darash's face and raised it once in gladiator fashion to the crowd to signal the fall of yet another opponent. He called for the next challenger, Darash already forgotten.

Darash picked himself up from the dusty surface of the hard-packed dirt and shook out the back of his tunic. He rubbed the spot on his side, knowing it would become a handsome bruise by morning. The goal of the game was to force one's opponent to the ground, not cause injury. Still, injuries did occur.

Darash kept his head down. His black, stringy hair fell before his eyes as he removed himself from the field of battle. Darash pushed through the row of teenage boys, avoiding glances of disgust or pity. He turned away from the girls who had escaped their mothers' charges long enough to sit with their friends on a low wall and watch the masculine display of strength. They whispered and snickered amongst themselves, bare feet and sandals dangling inches above the ground.

Darash gathered his robe from one of the boulders lining the edge of the open lot, which had once housed a collection of ramshackle homes. Once the edifices had been torn down and looted for spare materials, the town children claimed it for their own.

He moved away from the crowd.

"Darash!"

His shoulders sank at the sound. Darash turned and caught the eyes of his friend, Chaphash, a young man several years his senior.

"I did not know you were here," Darash stammered.

"Do not be discouraged, my friend! You will be victorious next time."

Darash nodded and tried to smile, but the pain in his side discouraged any hope he might have in future battles. He moved away, making a concerted effort to walk normally, holding his breath and fighting the temptation to hobble or grip his ribs.

"You only got what you deserved," his mother would say had she been witness to his foolish challenge of the stronger, more experienced stick-fighter. "What did you expect would happen? 'Pride goes before destruction.' Besides, you no longer have the luxury of playing in the streets like a child now that your father is dead. Our family's survival is your responsibility. You have far more important battles to face."

סֶלָה

Darash led his heavily-laden donkey through a narrow street toward the lower shuk, the southern market in Jerusalem's Lower City, called the agora, in Greek. One piece of leather had come loose from his sandals and flopped about as he walked. It must have snapped when he fell in this morning's dismal stick-fighting attempt. He sighed.

Imah will not be happy about this, he thought again of his mother, Revayah—Imah being the Hebrew word for mom. *Now I am going to have to tell her what I did... or come up with some other explanation.*

It was yom rishon, the first day of the week and the first day of the month of Kislev. Shabbat had just passed. He crossed paths with robed women, balancing clay jugs on their heads. Male pastry sellers sported baskets of honey-glazed cakes and sweetmeats, calling to passersby as they moved through the congested streets.

Mmmm.... That smells good.... Maybe I can tell her it just broke on its own....

The street of the Lower Market, lined with shops of dizzying variety, billowed with color and undulated with masses of bodies. Though always busy on the first day after Shabbat, today the heart and lifeblood of the city buzzed with new excitement. Despite the biting cold, the sounds of intense voices and rapid paces of sandals on stone filled the market streets and the small square where one of the city wells resided.

Or, that Nekoda stepped on it as we walked and tore it....

He led his small donkey, Nekoda, to the far end of the square. His little sister had named his father's donkey after the many spots on her rump. Darash entered a narrow alley—a far from ideal location for a merchant. Putting aside his worries, he turned his attention to the conversations around him as he began to unload. Nib'haz, a blind seller who occupied the place next to his, spoke to the man who supplied him with reeds for basket weaving.

"When did it happen?" Nib'haz asked in Aramaic.

"Sometime last night," came the reply. "It was very late. A woman who lives in the area found her body this morning."

"And no one saw anything?"

"I know not. I believe Pontius Pilate has been alerted. One of the Roman magistrates started asking questions."

"What a shame," Nib'haz sighed.

"Yes, I agree. It would be better if one of our people conducted the search. We know Yerusháyim far better than they."

"No! I mean, it is a shame that such a tragedy has occurred."

"Oh."

"What of her family?"

"They have been notified, of course. They are Greeks and live not far from where she was found. That is all I know."

"Odd that she was killed just after the close of Shabbat then, no?" Valad, a seller of goat milk and cheese, said from his usual place directly across the narrow alleyway.

"Are you suggesting that a Jew was to blame?" the reed seller asked, voice hard and elevated with indignation. "That he would keep Shabbat but then commit a murder? Ludicrous!"

"What a shame!" Nib'haz said again and hung his shaggy head, shaking it back and forth more vigorously than a sighted person might. "So young!" Nib'haz muttered something to himself under his breath.

"Yes.... Well, Nib'haz, do you want these reeds or not? It is the usual supply."

"Yes, yes, my friend," Nib'haz replied. He finished his transaction and turned to Darash. "Did you hear?"

"A girl was killed last night?" Darash asked, resorting to Hebrew.

"Yes! Head smashed in with a rock! Killed at only fifteen—same age as you. Such a waste!"

"Does anyone know why?"

"No.... Who would do such a thing? And in Yerushaláyim, too! What is this city coming to? It seems every couple of weeks someone is getting crucified or stabbed or— Oh! I am sorry, my young friend! For a moment I forgot who I was talking to! Please forgive a forgetful old man!"

"It is alright, Nib'haz. It has been eight months since my father's murder."

Nib'haz paused. "But it never gets easier to hear such things, does it?"

Darash shook his head, but then remembered who he was talking to. Being blind, Nib'haz could not see Darash's bodily response, so the boy responded aloud. "I suppose not."

Nib'haz nodded in the boy's general direction, but said no more and began counting baskets, broom handles, and reed mats with his fingertips. His unseeing eyes stared straight ahead.

Darash had no idea how long Nib'haz had occupied this spot. He only knew the old man was usually here before he arrived and left long after he packed up and went home. If Darash had to guess, Nib'haz was in his late sixties—possibly older—and lived alone on a steppe somewhere in the New City. Once, when Darash arrived unusually early, he had seen Nib'haz walking to market, carrying a bundle of baskets piled high on his back and shoulders. He knew the way so well he needed neither staff nor assistance. He simply called out, "Coming through!" and people knew to get out of his way.

"Nib'haz, why do you come all the way to the Lower City market when you live so much closer to the Sheep Market?" Darash had once asked.

"They already have enough blind people there," he answered, as if everyone should understand this.

Nib'haz's unkempt mane of hair had long since grayed and now bore streaks of white. Three teeth had gone missing in front. Sharp, aquiline features accentuated eyes white with cataracts. Though thin, he was not frail, and, though poor, he always made certain to clean his cloak and keep it free of holes. Like his person, he kept his spot on the square neat and orderly, making sure each item was in its proper place, murmuring to himself as he did so, as was his custom.

Darash unloaded his balance, weights, and wares—sacks of grain, wool, lentils—even bitumen. He also sold weapons, jewelry, metal tools, and anything else he could get his hands on. He tried to avoid selling baskets and reed items, however, as a courtesy to Nib'haz.

Today Darash hoped to sell a decorative, Egyptian cedar box he had gotten off a traveler who wanted to lighten his load. It was old and surprisingly heavy, but an unusual item due to its origin and intricate beryl, carnelian, and mother-of-pearl inlay. It bore a cracked but still beautiful depiction of a man pushing a reed boat on the Nile amongst crocodiles and hippos—both considered sacred beasts—surrounded by various flora. The sides and top bore simpler designs of flowers, reeds, charmed river animals, and symbols he did not understand.

Examining the artwork made him think of life as both dangerous and magical. Neither of these ideas appealed to Darash. He did not believe in magic, and danger frightened him. His mother, of course, would have loved the small chest for both its beauty and price. So Darash had made sure to hide it from her on the roof under some bags and a blanket. He needed it to fetch a good price.

"Feh! Here comes Pertho," Valad said as Darash positioned the box in a prominent position in the center of his mat.

"I know," Nib'haz replied. "I could sense his evil from here."

Despite the older man's blindness, he noticed a great deal. Nib'haz could tell if his customer carried Roman gold, the silver coins of Tyre, the bronze, less valuable coins of Judea, or some combination of the three. He could identify his regulars simply by the sound of their sandals on the stones, catch snippets of conversations from far away, and tell a truthful man from a dishonest one by the tone of his voice and his choice of words. He often knew where a person was from simply by the smell of their garments. A pungent, sweet-sour aroma, Nib'haz claimed, spoke of the vineyards that dotted the steppes and hillsides surrounding the city. A dry, musty smell spoke of the fields and tall grasses of the Negev. The smell of sheep differed from the smell of cattle or of donkeys and so on.

"You could smell him, you mean," Valad laughed.

"Sometimes it is difficult to smell anything beyond you."

"What? What are you saying, old man? I have no smell!"

"You smell of goats and sour milk."

"That is only because I make cheese from goat milk! Everyone knows this!"

"True, but you most certainly have a smell. And a strong one. But sometimes I also get a hint of fig juice from your direction."

"So I like figs. There is no harm in this. And fig is a very pleasant smell."

"True. Unfortunately, it cannot make up for the smell of goat, which is not."

"You blind, old—!"

"Shhh!" Darash cut in. "Pertho is looking this way."

Valad changed the subject, immediately forgetting his irritation with his friend. "I would not be surprised if it was he who killed that poor girl last night. It would not be the first time a woman died at his hands."

"What?" Darash asked.

"Ah, young one," Nib'haz sighed. "There is much that goes on in this world that is best you never learn."

"Who did he kill?" Darash insisted.

"Well, no one could prove it, but..."

"His wife," Valad interrupted. "Five years ago. He beat her for years—her, the servants, the animals. Everyone knew it, but no one could do anything. He claimed she died from an illness, but everyone knew it was from her injuries."

"Silence! Finish setting up," Nib'haz ordered. "He is coming."

By observing Nib'haz conduct business for the better part of a year, Darash had learned a great deal about the powers of observation but he was still amazed at the older man's mastery of his senses. Darash hoped to learn his mentor's skill with sound and smell, and eventually apply these same concepts to what he saw. Unfortunately, at the moment he saw a large, bald, harsh-looking man approaching.

Pertho was known to Darash and, indeed, to most of Jerusalem, for his filth as much as for his cruelty. In a city full of Adonai's People, who obsessed about cleanliness in every facet of personal and religious life, Pertho stood out like an ugly, penetrating stain—a blemish that could not be removed. A noxious stench followed him like a shadow which, by itself, would have made him unwelcome in every Jewish shop in the city, and most others as well. However, his overpowering aroma came secondary to his bad temper and an uncanny ability to avoid legal prosecution.

Today, a young Hebrew girl of about eleven or twelve followed the hulking Greek, struggling to keep up under a large sack. The child kept her head down. Stringy brown hair spilled about her face, hiding her features. Boney arms and legs protruded from a smock that looked more like a rag than a garment. The sight of this girl made Darash think of his own little sister, Tsarah, now eight, and he seethed.

"Who is that girl following him?" Darash whispered to Nib'haz.

"Is there a girl? ….Ah! I have heard he had a young, Jewish slave, but she is rarely seen."

"How did a man like that obtain a Jewess for a slave?"

"Her father was his bondsman," Valad interrupted, speaking quickly and keeping one eye on the rapidly approaching man. Pertho now headed directly toward Darash, eyes fixed on the Egyptian box. "She was born into her position and, when her father died, she had no protector."

"But what of her mother?"

"No one knows," Valad said under his breath, for at that moment Pertho reached them.

Darash swallowed and sat back on his haunches, trying to avoid staring in the direction of the staggering child and the muscular, intimidating man. Pertho grabbed the box, knocking over a few other items in the process.

"Ah! Egyptian, I see!" he declared in Greek, more loudly than was necessary for such a sparsely populated corner. He spoke in Aramaic, the common trade language. "I will give you two denarii for it." Without waiting for a response, he shouted at his servant girl, "Amah, come take this box!"

The child called merely *amah*, female slave, hobbled forward. She already carried more than she could reasonably manage. When she glanced up, Darash noticed a large bruise on her left cheek and a cut above her right eye. As if by instinct, he raised a hand in protest.

"I will take no less than eight denarii for this box," he said with a confidence that surprised both Pertho and himself.

Nib'haz's head turned slightly toward Darash. Valad starred unblinking.

Pertho's surprise became anger. "Eight denarii? You must be mad! I offered you two days' wages… more than adequate payment for this beat up, Egyptian castoff!"

Darash swallowed again, but squared his jaw with resolve. With a hand, he brushed the hair out of his eyes and said, "It is quite obvious many weeks of work went into the construction of this box. Eight denarii is like giving it away for free. But, since you like it so much, I will take seven."

Pertho glowered at the scrawny, young man. "This box is old, cracked, and scuffed up! ...I will give you five denarii, and you will consider yourself lucky!" He began digging into his money pouch.

Five denarii was more than twice what Darash had paid but there was nothing about this man he liked.

"Egypt is far away," he said, hoping his voice sounded calm and steady. "If you think you will find another box like it, feel free to take your five denarii and look."

The other merchants and customers in the area ceased their bargaining and watched to see how this encounter would end. Pertho stopped digging and eyed Darash, taking in every detail of the youth's skinny frame—from his worn, broken sandals and faded brown cloak to the straight, dusty, black hair and dark eyes.

Darash met his gaze but tried to adopt a relaxed, uncaring expression, despite the fear growing inside. For what seemed an eternity, Pertho tried to stare him down, but Darash filled his thoughts with the little amah's bruised face.

A slow smile spread across Pertho's lips, never reaching his eyes. "You are far too young to be playing such games," he began and paused. Then, pulling seven denarii from his pouch, he added as if to the crowd, "But I will humor the child... this time." Then he turned to his servant. "Amah!" he cried, holding the box out to her.

Darash leapt up. "Let me help you carry the box back to your home," he offered. Without waiting for an agreement from Pertho, he took the box from Pertho's hands and glanced back at Nib'haz, who seemed transfixed by the course of events. "Nib'haz?"

"Huh? Oh, yes, yes, of course! I will take charge of your things while you are gone," he said.

Darash followed Pertho and the slave girl back toward the main square.

"You are a fool to leave your belongings in the care of a blind man," Pertho barked. "And here I almost thought you were clever."

"Nib'haz sees more than most," Darash replied.

Pertho only grunted.

Darash followed closely, watching the girl. Despite her despondence and unhealthy appearance, she was a beautiful little thing. He could only imagine what a horrible life she led and wished there was something more he could do for her. Amah teetered under her load, and he almost offered to carry hers as well, but feared she might suffer reprisal for the kindness.

They left the shuk and headed down the same street Darash would later take home, but two streets later they turned left and angled through a dusty path, entering a predominantly Greek neighborhood.

Even before seeing the source, the stench of death accosted Darash's nostrils. It emanated from the carcass of a bloated dog on the side of the road, evidently trampled by a horse and left to decay in the sun. Flies swarmed loudly above it, and maggots crawled amidst the red-brown, rotting flesh. Darash's stomach lurched.

Do Greeks not care about the revolting odors seeping into their homes at all hours of the day and night? Or about the health of their children? Such a thing would never happen in a Jewish neighborhood!

Darash felt the familiar seething in his chest against this entire race of filthy, drunken, wife-murdering idolaters. Normally, a Jew would not even venture into this section of the city, let alone go to the home of a foreigner. Of course, that meant it was unlikely Darash would be seen here by anyone who would recognize him.

They came upon a small, run-down home. Though the dwelling may have been nice at one time, years of neglect showed in the chipped brick edges, the tattered remains of a roof-top lean-to, and the broken fencing surrounding a small, abandoned sheep pen. Shards of broken pottery lay strewn about the path and the long dead and overgrown garden. Weeds partially hid the unusually large rubbish heap leaning against the southern wall. Filled with everything from chicken bones and rotting food to human excrement, it welcomed all who ventured near with a putrefying stench that rivaled that of the dead dog.

Loathing rose in his chest, darkening his eyes and hardening his features. Yet, despite his repulsion at witnessing this painfully unclean home, his greatest feelings of loathing came from seeing a filthy Greek owning and abusing one of the People.

Darash slowed, finding it difficult to will himself any closer, but about that time Pertho turned and snatched the box from his hands. Evidently the man had no intention of inviting the youngster any nearer, which suited Darash perfectly. Without another word Pertho headed inside, Amah following closely. Darash tried to catch the child's eye to offer her a smile, but she never glanced his way.

Chapter Two

A City at His Feet

Darash was surprised to hear his name as he returned to the square. Several shoppers looked up as he passed and snickered at some private joke. A few, who had never before acknowledged him, now stared and nodded in his direction.

"What is going on?" he whispered to Nib'haz in Hebrew as he again planted himself on the ground and brought a knee up.

"No one has bested Pertho in a sale before," Nib'haz said with a chuckle.

Valad laughed as well. "I never would have believed it."

"Seven denarii was a fair price," Darash defended himself, unsure how to respond to the unexpected merriment. He had never been one to crave the attention of others, much preferring to observe.

"Fair?" Valad laughed aloud. "Perhaps... perhaps... But I happen to know you paid only two—and—" he added with one finger held aloft and waited to make sure he had the attention of all. "There was a large crack in the bottom! I could almost put my finger in it!"

"That is not true!"

But they merely laughed, and several others joined the fun.

There had been a crack in the bottom but only a small one, and Pertho had noticed the defects before he bought it. Surely the buyer expected used items to have their share of imperfections. Darash glanced at Nib'haz, worried his older mentor would be disappointed in him, but Nib'haz smiled broadly.

"That is alright," Valad said in a consoling manner. "About time Pertho got some of his own back!" Others nodded in agreement. "He has cheated me so often I refuse to sell to him anymore!"

"I saw you sell him a large block of cheese just the other day," a woman said, "and for half what you could have gotten for it elsewhere."

"Well..." Valad began, "I mean, I was thinking of refusing to sell to him anymore."

That sent up another round of raucous laughter. All the merchants knew Pertho's powers of persuasion. His was a cruelty not easily contained, and no one wanted a piece of it.

"Seven days' wages in less than four minutes," Nib'haz sighed happily, shaking his head. "And from Pertho, too! You may become a successful merchant after all!"

Darash ventured a smile.

סֶ לָ ה

Darash's stomach knotted and whined in hunger. His mother and sister would have already eaten by now, but perhaps they saved him a bowl. He imagined the stone ledge behind their fire pit and a bowl of lentil stew, seasoned with onions and black cumin with a delicious-smelling steam rising from its center. His stomach growled again at the thought. But then he remembered something else. Ever since their house servant, Huldah, had left and Revayah had taken over the cooking, the meals in their home had been far from delicious.

His stomach growled a third time, sounding like a heavy door creaking on iron hinges.

Well, at least it will be filling.

Darash quickly finished tying his baskets and bags to the back of Nekoda. Little else had sold that day, but a profit of five denarii was more than enough to get them through the week. Mother would be pleased.

"I shall see you in the morning, Nib'haz," he said in a tired voice.

"Yes, young one. Yes." Nib'haz remained, counting his earnings. Neat piles of baskets crowded all around him—piles that never decreased in size, since he spent the time between sales weaving more.

Darash summoned Nekoda to action with a click of his tongue and led her back through the shuk toward home. As Darash passed the city well, which marked the center of the Lower Market, Nekoda turned her head toward the water source and came to an abrupt stop. She kicked her head back, tugging against the rope. Darash sighed and relented, allowing his stubborn companion a quick drink from the stone trough that jutted from the well.

As he waited, he noticed Nakal and Hathal, his father's former business associates, standing not six arm-lengths away in a group of men. Darash's shoulders sank. These men had caused him nothing but trouble since his father's passing, and Nakal was also Elias's uncle—another reason to avoid them. No doubt Elias bragged to his uncle about his many victories. Darash jerked on his Nekoda's rope. She shook her mane at him, yanked back, and continued drinking.

When Darash took over his father's merchant business eight months ago, Nakal and Hathal had forced him out. Now Darash occupied one of the least visible places in the Lower Market, though his father, Tuwr, had occupied one of the most prominent. Tuwr had shared a large shop in the Upper Market with these men, who now stood with their backs to him.

Upon Tuwr's death, these men insisted he pay his father's debt. They claimed Tuwr owed them forty shekels—four months' wages. They had proved Tuwr's debt with a scrawled message bearing a suspicious-looking mark of Tuwr and the testimony from a third witness who disappeared from the city the following day. Due to his youth—only fourteen at the time—and lack of powerful contacts, Darash had no recourse but to agree to their demands. Since he could not pay, they took ownership of Tuwr's portion of the shop and rented it out to another man for a profitable fee.

Darash often went over the problem in his mind, considering it from every angle, but getting no closer to an answer.

The magistrate believed them.... But surely, Abba would not have promised me the shop if he had accrued such a debt.

"This will all be yours one day, my son," his father had told him on his thirteenth birthday.

The week of Darash's thirteenth birthday, they went to the synagogue on Shabbat to hear the reading of the Torah. That meeting had been special. After the regular readings, the prayers, and the teachings, the Rabbi called him and his father to the front of the congregation. Tuwr placed his thick, heavy arm around Darash's scrawny shoulders and introduced him to those in attendance. Of course, everyone knew him already, but that made no difference. His father now introduced him before them for the first time as a man.

Despite that he had been preparing for this an entire year, Darash still felt nervous. But then he remembered his father's words of that morning. "Do not hang your head, as you so often do. Stand up straight. Look them in the eye. You are a man now and must take your place among men. From this day forward, the vows you make are legally binding. You can stand in front of the People and read from the Torah. You can take your rightful place in all religious and political life. You can even get married! But, best of all, I am no longer responsible for all of your nonsense." With that, he laughed and tussled Darash's hair, already forgetting that grown men do not get their hair tussled.

Darash smiled.

So, on that special Shabbat, Darash looked into the faces of the other Hebrew men. He was surprised to find them less intimidating than he had imagined, for they nodded in agreement as Abba and the Rabbi took turns saying the blessings over him.

Even before the ceremony, a few days earlier on the actual thirteenth anniversary of his birth, Tuwr had pulled him aside and said, "Now that you are a man, you must learn how to travel this city alone. I know you are familiar with the Lower City, where we live, and the Temple Mount, but I fear you would get lost if I sent you to the Upper Market or the Sheep Market alone. It is time you learned those roads."

"I know how to get to the Upper Market, Abba," Darash protested.

"Do you, now?"

"Of course! I go there all the time."

"Then lead the way!"

The Upper Market, located in the Upper City, provided the ideal location for a merchant or shopkeeper. The Upper City occupied the southwestern corner of Jerusalem and had been walled in by Herod the Great. It topped Mount Zion and its market was frequented not only by Jerusalem's elite, who lived nearby, and the many travelers and dignitaries who entered Jerusalem's gates, but also by royalty. Herod's palace and theatre, as well as the Hasmonean palace, graced its wider streets, along with their adjacent swimming pools, baths, orchards, and ornamental gardens. These roads passed grand, whitewashed stone homes, tiled porticos, and the scandalous bathhouses frequented by the Romans. To the south lay the Essene Quarter. High Priest Caiaphas resided there. Less formal meetings of the Sanhedrin, the Jewish court, were sometimes held on his extensive properties.

But getting there from the Lower City, despite that the two bordered one another, proved much more difficult than one might expect. As Jerusalem had been built amidst the mountains, travelers had to contend with frequent changes in the levels of terrain. Darash skillfully led his father through one narrow street after another, weaving between pedestrians and the stock animals driven by their owners. A high, rocky escarpment separated the Upper City from the Lower City and, unless one was ready for a steep climb of several stories' height, travelers from one section of the city to the other found it necessary to go out of their way to locate the road connecting the two levels.

"Here it is," Darash said in triumph, and Tuwr nodded to his partner, Hathal, who then tended the shop.

"Well done, my son!" Tuwr said, putting a hand on his shoulder. He bent to look Darash in the eyes—but only slightly, for Tuwr was not a tall man and Darash was quickly gaining on him. "Now. Take me to the Sheep Market. Can you do that as well?"

Darash thought a moment. "I know one must travel north..." he scanned the streets. "That way."

"Very well! Let us go!"

The terrain sloped down once again as they traveled north. They passed through a large gate in the wall northeast of Herod's Palace that let them out into the Second Quarter—once a rocky wilderness but now part of the city itself. A fair number of Greeks had taken up residence here, as well as Romans—mostly military, due to its proximity to the Roman fortress.

Shortly after passing through a second gate and entering the New City, Darash stopped to think, and his father waited for him to get his bearings. Darash spotted one of the towers of the Antonia Fortress, and forged ahead.

The Antonia Fortress, the focal point of the New City—the region of territory—was now being enclosed by Herod Agrippa's ongoing construction of a thick city wall. The fortress was a massive, foreboding, stone structure with oversized towers at each corner. Roman governor, Pontius Pilate resided here, and no end of Roman sentries, centurions, and members of the Praetorian Guard streamed from its wide gates. This final section of Jerusalem, encompassing the northern slopes, boasted the most pools and the monument of King Alexander Janneus. The Pool of Bethesda had been locally renamed The Sheep Pools, due to their proximity to the Sheep Gate. A large market area—the Sheep Market— surrounded the waters, and this was the very market which Darash now sought.

"Is that it over there?" Darash asked, unable to see past the buildings, but hearing the noise of distant voices and livestock.

"Very good! You are using more than just your eyesight to find your way!"

"You have brought me here before. I remember this place," Darash said as they rounded a corner and took in the sight. Colorful booths dressed in reds, blues, and yellows enticed the eye, and exotic smells filled the air. The sounds of haggling, loudly shouted advertisements, and animals bleating and braying filled Darash with a sense of awe and excitement.

This will be my world.

"I come here twice a week, sometimes more," Abba said, leading him, one hand on his back. The closer they got to the noise, the closer he bent toward Darash's ear. "The animal pens are all set up in that area over there," he pointed to a vast array of fences, posts, and ropes. Unable to make out where one pen ended and another started, it seemed to Darash that animals of all varieties mingled together in a large, tangled, beautiful mess. Donkeys, camels, horses, emus, and, of course, sheep of every variety paced about nervously, lazed in the sun, or tugged impatiently at their restraints.

"That is where I purchased Nekoda," Tuwr said. "The seller wanted twice what I was willing to pay! But I succeeded at last!"

"You did well, Abba. She has been a good donkey."

"Yes, I suppose so… as donkeys go, anyway." Tuwr's free hand moved to his left, upper thigh—a spot he had once been roughly kicked by their good donkey. He rubbed it without realizing what he did, but Darash snickered.

They entered the Sheep Market and saw the Sheep Pools at the center of the bustling world of commerce. The waters composed one large, rectangular pool with a dam and wide walkway built down the center, separating them into two halves. Five covered colonnades surrounded the pools. The market milled with activity, but the noise and busyness came to a halt at the edge of the waters. This was not for lack of bodies. People of all ages, genders, and ethnicity surrounded the manmade ponds and littered the center walkway. Despite the people's obvious differences, all shared something in common. Some deformity or illness afflicted them all. They sat with blank faces, staring at the waters, waiting… always waiting.

"Have you ever heard of anyone being healed in these pools, Abba?" Darash asked.

"Oh, yes. There are stories," he responded. "I heard of a man whose beloved wife died. But, before she died, she gave him a son. This man loved his son more than life itself—just as I love you. But, tragically, when the boy was about ten years old, he ran out into the street and was trampled by a Roman horse and chariot. The man wept bitterly, for the accident had left his son paralyzed in both legs. The Roman soldier did not even send for a doctor, but continued on his way."

"How awful!"

"Yes, it was. But the father brought his son to this very spot, to the Pool of Bethesda." Tuwr motioned toward the large, flat tiles that surrounded the water's edge and the people sprawled there. "They sat here for days, weeks, months, waiting for a miracle."

"What miracle, Abba?"

"They waited for the troubling of the waters."

"What does that mean?"

"Darash, life is very hard. It is especially hard for the Jew. We must learn to deal with it the best we can. But, from time to time, Adonai takes pity on his People. When He sees great suffering coupled with great faith, it is said that Adonai will sometimes send His angel to this pool. The angel will touch the waters and make them capable of healing any variety of ailments."

"What does this angel look like?" Darash asked, voice full of amazement.

"No one can see the angel," his father answered, "but they can see the ripples in the water made by the angel's hand."

Darash's eyes opened wider as his mind filled with understanding. "So that is why the people sit here and watch the waters."

"Precisely, my son!" Tuwr squeezed Darash's shoulder. "They watch and wait, afraid to take their eyes from the water. Because, when the waters stir, that means the angel is present and they can be healed. The first person who climbs into the water after the angel touches it will be healed."

"Just the first person, Abba?"

Tuwr nodded.

"Why not all of them?"

"As I said, we Jews suffer greatly. And, our suffering reminds us that we need Adonai. If everyone could be healed, we might forget that."

Darash gazed on the people. An elderly man, eyes completely white with blindness, sat near a younger man, most likely his son. The son watched the waters as the father reclined against a stone pillar, listening to the sounds of the market. A woman dressed in a torn robe sat with her daughter—a child of perhaps six years old—whose left leg was badly twisted. A woman on the other side of the pools leaned on a stick, her upper back bulging severely beneath her cloak. Some lay on mats, their heads on the laps of a family member. Some sat in heaps of ragged clothing, waiting and watching intently for their miracle. Others took some time off from their staring to hobble about the square and beg prutot—small, Hebrew, copper coins—off the shoppers.

"Then suffering is a good thing, Abba," he stated.

"Of course not!"

Darash, confused, looked away from the people and into his father's eyes.

"Whatever gave you that idea? Suffering is a terrible thing. Avoid it when you can. Come, I will buy you a present for this special birthday. Let us find something here you would like."

Tuwr and Darash walked the length of the market, perusing the shops, booths, and pallets of goods spread out on the ground, searching for the perfect gift.

"So what happened to the boy, Abba?"

"What boy?"

"The boy in your story. The one whose legs were crushed by a horse and chariot?"

"Did I not say?"

Darash shook his head.

"Ah, well, he was healed, of course." Tuwr looked to his left and then reached beyond a stack of clay bowls. "Here, what do you think of this one?"

He pulled out a new, beautifully crafted set of weights and measures. The balance was large and made of bronze, and each perfectly rounded stone weight bore the appropriate symbol carved into one side.

"They are too expensive, Abba," Darash protested. "I can just use yours."

"No, my son. You are a man now and must have a good set of your own."

Darash smiled broadly as the seller wrapped the brilliantly polished scales in a piece of white linen and placed them in his hands. Tuwr haggled some, but not nearly as much as usual. Still, he paid the man cheerfully and slapped Darash on the back with pride.

"Thank you, Abba," Darash said, cradling his gift and hardly able to believe his good fortune or his father's extravagance.

"It gives me joy to do this for you," Tuwr said. "Come, it is time we headed back home. You will lead us again, but this time let us go by a different route."

Directly south of the Sheep Market and Pool of Bethesda lay the Temple Mount, topped by the magnificent Holy Temple—the focal point of Jewish existence, both past and present. Despite that Herod the Great had been a senselessly cruel man, none could deny his visionary skill and near obsessive attention to detail in whatever building project he undertook. When he decided to improve and expand the Hebrew Temple, he did so with meticulous precision, building new portions like a shell, one section at a time, and then dismantling the older sections. He spared no expense and insisted that his laborers create a masterpiece worthy of every Hebrew religious tradition and ritual so no one could complain.

"This way," Darash said, and his father followed with a nod.

They traveled south between buildings, dodging crowds of people coming and going from the market area. They passed the large Pool of Israel to their left and walked through the Sheep Gate into the Temple grounds. A sense of reverence and awe descended on Darash as they neared the enormous, brilliant white building with gold accents. Here the Holy One of Israel dwelled. Seeing the Temple reminded Darash of their earlier conversation near the pools.

"Abba," he said, "who was the man whose son was healed at the Pool of Bethesda?"

"I know not. It is an old story."

"Have you heard of anyone else who has been healed by the angel?"

"Let me see… I think there was a woman healed there once. She had been born without the ability to hear. …And some tell of a man who had been healed of blindness. There are always stories."

"Do you believe them?"

Tuwr took a little time to respond. Whether it was because he was thinking or simply trying to avoid a noisy group of women walking toward them, Darash could not tell.

"I believe miracles have happened in the past," he said at last.

"But not today?"

Again, Tuwr took a while to respond. This time Darash knew it was because he struggled to find the answer.

"I have heard stories of miracles happening today," he said at last. "But I am not sure what they mean. There is a man who people say has been healing the sick, making the lame walk again, and even raising people from the dead."

"Who is this man, Abba?" Darash's voice rose in immediate interest.

"He is called Yeshua, but do not tell your mother I mentioned him to you."

"Why not?"

"She believes he practices witchcraft in order to draw the People away from the true religion."

"Is that what you think, Abba?"

Tuwr paused again. "I do not know. It is possible."

They now neared the southern end of the Temple Mount, having traveled along its eastern edge, just inside the outer wall of Jerusalem that overlooked the Kidron Valley. They passed through the Huldah Gates and down an expanse of stone steps from the Temple Mount into the City of David.

Centuries ago, the City of David had been built atop the Eastern Hill, a southern extension of Mount Moriah. This part of Jerusalem formed a narrow section of both historic and modern buildings, running along the southeast corner. Here King David had established his capitol, built his palace, and ruled the Hebrew people under Adonai's blessing and authority. One could still visit the tombs of the long-dead kings, peruse the rose gardens, or take a dip in the Pool of Siloam, a large pool fed intermittently by the Gihon Spring and the reason for Jerusalem's continued existence.

Aside from these reminders of Hebraic history and blessing, the location had since been transformed to a region of palaces for foreign royalty. Here, Queen Helena of Adiabene, a member of the Assyrian royal family, had built palaces for herself and her sons after she converted to Judaism three years ago. Despite her foreign origins, the Jewish people knew her as the generous Heleni HaMalka, for her large donations to the Temple.

As Darash led his father through these ancient, but meticulously cleaned, streets and passed massive, modern constructions, he prodded for more information.

"Have you seen the man Yeshua perform any miracles, Abba?"

"I have seen some strange things, yes." Tuwr scratched his chin.

"What was it?"

"You must promise not to mention this to your mother," Tuwr said as he guided his son across the street after four soldiers on horseback passed by. "She would not be happy I told you."

"I promise."

"As you know, I go to the Sheep Market at least twice a week to trade there. Many travelers passing through Yerushaláyim stop there, but do not make it to the other markets. So one day I was haggling with a caravan driver over some decorative pottery from Susa. It was a spouted jar with some beautiful designs in square patterns on the side. I remember it well. It fetched me a good price from a wealthy Sadducee customer."

Darash waited patiently, knowing well his father's propensity to get side-tracked by his passion for the intricacies of his business.

"I had just concluded the transaction when I witnessed the most amazing thing I have ever seen before or since. As I passed by the pools, I overheard a man questioning one of the cripples. He spoke with a funny, Nazarene accent, saying, 'How long have you lacked the use of your legs?' The man responded that he had been an invalid for 38 years—a very long time, indeed. I knew this to be true. The man has occupied that same place for as long as I have been coming to market— since I was a small child. The stranger questioned the invalid again, 'Do you want to get well?' Some of us laughed at that. Of course the man wanted to get well! Why else did he spend his days by the healing waters?

"The man answered in the affirmative, but then said, 'Sir, I have no one to help me into the pool when the water is stirred. While I am trying to get in, someone else goes down ahead of me.'"

Tuwr stopped speaking, staring not at the path ahead, but into the recesses of his memory.

"So what happened?" Darash prompted.

"I keep going over it and over it in my mind," Tuwr responded. "The Nazarene just looked at the cripple and said, 'Get up! Pick up your mat and walk.' I actually saw the man's legs transform from thin and sickly to strong and healthy before my eyes. They straightened out and filled out with flesh and muscle and color. The man was cured! As we all watched, unable to believe our own eyes, he pushed himself up on two legs, picked up his mat, and walked over to where Yeshua stood."

"Then what happened, Abba?"

"Well, as you can imagine, the crowd began to talk loudly in amazement at what they had seen. I, too, could not contain my astonishment. But some in the crowd approached the man who had been healed and chastised him for carrying his mat. 'It is Shabbat,' they said. 'The law forbids you to carry your mat.'"

"It was Shabbat?" Darash asked in astonishment. "But is it not forbidden to buy and sell on Shabbat?"

Tuwr colored, then sputtered, "Do not fret about it. I was not doing business with a Jew. And, since they do not honor Shabbat, I was causing no one else to sin…. So it is less of a problem… but do not mention that to your mother, either."

"Yes, Abba."

Darash and his father passed through yet another gate out of the City of David and into the Lower City to the west. They passed through the Tyropoeon Valley, their legs now tiring from their long day's trek up and down the mountainous terrain that made up Jerusalem. This region separated Mount Zion from Mount Moriah and emptied out into the Hinnom Valley to the south. Darash and his family lived in the Lower City, an area of densely packed buildings. Herod the Great had built his hippodrome in the northeast corner, where wealthy infidels enjoyed horse and chariot races, but most of the Lower City served as a residential area.

"What did the Jews do to the man Yeshua healed?" Darash asked.

"They questioned him about what had happened, and the man told them the story we had all witnessed. They then asked, 'Who is this fellow who told you to pick it up and walk?' But neither the man nor any of us knew who the Nazarene was and, when we looked for him, he had disappeared into the crowd."

As their home came into sight, Tuwr slowed and stopped Darash with a hand on his shoulder. He bent to look in his son's eyes. "Now remember, not a word about Yeshua or my Shabbat dealings to your mother. Let us not ruin your special day. Are we agreed?"

"Of course, Abba."

"Very good." Tuwr paused, still looking into his son's eyes. He softened for a moment and said, "I am very proud of you, my son. You have proven to me that you know this city far better than I thought. You have a good memory, a sharp eye, and a quick mind. These are most important for any merchant. This whole city is laid out before you. Go forth and conquer it!"

Chapter Three

Murders and Miracles

Seeing his enemies raised a flame of anger in his chest. Darash could wait no longer. He pulled at Nekoda's rope, willing her to cooperate. She was enjoying her long drink and knew she was stronger than her spindly youth. A tugging match ensued, from which Darash knew not how to escape. The battle began to draw attention—the last thing he wanted. Now, if he let go, his foolish donkey would run off and he would have to catch her.

"Ah," Nakal said turning to look. The short, round-bellied man had wide-set eyes, a bulbous nose and a thick beard, which he allowed to grow so far down his neck that he looked like an overfed wolf. "It is Darash, son of Tuwr."

"Indeed, it is," Hathal said slowly, eyes lighting up with interest. Hathal stood nearly head and shoulders above his bantam friend. He had small eyes, a thin, patchy beard, and a receding and graying hairline. "Looks as though he is having a disagreement with his friend."

They laughed as Darash tried to gain control over his stubborn beast. As the circle of men amused themselves with his predicament, Darash managed to regain Nekoda's cooperation by loosening his tension on the rope and placing a hand on her snout.

"We heard how you cheated Pertho today," Nakal called, walking over with Hathal, interrupting Darash's attempt to leave. The other men dispersed, heading off into the gathering darkness. Darash envied them.

"I cheated no one," Darash answered, feeling a surge of anger but forcing himself to sound bored with their accusations.

"Oh, do not worry about us!" Hathal said in mock self-defense. "We think he got exactly what he deserved. He is a wicked man."

"Very wicked," his friend agreed.

They paused and, assuming they were finished, Darash turned to go.

"I suppose you think you are very clever," Nakal said. Despite his wolfish appearance, he had an unusually high voice for a man. As a child, Darash had always found it amusing. Now it grated on his nerves.

Darash sighed. His stomach growled. He eyed them for a moment, thinking. Either he could deny his cleverness which would no doubt elicit a great many patronizing comments from them, or he could agree, making himself a fool. He decided to sidestep the issue entirely.

"Like all the merchants here, I try to get the best deal I can for every item I sell. It is no more and no less than you yourselves do. Shalom to you." Again he turned to go.

"So you think you are like us? You think you are a good enough merchant to sit in your father's old place without having to earn it?" Hathal accused, his venom plain. He looked down at his friend and spoke with large hand gestures, "Nakal, did we not explain to him how every new businessman starts out at the outskirts and slowly earns his way to places of prominence? Unless one inherits that place from his father and is able to pay for it—which the boy cannot—everyone must start at the bottom! Why does this young fool not understand? He still thinks he deserves a place in our shop simply because of who his father was! The young always want the best now. They do not understand the value of working one's way up!"

Darash knew Hathal had not so much worked his way up as cheated his way in, but it was not his place to correct an elder.

"It is a shame the young are so impatient," Nakal agreed. Then to Darash, he said, "Your father was a good friend and a good merchant, but even he had to work many years before he could afford a shop. Do not think you are so clever as to merit it now. You will need far more money than what you can swindle out of Pertho for that!"

סֶ לָ ה

"Friends and countrymen! Hear my plea!" The speaker stood on the edge of the well at the center of the shuk two days later on yom shli'shi, the third day of the week, and shouted over the crowd to make himself heard. He wore an expensive, Greek toga. Thick, ebony hair topped his head above dark green eyes. His clean shaven upper lip and jaw set him apart from the Jewish men populating the square, who, once married, allowed their beards to grow thick and long. Though the man bore a certain elegance of manner and dress, his shoulders slumped and his voice sounded flat and dull.

Seeing he had attracted attention, he continued in Aramaic, "I am Barus. The girl who was murdered three days ago was my daughter, Aphiemi. She was my only child. I come to you today to ask—to beg—for your help! After three days of searching, the magistrate has found nothing."

Of course not, Darash thought, listening from the sidelines. *That same man gave Nakal and Hathal my shop without even investigating their flimsy evidence.*

"He says no one saw anything because it was such a cold night and everyone slept indoors. He says he can find no one and nothing to help him find my daughter's killer. He has given up! But I believe someone must have seen something! My friends and neighbors!" The man's face contorted in grief and desperation. He reached his hands out in supplication, taut fingers bent with pain and longing. "I know you owe me nothing. I know we are different people. We have different beliefs, different customs, different traditions. But we all have sons and daughters, do we not? We all love our families! We all work and sacrifice so they can have a safe place to grow and prosper! Is this not true? Then hear me, please! My daughter is dead! My only child!"

He sucked in a breath, torn with pain, but pushed on. "She is dead while her killer goes free! Can you tell me your daughters are safe? Can you go home tonight, tuck your children into their beds, and know you will see them again in the morning? Do you not want them to be safe?

"I come to you to beg for your help! If you saw something or heard something or know anything that might lead us to my daughter's killer, I beg you to come forward and tell me. I know you are good people and you want your children to be safe, so you would help me if you could. But I also know your time is precious and your efforts worthy of recompense. So know that your efforts will not be without reward. I am a wealthy man! I will greatly reward anyone who can bring me information that leads me to this evil person—the one who killed my daughter and threatens yours!"

Darash had never witnessed the shuk so still or so silent. All eyes gazed on this desperate father. All ears clung to his words. All hearts felt his grief. But it was hopeless, of course. Barus stood on the well for hours, searching the crowd, waiting for a response, sometimes speaking and crying out for justice, sometimes making individual supplications. But no one came forward. No one answered his plea. No one helped.

As Darash listened, the deep recesses of his mind began to circulate on an idea.

A reward. A reward from a very wealthy man.... What if? What if I could find something... some evidence... some clue that might help this man?

As soon as the idea presented itself, Darash pushed it away. It was foolishness, of course. If the magistrate could find nothing, and if no one in the square had any helpful information, what could he—a boy of barely fifteen years—do? He was a fool to even think it.

סֶ לַ ה

By the time Darash unloaded his belongings that evening and stored them under the lean-to on the roof, he was exhausted. He expected his mother and sister to have retired to their beds but, as he opened the door to his home, he heard a man's voice coming from inside. Entering, his nostrils detected a delicious aroma that made his mouth water. He found his mother and sister sitting with a young couple. The stone floor of the house had been meticulously swept, the room cleaned and organized, and at least five lamps burned brightly about the room, casting a warm glow on the faces of Revayah and her guests.

Revayah had painted her eyes with black kohl, colored her lips red, and rubbed olive oil into her skin to make it shine. She wore no head-covering, but instead had plaited her hair, wound it about her head in a becoming pattern, and then finger-curled smooth, black tendrils to frame her face. Copper earrings dangled nearly to her shoulders, matching a copper necklace that graced her neck. She wore her best, blue linen tunic, topped with a purple, decorative mantle fringed in white—a gift from her husband and one of her last remaining possessions from a wealthier time. For a woman who, even without the use of paint or finery, ranked among the most beautiful women in Judea, Revayah's efforts on this evening most certainly elevated her past them.

The low table, too, had been decorated with her brightest, white linen cloth. They had just finished a meal... without him. Thankfully, plenty of food remained.

"Ah, Darash, my son," Revayah said.

Darash recognized the young man as Shavah, the son of one of his father's friends, but he could not recall the name of the man's wife.

"You remember Shavah and Teshuah, his wife," his mother supplied.

"Of course," he said and greeted them both. While greeting Teshuah, he noticed her large, pregnant belly.

"They will shortly be blessed with their first child and have come to share the good news with us," his mother dispelled all possible awkwardness, ever the gracious hostess. "Teshuah has also asked me to help when it is time for the birth. I have agreed, of course."

Darash smiled and nodded at their guests. "May you both be blessed." He then bent to remove his sandals and wipe his dusty feet with a cloth. Unfortunately, though he had managed to hide the fact of his broken sandal thong for the past few days by removing them quickly and concealing the broken one beneath the good one, now all eyes were on him, particularly those of his mother. When he rose to approach the table, she caught his eye. She was not happy.

Shavah, not noticing the silent interchange, smiled broadly, "I know it is not customary to celebrate until the child is weaned, but I simply cannot contain my joy! We have been making the rounds to all our friends to ask for their prayers."

Teshuah, a shy woman, beamed at her husband, her love for him and her excitement over their coming child written in her eyes and smile.

"Of course, we will pray for you," Revayah promised, again focused on her guests. "Your joy will be our joy! Come, Darash, have some food. And, no need to get up, Shavah and Teshuah. Relax and enjoy yourselves a little longer. I would like to hear more news."

Darash joined his sister, Tsarah, and helped himself to a heaping bowl of stewed lamb, leeks, and chickpeas, flavored with caraway—an expensive luxury of a meal, considering how tight money had become. He did not want to guess what his mother had sold in order to procure the ingredients, nor how much she had paid the neighbor to come help her cook it. But he still felt the weight of the six denarii in his belt so he reached for two of the kneaded cakes.

Tsarah, having long since finished her meal, looked bored with all the adult talk, but remained seated and quiet, remembering her manners before her mother's guests. Her hair, which Revayah rarely trimmed, usually hung very long, passing her waist, black as pitch like her eyes and long eyelashes. Tonight, though, Revayah had taken special pains to plait and arrange Tsarah's hair about her head, though loose bits had since relaxed and stuck out from their desired locations. She resembled her beautiful mother, with smooth, unspoiled skin, large, penetrating eyes, and perfectly shaped lips. She wore a clean, pale blue tunic and a simple chain about her neck. Darash smiled at her around a mouthful of lamb. She smiled back.

"What you were saying about that new religious sect, Shavah," Revayah began, "is quite true. It has caused trouble, but I think it is nearing its end. Others have claimed to be the Messiah before this and there will be more to come. Eventually they are all forgotten."

"I do not know, Revayah," Shavah said. "I thought so, too, at first—especially after their leader was crucified and the Romans remained in control of Judea. However, since they claimed he came back from the dead and the tomb found empty, the rumors have begun to change. I heard there are groups of Jewish believers meeting in various homes in the city, and more are coming to this faith every day."

"I suppose the priests and Pharisees will find a way to deal with them in time. Is it true they are no longer allowed to preach in the Temple and synagogues?"

"I believe so but that has not stopped them from gathering there," Shavah said, tearing off a small piece of bread, which he munched thoughtfully. "I admit I have found this sect most fascinating—

blasphemous, of course," he added quickly, eyes darting to Revayah's face momentarily, "but most fascinating."

"How so?" Darash asked, earning himself a look of impatience from his mother. Though he was the man of the house now and had every right to enter into adult conversations, his mother still considered him a child. The transition from relying on her husband to relying on her son had been a difficult one, due in large part to Darash's inability to cover their many expenses.

"The men who followed Yeshua the Galilean are coming under attack by the Pharisees, Sadducees, and even the infidels, but they still go out and preach at every opportunity. I have heard they even perform miracles, healing the sick as he did."

"Sorcery!" Revayah spat.

Shavah nodded but said nothing. Teshuah looked embarrassed.

"It is a shame our beautiful city has to suffer under such misguided religious zealots. The Romans and Greeks cause enough trouble," Revayah said but added in a lighter tone, glancing at Teshuah's expansive middle, "especially now that you have a darling child on the way." Teshuah's smile returned. "Let us forget such nonsense and focus on Adonai's blessings instead, shall we?" Both Shavah and Teshuah nodded. "Now, tell me what your families said when they heard the news."

"Oh, my parents were quite ecstatic!" Teshuah spoke the first words Darash had ever heard from her lips. He liked her soft, feminine voice. "This will be their first grandchild."

"Oh, what a wonderful blessing!"

"My family was equally joyous," Shavah said. "Of course, you know they already have grandchildren from their real sons... but my mother loves babies and was very happy for us." Seeing the question in Darash's eyes, he added, "You see, I was adopted as a child. They already had two sons before they took me in."

"Ah! That is right," Revayah said. "I had nearly forgotten." Darash recognized the lie. His mother never forgot such juicy details. She and her friend Sapphira often got together to share any gossip they managed to turn up. "You were, what, three or four years old when they found you?"

"Yes, three, I believe, but even I am not certain."

"And what do you remember of your life before that?"

"Very little, actually. I remember moving around a lot, traveling. But I barely remember my real parents, and I have no knowledge of what happened to them. My father tells me he found me wandering outside the city gates all by myself. He asked around and, finding I had no family, took me into his home where he and my mother raised me as their own."

"What wonderful people!"

"Yes. Yes, they are." Shavah smiled.

"Now, that is what I call a real miracle, unlike what Yeshua's followers pretend to do," Revayah said. She hesitated. "Forgive me. I did not mean to return to that unsavory topic. But if it were not for that heretic and his conflict with established religion, my husband might still be alive today."

"What?" Darash asked, unable to mask his shock. He swept his hair from his eyes.

Seeing their guests' discomfort, Revayah said, "Ah, but what does it matter now that they are both gone? What vengeance is to be had? Besides, vengeance belongs to Adonai."

Shavah and Teshuah nodded in solemn reverence, impressed with her piety. Darash rolled his eyes.

"So let us not discuss these things any longer," she continued, giving Darash a warning glance.

He stifled his tongue, longing to ask more but knowing he would get no answer in the presence of guests.

Shavah and Teshuah stayed late into the evening conversing with Revayah and Darash but mostly with Revayah. By the time they left, little Tsarah lay slumped next to the table, head on Darash's lap, fast asleep. Revayah announced how tired she was and turned toward her room. Over her shoulder she said, "Pick up your sister and put her in bed. And I hope you made some money today, because tomorrow you must pay back that fat, ugly dog Nakal the seven denarii he loaned us and get your sandal repaired, as well."

What loan? Why is Mother borrowing money from Nakal, of all people! And how can I get another denarius by tomorrow?

But there were more important questions circling Darash's mind at the moment, so he let the matter of the money go and instead asked, "Imah, please explain something to me about what about what you said earlier. You said the criminal Yeshua had something to do with Father's death?"

Darash slipped out from under Tsarah to follow Revayah. She turned to face him at his approach.

"Darash, I do not think you should worry about that. I am sorry I even said it." She turned from him again, but he stopped her by blocking her path with his body.

"Imah, please. He was my father, and I have a right to know how he died."

"Hush! You will wake your sister!" She pushed out an angry sigh and drew her lips into thin, tight lines. But after a pause, she relented. "I never told you because your father would not have wanted you to know. He did not want to tell me either, but I made him. You see, Yeshua, the Galilean, and your father had an... an altercation only two days before your father was killed. I immediately suspected that marauding lunatic of his murder, but when he was arrested and put to death so quickly, what could I do? The magistrate and the Jewish rulers of law looked into your father's death for weeks after that, but when they turned up nothing, I knew the killer had already been silenced."

Chapter Four

Visiting a Greek

That night Darash dreamed of his father. Tuwr stood at a distance, peering out at him from deep shadow. He looked sad, hopeless. Darash reached for him, but Abba turned and walked away, farther and farther down the alley. Darash cried out to stop him, knowing evil waited in darkness, but his father disappeared around a corner. Darash followed, running in desperation, heart pounding, breath coming in gasps, chest tight.

"Abba, no! Stop, Abba! Please! Come back!"

When he arrived, he was too late. His father lay in a pool of blood, breathing his last. Darash turned to look for the killer but saw no one. He ran down a narrow alley but, instead of finding the murderer, he came upon another corpse—that of a murdered girl. He looked and he was surrounded. Corpses lay everywhere. The whole city lay slain at his feet, and he stood in a sea of blood.

The spirit of his father appeared before him, a look of sorrow and disappointment on his face.

"I will find your killer, Abba!" Darash said, anguish in his voice. "I will bring you justice!"

Tuwr shook his head in defeated disapproval and stepped aside to reveal a small, gaunt child. Tattered, filthy rags covered her sickly, emaciated frame. At first she bore Aman's face, the child slave of Pertho. But then she lifted her head, and Darash looked into the eyes of his little sister, Tsarah.

"How can you help me in death when you cannot help your mother and sister in life?" Tuwr asked.

Darash jerked awake, sweat streaming down his temples and dampening his tunic despite the chill in the air. His heart pounded and his breath came in hard puffs. He closed his eyes tight and tried to push the awful images from his mind, willing his chest to stop heaving.

If I do not do something soon, my family will starve. I need to make some real money, and soon! But how?

His mind returned to Aphiemi's father, Barus—a man willing to pay for justice. Barus's hope of finding his daughter's murderer was probably foolishness, the hope of a desperate, grieving father.

What can I do? Where would I even start?

At the edges of his desperation, Darash realized he had to try. He would likely fail. But he must try. Perhaps some clue existed, something the magistrate had overlooked, something small. And did not his blind mentor Nib'haz often tell him how easily sighted people ignore the details? Even if he could find something worth a few denarii to Barus, it would be enough to see his family through the week. He had nothing to lose.

The wild pounding of his heart smoothed and his breathing relaxed. He tried to think. Think....

Where would I even begin? I could speak to Barus. Then perhaps I could speak to the magistrate, Quintus Arrius—not that that lazy Roman will be of much help. Still... if I start asking questions I might find something... perhaps not. Beyond that....

Darash dreamed again. This time it was a jumble of sounds and images—hard faces, Nekoda's bucking head, Nib'haz's muttering, the Temple, darkness when it should be day, and then nothingness.

סֶ לָ ה

Darash did not go straight to the shuk the morning of the fourth day of the week, yom revi'i. Instead, he searched out Barus. He ducked out of the house without breakfast, hoping to avoid a confrontation with his mother. He took the six denarii. Somehow he would have to add to it before paying his mother's debt this afternoon, and there was no way he would be able to repair or replace his broken sandal now.

At Barus's home, a mournful looking woman opened the door and looked at him quizzically.

"I am here to see Barus," Darash told her in Greek.

"I will fetch my husband," she said, standing aside to let him enter.

Darash hovered at the stoop wondering what to do. He did not want to offend a grieving woman by refusing to enter her home, but his mother's teachings returned to him with force.

"It is a disgrace to enter the home of an idolater. We do not make friends with them or eat with them, and we only do business with them out of necessity. You make yourself unclean when you associate with them."

Barus's wife blinked, waiting. Darash nodded and entered.

This is business.

She left him standing in an elegant, whitewashed front room, with higher ceilings than those in his home, and returned shortly with Barus.

The tall Greek looked hard at Darash.

"Sh-shalom," Darash began, feeling he had made a terrible mistake. "Forgive me for this intrusion, but I-I heard your plea last night in the lower shuk and I came to—"

"Are you not the son of Tuwr?" Barus interrupted.

Darash paused, surprised, and then rushed ahead. "Yes. Tuwr was my father."

Barus sighed and nodded. "Ah, yes. You have grown since I last saw you, but I remember you. Your father and I were friends. He was a shrewd and clever man, and he once performed a service for me—which I never had the chance to repay." He paused. "I am sorry for your loss. His death was quite tragic."

"Thank you," Darash said with a bow.

Thankfully, at that moment Tuwr's wife dispelled the awkwardness by ushering him into the main room and offering him food and a place to recline at a low table. He stared at the food, knowing he should not eat with idolaters.

I have already compromised myself by entering their home, but how can I sit and eat with them?

Barus cleared his throat. "Your father often shared a meal with us," he said. "Having you here reminds me of his many visits."

Darash nodded and took a seat on a cushion near the low table. By now his middle had knotted with hunger, and the delicious smells beckoned him.

Well, if Abba thought it was alright, then....

"Tell me again the purpose of your visit," Barus said, joining him. "You say you heard me in the shuk this evening past."

"Yes. I am young and may be unable to help. But I came to offer to try."

Barus smiled, the edges of his mouth turning in a moderate expression of pleasure, mixed with a good degree of hopelessness. "I am honored that you would want to help," he said, sounding sincere in his gratitude, but doubtful.

Sitting on pillows, Barus, his wife, and Darash drank good wine and helped themselves to the meal. They ate boiled eggs, toasted bread topped with a lentil spread, olives, and dates. But Darash also noticed slices of ham on the table as well. He felt immediate revulsion upon seeing the cooked flesh of an unclean animal.

"Oh, no! I must apologize!" Barus's wife said in alarm. Seeing his discomfort on his face. "Please forgive me! I will take this away at once!" She grabbed the plate of ham and whisked it from the room.

"Young man," Barus said, "I apologize for my wife's oversight. Please do not take offense at the mistake of a grieving woman."

Darash reached a conciliatory hand in Barus's direction. "Please. I am not offended."

Darash tried to wave away the incident. However, he resolved never let his mother catch him entering the home of a Greek family.

Perhaps she is right after all. These people are so very different and have no reverence at all for Elohim's laws. Would Elohim bless such an alliance? And what if one of our friends or, worse, a Pharisee, sees me leaving this place? Imah would never forgive me!

But then Darash thought of his father.

He often came here himself. This is business, he told himself again.

As merchants, both he and his father had often dealt with Greeks. But this felt different. Here he sat in a Greek dwelling, surrounded by them, eating their rich food and gazing upon the evidence of their opulent lifestyle—decorative tapestries, soft, full pillows, large, decorative, clay vases. Odd, though, that he could find not a single foreign deity depicted in either the tapestries or in the pottery—something one might expect in the home of such a wealthy Greek.

Nevertheless, Darash felt trapped. He had made a vow to help a Greek. Elohim demanded that Jews fulfill their vows, but what if that vow had been foolishly made to an enemy of Adonai?

Darash forced himself to continue eating, hoping his actions would put both himself and his hosts at ease.

Elohim might curse me for associating with idolaters, but there is nothing I can do about it now. All I can do is help Barus, if I can, and earn a little money.

Barus, seeing Darash eat, relaxed as well. It would have been impolite to bring up the murder while eating, so Darash waited. As they finished the last few bites, Barus said, "I was sorry to hear of your father's death." He paused, a question playing at the corners of his mouth. "Your father's killer was never found?" he asked at length.

"No," Darash admitted, conflicted.

I have not even found my own father's killer. Why should he believe I can find the killer of a girl I have never met?

"Forgive me," Barus said. He sighed and wiped his mouth with a cloth as he reclined. As if on cue, a servant girl entered and cleared away the empty dishes. Barus nodded his approval, and she disappeared around the corner.

Darash felt he should push for more information about Aphiemi. That was why he had come, was it not?

"I know this seems like a hopeless situation," Darash began, "and maybe it is, but as you said last night, what could it hurt to try? Perhaps, if we work together... ask questions...."

"I have already asked questions," Barus said, his frustration showing. "The day before you saw me, I spent an entire day in the Upper Market, making the same plea. No one responded then, either. I have come to see that there are no answers."

Darash eyed Barus carefully for a moment. Everything about this man surprised him. Unlike Pertho and other Greeks he had known and despised for their carelessness, dishonesty, and unclean habits, Barus appeared intelligent, upright, and thoughtful.

He is caught in the throes of sorrow and hopelessness, yet he treats his wife and servants with kindness. He runs a clean and orderly home. His wife is generous and hospitable. Even his servant girl genuinely desires to assist him.

Nothing in this man elicited anything but respect, and Darash began to understand why Abba had chosen him as a friend. But how quickly Barus's desperation of last night had turned to hopelessness! Darash thought of Amah—Pertho's young servant who he wanted to help but could not—the girl with no name.

I cannot help her… but perhaps I can help Barus.

He sighed.

And this is about more than money… more than business. It is about justice. Even a Greek deserves justice.

"I can make no promises," Darash ventured. "I cannot assure you I will find answers where you have not. However, you lose nothing by having another person asking questions. Perhaps someone saw something, but is afraid to tell you or the magistrate. But what would they have to fear from a simple youth like me?"

Barus looked at him for a moment and smiled.

"You are your father's son," he said at length but then allowed his gaze to travel to an intricate, colorful tapestry hanging on the wall to Darash's left. Soft blues, deep reds, and brilliant yellows, interspersed with pure white highlights, combined to depict the image of a woman standing in a field of flowers, arms outstretched as if to embrace the beauty around her. "My daughter made that," he said. "It is beautiful, is it not?"

"Very." Darash paused, wanting to ask more about his father. Instead, he asked, "Would you tell me about her?"

Barus smiled and his eyes glimmered with unshed tears. "She was only fifteen years old and a very beautiful girl. She worked hard around the house and was a great help to her mother, but she liked to weave most of all. She became quite a skilled weaver, as you can see. She used to sit for hours at the loom.... On his last visit, my brother told me he would be willing to sell her rugs and tapestries in Macedonia.... He is looking into business opportunities there even now. He does not yet know what has happened."

"Tell me about her friends, the people she knew."

"She had a few friends who would come by once in a while. Greek and Hebrew girls, mostly. The one that came over most often is named Mareh. She lives three houses down." He gestured in a westerly direction. "Aphiemi used to visit her often, as well."

"Any young men?"

Barus shook his head. "No. None."

סֶ לָ ה

"...two... ah, yes... another... this one there... too many... yes... I think that will—Ah! Darash! There you are! I had begun to believe you would not come today."

"Shalom, Nib'haz," Darash said, Nekoda following, as he entered the alley to his obscure place of business. "I went to go talk to someone."

"And who would that be?" Nib'haz asked.

Darash paused, but then confessed, knowing Nib'haz would get the truth from him eventually. "I went to see Barus."

"The dead Greek girl's father?" Valad asked. "What could you possibly have to say to him?"

"Nothing, really." Darash hoped they would drop the subject.

"Ah.... Are you hoping to help this man find his daughter's killer and reap the reward?" Nib'haz said. To Darash's chagrin, his words drew the attention of several who stood around.

Darash colored at their looks and snickers. He led Nekoda to a post near several other draft animals that were kept there throughout the day as their owners worked. He retrieved a bundle of straw from one of the baskets on her back. She stood, munching her food in slow, thoughtful motions as Darash began unloading. He wished it was legal in Jerusalem to use carts, even a small one, as that would allow him to bring more items to sell and it would be easier on his animal. However, their leaders believed it would congest the narrow roads too much and create an unnecessary nuisance and danger.

"I think this is an excellent idea!" Nib'haz continued. "If everyone in the city kept their eyes and ears open as you do, no more killers would go free! You have a quick mind, Darash, and good instincts. And I will help you. ...So you have spoken to the Greek. And who is the girl's young man?"

"He said there was no young man."

At this Nib'haz laughed, as did Valad. "Of course, there was a young man!" Nib'haz said. "Otherwise, what would she be doing sneaking around in the middle of the night in the darkest corners?"

"Well, I had that thought but—"

"But you did not want to tell a grieving father that his dead daughter had been deceiving him." Nib'haz sighed loudly and shook his head a little too vigorously. "I understand, and you did right by holding your tongue. Still, know that strong emotion blinds us to the truth and grief elevates the dead. So stifle your tongue, but not your mind. Do not allow the blinding emotion in others to bind you as well." He reached unseeing hands across his stacks of baskets, straightening already straight piles.

Darash considered his words and nodded.

"Being a seeker of the truth is dangerous business," Nib'haz continued. "The truth does not set itself up to please any man. It simply is what it is, whether we would accept it or not, whether it should be or not. Is this Barus ready to find the truth he seeks?"

"Yes.... No.... I am not sure. I do not think he is."

"Ah, well. I do not suppose you can do anything about that."

"No, I can only do what I must—try to find some clue to Aphiemi's killer, no matter what the outcome."

"True, true. So... let us see.... This girl went to see her young man," Nib'haz said, "and she did it in secret. You say the father does not know about this young man, so we must ask why would she hide this from him? Perhaps she knew her father would disapprove of him. Ah! Yes... disapprove...." Nib'haz began muttering to himself again. "He would disapprove if the man were too old, too young, too poor—possibly if he was not Greek or followed the wrong gods.... too ugly... heh... heh... heh... no, no.... too not like her father .. too married... heh, heh, heh... or—Ah!" he cried, coming out of his personal reverie. "Was she already betrothed to someone?"

"I do not know," Darash said. "He said there were no young men. I just assumed—"

"You did not ask?" Nib'haz said, incredulously. "How are you going to find out anything if you do not ask?" He shook his head in disgust.

"He said she had a good friend, though. A Hebrew girl."

"Ah! Good, good! You can ask her, then. She will know more than the father, anyway."

Chapter Five

Longing for Freedom

"What is this?" Nakal asked and spat in disgust. "You owe me eight denarii, not seven and a half!"

Darash took a step away from the glob of mucus that landed near his damaged right sandal. Nakal stood before him in a tunic with his thick cloak open. He wore no belt. The tunic spread taut across his expansive middle, creating an indentation in the material at his date-sized navel. His breath smelled of cheap wine and olives, and his body radiated heat and the foul odor of sweat and dirt.

"That is all the money we have, Nakal," Darash said, trying not to breathe in too deeply. "I will get you the other quinquessis by tomorrow evening."

"But you owe me half a denarius tonight! If you wait until tomorrow, you will owe a full denarius! Consider it a quinquessis with interest."

Darash realized it had been a mistake to visit Nakal by himself. If his mother, Revayah, had come, he had no doubt Nakal would have extended the loan without additional interest applied. Revayah's flawless complexion, unusual gray eyes, and full lips made her a striking beauty. Though Darash did not like to admit it, her skill at charming men often procured the results she wanted. Nakal would have been clay in her hands. That gave Darash an idea.

"Very well, Nakal," he said and added a nod of respect for added effect. "I will go home and ask my mother if she has anything I can sell quickly in order to pay you back tonight—a bracelet or her head covering, perhaps. I am sure she will understand. She always speaks so highly of you and of your generosity. She would not want to impose any longer on—"

"Wait, wait," Nakal scratched at the back of his neck and then waved him off. "For your mother's sake, I will give you an extra day to pay me. But be sure to pay me no later than tomorrow evening, do you hear?"

"Yes, Nakal. Thank you." Darash turned to go, trying to hide the smile on his face.

"And be sure to tell your mother of my generous extension on your loan," the wolfish man called after him.

סֶלָה

Again Darash dreamed of his father's murder. And again, in a horrible twist on the original nightmare, the city, too, lay slain at his feet. Then another figure entered the dream. Darash saw the likeness of a man standing at the far end of the alley shrouded in darkness. But when Darash moved to follow, the stranger turned and disappeared into the abyss of night.

סֶ לָ ה

"Shalom. I am here to speak to your daughter, Mareh. I believe she and Aphiemi were friends."

The Hebrew man eyed Darash, no doubt wondering if he was simply making up an excuse to charm his daughter.

"My daughter is very upset about the death of her friend," he said at last. "She has not entertained visitors nor left the house since. Maybe if you were to come back another time...."

Darash shivered as a cool morning breeze played with his stringy mane of hair and reached thin, icy tendrils down the back of his cloak. It was the morning of yom khah'mi'shi, the fifth day.

"I am sorry for your daughter's loss," he chattered in the cold, "and it must seem strange to have a boy of my age come by asking questions, but I promised Barus, the murdered girl's father, to find out what I could. So I was hoping to speak to you and her together."

"Barus is a good man," Mareh's father conceded, "a Greek, but a good man."

Darash raised his eyebrows in surprise.

"Such tragedy should never have come to him," the man continued with feeling. "Come inside. I will fetch Mareh."

Darash nodded and followed him, thankful both for the welcome and the chance to get out of the chilled air. Shadows dominated the room, in contrast to the brightness of the crisp morning. Voices from the next room and the shuffling of feet met his ears as he waited in the modest quarters. Finally, the Hebrew man reemerged, followed by a plump, smooth-featured girl. She nodded to Darash and took a seat. Darash sat across from her. Her father stood protectively nearby.

"I am Darash ben Tuwr. I am here on behalf of Barus to find out what I can about Aphiemi's death."

Mareh nodded, but she slumped a little further into her cushion and took a ragged breath.

I hope she does not start to cry.

"Could you tell me of Aphiemi's other friends?" he asked.

Mareh nodded and cleared her throat.

"There were two other girls she considered friends, but she and I live—lived—closest to each other, so she spent most of her time with me."

After asking for and receiving the names of the other girls, Darash noted, with surprise, that they were all Hebrew. Strange that a young Greek girl had become such close friends with the daughters of Hebrew men.

What is it about this singular Greek man and his family? They make friends where their countrymen would find only enemies.

Darash had one more question. "Did Aphiemi have a young man she was seeing?"

Mareh's eyes grew wide for a moment and she glanced nervously at her father. She swallowed before answering. "Oh, no," she said. "Aphiemi only had girlfriends."

Darash considered her response for a moment—the widening of the pupils, the glance at her father, the nervousness in her voice, how she had clasped her hands together, her unwillingness to look him in the eyes as she spoke those last few words.

What would Nib'haz think of her response? Hmm.... Nib'haz would say she was lying. And he would be right.

סֶ לָ ה

"She did not want to tell on her friend in front of her father," Nib'haz summed up after Darash recounted the visit to him. "Obviously, Aphiemi was seeing someone, but swore Mareh to secrecy. Now Mareh knows she will get in a lot of trouble if she admits she has been lying to her parents and Aphiemi's as well."

"What if Mareh was not thinking of Aphiemi's young man, but of her own? Maybe her nervousness comes from being afraid she will bring questions about her own secrets by revealing her friend's. Could that also be true?"

"Hmmm," Nib'haz said. "Perhaps... but no. I am right. You are wrong."

Darash forced the air from his lungs in frustration, but decided Nib'haz probably spoke the truth.

"The simplest answer is often the correct one," Nib'haz added.

"So now what?"

"You have to get Mareh alone if you want to have any chance of her being honest with you," Nib'haz said.

"How am I supposed to do that?"

"How should I know? Do I look like someone who chases after young ladies?"

Valad, listening in on their conversation as always, laughed but mercifully kept his comments to himself. Nib'haz, in tidying up a row of baskets, noticed one with a stray reed.

"And what did Magistrate Quintus Arrius say when you spoke with him?" Nib'haz asked as he dug around in his satchel for a tool to clip the unkempt edge.

Darash sighed. His visit with the magistrate that morning, just after his talk with Mareh and her father, had been brief and humiliating. Still, it had rendered some good information.

"First he wanted to know why I was so interested—thought I might be a relative or maybe the murderer himself. But when I told him I was hoping to help Barus by finding out more, he told me what a fool I was to think I could find answers where he could not. I had to remind him of my father's unsolved murder before he would say more."

"Ah, good. A little guilt can go a long way. Go on."

Nib'haz sheered away the rough edge of the reed as he spoke.

"He said he asked at every house in the entire area," Darash answered, "including all the guard towers, and no one saw anything. It was very late when it happened, so everyone was asleep, and it was a very cold night, so no one slept on their roofs that evening."

"Sounds convenient for the murderer, does it not?"

"There was something odd about that, though."

"Oh?" Nib'haz asked, hands ceasing their work.

"There is a watchtower directly overlooking the place she died. Usually it is unmanned, so perhaps the killer did not expect a guard to be there. But on that night, a man had been assigned to it. The Roman governor is concerned about the growing unrest caused by the followers of Yeshua, so they are taking extra precautions."

"And, what did this guard have to say?"

"Nothing."

"Nothing?"

"Nothing," Darash confirmed.

"Hmm…. That is very strange…." Nib'haz let his hands return to their tasks of searching for more undesirable qualities that might mar his wicker merchandise.

"The magistrate also said the killer had probably left the city by now, but he is wrong about that."

"Why do you say that?"

"Because Barus would not raise his daughter to go off into dark corners with a stranger, and she would have screamed and been heard if she had been dragged there. No. She knew this man and knew him well. He lives here."

Nib'haz smiled broadly. "Ah! Now you are beginning to use the mind good Adonai gave you. Anything else?"

"Yes, but I doubt it will be much help."

"You never know. What is it?"

"He said he found the chain of a necklace lying broken on the ground, but—"

"Was there an amulet on it?" Nib'haz asked.

"No," Darash answered.

"Gold, silver, or copper?"

"Gold."

"Ah! Expensive! Did you see it?"

"He showed it to me," Darash said. "It looked costly but not unusual. He asked around to see if anyone recognized it, but no one has."

"Well, maybe they have, maybe they have not. People often lie."

Darash did not respond.

Nib'haz muttered something under his breath, but then said, "A gold chain... chain of gold. Broken on the ground. Hmmm.... Something like that breaking... pulled off... yanked off.... That would leave a mark, would it not? On the killer's neck, and perhaps on her hand, as well. Did the magistrate say anything about the condition of her body?"

"Not really. Only that the right side of her head had a big gash in it."

Nib'haz grew very quiet.

"Wait…." Darash said. He lifted his right hand, made a partial fist, as if holding a rock, and swung it through the air a few times. "That is odd…." He repeated his motions, this time with his left hand. "If she was facing her attacker, he would have to use his left hand to hit her on the right side of her head."

Nib'haz rocked back and forth, a sort of nod. "But if she was facing away?"

"No. She must have been facing him. The magistrate said the body was on her back. If she had been hit from behind, would she not fall forward? Also, she ripped off his chain. It would be very hard to do so if she was facing away from him."

Nib'haz smiled. "Very good, young one!" He paused. "Still, much remains hidden. You must go to the place the girl died."

"But that area is unclean, Nib'haz!" Darash said, repulsed.

"So do not touch anything," Nib'haz said with a shrug. "To get to the end of a problem, you must start at the beginning."

סֶ לָ ה

The noon hour came and went, and took with it the majority of shoppers. When the time of afternoon rest descended, folks went home to find a meal, reconnect with their families, and, perhaps, take a short nap before returning to their labor. In summer months, the heat drove people indoors, but though the winter climate was considerably less wearisome, the custom continued.

Darash loaded up Nekoda once again—a bothersome thing to do so often during the day, especially when the weather was nice—and started home, wishing, as he often did, that he could just lock up his possessions in his father's shop. However, before Darash got more than a few blocks, he settled on a new destination.

Mother will not miss me.

He sometimes did not return home at midday if a new business opportunity presented itself. But most others would have done so, leaving the streets largely deserted.

I could go visit the place of Aphiemi's death, as Nib'haz suggested.

He did not like the thought of it. Contact with a dead body made a Jewish person ceremonially unclean. Of course, the body would no longer be present, but the Pharisees and chief priests loved to find minute reasons to demand ceremonial washings which cost a denarius each time.

The good news, of course, would be that, since this was a Jewish and Essene neighborhood, no one would have ventured to where the body had lain for quite a while. That, at least, assured him that the scene had remained largely undisturbed since the murder, except for the fruitless visit from the magistrate.

As Darash approached, he took in the southern end of the Upper City. Much activity occurred within the narrow, house-lined streets, but the busyness and noise diminished considerably as he drew near the city wall. Many residences had been built at the base of this 20-cubit-high wall, actually using it as the back wall of the dwellings. Such construction saved space and materials and made breaching the city wall considerably more difficult, even if war machines were used.

He walked along this row of homes searching for the area near the tower where Magistrate Quintus Arrius said the murder had taken place. As Darash approached the tower, he noticed a break in the line of homes. A small stretch of city wall stood free of edifices to allow easy access to the guard tower. This tower stood at the intersection where the southern wall overlooking the Valley of Hinnom met the wall that bordered Jerusalem's western side. Three of the homes in this area had been built near the wall, but not right up against it. Between them and the wall ran a narrow alley for about a quarter of a stone's throw. Here Aphiemi lost her life.

Darash looked down the alley. Knowing what had occurred here, he did not want to venture in alone, even in broad daylight. He studied the location. Despite the torch sconce at the corner, now empty, the privacy of this place would be difficult to find elsewhere in the city. None of the houses had windows facing the alley. The risk would be the guard tower.

From where he now stood, he could see the guard who now manned that station. Catching the man's eye, he knew the guard could see him as well. Thankfully, the Roman evidenced only cursory interest in the curious youth below and turned back to surveying the valley.

Of course, if Aphiemi and her killer met here often and were used to the tower being empty.... And the murder occurred at night, when the guard would have been almost impossible to see without climbing up to check.... But neither fact solves the problem of why the guard claims to have seen nothing.

Darash glanced back up at the guard, but saw no sense bothering him with questions. The man who now manned the tower would not be the same one who had been on duty that night. Darash would have to return later if he hoped to catch the night watchman who should have witnessed the murder.

Darash took a deep breath and started down the narrow alleyway—a rocky path, lined with barrels, old fence posts, and large washing pots stored here by the people who lived in these homes. When he neared the center, he saw something that made him recoil. Blood.

A large patch of dried blood marred the dirt and rocks at his feet. Darash covered his mouth with a hand. Aphiemi died in this very spot. He turned away from the grisly scene and closed his eyes. He took a deep breath before opening them, and that is when he noticed it. The guard tower had disappeared. Because of the angle of the wall, where the guard tower stood, and the angle of the last roofline, a lean-to erected on the southern edge of a nearby roof completely blocked the alley from view of the tower.

I wonder how long that lean-to has been there.

The sun dimmed and cast Darash in shadow. He saw thick clouds gathering in the east. Rain would soon come, and from the looks of it, it would be a torrent. Soon the scene of Aphiemi's murder would be washed clean. It would be a good thing, he thought. But if there was anything else to find, Darash knew he should find it now. He took another deep breath, prepared himself, and turned back around.

He saw nothing new at first. His eyes traced the rocky path, the dried blood mixed with dust, and a place where a great deal had soaked into the dirt, leaving a black, sticky mess. The blood-painted rocks he saw measured no larger than the tip of his thumb, but he noticed a larger rock about three times the size of a pear. He knelt over it and picked it up, but immediately dropped it again. It, too, bore a deep red stain. It rolled to a stop and Darash noticed several black hairs clinging to the dark red blemish. The killer had held this same stone in his hands. With it, he had crushed her skull and driven the life from her body.

Darash shuddered, rose, and backed away. He took a few steps around the area, looking for anything else that might help him recreate the past, but saw nothing. He was about to leave when, for a brief moment, the sun poked through the clouds overhead. Something shimmered amid the rocks, about four paces from where the blood had collected. Darash kicked aside a few pebbles, looking for what had caught his eye. He bent and retrieved a flat, gold amulet bearing the image of an olive branch.

Darash remembered the gold chain the magistrate had found.

Does this amulet go with the chain? Had the amulet been flung off when the chain broke, or had it been dropped there earlier by someone unrelated to the crime?

Darash clasped the amulet in his hand and headed out of the alley. After a quick glance up at the corner wall, he began following the road back to where he had tied Nekoda. As he left the first row of buildings, chilling drops of rain rebounded from his arms, shoulders, and the back of his neck. Normally, Darash would have found the rain bothersome but this afternoon, despite the cold discomfort, the rain brought a refreshing sensation after the dark, dirty feeling of the alley. Elohim in His heaven had sent the rain, like the tears of a thousand angels, to cleanse all that had been made unclean.

Chapter Six

The Grip of Fear

That evening Darash neared his home on tired feet, feeling the rain soaking through his cloak and tunic at his neck and shoulders. He regretted his decision to leave his head covering at home. Nakal had made him stand in the rain, waiting at his door to pay the final half denarius he owed. Now he could feel the cold and moisture making its way down his back and buttocks to his legs. Worse still, no money remained—none for food and none to replace what he had sold.

He pushed open the heavy, time-smoothed wooden door in the outer wall and the warm glow of one of his mother's clay oil lamps greeted him from the front window of their home. He sighed.

For now, at least, Elohim still provides.

Darash could not remember a time when her light had ever gone out. She kept at least one lamp burning, even throughout the night.

Darash's father, Tuwr, had inherited this home from his parents upon his father's death nearly ten years ago. Until that time, they had all lived here together. Of course, Tsarah had not been born yet, so she did not know her grandfather, but she remembered her grandmother well. After Grandfather's death, Grandmother had remarried. She married an old family friend, a widower, and moved to Hebron to live with him and his family.

Darash and his family used to visit her often until Abba's death. Darash simply could not stop working long enough to make the journey. Hebron lay a full day's journey to the south. With Tsarah along, it would take longer, requiring a night's lodging in one of the roadside inns. Even so, this would not prevent Revayah from taking Tsarah down for a visit, as they often had friends traveling that way, but his mother had never gotten along well with her mother-in-law, so chose not to make the effort.

The house itself had been built of limestone—thick walls covered in clay-rich mud and white-wash kept out the cold in winter months and the heat in summer. A single window built high into the front wall allowed the fresh air in. When necessary, they covered the small opening with a sheepskin to keep out the rain. A high wall surrounded the front of the home and connected to the back of the house, creating a space for animals and a garden. The outer wall also bore a wooden door which they could easily lock from the inside by placing a beam across it.

Darash entered the yard and led Nekoda along the worn path past the stone staircase on his left that led to the roof. It, too, had been plastered in mud and white-washed, to match the rest of the dwelling and outer wall. The steps sagged in the middle from much use, and the mud had cracked and broken off in some places, exposing the stones beneath. Darash locked Nekoda in their small stable, a domicile that shared one wall with Revayah's room.

Revayah's chamber used to house Darash's grandparents, as it was the only private bedroom. This room met up with the outer wall of their main living space, the lower floor of the two-story edifice. Though it had once been used for animals, it had long since been converted into a family room, where they cooked and ate their meals, completed their daily chores, and relaxed together. Darash and Tsarah slept upstairs on low, wooden beds covered with simple mattresses and wool blankets.

On the other side of the property, in the corner, an old olive extended its branches well over the wall and the roof. It provided shade for animals and people alike in the heat of the summer afternoons. In the summer, Revayah and Tsarah often sat here to grind grain into flour, wash and prepare vegetables, or comb one another's hair. It stood between the main room and the right wall. Further along that wall, to the right of the outer door, lay Revayah's immaculate vegetable garden. Tuwr had built a secure fence around it to keep their animals from getting at her developing leeks, melons, and cucumbers.

"Ah, Darash, I am glad you are finally home," Revayah greeted him from the door, breaking the silence that had risen between them since his unwelcome questions about his father's killer. He looked up at her with a smile. But then she pulled her cloak over her shoulders and grabbed a basket.

"I must go out. You will take care of your sister."

"Where are you going?"

Revayah hesitated. "I have business I must attend to."

"Business? At this hour?"

"A friend. A friend is ill and I must attend to her."

"Who is ill?"

"Forgive me, Darash. I do not have time to answer your questions. I must go. I might be back very late. Do not wait up for me."

Darash watched as she bundled her cloak around her head to protect herself from the rain, cross the yard, open the wooden doors, and disappear beyond them.

Where could she be going? And why did she not just give me the name of this sick friend? ...If there is a sick friend.

סֶ לַ ה

A few hours later, as dusk settled over Jerusalem, the rain dispersed leaving the streets wet and muddy, but not unmanageable. Darash had almost given up going to see the night watchtower guard that evening once he realized he would have to care for his sister; however, he changed his mind with the change in weather.

A little walk will not hurt her.

Of course, that walk would be about ten furlongs through the city at night, but as long as Imah did not find out....

"I am cold," Tsarah complained by the second block.

"Pull your cloak tighter around your neck," he said helping her adjust it as they walked. "This will not take long."

"Where are we going?"

"I have to ask someone some questions."

"What kind of questions?" she wanted to know.

"That is none of your concern."

"Is it about the murdered girl?"

"How did you find out about that?"

"Imah told me."

Darash sighed. His mother did not shield eight-year-old Tsarah from things he believed should stay in the adult world. Only this morning, Darash had awakened to find Revayah sitting with Tsarah, combing her hair, and saying, "There, that is much better. You are a very pretty girl. We will have no trouble finding a husband for you! As long as you are pretty, you will never have to worry."

"Worry about what, Imah?" Tsarah had asked.

"Oh, about money or having nice things or losing your husband's love."

"I do not want to get married."

"Of course, you do! You are very beautiful. We will find a wealthy husband for you."

Darash tended to agree with his sister when it came to the subject of marriage. Why would he want some woman in his home who nagged and demanded and then burst into tears whenever she wanted something unreasonable? He had seen enough of that in his parents' marriage. And he knew that what a couple pretended to be in public or at the synagogue might be something altogether different when they were home. But in a strange way, his parents had loved one another deeply... though he never understood why.

"Yes, it is about the murder," he answered with a sigh, hoping she would let the matter drop.

"Who killed her?"

"That is what I want to find out."

"What are you going to do when you find out?"

That gave him pause. "Tell the magistrate, I suppose."

"Imah says she was probably killed by her husband."

"What?" Now he was angry. "That is not true! She was not even married." He wanted to add how Imah should not say such things, but held his tongue.

Imah had gone too far. She often went too far, he realized, but did not know how to make the situation better. As their mother and only parent, she had the right to instruct them as she saw fit. However, since Darash had become the man of their home, he felt his responsibilities should extend farther than simply bringing home money.

Tsarah drew silent for a moment, and Darash took the opportunity to say something to counteract some of her fears, as well as shift the topic of conversation away from Aphiemi's grisly murder. "You know, husbands are not all bad," he said. "Look at me. Do you think I would make a bad husband?"

Tsarah snickered at the thought. "No. You would make a funny husband!"

"What?" he said, feigning injury.

She laughed harder. But after a moment, she clouded up again. "But what if I marry someone who is not good like you?"

Darash put a hand around her tiny shoulder. "Do not worry. I am the man of the family now. I get to decide who you marry, and I will make sure he is good. I promise."

סֶלָה

Thick clouds hid sparse moonlight, deepening the night. As Darash approached the area of Ahpiemi's murder, he remembered the death of another, which was also marked by darkness—the death of Yeshua the Galilean. Only that death had occurred at mid-day. Darash did not know quite what to think of the strange phenomenon. His mother had dismissed it as a coincidence. The Pharisees suggested it was a trick of the devil. The Sadducees refused to acknowledge the occurrence at all. But Darash remembered. He remembered the fading light, the cooling winds, and then how darkness simply swallowed up the sun as it hung in the sky. In the middle of the day, Jerusalem succumbed to darkness. The light, hidden. Day became night.

Strange how death and darkness are such frequent companions.

His own father, murdered in a dark alley. Aphiemi killed in the darkness of night. But Yeshua… Yeshua…. Darkness simply showed up for that one.

"I am frightened. It is too dark here," Tsarah whimpered, glancing about her at the shadows.

"Do not fear. There is torchlight, and I will not let you out of my sight."

Darash swallowed hard, thankful for the lit torches at the street corners, despite their failure to reach into the corners. The firelight flicked and danced about the road and stone walls, casting the world in greenish-gray. As they walked, Darash and Tsarah's shadows lumbered against crude brickwork and grew to giant sizes—like cursed, pre-flood Nephilim searching for victims. He swallowed again and squeezed his sister's hand more tightly. As they rounded the corner of the furthest alley, he noticed that the center—the very spot where Aphiemi had met her end—remained bathed in shadow. A place of utter darkness no eyes could penetrate.

Instead of proceeding to the guard tower, Darash took Tsarah's hand and led her back toward the house with the lean-to.

"Where are we going?" she asked.

"I have a question for the person who lives here."

Darash knocked on the door, and a gruff voice met him from inside.

"Who is it? What do you want? You should know that I have a sword!"

"Forgive me, brother, and shalom," Darash addressed his countryman. "I am only a youth, but I have a question for you."

After a good deal of wood on wood commotion, a middle-aged, bearded man dressed in the short-sleeved, colorless tunic of the Essene opened the door. He held an old, rusty sword, which he let dangle next to his right thigh.

"Ah. Forgive me, but Yerushaláyim has become a dangerous place to live." He glanced over Darash's shoulder at Tsarah. "And, you children should not be out after dark. What could you possibly want at this hour?"

Darash bowed in respect to his elder. "This was the only time we could come. We seek information, and it is I who should be asking forgiveness for disturbing you. I will be brief. The night of the murder, was your lean-to on your roof?"

"Yes. That lean-to is always there."

Darash's heart sank.

"No... wait...." The man scratched his beard, thinking. "That was the night Shabbat ended, was it not? The first very cold day of winter?"

Darash nodded. "Yes. That same night."

"Ah... I had taken it down to clean it on the day before Shabbat. I remember because I always clean it this time of year, but I waited a little too long and could not get it up before Shabbat began."

"Did you put it back up that evening?"

"No.... I meant to, but it was very cold that night, so I did not bother with it. The next morning, I went up on my roof to put up the lean-to and from there observed the men who came to take away that poor girl's body. I had not heard about her death until I saw them carry her away. I have daughters of my own. I have been boarding up our door every night since then. Very sad... very sad."

"Yes, it is," Darash agreed. "One last question, if I may. Could you tell me the name of the centurion who mans the watchtower above your home?"

"Uh... let me see." The man again fondled his beard and stared at the hard-packed, dirt floor. "He is called Servius... Servius Aurelius.... Interesting sort, he is. He was one of the guards at the garden tomb the morning they claimed Yeshua came back to life."

סֶ לֶ ה

Darash looked up at the stone tower rising from the apex of the city wall silhouetted against the night sky and ringed in stars.

"I will not be long," he promised his sister. "Just sit down right there in the torchlight, and I will be able to see you the whole time. And I will be able to hear you if you call me, alright?"

"Yes, brother," she said in obedience, though her eyes betrayed uncertainty. She huddled against the side wall of a house near the base of the ladder.

"Hail!" Darash called up to the tower in Latin. "Guard, I must speak with you!"

Darash waited for a response but received none. Again he called.

"Hail! Night watchman!"

Again, no answer.

Has the Roman government again decided this tower need not be manned? Strange, considering the murder that just took place beneath it....

Darash decided to find out. He had planned on climbing anyway, since the guard could not leave his post; however, Darash had hoped to get permission first. Roman soldiers never appreciated being approached without fair warning, particularly at night. Darash took a deep breath, squared his shoulders, and began to climb, hand over hand, rung after rung. About two thirds of the way up, he expected to see the head and shoulders of the guard come into view. But he saw no one. He called again with no response. Darash climbed a few rungs more.

Nearing the top, he saw a sandaled foot near the narrow, brick-lined entrance to the tower. The guard was there, reclining against the low wall of the guardhouse, eyes closed. Soft, deep breaths wafted regularly from slightly parted lips. He wore a red cape, thick, leather armor covering a red tunic, and a red, plumed helmet. The helmet was forced to an odd angle on the man's head by his position against the wall. Darash knew immediately he had come upon no mere foot soldier. This man was a centurion in the Roman army.

Darash climbed inside and shook the man's foot vigorously. The man woke with a start and leveled eyes on Darash in confusion. He jumped up and reached for his sword.

"Wait, please! I mean you no harm!" Darash cried.

"Who are you?" The soldier demanded, eyes wild. He placed the tip of his sword against Darash's neck.

"I am a Jew! I live here in Yerushaláyim—the city you protect. I just want to ask you some questions."

At the mention of Jerusalem, the centurion realized where he was. His memories of old battles left him, and panic took their place.

"Oh, no! Ahhh, no!" He cried in Latin, gripping the low wall's rim for support. "I will be put to death for this!"

You claimed to have gotten away with it once before, Darash thought, remembering the scandal that had arisen after the incident at the tomb of Yeshua.

"No, please, do not fear," Darash said, also speaking Latin. "I will not turn you in to the authorities."

The centurion's breath erupted in furious gusts. He put a hand to his forehead as though to assuage a throbbing headache and tried to clear his head. For the moment, he was vulnerable.

"You have nothing to fear from me, but you must answer my questions," Darash added, seeing his opportunity. "But… perhaps we could help one another."

Before the man could respond, a sound from below reached their ears. Darash glanced down toward where he had left his sister and saw that a woman had come along and noticed Tsarah. No doubt worried to find a child alone outdoors at night, she had stopped to ascertain the child's condition. Though he could not make out their precise words, he observed Tsarah pointing at him and the woman's gaze following. He waved to reassure her that Tsarah had not been abandoned.

The guard, too, noticed their company below.

Darash pressed on, "I have come to ask you about the murder that took place a week ago. Were you here when it happened?"

The square-jawed man looked Darash in the eyes, expression both hard and broken. Then he turned from Darash to look over the valleys and hills beyond the city. From there they could see the Essene Gate, aglow in lamplight. The light-splashed contours of the earth marked out the beginning of the road that wound through the Hinnom Valley toward Hebron. A glance to the right revealed that indeed, if the lean-to were removed, they would be able to see directly into the alley. Despite the darkness, movement could no doubt be seen, as well as anyone coming or going.

"I saw nothing," he responded at last. "I saw nothing."

"Perhaps you were asleep," Darash answered, annoyed.

"No!" The centurion turned back toward him with such conviction that Darash began to wonder if he should have questioned the large soldier.

All he has to do is throw me over the wall to the valley beneath. If it were not for the witnesses below....

"I was awake," the guard insisted. "I remember. I was awake that night. I just... did not see anything."

"Did you hear anything?"

"No." He turned away and seemed to be struggling with his memories. "I was awake, though."

"How can you be certain?"

"I have never fallen asleep at my post before that night. It was not until the night after the murder that this... this... sickness came upon me."

"Never?" Darash asked. "Were you not among the twenty who guarded the tomb of Yeshua some months ago?"

"No, I did not—!" The man stopped, recognizing the trap. He turned back to Darash, his eyes wide. "You do not know what you speak of!"

"Did you and your comrades not all claim to have fallen asleep that night?"

"You do not understand! You could not possibly comprehend what happened that night!" The Roman again turned away. He drew a hand roughly over his face. "No one could."

"Then help me understand what happened the night the Greek girl was killed at the base of this very tower."

"I will not speak of the night at the tomb! ...And I did not sleep on the night of which you speak. But since then... I have not been able to control myself. It is as though I have been put under a curse. Each night since, I have awakened here in my tower in a great fright. I do not even recall feeling drowsy. And I know what the penalty is! Who could sleep with the threat of death hanging over them?"

You, apparently. And more than once.

Chapter Seven

Shabbat Descends

"I do not understand, Nib'haz. Why would he lie?" Darash asked the following morning between customers, enjoying the comfort of speaking his mother-tongue. It was yom ha'shi'shi, the sixth day.

Nib'haz scratched his bearded chin. "Maybe he is not lying."

"But he must have seen something," Darash whispered, realizing how much trouble could ensue for the guard if anyone overheard. "He had a clear view of the alley from where he stood. If he was awake, as he claims, he must have seen something. But if he indeed fell asleep on that particular night, why would he lie about it? After all, he admitted he has been falling asleep every night since then."

"It is strange. You are right." Nib'haz muttered something and then continued, "There are only two possible answers. Either he is lying or he is telling the truth."

Darash sighed. "Either he is lying or he is telling the truth? Is that not true for everyone, Nib'haz? How does that help me?"

A condescending and infuriating smile played at the edges of Nib'haz's lips. "Young one, you say you know it, but you do not. You say he must be lying. But perhaps he is telling the truth—that he truly remembers seeing nothing. But if he is lying, he would have a reason. I see no reason for him to lie about sleeping. So, you must ask yourself: Why would he lie about seeing a murder?"

"Perhaps he is protecting someone."

"Ah! Perhaps so. ...Or, perhaps not. You do not know."

Darash groaned in frustration.

"But," Nib'haz continued. "If you want to know what motivates this man, then you should find out more about him."

"And how do I do that?"

Now it was Nib'haz's turn to sigh in annoyance. "Surely you can answer that one for yourself."

סֶ לָ ה

Darash slipped a hand into the folds of the cloth belt that cinched his cotton, V-neck tunic and fingered the coins he had earned that day. He had sold a decorative clay jar, a set of second-hand, iron wood-shaving tools, and two bronze bracelets polished to a bright sheen. He had earned enough to feed his family through the better part of next week, but he worried they would not have the half shekel tax his mother would owe the Temple later this year.

Being under the age of twenty years, he would not have to pay the Temple tax, but his youth did not stop the Roman government from collecting income and sales tax from him each month. If he was making any money at all, they claimed a right to a portion of it, regardless of his expenses. Though he worked hard each day to purchase and resell marketable goods, money flowed out much faster than it flowed in. He had not been able to save any of it. When they were forced to sell something to pay for food, the items never got replaced.

Darash removed his hand from his belt and fingered the dusty, worn material of his outer cloak. It was a thick, handsome garment, bearing multiple shades of blues and reds. Made of wool, it kept the rain off and the cold out during winter months. Its long sleeves made it more valuable, for it covered the bare places Darash's short-sleeved tunic missed.

I wonder what price it would fetch.

He owned little else of value, aside from his small tallit, an undergarment of purplish-blue cotton with four tassels worn by Jewish males as a sign of separation to YHWH. Of course, he would not think of selling this.

Darash drew Nekoda toward the well to allow her a final drink before heading home. The noon hour had come and gone and most people had already wrapped up their morning affairs to head home for the traditional afternoon rest. Today, the day before Shabbat, many would spend their time at home vigorously cooking and cleaning, for none of this could be done tomorrow. Later, some of them would return to work and to shop, but none of the People would work until sundown, as they normally did. Shabbat would begin at sundown, and no Jew wanted to be caught working or even walking too far a distance.

As Darash neared the well, he spotted his friend Chaphash coming toward him at a near run. At first he said nothing, remembering how Chaphash had witnessed his humiliating defeat to Elias earlier this week. Chaphash, though, did not hesitate to call out a greeting as soon as his eyes landed on Darash. Darash smiled and moved toward his friend.

Darash had first met Chaphash many years ago at the synagogue school, called "the house of the book," held in the home of one of the priests. Chaphash, a round-faced, pleasant young man with friendly brown eyes, was nearly six years older than Darash. Unlike the other young men his age, he had time for everyone. Darash remembered the many times Chaphash drilled him on his memorization of the Torah. It was not long, however, before Chaphash began asking Darash for help with his sums. Chaphash had helped his younger friend avoid trouble with Zahar, their priest and teacher, a brilliant but strict man, by putting in a good word for Darash.

Now, however, Chaphash dealt with struggles of his own. About four years ago, Chaphash's father died, leaving a great deal of debt for him and his brothers to pay off. In order to help settle that debt, Chaphash had indentured himself as a servant to his father's creditor, Gabahh, a wealthy Sadducee. Chaphash lived in the servant's quarters of Gabahh's large home and now approached from that direction.

"Ah, Darash, it is good to see you!" Chaphash smiled brightly, despite a line of worry crossing his brow. He slowed, but did not stop moving. "Do you by chance have any cheese to sell? I was sent by my master to get some, but the Upper Market is already closed, and I am almost certain the Lower Market cheese sellers will be also gone by the time I get there."

Darash felt annoyed for his friend. Gabahh and his wife regularly gave Chaphash impossible tasks and then severely punished him if he failed.

"It is. And, yes, I have a little. I traded it from Valad today and was going to take it to my mother, but she is not expecting it. I could let you have it for a few gera."

"Excellent!" Chaphash said, coming to a complete stop.

As they exchanged the cloth-wrapped cheese and coins, Chaphash launched into further news. "You will never believe my good fortune! I will soon be getting married!"

"What? That is wonderful! ...But what about—" Darash gestured toward the Upper City where Gabahh's home resided.

"My indentured servanthood? That is the best part! In only one week, I will have earned enough to pay back the rest of my father's debt—with the help of what my brothers have already paid, of course. That is two years' worth of wages in silver and copper, but soon I will be free—and a married man! You must come to the wedding celebration, you and your mother and sister!"

"Of course! I will shout the loudest in your wedding procession!"

"No louder than I, my friend!" he beamed.

"What did your master say when you told him?"

"Ah, well," his smile faded a bit. "He said he was happy for me, but I could tell he was disappointed. He has grown accustomed to my presence and relies on me for just about everything."

"What master would not? I have seen how well you serve him. A better helper cannot be found."

"I am sure, with the money I will give him, he can hire anyone he likes."

Darash nodded. Chaphash's smile returned. "You have to meet my wife-to-be," he said. "Her name is Hadassah, Queen Esther's true Hebrew name in the Holy Scripture. Her father says we can arrange a legal betrothal as soon as I am a free man. She is the most beautiful creature in the world, Darash! I am told she resembles her great-grandmother, a woman who was known all across Judea for her beauty. She, like Hadassah, has blue eyes. Blue! Odd, is it not? Neither of her parents and none of her siblings have this trait. There may never be another like her!" he added with a laugh, and Darash laughed, too. "Why she agreed to marry me, I will never know. Me! A mere servant!"

"You are no mere servant, Chaphash," Darash said. "You are a godly man, and Elohim has rewarded you by blessing everything your hands touch, just like Joseph. You have had some hardships, but those days will soon be over. We should celebrate!"

"Yes, yes, of course! I will have you over to my mother's house within the month, I promise! But now I must hurry back. I have already been gone too long."

Darash watched his friend sprint back toward the road that navigated around the escarpment to the Upper City and Gabahh's large home. Darash worked the lever on the well, raised some water, and poured it into the adjacent stone animal trough. He watched Nekoda as she slurped and thought of his friend.

No matter how much Chaphash is willing to pay for his freedom, Gabahh will be getting a very bad deal indeed.

סֶ לָ ה

When Darash entered their home he found his mother had already spread a white cloth over the table and laid out two challot—braided loaves—covered with an embroidered cloth, a clay flask of wine, and two unlit, clay oil lamps. Three more glowing oil lamps dotted the room. She busied herself near the fire, adding extra wood to keep it burning longer. Once it went out, there would be no refueling it.

"Shalom, Imah," Darash said, dropping his satchel of weights and measures near the door.

"Oh, not there, son," she chided. "Take that to your room and put it out of sight. I have washed and laid out your best tunic."

Darash retrieved his satchel again and went up the stairs at the back of the main room that led to the upstairs room he shared with Tsarah.

Upon entering, he found that it, too, had been swept clean and organized. His best tunic—used only for special occasions—lay spread on the bed and a basin of fresh water, a small vial of oil, and a clean cloth had been prepared for him on his small, wooden dressing table.

He hid his satchel beneath a cloth in the corner of his room. It was tradition to keep all tools, money, and utensils hidden during Shabbat, lest they remind one of working and become a temptation.

Darash removed his robe and tunic and dipped his hands in the water. Leaning forward over the basin, he scooped handfuls of water over his head and hair. Once wet, he poured a dab of olive oil into his right hand and vigorously scrubbed his scalp with it, using his fingers and both hands to work the oil all the way through.

Another good rinse and scrub with water left him feeling refreshed. He took the cloth, mopped up the extra moisture from his hair, and then dipped the cloth in the water. Next, he scrubbed his body with the wet cloth, starting with his face and neck and moving down his body to his ankles. He again used the oil, rubbing it into his skin and then scrubbing himself again with the other side of the cloth. He donned his fresh tunic, moved the basin to the floor, sat on the side of his bed, and washed his feet. A door from the upper room opened up onto the roof, so he went outside and tossed the now dirty brown water down to the yard below.

"Ah, much better." Revayah smiled in approval when he returned to the family room. "Wait," she said, nearing. "What is that?" She bent closer, staring intently at his upper lip.

Darash took a step away, self-conscious.

"It is time you begin to shave, my son."

"I have already shaved," he answered. "Abba taught me last year."

A look of something, he could not tell precisely what, crossed her face, and her shoulders lowered. Hearing her husband mentioned always affected her. She straightened and then turned and moved back to her fire.

"Perhaps you should consider doing it more often," she said. "And I see that you have yet to fix your sandal. But never mind that now. Our supper is almost ready. It is a little sparser than usual, but it will suffice to welcome in Shabbat."

At that moment, Tsarah entered from Revayah's room. She, too, had dressed in her best tunic, smelled of olive oil, and her hair had been washed, combed, and braided.

"I heard your voice," she said to him, approaching with a smile.

Darash, still standing at the door, now bent to remove his sandals. "You look very pretty this evening," he told her.

Her smile grew and she swayed from side to side. "Do you like my hair?" she asked and turned for him, lightly touching three white flowers that had been braided into it. "The flowers were my idea."

"Ah! Very pretty, indeed!"

"Come," Revayah beckoned them, placing a bowl of stew and a plate of small, cheap fish on the table next to the bread. "It is time to welcome Shabbat."

Tsarah and Darash took their places at table and folded their hands in their laps. Revayah ceremoniously took a thin stick and lit it in the fire. Then, shielding it as she walked, she returned to the table and lit the flax wicks of the two clay lamps. Finally, she went about the room, extinguishing the other lamps, bending forward to blow on them while holding her long, black hair against her shoulder with her right hand to keep it out of the flames. Then she sat as well and smiled at her children.

Revayah waved her hands over the lit lamps to welcome in Shabbat, then closed her eyes and covered them with both hands so as not to see the flickering lights before the blessing had been said. Still smiling, she took a deep breath through her nose and began to recite the prayer of blessing.

"Blessed are you, Adonai, Eloheinu, sovereign of the universe who has sanctified us with His commandments and commanded us to light the lights of Shabbat. Amen."

Revayah then removed her hands, opened her eyes, and looked into the flames, completing the ritual of the Shabbat lamp-lighting ceremony. Even as she did so, they heard the sound of distant trumpets. The joyous sound filtered from the Temple Mount into the crowded valley where they lived.

Despite the difficulty imposed on the People by the Pharisees and chief priests regarding how to keep from breaking Shabbat, it nevertheless remained the Jew's favorite day of the week. They looked forward to it during their days of labor and welcomed it with joy. Revayah, in particular, anticipated this day like no other, and it was the one day the children could count on to catch her in good spirits. Indeed, they had gotten into the habit of saving their requests of her for this day, knowing their chances for success would be much higher.

But the time had not yet come for requests or further confessions, as more ceremonies remained—the individual blessings and the meal itself. Usually, it would be the father's turn to say a blessing; however, since Tuwr's passing, Revayah had assumed that responsibility.

She placed her hands upon Darash's shoulders. He looked in her eyes as she said, "May Elohim make you like unto Ephraim and Manasseh." Removing her hands from Darash, she turned to her daughter and placed them on her shoulders. "And, may Elchim make you like unto Sarah, Rebekah, Rachel, and Leah."

Tsarah's mouth opened in a wide, toothy grin and she wiggled in her seat. Revayah smiled at her, but quickly regained her attitude of solemn reverence.

Normally, the husband would then turn to his wife and recite a passage from Proverbs—the one which began, "An excellent wife, who can find? For her worth is far above jewels…" But it had been a long time since Revayah had heard herself praised or blessed in this way.

Two more special prayers remained. The first, the Kiddush, was a prayer of sanctification of Shabbat. Revayah took the wine, poured it into a single cup, and lifted the cup before her. Again, she closed her eyes and recited, "And there was evening and there was morning, a sixth day. The heavens and the earth were finished, the whole host of them. And on the seventh day, Elohim completed his work that he had done and He rested on the seventh day from all His work that He had done. And Elohim blessed the seventh day, and sanctified it because in it He had rested from all His work that Elohim had created to do. Blessed are you, Adonai, Eloheinu, sovereign of the universe who creates the fruit of the vine. Amen."

She took a sip of the wine and passed it to Darash. He took a sip and passed it to Tsarah, who also partook. Revayah took the cup from her daughter, closed her eyes once more, and recited the second half of the benediction, "Blessed are you, Adonai, Eloheinu, King of the Universe, who sanctifies us with His commandments and has been pleased with us. You have lovingly and willingly given us Your holy Shabbat as an inheritance, in memory of creation because it is the first day of our holy assemblies, in memory of the exodus from Egypt, because You have chosen us and made us holy from all peoples and have willingly and lovingly given us Your holy Shabbat for an inheritance. Blessed are You, who sanctifies Shabbat. Amen."

All three rose from the table for yet another ritual before beginning their meal. On a small table by the wall, Revayah had placed a clay jug of fresh water, an empty basin, a cup, and a clean cloth. One by one, they approached the table, filled the cup with water from the jug, and poured it over the top and bottom of each hand, starting with the left, and catching the water in the basin. As they did these things and before wiping their hands with the cloth, they each recited this prayer, "Blessed are You, Adonai, Eloheinu, King of the Universe, who has sanctified us with His commandments and commanded us concerning washing of the hands."

They returned to the table with clean, dry hands, and Revayah removed the cloth from the two challah loaves and lifted them, one in each hand. She then pronounced the Ha-Mosi.' "Blessed are You, Adonai, Eloheinu, King of the Universe who brings forth bread from the earth. Amen." She returned one to the table and ripped the second into three, large pieces, one for each of them.

With the ritual prayers and benedictions completed, they now relaxed together at the table, helped themselves to the small, brine-soaked fish and vegetable stew, and began to talk about the day.

Darash opened one of the fish with a knife and spread its white flesh across his piece of bread before taking a bite.

"Be careful with the bones," he told his sister as she fidgeted with her fish.

"It is too slippery," she said.

"Here, let me," Revayah took command of the fish cutting and spreading process. "I think we shall stay home this evening instead of going to the evening services at the synagogue, if that is alright with you children. It may rain. So let us now sing the Zemirot," she said, referring to the joyful Shabbat table-hymns sung to celebrate the day. "Who shall begin?"

Chapter Eight

Shabbat

It did indeed rain that night, a light but steady drizzle. The next morning they slept in and arose after the sun, listening to the last drops of rainwater loosing themselves from the eaves and tree branches to rebound off stone or thud into hard packed dirt.

Breakfast consisted of leftover bread and cold stew from the night before. After their meal, they walked together to the Temple. Though they normally went to a small, neighborhood synagogue, today they decided to attend the three-hour morning Temple service to watch the ceremony of the replacement of the showbread, listen to the reading of the Torah, participate in the worship service, and watch the Shabbat sacrifice that honored the day of rest.

Darash left his mother and sister in the Court of the Women, passing through the Nicanor Gate which opened into the Court of Israel, now billowing with smoke from the now blazing altar. Just off to his right, he spotted Gabahh entertaining an audience of four men. Chaphash was not among them.

Darash had never liked Gabahh. Aside from mistreating Chaphash, he and his wife Nasha loved nothing better than to parade themselves about the Temple in their fine clothes on Shabbat. They gossiped with their Sadducee brethren and argued with the Pharisees over religion and politics. The couple made great boasts about their strict adherence to the Torah, their lenience and generosity toward the poor, and their Zadokian heritage, all which they then undermined with immoral and extravagant indulgences except, of course, on holy days. On those days, no one could hope to surpass their piety, pray more loudly on the street corners, dress in more ragged garments, nor rival the amount of ash Gabahh managed smear upon his head.

"Yes, yes," Gabahh addressed a man with a sparse beard and a coarse mustache poking out from beneath a hooked nose. "It has been both a blessing and a curse, you might say. Our ancestor, the High Priest Zadok has left us a great heritage, to be sure. And what other calling could be higher than to be Elohim's priests and servants? Of course, there are some among his descendants who prefer to put their hands to different tasks. They find themselves obligated by birth to fill Sadducean roles, seats on the council, for example. For my own part, I think they should take the responsibility as a privilege and a holy calling, as I do; however, it is also hard to watch their dreams—which are not, in and of themselves, unholy—fall by the wayside.

"For example," he continued with vigor, "the son of a cousin of mine has a great aptitude for metallurgy but no desire or charisma, truth be known, to stand up in front of others and be heard. Should he be forced to serve in the Temple due to his birth? And what of those with other practical or artistic skills? Ah! That reminds me!" He turned to a tall, lightly bearded man with thinning hair who stood to his right. "My neighbor here, Ibnei'ah, is a fine artisan. And, though he came from lowly beginnings, his artistry is sought after by some very prominent members of our sacred sect. You should see the work he did for High Priest Caiaphas with colored stone! Beautiful mosaics that give tribute to the most beautiful and beloved of Elohim's creatures! He can recreate birds, flowers, pomegranates, fawns—anything you can imagine! In fact, only yesterday I asked him to create a large mosaic on the floor of my courtyard—even larger than the high priest's."

The others nodded and smiled in approval, impressed with Gabahh's wealth and his condescension to associate with a mere artisan, as artisans typically learned their trades during their tenure as servants or slaves. Once a slave, always slavish. Still, even slavish artists, if their skill was as renowned as Ibnei'ah's, could be acknowledged in public. Religious settings offered the best opportunity for these interactions, as such notice could be considered an act of charity rather than a personal association with a baser member of society.

"So, if you visit within the next few months, you will understand if that area is off limits. I have already begun to clear the space. Of course, I am sure you will be quite impressed with the work once it is done."

He beamed at them and then slid an arm around Ibnei'ah's shoulders. Ibnei'ah's body remained stiff and he leaned slightly away from Gabahh. Gabahh did not seem to notice.

"Let me warn you, though, my friends," he continued, "this man's work does not come cheaply! It will cost a great deal of money and will probably take quite some time to complete but who could expect less for such beauty? He earns every lepton, I assure you! But would it not be a shame if this artist could not share this beauty with the world only to fulfill an obligation tied to him from his infancy?"

Darash moved on, tiring of the sound of Gabahh's voice. He wondered, though, how Gabahh could afford such a mosaic. Darash had seen such work only once, and it had been at the home of a wealthy Roman dignitary when his father had taken him along on a business venture some years ago. There they found the floor of the main hall covered in an elaborate mosaic of a man and woman in a garden, surrounded by very intricate and deccrative borders. When Tuwr had praised the beauty of the artwork, the Roman had boasted that it took close to a year to complete and nearly two years' wages. Yet that man's floor was quite a bit smaller than Gabahh's courtyard.

How large will this new mosaic be?

Darash knew Gabahh to be a wealthy member of the aristocratic Sadducees. But he was not a priest, nor even among the elite of his sect, despite his pretentions. He had money, certainly, but that much? Darash remembered Chaphash telling him how he would soon pay off his debt, and suddenly it made sense. No doubt Chaphash's final, rather large payment would help pay for this extravagance.

Shortly before the services began, Darash spotted Chaphash at the far end of the courtyard.

"Shalom! Only a few days more until you are a free man," Darash said with a congratulatory smile. Then he sneezed violently, for the smoke had grown thick in this corner of the courtyard, thanks to a slight northeasterly breeze.

"Yes! It is almost too good to be true," he beamed, but then, in a sudden fit of frustration said, "Agh! If I had only seen you sooner I could have introduced you to the girl I am to marry. She is out in the Court of the Women this moment with her family."

"I look forward to meeting her," Darash smiled.

Chaphash's smile returned, interrupted momentarily by a sneeze of his own. "You will stay then? Good! Good! Let us move in closer. I hear the Levitical choir getting ready."

The two young men headed forward, searching for a place where they could see into the Court of Priests beyond the crowds. Moments later, they watched High Priest Caiaphas, flanked by two other priests, ascend the wide sweeping steps leading to the Temple. They wore no sandals, signifying that the ground upon which they tread had been made holy by Elohim's presence.

As they climbed, they sidestepped an ugly crack that ran up the center of the steps, a wound remaining from the earthquake that shook these grounds earlier this year at the moment Yeshua had died.

The high priest wore a deep blue, short-sleeved tunic over a long-sleeved, white linen one. When the people remained quiet, the jingling sound he made when he walked could be heard. He wore small golden bells, interspersed with metal pomegranates in blue, purple, and scarlet sewn to the hem of the shorter, blue tunic.

The ephod, an apron-like garment embroidered with blue, purple, scarlet, and gold, topped his tunics. Strapped to his chest, he wore the Breastplate of Judgment bearing the most visible representations of the original twelve tribes of Israel, twelve precious stones which gleamed in the morning sun as he moved. In addition to this, two onyx stones, each inscribed with six of the twelve tribes, twinkled from each shoulder.

Three barefooted priests followed several paces behind Caiaphas and the first two lesser priests as they ascended the stairs. The first three stopped upon the wide porch and turned toward the people. The others remained about five steps below the porch throughout the morning benediction. The five lesser priests raised their hands to heaven, but Caiaphas only lifted his as far as his chin. He wore a gold-banded mitre, a turban-like crown, which bore the words "Holiness to YHWH." It would not have been right to raise any part of himself above Elohim's Name.

As Darash watched these proceedings, nagging questions surfaced—questions that had nagged at him for months.

I wonder if they repaired the curtain. If it ripped down the center during the earthquake, as rumor has it, how do they make sense of these rituals now? No priests were killed when the curtain tore.... So does that mean that the Holy of Holies is now empty? Has Elohim left us?

The Temple stood at the western end of the Court of Priests where they stood. Directly in the center of this courtyard rested the stone altar—a massive, raised platform on which a raging fire had been kindled. A ramp, wide enough for several wagons to be driven up simultaneously, led to the top of its southern side.

Darash fidgeted as the priests gave their Scripture readings and prayed for the blessing of Israel, Elohim's acceptance of their offerings, and for freedom from their heathen overlords.

How can you be sure He hears?

When they finished the opening benedictions, the Levirate choir, standing on wooden risers in the southeastern corner of the courtyard, regaled them with a song. Today they sang a Psalm which spoke of Elohim's mercy enduring forever. Their beautiful voices harmonized with the music created by a variety of musical instruments—largely cymbals, lyres, and wind instruments, including the halil and the hatzotzrot.

When the ceremony ended, Chaphash and Darash made their way through the crowds toward the exit.

"Will I see you later this week?" Darash asked.

"Perhaps. My master's wife, Nasha, plans to visit her relatives in Lydda over the next Shabbat, so I have been running back and forth to the Upper Market to fulfill every last minute need. However, I expect things will settle down while she is gone."

Darash smiled. "You must be looking forward to having one less person hurling orders at you."

Chaphash chuckled. "Yes, I confess I am. But I am surprised you have not heard of her leaving. My master has been speaking of little else for the past week and a half. It seems he has told every friend, neighbor, and relative, some of them twice."

"Is this a special trip?"

Chaphash shrugged. "One would think so by the way he goes on, but I see no reason it would be."

"How long will she be gone?"

"Only a few days. It is a day's journey there and back. She leaves the morning of the fifth day, yom khah'mi'shi and returns on the evening of first day of the following week, yom rishon."

"Just visiting relatives?"

"Yes. Her brother's family."

"A wedding? A birth?"

"No. Nothing special."

Darash shrugged, and Chaphash copied him, but then followed up with a very boisterous sneeze. Darash looked at him and they laughed.

Once the Shabbat sacrifices concluded, Chaphash introduced Darash to Hadassah, his bride-to-be. There could be no mistake that she only had eyes for Chaphash—beautiful blue eyes. But when her betrothed looked at her, she turned away shyly, only to steal glances at him when she thought no one saw.

Hadassah's family, a large one, numbered her as the fourth daughter of seven and the next in line to be married. Two of her older sisters had attended the ceremony with their husbands, listening from the Court of Women as their husbands enjoyed it from the Court of Priests. One sister carried a child on her hip, and the other struggled to keep her balance carrying a babe in her arms with a second child clinging about her legs. Hadassah had a brother, too, a boy about Darash's age, but Darash could not place him in the sequence of girls. The family chatted with Darash warmly, and at the end of a half-hour, he felt glad his friend would soon be one of them. In fact, Darash began to look forward to being able to mingle among them again, stretching out at leisurely dinners as Chaphash's boyhood friend. Surely the meals in a home with so many women would be delicious!

סֶ לָ ה

Late that evening, after Shabbat officially ended, a spindly woman named Sapphira, came and knocked loudly on the door. Revayah relied on Sapphira as a valuable source of gossip. So, when she came in, eyes wide, Revayah made Tsarah fetch a clay flask of wine, and they settled in for a nice long talk. Darash and Tsarah sat on cushions nearby listening.

"I have witnessed the most amazing thing I have ever seen in all my days!" Sapphira began, gesturing broadly with bony hands. "My husband and I were at the Temple this afternoon. We arrived early, so we decided to take a short stroll together until it was time for the afternoon prayers to begin. We found ourselves just inside the Beautiful Gate when we saw two men coming our way, about to enter. My husband recognized them as men he had seen with the Galilean, Yeshua, who was lately crucified and of whom there is so much wild speculation as to why his grave now lies empty."

"Lies! Rumors!" Revayah spat. Once leaning forward in anticipation, she now reclined, leaning away from her friend and crossed her arms.

"Y-Yes, of course, you are right," Sapphira stammered. "So, then, uh.... Well, let me see.... We were walking and...."

"So these men were....?" Revayah prompted.

"Ah, yes! Ananias pointed them out and said, 'My wife, do you remember those men there?' And I said I did not, for in truth I had no recollection of them at all. There are so many men in this city and more people coming all the time. How am I supposed to—"

"Yes, yes, of course," Revayah interrupted again. "But what were their names?"

"Ah! Let me see.... There were two of them. They were very sun-browned, but one was quite a bit larger than the other. He looked something like a bear, with those broad shoulders and that thickly bearded face. That one was Peter. The younger one was John. They are known to have been some of Yeshua's closest friends, at least they were before he disappeared."

"Was killed, you mean," Revayah corrected.

"Oh, yes, certainly."

"I know of these men," Revayah said. "My husband spoke of them on many occasions, and I have seen them about the city. They are known trouble-makers."

"But they have performed miracles," Sapphira stated in a quiet, timid voice.

"The only miracle is that they were not crucified along with the leader of their sect!"

"Ah, but wait until you hear what they did this very afternoon!"

Though Revayah's eyes were little more than slits, Darash could see her curiosity engaging. Her jaw relaxed and she leaned in again ever so slightly.

"As I said, my husband and I saw them entering the city, but then they stopped just outside the gate. We heard them talking to one of the beggars who sits outside asking for money from everyone who passes by. You have probably seen him yourself, as he is always there. You know, the lame one who never quite looks you in the eye?"

"Yes. I remember."

"But you will not see him there any longer!" Sapphira announced. Revayah's eyes opened a bit wider. "When he asked these men for money, the large one, Peter, looked right at him and made him look at them, too. Peter told him he could not give him money, but he could give him something else. And then you will never believe what he did next!"

Sapphira looked expectantly at Revayah, over at Darash and then back at her friend, who said nothing. Sapphira's long, bony fingers spread wide with wonder as she continued.

"He said, 'In the name of Yeshua Messiah of Nazareth, walk.' And then—oh, Revayah! Then he did! I could not believe what my eyes saw! That lame man walked! Peter leaned over, took him by the hand and simply raised him to his feet." Sapphira, now quite aglow with excitement, put a hand to her chest to still her gasps. "I was so amazed! I have never seen anything like that before! Of course, I have heard the stories, but I never really…. Well, you know how some people will make things up just to have a good story to tell."

"I certainly do," Revayah said, looking hard at her friend.

"Oh, Revayah! If only you could have been there! It was a miracle of Adonai—performed right before my very eyes! I saw that man pick up his mat and stand for the first time in his life! At first he was a little wobbly, to be sure, but soon he was running and jumping like a newborn colt! He praised Elohim in a loud voice and took hold of Peter. The three of them made their way to the Temple courts where he made such an uproar!"

Sapphira laughed in joy at the memory, but then her smile faded and her brow furrowed. "Oh, but things got very bad after that, I am afraid," she continued, twisting the front hem of her robe with scrawny, nervous hands.

"What happened, my friend, my sister? What went wrong?"

"The lame man—I mean, the man who had been lame—nearly dragged the much larger man, Peter, to Solomon's Colonnade and refused to let him go. He wanted everyone to know what had happened to him and a large crowd began to gather. Many recognized him as having been lame from birth and seeing him there on two strong legs—well! Everyone wanted to know what had happened, as you can imagine! Many of them seemed to think Peter and John must be sorcerers, so Peter spoke to those of us who were standing about and said that it was not by their own power that this miracle was done, but by the power of Yeshua the Christ, who we... we...."

At the mention of Yeshua's name, Revayah's face hardened. Sapphira swallowed hard.

"...who we put to death....."

"And? Is that all?"

"No... He also said we should repent from our sins and believe in Yeshua and that He—"

"I have heard enough!" Revayah stood abruptly and paced. "Surely you did not stand there to listen to all of this! Surely your husband, Ananias, a good Jewish man, was wise enough to take you home and refuse to listen to such heresy—and in the Temple courts, too!"

"Uh... actually, we stayed a little longer, Revayah. You see, the priests, some Sadducees, and the captain of the temple guard, aroused by the commotion, came over to put a stop to it all."

"That, at least, is good news! Such blasphemy cannot be tolerated! And what happened then? Were these men arrested?"

"Yes, Revayah! The temple police seized Peter and John, not the healed man, though, and took them away. They are probably in jail as we speak!"

"Ah, good!" Revayah returned to her seat. "Hopefully those men will learn to never again spread such deceit to Elohim's people! Such things should not be allowed to happen. Do you not agree?"

"Yes, Revayah... of course."

Revayah eyed her friend carefully for a moment. Sapphira squirmed.

"You were not taken in by their witchcraft, were you my friend? Tell me you and your husband cannot be so easily swayed!"

"Ah, we... ahh... we were quite amazed, of course.... but, we... I do not think we really knew what to think. It all happened so quickly, you see, and then the temple police escorted the men away. Those of us left behind just stood there amazed, talking about it. We only just left there, in fact, and I came right over to tell you, ahh... to find out what you thought of it."

Revayah smiled wisely and patted her friend's knee as a mother might a daughter who had just come to her for advice.

"I think what any good Jewish woman should think. We must not allow ourselves to listen to anyone who claims to be the long awaited Messiah, unless he really is the king he is supposed to be! This Yeshua was not a king—this we know! If he were, why are the Romans still in control? And where is he? He was the son of a carpenter—from Nazareth, of all places! And now he is dead and buried!"

"But he is not buried. He—"

"He was a pretender and his followers are nothing more, my friend!" Revayah interrupted sternly, but softened a bit and allowed her friend a condescending smile. "I know you are confused by these things. Many are. But heed my words. Do not allow your heart to be swayed from the true religion. And, though I do not always agree with what the Sadducees do and teach, I think it is good they took those men away. Just continue as you always have and let us think no more on these things."

Revayah and her friend talked of other topics, but the excitement had gone out of the conversation. Before long, Sapphira declared she had to get back home to her husband and took her leave. When Revayah closed the door on her friend, she sighed heavily, shook her head and turned to her children.

"Can you believe that?" She cried in disgust. "That woman is in great danger of becoming one of those heretics, believe me! She is easily swayed, that one. And her husband is little better! Before you know, it they will be sneaking off to those clandestine meetings held by the Followers of the Way. You must not pay any attention to such talk, my children. That woman is not to be trusted! Believe me! I have known her for years, and she always makes her stories seem much larger than they really are!"

Chapter Nine

Glimpses

By the time Darash arrived at the shuk on the morning after Shabbat, the sun had climbed midway up into the cloud-painted heavens. The bright rays chased the frost away, but the chill in the blustery wind remained. Darash had slept later than he intended and skipped breakfast to quickly ready Nekoda for the trip to market. Now he felt weak from hunger. Darash stopped and bought three braised chicken legs and a dozen boiled eggs, all wrapped in a scrap of cloth. He tore into the tender chicken flesh with hardly a breath between bites as he continued toward his spot and Nib'haz.

"The days since the murder are passing very quickly," Nib'haz said before Darash even got out a greeting. "The longer the killer goes free, the harder it will be to find him."

"Shalom to you, as well." Darash replied. "I have been busy. Things keep happening that rob me of my time and put no money in my pocket. If I do not sell enough today, there will not be any food tomorrow. I just spent my last lepton."

"Yes, I can smell it... chicken and... boiled eggs?"

"How can you tell with Valad's cheese smelling up the whole street?"

"Feh!" Valad interjected, waving a block of it about for effect, "my cheese is the freshest from here to the sea in any direction."

"It was a new smell," Nib'haz answered. "I am used to the smell of cheese."

Valad eyed Darash's stash of boiled eggs. "I will trade you this block of cheese for six of your eggs."

"Four."

"Five."

"Agreed." Darash handed over five eggs and received the cheese in return. It made a tasty addition to his remaining chicken leg and three eggs.

"What happened to all the money you took off Pertho and made since?" Nib'haz asked, returning to the original topic.

"It has all been spent on debts, food, or taken by my mother," he answered, feeling somewhat ashamed of the fact, but lacking the energy to come up with a better excuse.

"Women!" Valad spat with theatrical vehemence. "Speaking of women," Valad added in a completely changed tone. "I saw that little mud flower of Pertho's this morning."

"What?" Darash asked.

"That little dirty slave of his who you took such a liking to."

Darash colored. "Do you mean the one he calls amah?"

"Is that all he called her?" Nib'haz asked. "The one who came with him the day you lightened his belt? Do you remember?"

"I remember." Darash remembered her well. Little, unkempt Amah, teetering under a load far too heavy for her. He had thought of her often since that day. He turned back to Valad. "Where did you see her?"

"She was just over there only a moment ago." Valad strained to look. "I do not see her now, though."

Darash looked in that direction, but saw only the regular shoppers and several strangers. He quickly set out the last of his belongings and began to head in that direction. "Nib'haz?"

"I will sell for you, but do not be long this time," Nib'haz responded.

"Thank you."

Once in the open market area, Darash scanned the undulating crowd. It was a busy morning. Several caravans of foreign merchants had arrived over Shabbat, and the People were interested to discover what novel goods might be obtained.

She is so small. I will never find her among so many people.

Darash lowered his gaze and looked for someone wearing rags. After a moment, off to his left and only about a block away, he noticed a small figure with her back to him standing near a table of produce. She waited her turn to speak to the seller, a large, buxom woman whose head was wrapped in a brilliant red and yellow scarf.

I am a fool! What can I possibly have to say to her? Would she even remember me? And what will people think?

Darash wasn't even sure if it was appropriate to speak to her. He feared she might get in trouble with Pertho if caught making friends— particularly with a boy. But Pertho did not seem to be present. Amah had been sent to the market alone. He inched closer, close enough to overhear the seller.

"You can have it for a quarter-shekel and not a lepton less," the brightly-clad seller said to a frightfully thin elderly woman opposite her.

Darash watched the old woman rustle around in her belt for the money as the seller sighed in exaggerated impatience. She opened her mouth and began to say something to hurry her customer when she spotted Amah. Upon seeing the unkempt, dirty child, her eyes narrowed and she scanned the tabletop. Indeed, something was amiss.

"Thief!" she cried, eyes blazing with contempt. "Where is the pineapple that was just there? It is the only one I have, and now it is gone!" She thrust out a fat finger to indicate an empty space.

Amah stood in shock and took a step back. Quite obviously, she had no pineapple hidden anywhere on her skinny frame.

"You return it this instant, or I will call the guards! Where is it?"

Darash moved a few steps closer and leaned over to search beneath the table. Amah moved back to give him space, but the seller leaned forward to watch his movements. Baskets of fruit, earthenware jars, and discarded husks and seeds littered the ground, but it took almost no time to locate the absconding pineapple. He brought it up in sight of them all and placed it back on the table from which it had fallen.

"Ah, well, there it is," the seller said in a modified tone, though far from apologetic. "Be more careful next time," she admonished Amah, "or you might lose a hand!"

"I suggest you also take care," Darash told her, sweeping the hair from his eyes so there could be no mistake in his meaning. "If you mistreat Pertho's servant, he may have to come deal with you himself."

"What?" The woman's haughtiness evaporated. "This girl belongs to Pertho?"

Darash nodded.

"Here, child. You can have the pineapple for nothing—just so you know there are no more worries. Here, come and take it.... Child? Where are you going?"

Darash turned just in time to see Amah slipping away into the crowd. He moved to follow, but she had vanished.

$$ \text{סֶ לָ ה} $$

Darash passed the well and rounded a corner to return to rescue Nib'haz from the burden of guarding a second set of merchandise. A sudden jolt and a cry met him on the other side.

"Look what you have done, you stupid child!"

Darash stared into the angry face of a well-dressed servant. The man held a spouted jar that dripped a blood-red liquid. The liquid had also covered the right side of his chest, and was soaking through his tunic.

"Calm yourself," another servant said. He stood just behind, carrying a large tray of dates, pomegranates, and sweet breads. "It was not his fault."

"But, Malchus, this wine is expensive! And now half of it is ruined! The high priest will have my head!"

"There is plenty left. We can add a little of the cheaper wine. He will never know the difference."

"Of course, he will know! He always knows!" The angry servant shot Darash a menacing stare, eyebrows pulled together, jaw tight. "If this banquet is ruined, I—!"

"Peace, brother, peace!" Malchus interrupted. He turned to Darash. "Forgive us, young one. And, if you cannot get the stain out, I will give you the cost of a new tunic. Come ask for me at the home of High Priest Caiaphas. Ask for Malchus."

Malchus took the lead and the two men hurried on. Darash watched them go, feeling the uncomfortable moisture on his breast seeping down toward his bellybutton.

That is him! There are stories about that man. That is the man Yeshua healed in the Garden of Gethsemane after Peter chopped off one of his ears. ...His ears look fine to me.

סֶ לֶ ה

Darash walked through the door of his home that night and saw his mother preparing to leave, her back to him.

"Shavah was just here. Teshuah is about to have her baby," she explained. "I wish I knew why babies always want to come at night! I have never heard of a baby who came in the afternoon… except one—Sapphira, which is odd because she has made herself troublesome ever since. I have to go." She turned and her mouth opened at the sight of him. "Darash! What have you done? Are you alright?"

"It is just a stain. I was just walking in the market and someone ran into me carrying wine."

"Oh, Darash! I thought it was blood! But why can you not be more careful?" She raised one hand in the air in exasperation, but then shook her head. "I do not have time to deal with this right now. You will have to soak it out yourself." She hustled past him to the road, and threw back over her shoulder, "I do not know when I will be back. Could be late. Could be tomorrow. Take care of your sister. And no long walks, do you hear? Oh, yes! She told me about your ridiculous trek the last time I asked you to watch her. Stay inside! The city is dangerous at night."

Revayah dashed off, closing the outer door behind her with a bang. Darash went to the upper room and changed into his thinner, summer tunic and set to work on his soiled one. The blood-red stain took longer to wash out than Darash had thought. Cold water alone would not do it, so he stoked up the fire and boiled it. Despite his fascination with the story of Malchus's miraculous healing, he had no intention of visiting the high priest's home, let alone ask for money.

That night, Darash shivered in his sleep and rolled over, pulling the blanket tighter, trying to tuck it about his frozen feet. Moments later, though, he rose from his pallet and, still wrapped tightly in his blanket, hobbled to the peg in the wall where his robe hung. This he used to bind up his feet, finally bringing relief from the biting cold. He hated getting up in the night. He always found it difficult to fall asleep again. He closed his eyes and tried to recapture an elusive dream, but found his mind sifting through all he had to do the coming day.

Darash rolled over and squeezed his eyes tighter, trying to push the busy thoughts from his mind. He yawned and forced himself to relax, hoping to reclaim the drowsiness he had lost, but the cold air threatened to wake him further. He sank deeper under his covers and drew his knees up to his chest. A few deep breaths later, his mind had relaxed into a new, sleepy pattern. But he started at an unexpected nudging on his left shoulder.

"Wha—? Huh?" He rolled over to find Tsarah standing over him, wrapped in her blanket and shivering.

"Can I sleep with you?"

"Huh?"

"Can I sleep with you? I am cold." Her words came with short breaths pushed through chattering teeth.

"Can you not sleep with Imah?"

"She is not back yet."

Darash gazed groggily at her for a moment and then released a combined sigh and moan. He scooted over and lifted the blanket for her. A great swoosh of cold air penetrated his tunic. Tsarah eagerly climbed in beside him, but he immediately jumped at a painful, shocking sensation.

"Ahh! Your feet," he cried. "Keep them off my legs!"

"Sorry," she said, but snuggled up closer until he felt bony elbows and knees at his back.

With one arm, he spread her blanket over both of them and then huddled back down, still trying to rid his body of the cold shock. Within moments her breath came in slow, steady puffs on the back of his neck. At least one of them would get some sleep.

סֶ לֶ ה

"Oh, calamity!" Revayah wailed, as she walked in the door early the next morning. She had returned from Shavah and Teshuah's home where she had helped deliver their child. "How could this happen? Now we will no longer be able to associate with them!"

"What happened, Imah?" Darash asked, rising from his seat on the low couch.

"That woman is an adulteress! That is what!" she said and spat. "The baby she bore our dear friend Shavah is not his child at all!"

"What?"

"It is true! You can tell just by looking at that child that he is no Hebrew baby! He is the son of a foreigner! A northern merchant of the Orient, no doubt! Those squinted eyes! I always knew there was something wrong with that girl!"

Darash glanced over his shoulder and saw Tsarah listening at the base of the stairs. "Tsarah, go back upstairs," he ordered. She obeyed but could no doubt still hear their mother's resonant lament.

"What a tragedy! That woman should be stoned!"

"Imah!" Darash had never raised his voice to his mother before.

Revayah leveled angry eyes on him. "Do not speak to me in that manner, Darash! You will show respect!"

"Imah," he said again, holding his ground but forcing his voice into a steadier, softer timbre. "How can anyone be certain of Teshuah's unfaithfulness? I find that difficult to believe. Does she admit to this?"

"Oh, of course not! The little whore is nothing but a pile of tears and supplications. She insists she has been with no one but her husband, but who could believe such an obvious lie? She will be stoned before the week is out, and that child will be left by the roadside, mark my words!"

"Shavah doubts her this much? And what of their parents? Have they already given her up?"

Revayah considered for a moment. Her reply lacked her former passion, "Ah, they hardly know what to think. This unwelcome news is still very fresh. Both mothers are all tears. Her father pleads her case, though even he is beginning to doubt. And Shavah's father, Chamal, sits in the corner bearing a very mournful look. It is clear he wants to take the child in his arms and welcome it into the family regardless—the man has no scruples at all! He is a soft-hearted one, to be sure. It was he who took in Shavah, if you remember. That man would take in a wolf, if it had a limp. He— Where are you going?"

Darash, half-way out the door, now moved in a sudden rush. "I will be back soon, Imah. Do not hold supper for me!"

"I should think not! How dare you walk out on me!" she cried after him.

Chapter Ten

Joy and Shame

The home where Shavah and his wife lived with his parents appeared deserted compared to the bustling neighborhood, yet Darash's knock barely had time to echo through the inner rooms before a servant girl opened the door to him, wiping wet hands on a cloth. He waited outside as she announced him but was disappointed when she returned and asked him to come back another time.

"I know there has been much trouble here," he persisted, fearing his mother's reaction had made him unwelcome. "It is on that account I come. Please. I must speak to Chamal. It is important."

The servant girl made a face of annoyance, reluctant to disturb her master again and risk reprisal, but disappeared once more and, after a long wait, Chamal emerged in the entrance. This man, normally jovial and welcoming, appeared much changed. Above his thickly bearded chin, his usually sparkling eyes now looked dull, reddened, lifeless.

"Forgive me," he said with more formality than was his custom, "we have had much trouble of late. I cannot at this time—"

"Please," Darash interrupted. "It is because of your troubles that I have come." He glanced around to be sure no one overheard and lowered his voice. "I do not believe your daughter-in-law to be guilty of what she is accused."

Chamal's brows rose in question, and his eyes searched Darash for reason to hope. He waited for an explanation.

Darash glanced over at a woman who now walked along the road behind him, quite within earshot. "Might we go somewhere more..." he trailed off.

Chamal caught his meaning and, giving a quick nod, ushered Darash through the outer gate and main building and then outside again to the inner courtyard. Chamal gestured to a low, stone bench, but Darash remained standing and said, "Please forgive me for inserting myself into this delicate family matter, but might I see the child?"

Chamal hesitated, but then called for a servant. The same girl who had met Darash at the door emerged.

"Bring the child," he said and, within a few moments, she returned with the tiny, newborn in her arms.

Darash approached, pulled back the cloth and examined the infant's features. Indeed, the eyes seemed much more slanted than those of a Hebrew. His skin, too, was lighter, but his hair was jet black like that of his parents. Darash asked if he might hold the baby. He knew Chamal had not yet taken the infant in his arms because to do so would be to accept him into the family. Custom dictated, though, that if Chamal refused to take the baby to his bosom within the first three days of his life, the rest of the family must also reject the child. They must take him from the city and leave him by the side of the road to die or, by some miracle, be adopted by a passerby.

Chamal nodded his assent to the servant girl, and she handed the baby boy over. Chamal waved the servant girl away. Darash cradled the tiny child in his arms, remembering how he had often held Tsarah when she was just this size, brand new and completely vulnerable. The baby attempted to wiggle at being disturbed from his slumber, but the tight swaddling clothes, intended to keep his arms and legs growing straight, prevented much motion. Darash noticed the smell of olive oil that had been mixed with salt and water and rubbed into the child's skin to keep him healthy. At least the baby was being cared for.

"Chamal," he began, considering the little one's face as he took a seat on one of the benches. "Tell me the story of how you came to be Shavah's father."

Chamal sat on a bench across from Darash with a sigh. "I was on my way home from Gophna in the north. I had gone there on business and had stayed a few extra days with my sister's family. The mighty walls of Yerushaláyim had just come into view over the last hill when I heard a noise. It sounded like a wild animal, something injured or dying. I thought to investigate, but my exhaustion got the better of me. It had been a long day and injured animals can be dangerous, so I decided not to stop. I kept going but heard the sound again. Finally, curiosity prevailed. Still determined not to stop, I sent my servant to search the brush. Neither of us was prepared for what he found, though. He came from the brush, eyes wide and filled with great concern.

"'What is it?' I asked. 'It is a small child of about three or four,' he said. I jumped down from my horse and went to see. On the ground sat a small boy. Dirt and ant bites covered his skinny, naked body. I went to pick him up, but he cried out in fear and ran from me. He was frail from lack of food, so I easily caught him, but how he fought! Kicked and screamed. Tried to scratch me and bite me! Poor little thing. I had to hold on to him very tightly while my servant fetched food, water, and a blanket for him. Despite his hunger and thirst, he still fought me until I had him wrapped securely in the blanket. In time, as I talked softly to him, he began to calm down and let me feed him.

"I got him back to the house and my wife and I together washed him and dressed him and made sure he had plenty to eat. We made a bed for him, but at first he was unable to sleep in it. He could not fall asleep unless someone was holding him and no sooner would we put him down than he would wake with terrible screams. For several weeks, my wife and I took turns holding him throughout the night as he slept."

Darash waited for Chamal to continue, but he only stared at the babe, now asleep again. Chamal did not really see the child resting in Darash's embrace. His eyes instead stared unseeing and moistened with sorrow.

"What did you find out in town about him?" Darash prompted.

"I asked around to see if anyone had lost a child. I reported him at the Temple and to the council and even with the Roman magistrates, but several weeks went by without anyone coming forward to claim him. Eventually, the priest told us we could adopt him as our own if we wished, which we did. And the rest you know."

"So nothing was ever discovered of his real parents?"

"No, nothing. At least, nothing that could be proven. There were speculations, but..."

"Such as?" Darash asked.

"There had been some reports of bandits robbing and killing travelers, as there always are. We could only assume Shavah's family had been killed or chased away by bandits, leaving him behind."

"And he was found along the northern road from the city?" Darash prompted.

"Yes, as I said."

"And were there many travelers coming and going during that time?"

"Yes. Passover approached and, as you know, Passover attracts many people, not only Jews. There is much money to be made that time of year."

"And these merchants from the north... were there any who may have come from the Orient?"

Chamal stopped and grew pensive. "I do not think many came from the Orient directly," he said, measuring his words to match his best recollections. "However, it is well known that quite a few men from the north find Oriental wives to be desired.... I have seen several such travelers...."

Darash waited, saying nothing.

"Is it possible?" Chamal finally asked. He spoke to himself—to the beliefs of his heart, as he stared at the sleeping baby in Darash's arms. "Could a child from such a union pass for Hebrew?"

"I have witnessed such things," Darash said, also looking at the child. "Sometimes certain traits of a parent like blue eyes, for example, might not show up in their children. But, later, a grandchild or a great-grandchild might be born with blue eyes. So, when I heard of your family's troubles, I thought of how Shavah's natural heritage is in question. And, considering Teshuah's impeccable character...."

Darash glanced up as a great sob escaped Chamal's lips. The man's face contorted with emotion and he put a hand to his mouth. After a moment, he opened his arms. "Give me the child!" he cried.

As Darash moved to hand over the baby, a door burst open and a woman's cry of joy was heard. Chamal's wife rushed toward them, followed by Shavah and several servants. They watched with tears streaming as Chamal took the child, cradled him in his arms, and kissed his tiny head.

"This child is my own grandson," he announced in a loud voice. "He is a part of this family from now until the good Lord takes him!"

סֶ לָ ה

"What? Where did you get those animals?" Revayah asked, seeing Darash leading three calves and a donkey foal through the outer door of their home.

"Chamal has accepted the child. The baby is truly Shavah's son, and in his joy he gave me these animals."

"What? Accepted the child? But it is obviously the child of a foreigner!"

"And so is Shavah, Imah. Do you not remember how Chamal found him? Once the child is a little older, the resemblance will become plain. At least now the child will live long enough for everyone to be certain."

For a moment, Revayah stood eyes wide, face drawn, and mouth speechless. But, as she watched him pen up the new young animals and fetch feed for them, her features relaxed and she smiled as one who has just guessed a secret.

"This is a very nice gift, Darash. I know Chamal is a reasonably wealthy man, but these animals are worth two months' wages."

Darash gave a slight shrug.

"Come now, my son. What did you do?" She leaned toward him, one hand on the stable fence, her voice soft and compelling.

He looked down and away. "Very little, Imah."

"Surely you did something," she coaxed. "Chamal did not give three calves and a donkey foal to everyone who visited, now did he? You convinced him to keep the child, did you not?"

"I only helped him see what he already knew."

"What he wanted to believe, you mean," she said and laughed. "I knew it! I knew that old man would not be able to send them away." She laughed again. "Ah, well. So much the better, I suppose." She stroked one of the young calves as it slowly chewed a knot of fresh hay. "It is unfortunate, though, that no one will know of your service to them. Surely Chamal does not want the whole city to know they suspected their own daughter-in-law of adultery, despite that she has since been so mercifully vindicated."

"It is better that way. You know how people are," Darash said.

"Oh yes! Such gossips! No one would believe in her innocence once such a notion got into their heads. People always want to believe the worst." She picked up a handful of hay and tried to feed the donkey foal who had not yet noticed the provisions. "But you, my son, always want to believe the best of everyone." She paused. The foal finally took a small nibble. "It has worked in our favor this time. But beware… Such an attitude is much more likely to empty our pockets than fill them."

Chapter Eleven

A Step Closer

"I shall be busy today, Darash," Revayah announced as Darash sat eating a late breakfast with his sister. "I need to purchase some food and some items for the house, so I am going to sell one of the calves to Ananias. Sapphira will likely expect me to stay the afternoon. I need you to watch your sister."

Darash sighed and made a face, but Tsarah grinned broadly in his direction. She liked accompanying him to the shuk or anywhere. He smiled back.

The market provided a place of endless entertainment and business. Women walked along carrying baskets of cakes or fruit on their heads, the streets boasted items of every kind and color imaginable, and sellers called out to passersby about their on-time deals. Although the Jews hated seeing so many foreigners in Jerusalem, the Jews interacted with them when the situation demanded, and nearly all such interactions occurred within the market area. In the shuk, far more than buying and selling took place. Men came seeking employment or business advice. Others chose the shuk as a meeting place or a place to stage public events or make an announcement.

However, Tsarah enjoyed the market for another reason. Plenty of children accompanied their parents and sought one another out to play. They invented elaborate games, made dolls or toys from the scraps of whatever items they could charm from the vendors, and chased one another between the booths streaming peals of laughter in their wake.

A half hour later, Darash and Tsarah said goodbye to Revayah at the dyer's booth and, within moments, began unloading their wares next to Nib'haz. Tsarah approached the older man and gingerly tapped him on the shoulder. Darash knew Nib'haz had heard her coming, for he had seen the blind man's knowing smile at their approach. But Nib'haz had his own way with children.

"Who has come to bother me this morning?" the old man asked in mock annoyance.

"It is I!" she announced merrily. "Tsarah!"

"Tsarah? That little child who never leaves me be?"

She giggled and tapped his shoulder more vigorously.

"Stop it, now, child! Be still! If you are going to be so troublesome, I am going to put you to work. Now, sit down here," after finding her feet with one hand, he placed a hand on each of her hips and pulled her down beside him. He then tried to settle her wiggles by placing a half-formed basket in her lap. "There, now... take hold of this piece of straw... just like that.... Weave it around just so.... There you are. That will teach you to make trouble for an old man!" But he smiled at her giggles.

Darash smirked. Evidently, Tsarah had decided against playing with the other children today in favor of "helping" Nib'haz with his weaving, as she loved to do. The old man always encouraged her and told her how wonderful her work was, though he later undid the misshapen parts and rewove it. A few weeks ago, as Darash watched Nib'haz fix a lopsided basket, Nib'haz said, "Ah! Tsarah is a beautiful little girl!"

Darash asked, "How do you know she is beautiful? You have never seen her."

"Beauty is not only seen, my friend," he replied. "Beauty is breathed."

Darash still did not really understand what the old man meant.

He sat for a long while without drawing a single look of interest for his wares. The cool air and hidden sun did not hold out promise for better. When the pain in his buttocks and lower back became intolerable, he stood to stretch. Rolling his head back to ease the tension in his neck, he examined the sky. Clouds, ringed with gray, gathered in the east. The sun struggled to penetrate them. Though growers and shepherds relied on the rainy season, Darash and the merchants did not like what it did to business. Darash decided it was time for a stroll through the shuk. Nib'haz still entertained Tsarah and Valad could keep an eye on his belongings.

As he rounded a corner, he came upon Barus, walking and talking with two men. By their dress Darash knew Barus's friends to be Sadducees, members of the wealthy, aristocratic priesthood. The bearded one, speaking at the moment, appeared older than Barus. He wore a skull-cap with a great tallit head-covering draped across it. Made of white wool, it bore a purplish-blue emblem of a vineyard, bordered with black stripes, and a cord with eight threads and five knots to represent the number of commandments in the Torah. This drape hung long and loose about his shoulders and back, nicely matching his purple, long-sleeved robe. He carried a scroll in his hand, likely some holy writings.

The other man, a good deal younger, wore a similar, rust-colored robe, but no cap. He, too, wore a tallit draped, not on his head, but about his shoulders and the back of his neck, hanging down to his thighs in front. By wearing the large tallit at all times, they displayed their strong Jewish lineage; however, it was not at all unusual to see them interacting with Greeks, Romans, and other foreigners, or even entering into business with them—actions which drew no small amount of criticism from the Pharisees. Darash, too, and indeed most Jewish men wore the tallit as a reminder of their separation unto Elohim, but theirs were small and worn close to the tunic, often hidden from sight.

"Ah, Darash!" Barus greeted him in Aramaic. "Let me introduce you to my friends and business associates. This is Jacob and his son-in-law, Ratash."

"Shalom," Jacob and Ratash greeted the inferior youth out of respect for their friend. "Soon to be son-in-law," Jacob clarified.

"The betrothal was finalized only this week, correct?" Barus said.

Jacob nodded, his eyes on Barus.

"Forgive me for not attending the celebration," Barus continued. "I have had other matters...."

"No apologies, my friend," Jacob responded with feeling at the reference to Barus's loss. He placed a hand on the taller man's shoulder. "Our hearts mourn with you during this difficult time."

"Yes," Ratash added. "Your loss is ours."

Darash felt awkward in this personal conversation. Neither Sadducee had glanced his way since his introduction, nor would they later deign to recognize him if they passed him in the street even an hour from now.

"Actually," Barus said, "this young man offered to help me find the one who robbed me of my daughter."

Jacob's eyebrows raised in surprise. His glance made Darash feel chastised for involving himself in the matter. Ratash, however, had a different reaction. His was one of annoyance.

"This child has made you believe he can find the one who did it?" Ratash asked with a sidelong glance at Darash.

Barus sighed. "Not really. But I knew his father—a clever merchant with unusual insights. So I hope Darash might discover something... in time."

"How much is he asking in pay?" Ratash shot Darash a direct, accusatory gaze.

Darash glanced down and away.

"Nothing," Barus answered, his voice stronger, harder. "At least, no more than I promised as a reward to anyone who might lead me to the vile murderer. Perhaps you did not hear my pleas for help? I am sure if you had, you would have offered to help as well."

"Forgive my young friend," Jacob intervened, glancing nervously from one man to the other. "He did not mean to insult your ability to spot a deception. He is merely desiring your best—not wanting to see your hopes misplaced."

"And I am more than happy to help you in any way I can," Ratash quickly added. "I simply have no idea where to begin."

Barus smiled. "I understand completely. And, I certainly appreciate your concern on my behalf. But I am willing to accept anyone's help in this matter, Greek or Jew, wealthy or poor, young or old. I am sure you understand my desperation for answers."

"Of course, we do," Jacob answered. He handed the scroll to Ratash, who accepted it with his left hand. Then Jacob laid a hand on Barus's shoulder. "Of course, we do! In fact, I have already been asking around, but... unfortunately Adonai has not seen it fit to open my eyes to any truths that might help your cause."

"Perhaps in time He will," Barus replied. "But, if not, perchance He may see fit to open the eyes of someone else." He glanced at Darash, and the others followed his gaze. "After all, did not your prophet Isaiah say, 'He gives strength to the weary and increases the power of the weak'? Between the boy and me, we certainly fulfill the human requirements of those words."

Darash swallowed. The three sets of eyes leveled on him drew uncomfortable warmth into his neck and cheeks. Thankfully, they did not stand staring at him for long.

"Ah, my friend!" Jacob said. "Your understanding of our Scriptures has always impressed me immensely! You speak with great wisdom! Perhaps Elohim will reward you in your search. I would be interested in hearing the Greek perspective on Jewish prophesies and...."

Darash took a step back. Barus met his eye, nodded a friendly dismissal, and Darash slipped away. He rounded a corner. Sellers lined the street displaying and offering prepared food. He bought four honeycakes—two for himself and two for Tsarah and Nib'haz. Valad would have to fend for himself. Darash munched as he walked, deep in thought over the men he had just met and their relationship to Barus.

Barus mixes very freely within Jewish circles.

Before he could decide what to make of it, he recognized a young woman a short distance away. Mareh, Aphiemi's friend, stood looking over several tall stacks of flat bread teetering on a blanket on the ground. She appeared to be shopping alone.

"Shalom." Darash approached her with a slight bow of his head, using their common Hebrew tongue. "Might I have a word with you?"

Mareh's countenance, relaxed and thoughtful the moment before, drew instantly taut with worry. It was not proper for her to be seen speaking to a man in public, especially outside of the protection of her father. She drew a nervous hand up to grasp the edges of her head covering, and pulled it tighter about her head and shoulders.

"I will not take much of your time," he said, keeping a respectable distance and hoping to put her at ease. "I simply need to ask you one more question."

With a worried look about, Mareh followed Darash to an empty area next to a wall, still within the shuk but out of easy earshot.

"Who was Aphiemi's suitor?"

"I told you. There was no—"

"Mareh, do not worry. I will not tell your father you lied for her. But this is important. I know there was a young man."

Mareh's upper lip began to quiver and her eyes glossed with moisture.

Oh, no! She is going to cry!

She paused, and then spoke in a barely audible whisper. "You are right. There was a young man, but Aphiemi never told me his name." Mareh's eyes darted around, and Darash waited for her to continue. "I do not think they wanted anyone to know."

"But why? Aphiemi was free, was she not? Why did he not simply go to Barus and ask for her hand?"

"I asked her the same question. She said he would do so soon, but he never did. She feared he had received a better offer of marriage."

"Better than the daughter of Barus? He is no beggar! He could have provided a very nice dowry."

"Yes, but there is something else. As you know, Aphiemi was a Greek."

"And this man was not?"

"I am almost certain she spoke of him attending the synagogue."

"A Jew?"

"Yes."

Hmm.... That would certainly have made their relationship more difficult.

Intermarriages were not unheard of. Some Jewish men had married foreign women and raised Jewish children. Still, both Jew and Greek disparaged such alliances, and such families often faced continued harassment from their Hebrew brethren.

"Well, Mareh, thank you. You have been a great help." Darash moved to leave her, but she caught his sleeve.

"I promised Aphiemi I would not tell a soul," she breathed, again speaking in a low whisper. "But I think you should know one more thing."

Darash waited as she gathered herself to continue.

"A few days before she died, Aphiemi came to my house, greatly distressed. How she cried!" Mareh swallowed, and a tear trickled down her left cheek. After a darting glance around, she pulled him toward her and put her mouth to his ear and whispered so softly he almost did not hear.

Mareh then turned on her heel and rushed away, her robe and soft, blue sash flapping behind her as she moved.

Darash stood frozen with a knotted heart.

Aphiemi had been with child.

סֶ לָ ה

"Ah! There you are," Nib'haz called to Darash while he was still several paces away. "Come get your troublesome little sister! She is scaring away all my customers."

Tsarah giggled. "You have had no customers, Nib'haz!"

"Ah! And now you see why!"

Darash pulled out the remaining honeycakes and handed them to Tsarah to share. "Perhaps this will help compensate you for your trouble."

"Mmm... Smells delicious," he said. "Hand me some of that, child."

As they ate, Darash settled onto his reed mat. Apparently, he had received no customers either, but he cared more about what he had just learned.

Aphiemi, with child? Had her killer known this? Could her killer have been the unborn child's father? What kind of man kills the mother of his unborn child—making one murder two?

Such a situation would have disgraced them both. If the man were married, they would both be guilty of adultery and subject to punishment by law. Barus would have been within his right to have her flogged or, at best, sent away. Her lover could be forced to pay heavily, and his place in society would be severely weakened. Darash knew that some men in such a situation would see murder as an easy way out.

"Darash, you are very quiet," Valad said, drawing Darash's gaze through dangling hair. "What are you thinking of so intently?"

"I will share it with you another time," he said with a meaningful glance at his sister. Thankfully, Valad caught his meaning and did not press him further.

Darash watched the few milling shoppers and listened to the pleadings and "one time offers" of the sellers and shopkeepers desperate to redeem themselves in the afternoon for the slow business of the morning. He smelled frying lamb kabobs. The rich aroma melded with the ever-present smell of Valad's supply of cheeses and made his mouth water.

Darash leaned his head back against the stone wall and closed his eyes. The sounds of Jerusalem surrounded him—voices of sellers peddling their goods and wares, sandals on stone, the clattering of hooves, the snorting of donkeys and mules, the yip of a dog as someone chased it off with a curt shout. The city, though still busy, seemed somehow changed. Was it just him, or had Jerusalem become a sadder place since Aphiemi's murder?

Darash felt Nib'haz slap his forearm, and he opened his eyes. A familiar-looking man and his young daughter approached. The girl, about Tsarah's age, followed her father, walking with a slight limp, but then stopped to stand at her father's side. Tsarah and the little girl eyed one another with friendly interest.

"Shalom, Ibnei'ah," Valad greeted him. "How have you been these days?"

"El Roi is still watching out for us," he said, using the name given to Elohim by Sarah's handmaiden, Hagar, meaning 'God who sees me.' "I have plenty of work."

He stood with one protective hand on his daughter's shoulder. As Darash observed their exchange, he recognized the man as the mosaic artisan he saw at the Temple with Gabah on Shabbat.

"That is good," Valad said. "I was sorry to hear about your wife's passing."

The tall, sun-bronzed Jew with light brown eyes and thinning hair and beard, said nothing but nodded his head in thanks.

"Shalom, child, what is your name?" Nib'haz asked, no longer surprising Darash with his intuitive ability to detect the presence of unseen children.

"Ra'ah," the curly-haired, little one answered.

"What a pretty name! You must be a very perceptive young lady to have such a name."

"When she was born, she did not even cry. She just studied my wife's face for the longest time. That is how she got her name," Ibnei'ah explained. "Is this your little girl?" he asked Nib'haz, indicating Tsarah.

"This troublesome little thing?" Nib'haz asked with a smile and Tsarah giggled. "No. She is the boy's sister." He thrust his chin in Darash's general direction.

Tsarah put down a frayed basket. Stepping over a pile of brooms, she took Ra'ah's hand. "Come," she said. "I want to show you something."

Ra'ah glanced up for permission from her father. He smiled in assent, and Tsarah led her to a bag near Darash that was full of little dolls for sale at five prutot apiece, about half the cost of a loaf of bread. The girls were soon engrossed comparing the various tunic colors and hairstyles of the dolls, but Ibnei'ah surprised Darash by turning to him.

"Shalom," the man greeted him. "You are Darash, son of Tuwr, are you not?"

"I am," he said standing and bowing his head to his elder in respect.

"I have heard much of you of late," he said. "My wife was Chamal's cousin." By Ibnei'ah's tone and look, Darash could tell he did not want the circumstances of his interest known.

"A very generous and wise man," Darash smiled, "and a very good father and grandfather."

Ibnei'ah smiled. "Yes," he said. "Yes, he is." Ibnei'ah glanced at a jar of the natural, black pitch among Darash's wares. "I would like to purchase some bitumen," he said. "In fact, I intend to buy only from you... as you are so close to my family. I am an artisan. I decorate the homes of the wealthy with colorful stones for their floors, walls, and gardens. So if you think you can keep a regular supply...."

"Of course," Darash replied, happy at this unexpected blessing. "How much does your regular supplier charge?"

"Four and a half denarii for one ephah."

"Then I shall charge four."

Ibnei'ah smiled. "Very good, very good!" After finishing the transaction, he turned to his daughter. "Ra'ah," he said. "It is time for us to continue home."

The girls seemed reluctant to leave the dolls.

"Which one do you like the best?" Darash asked.

"This one," Ra'ah said, holding out a straw doll wearing a robe made from a blue scrap of cloth.

"Then it is yours," he said and the child rewarded him with an immense smile.

"How much for the doll?" Ibnei'ah asked, digging for his money bag again.

"Please," Darash smiled, waving away Ibnei'ah's gesture. "Consider it my thanks for your business."

סֶ לְ ה

"What has captured you today, Darash?" Revayah asked him after dinner that evening once Tsarah left to play across the street. Revayah stood near a pile of newly-washed dishes on a ledge, wiping out the last bowl with a cloth. "Why could you not play a game with your sister? She has been trying to get your attention all evening."

"Forgive me, Imah. I have a lot on my mind today."

"Well, that is plain," she said, slapping the bowl down and folding her cloth in fast, hard motions. "Having you here tonight is like having a stranger in my home."

"It is this trouble of the murdered girl," he confessed. For a moment, he considered confiding in her what he had learned that afternoon.

"Perhaps it is best that you put it out of your mind altogether," Revayah told him as she began sweeping up. She paused and gestured broadly with her hands. "You will never find the killer, that is certain, and neglecting your family will not make the person who did it confess. Besides, you should be using your time finding new business connections. Put this other business from your mind and focus on your own affairs!"

Darash sighed, akin to a growl. His mother had no understanding of how deeply he wanted to find the man who had killed Barus's daughter… and her unborn child.

Maybe she is right. Aphiemi was not just an innocent victim. She gave herself to a man not her husband! Had she been a Jewess, she could have been stoned for this! …Maybe she deserved to die.

The knot in Darash's chest grew tighter. He realized he had begun to like this poor girl—a girl his own age, who, by every description, had been very beautiful and talented and loved.

How could she betray her family this way? What would make such a girl throw away her future? …She must have loved him.

That last thought came to him unexpectedly.

…or believed she did …and trusted him, too. But a man who destroys a woman's purity and safety is not worthy of such trust. For there is no love in him.

Chapter Twelve

The Sin of Pride

Darash awoke to the acrid smell of lentils burning. His mother had been raised in a wealthy family, used to having a servant cook the meals. When she married Tuwr, he also secured a servant for her, a woman named Huldah, who had done the cooking. However, after Tuwr's death, Darash could not support the lifestyle to which they had become accustomed. Within a few months, they had sold their animals and greatly reduced their supply of wine, olive oil, and grain. Huldah, seeing their inevitable descent into poverty, left to find employment elsewhere.

Revayah found herself in charge of the cooking, cleaning, and mending—hardships she considered wholly Darash's fault. So, when he found holes in his robe or had to eat burned bread, he took it to mean his mother felt such menial tasks to be beneath her. Or perhaps it was her way of saying that, if Darash could not bring in a decent wage, he deserved to live like it. This morning he would once again choke down his overcooked lentils and pretend he liked them.

As Darash approached the shuk on yom shli'shi, the third day, he heard snippets of many conversations centering on Peter and John and the man who had been a cripple.

"I cannot speak for you," Valad said as he slapped his cheeses onto his reed mat with extra flair that crisp, energetic morning, "but if I had been a cripple for over 40 years and was healed by just a word, I would sit up and listen to anything they had to say! —That is, I would stand up and listen! Ha, ha! Believe me! I would not care who they claimed was responsible! I would believe every word they said from then on!"

"You speak heresy!" one of his regular customers, a middle-aged bondswoman, accused.

"Heresy?" Valad asked. "Heresy against what? Against getting healed? Feh!"

The woman squared her shoulders and glared at Valad but said nothing. In a huff, she marched off to purchase her wares elsewhere. Valad seemed not to notice.

"So you believe the stories?" Darash asked, tying Nekoda to her usual post.

"Sure I do! I saw the man myself this very morning as I passed by the jail on my way here. He was standing outside asking for the men they were holding—the men who healed him. He refused to go away until the magistrate himself came out and told him they had already been freed.

But he was standing, I tell you! Standing on two legs that are stronger than mine! That same man that has been sitting and begging at the gate for most of his life and all of mine. And now he stands! And walks and runs and jumps!"

Darash removed a bundle of supplies from Nekoda's back and carried them to his usual place. Nib'haz sat nearby, silently listening.

"Shalom, Nib'haz," Darash greeted him.

"Shalom, my young friend."

"What do you think of all this talk?"

"There is always talk."

Darash paused, wishing Nib'haz would state his true opinion. Nib'haz had never been especially forthcoming on the subject of religion. Though he followed the teachings of the Mishnah and the Torah, Darash had never seen him at a Temple or even at the synagogue. Blind men did not stand and talk in company with Pharisees or Sadducees in the market or courtyards of Jerusalem. Nor would Nib'haz offer an opinion touching religious piety or Shabbat practice, despite his keen knowledge of the Torah. He was simply absent from the shuk on Shabbat and present every other day of the week.

"Where are the men now?" an old man asked a Pharisee's wife, who had come down in search of a new comb.

"My husband attended their questioning before the Sanhedrin. Annas, High Priest Caiaphas, John, and Alexander, among others, brought them from the jail to be questioned. They wanted to know what they had been preaching and how they were able to heal that man. The meeting lasted most of the morning of the first day of the week and then reconvened in the afternoon. They were kept one night, but then turned loose the next day."

"Are these teachers and miracle workers Pharisees?" he asked.

"Oh, no!" she answered with more force than necessary. "They are but fishermen!"

"Fishermen? Fishermen who preach and go about healing people?"

"Well, fishermen who preach, yes, but no one seems to know by what power they healed that man. The teachers of the law ordered them to stop preaching in the name of Yeshua. …My husband seems to think they will not obey, though. So do not be surprised if these men find themselves in jail again."

Darash and his friends made more than their usual sales that morning. The excitement of the past days had inspired many to leave their homes and mingle in the shuk to hear more about the mysterious Yeshua and those who performed miracles in his name. But something else weighed on Darash's mind that he desperately wanted to discuss with Nib'haz—only, he did not wish to discuss it in front of Valad.

As the noon hour approached, Darash got his chance. Valad packed up a few minutes early for the afternoon rest, leaving them in relative solitude.

"Nib'haz," Darash addressed his gray, wrinkled friend. "I found out something about the Greek girl's death that I now wish I did not know."

"Ah, yes?" Nib'haz responded, turning his head and blind eyes toward the sound of Darash's voice.

"Yes. And, now I do not know if I should pursue this any longer."

"How can that be? What could you have discovered that would make you want to let her killer go free?"

Darash sighed. "It is not that I want her killer to go free, but... I wonder if anyone will desire to find him once they know the truth."

"Perhaps you should simply tell me what you discovered so I can better advise you."

Darash paused, searching for the right words. "Aphiemi was... The girl had been... What we did not know was that...."

"Darash, my young friend," Nib'haz cut in, "just say what you need to say."

Darash took a deep breath and blurted, "She was pregnant."

"Ah.... I see... A young girl... Ah, ha... Yes... This makes things clearer...." Nib'haz muttered to himself, mulling over this new information. But, unlike Darash, he did not appear shocked or scandalized by it.

Finally, Nib'haz turned again to Darash and asked, "So you believe that, if a man seduces a young, unmarried girl and causes her to become pregnant with his child, he then has the right to smash her head in with a rock—killing both her and his unborn child? That he commits no crime in this?"

"What? No! I...." Darash stumbled to a stop. "Wait. How do we know the killer was the child's father?"

"Tell me. Who else would have reason to kill her? And what other reason could there possibly be for an unmarried, pregnant woman to sneak out of her father's house to meet someone late at night?"

"Perhaps she was meeting one of those women who claim to make pregnancies like this one go away."

"No, Darash. A woman in that business would have no reason to kill her. To do so would be to eliminate her own source of income, and such women have no scruples about marital convention."

"Or, maybe, Aphiemi met someone to whom she confided her sin, like a rabbi or a friend of the family, and that person killed her for it."

"Darash, even the killer knew he did wrong. Otherwise, why lure her to a dark alley and strike her down in the dark of night? Why not drag her before the Sanhedrin and expose her sin to them?"

Darash paused, thinking. "Because this was not an act of justice.... It was an act of self-preservation."

"Yes, my young friend! Now you are beginning to understand what was in the killer's mind and heart!"

"He had something to lose—perhaps a lot to lose. If he had exposed her, he would have exposed himself as well."

"Yes! Very good! As you probably know, much of the time these girls are simply sent away to live with family in another village. Only rarely are they actually stoned. And the men who used them, although they are rarely punished, often lose respect within the community. People talk. Of course, if the man is honorable, he can marry her—even after the pregnancy is discovered. Life would be difficult for them, but it is not necessary for the woman to die for the sins of them both."

"But this man was not honorable. And he did not want to marry her," Darash said. "I do not think he ever truly loved her. It appears as if he cared more about his position and his plans than he did about her life."

"And the life of their child," Nib'haz added. "Keep going. What else can you surmise about this man?"

"He is... he is a religious man, I think...."

"Oh? And why do you think that?" Nib'haz asked.

"Something Valad pointed out the day we found out about the murder. The killer waited until Shabbat had ended to kill her.... And, the knowledge of her pregnancy must have given him a religious excuse to kill her—at least, in his mind. ...Even though he was the father of her unborn child."

"The killer you search for is a Jew," Nib'haz supplied.

"And a very strict one," Darash added.

"Strict in his religion, yes.... Yet he fails to see or understand Adonai."

Darash thought about this for a moment.

Could there be a difference between knowing Elohim and being faithful to one's religion?

The idea was foreign to him, and yet....

"Tell me. How did you find out about the girl's condition?" Nib'haz asked.

"I spoke to one of her friends—a Jewish girl, actually. She told me."

"So Aphiemi's parents did not know?"

"No. And they still do not."

Nib'haz relapsed into silence for a moment, muttering to himself again, but this time too quietly for Darash to make sense of his words.

"What am I to do, Nib'haz?" Darash asked. "Should I tell them? Should I tell anyone?"

"This is a great dilemma, indeed," his mentor said, shaking his head. "If you tell them, it will break their hearts, but at least they will have the answers they seek."

"But if I tell too many others, I risk ruining her family's name."

"You risk more than that."

"What do you mean?"

Nib'haz adjusted himself on his mat to angle his shoulders more toward Darash. "Darash, my young friend, though I have never seen your face, I have come to know you in these past months. You are a clever, thoughtful, and compassionate youth. You care deeply for your family, you work hard, you try to live in a way to honor Elohim, and you sacrifice much for the people you love. But, even you, just now, were almost ready to let a vicious killer go free because you felt the victim was somehow... tarnished."

Darash's shoulders slumped, knowing Nib'haz spoke the truth. A sour feeling formed in the pit of his stomach.

"What do you think the People would do if they knew the truth of her condition? Would they condemn the murderer? Or the victim?"

Nib'haz paused.

"Truly, Nib'haz, I am now certain the murderer should be punished for his crime. For it was a crime—and a terrible one. I do not think Elohim would be pleased by this man's actions, no matter her sins."

"Very, very good, young one! You show a wisdom beyond your years. It is a difficult thing for us to separate one person's sins from another's... but we can be certain that Elohim will."

"And that is your point, is it not, Nib'haz?" Darash asked, looking at his friend. "The chief priests will not be able to do this? They will assume that, because she was not perfect, her killer should not be punished, regardless of his crimes?"

Nib'haz nodded.

"But, if he is caught, he may tell them of her condition, anyway, to rid himself of some of the guilt of it."

"He well may," Nib'haz agreed, nodding again. "But then he will be telling on himself, as well. For whom, but the father of her child, would want them both dead?"

סֶ לֶ ה

It was too late to go all the way home for a meal and a nap, so Darash stayed in the market to hunt for something to eat. A few prutot bought him a small sack of dried dates and a small loaf of bread. He led Nekoda to the water trough and sat down nearby to eat. He pulled one knee up to use as an arm rest from which he dangled the sack, silently picking out dates one at a time to munch. He allowed his mind to go back over his conversation with Nib'haz, and again he felt the sting of shame for his own self-righteousness. Odd that it took a blind man to see it. Despite his deep thoughts, he finished his meal before Nekoda finished her drink.

"I suppose you must be hungry, as well," he spoke in soft Hebrew as she finished, water dripping from her snout. He stood to stroke her between her oversized ears. Small puffs of dust arose from the path his fingernails drew through her thick hair. He patted her neck, now releasing greater wafts of dust into the air. "Come with me."

Darash led Nekoda away from the crowds to find a suitable place for her to feed. Soon they came upon the clearing where Elias had defeated him. Despite the chill in the air, a new battle was raging, and again Elias dominated. Elias was broad in the chest and shoulders, and his arms boasted thick muscles. His hair was of a lighter hue than the other boys, suggesting mixed blood, but he dressed in a simple Jewish tunic. Nevertheless, the girls must have found him attractive, from the way they watched him and giggled together when he glanced their way.

I wonder what it would feel like for the girls to look at me that way.

Darash moved to the far edge of the children's make-shift arena and tied Nekoda to a young olive tree, making sure to leave plenty of slack in the rope for her to move her head. He removed some hay from a pack on Nekoda's back and placed it on the ground before her, barely watching what he was doing, so absorbed was he in the competition.

"Bring him down!" a boy called to Elias's opponent from the sidelines, fist clenched and raised.

"He comes for you, Elias!" another boy cried.

Elias stood opposite another youth in the center of the square, exchanging blow for blow with thick staffs, loud smacks of wood on wood reverberating off the stone walls of the surrounding homes, mingling with the sound of children yelling. The youths who had gathered to watch the spectacle shouted advice and cheered on their heroes.

Perhaps today Elias has finally met his match.

Darash eyed the tall boy facing off with the local champion. He stood taller than Elias, though was not as muscular, and dressed in the thickly woven, undyed tunic style of an Essene. Darash had never seen him before, but this newcomer was giving Elias everything he could handle.

Elias blocked a vicious blow that landed far too close to his skull. By the look on his face, Darash could see he was worried—perhaps for the first time. Still, Elias countered by sidestepping and swiping at the newcomer's side, narrowly missing. The other boy backed up to get out of the way, centered himself again, and renewed his onslaught. Elias found himself blocking more blows than he delivered. For a time, Darash and the crowd wondered how much more he could take. He kept getting pushed back to the line of spectators, but each time managed to regain his footing, even as he blocked one blow after another.

As the battle in the sun and dust raged on, beads of sweat began to appear on both their brows, but the newcomer began to heave more heavily with each attack, fighting for air. He was tiring. Even as this change became clear to some of the crowd, Elias had already begun his new tactic. No longer content to simply shield himself from blows, he acquired a new energy and launched his own attack. He was the stronger of the two and now released that strength in blows, cuts, jabs, and deflections.

The newcomer, now exhausted, found himself pushed out of the center of the square, losing ground quickly. And then, as their audience watched, the challenger lost his footing and dropped to one knee. Elias lost no time, jabbing him in the left shoulder with the tip of his staff, pushing him off balance, and forcing him onto his back.

The crowd erupted in cheers and cries.

"He won! He won again!"

"Elias is victorious!"

"Elias, the champion!"

Not all the cries were cries of victory. A small group of youths who had been cheering for the challenger now shook their heads in frustration, swiped dusty feet at the ground, and groaned.

Elias bent and rested his hands on his knees to catch his breath as the dust cleared, but then reached down to give his opponent a hand up. It was received and the former opponents' mutual respect renewed. Darash watched as Elias wiped his brow. He then raised his staff to the crowd, who gave a final cheer for him, and the two fighters walked from the square. Elias retrieved a gourd from a stone and took several long droughts of water, breathing hard in between.

The crowd settled a bit, but noisily discussed the intricacies of the fight, creating an excited cacophony of voices bathed in the afterglow of battle. Darash turned to see if Nekoda had finished her light meal. She still chewed, oblivious to the chaos of children, but little hay remained. Darash moved to untie her.

"To celebrate my victory," Elias announced, yelling to raise his voice above the din, "I will face one more opponent today!"

The children, who had begun to fill the square in their excited meandering conversations, now let out another cheer and moved back to their places.

"Who will it be?" Elias asked, his eyes scanning the crowd.

Darash saw his gaze moving near and stepped back. He turned away and pulled at the loose knot around the rough but slender trunk of the small olive tree.

"You! You, I say! What is your name?" The voice was getting nearer.

Darash pulled and the rope slipped free.

"You! Turn around!" The voice was now at his back. "I will fight you today!"

Darash finally turned and found Elias standing within arm's length and staring at him hard.

"No, no... I... I have duties I must—"

"Come! Fight me!" Elias challenged. "You will even have the advantage, for I am tired from my last battle."

The pack of insistent boys shouted at him, insisting that the show go on. Darash glanced at the line of girls who gazed at him with smiles and open curiosity.

Perhaps he is right. Perhaps I will finally be able to beat him.

Chapter Thirteen

Easy Prey

Ten minutes later, Darash arrived back at his spot in the shuk, head throbbing and hands bloodied from wiping at his swollen nose.

What a fool I am! To believe I had an advantage! Yes, Elias was tired, but that is precisely why he picked me!

"What happened to you?" Valad asked, snickering and pointing at Darash's face with the tact of a wild boar. "Did the Praetorian Guard find you sitting in one of their chariots drinking their wine?"

Darash refused to answer.

"What is it?" Nib'haz asked. "Darash, is that you?"

"I should have ducked," was all Darash would say.

"You should have run, you mean!" Valad laughed louder. "Who did this to you? Have you been stick fighting again?"

Darash unloaded his belongings, his back to Valad.

"What has happened to him?" Nib'haz still wanted to know.

"He has a knot on his forehead and his nose has been bleeding—quite badly, too. Someone must have smacked him right in the face with a big stick." Valad turned his attention back to Darash. "That is what happened, correct, Boy? You have been street fighting again. I warned you about that!"

"You never warned me about it," Darash insisted, letting his annoyance show in his voice.

"Then, I should have!" Valad laughed again. "Here, Darash. Here is your warning. No more stick fighting! You are bad at it! There. Think of the countless troubles I just saved you."

Darash sighed and dug into his pack for his flask of water. He stood to the side where he would not splash anyone or their belongings, and poured the water over his hands, using it to scrub away the blood. Unfortunately, it would not be so easy to get it out of his tunic.

Mother is going to have my head.

סֶלָה

As Darash walked home, he fell deep into thought, looking at the ground and allowing his hair to fall before his eyes like a curtain between him and the world.

Shall I tell Aphiemi's parents about her condition? Perhaps they are better off not knowing. It would be best to keep the secret among as few people as possible. Right now, only Mareh, myself, and Nib'haz know. Surely none of us will betray her reputation to public derision.

Darash paused. No, he had forgotten something. Someone else also knew of her pregnancy... her killer.

Thinking of him—whoever this man was—caused a knot of anger and desperation to develop in his chest. Such a man should not go free... but, despite what he and Nib'haz had managed to discern about his character, Darash could think of no way to track him down. There were many, many religious men in Jerusalem! How could he tell which of them, if caught in a clandestine affair with a Greek girl, might see their way to committing such a crime?

I will simply have to keep asking questions until the answers run out... which may be very soon.

He went over in his mind all the people who might shed some light on Aphiemi's tragic end. The guard should be questioned again, as well as his family. Following Nib'haz's advice, Darash wanted to learn everything he could about that man's character. He also wanted to speak to the magistrate again to find out if anything new had come to light but he worried he had already made enough of a pest of himself on that front.

Consumed by thought, Darash narrowly avoided running into a man who had stopped for a chat on the side of the road. He looked up with an apology on his lips, but the face he saw stripped him of all words. It was Hathal, his father's former business partner. And, the man with whom he had been conversing was none other than that wolf, Nakal.

"Ah!" Hathal said, annoyance and opportunism marking his countenance. "It is our young friend, Darash!"

"Ah, yes! Greetings, young Darash!" Nakal said. They spoke Aramaic, despite their shared Jewish heritage, apparently preferring the common trade language to the language of faith. "I see you have had some troubles today," he said, noting Darash's bruised up face and shooting a knowing look at Hathal. "That reminds me! I just heard a story from my nephew that you might be interested to hear."

Darash cringed.

"My nephew, as you may know, is quite a talented little fighter," Nakal continued. "He tells me today that he fought two opponents. One of them was quite skilled. Really gave Elias a tough battle. Of course, my nephew conquered in the end, as he always does. His second opponent was quite easy prey. Easily beaten, even though Elias had just exhausted himself fighting the other boy."

"Why do you tell us this story, Nakal?" Hathal prompted.

"I tell it because young Darash here was one of my nephew's opponents."

"Truly?" Hathal asked with interest.

"Indeed. Which do you think he was? The skilled fighter or the easy prey?"

"The skilled fighter, of course," Hathal responded, casting a sly, sideways glance at Darash. "Surely he fought well. He is always so sure of himself. No doubt he has reason to be."

"Ah, but there you will be disappointed, my friend," Nakal said. "Our departed friend's son was not the skilled fighter. He was the easy prey. He lost his battle almost before he stepped into the square."

"What a shame!" Hathal said, shaking his head and clucking his tongue. He looked Darash in the eye. "I suppose that explains that ugly bump on your head. But wait, young one. Do not leave yet." Hathal stepped into Darash's path as the boy tried to pass. "I have also heard some news about you that you might find of interest. Of course, I was just telling Nakal that it could not possibly be true! For even someone of your youth and foolishness could not possibly be foolish enough to make promises to a grieving father that would be impossible to fulfill."

Darash sighed and replied in Hebrew, "I have made no promises."

"Then it is true!" Hathal shook his head, sticking to Aramaic. "We expected better of you."

"Obviously, Hathal, we were mistaken," Nakal addressed his friend with a shrug of defeat. "We thought too highly of him, if it can be believed."

"A hard thing, indeed, as I have hardly thought of him at all."

Both men burst into uproarious laughter.

"So where is the murderer?" Hathal continued. "Surely you have him locked up in jail by now."

Darash moved around them and continued walking.

"Where are you going? We are very interested in hearing news of your progress," Nakal called after him.

"Yes," Hathal enjoined, finding it difficult to contain his laughter. "Please enlighten us as to how the easy prey will be able to solve such a complicated mystery! We only hope to learn from you! Could you not even spare a moment for your old friends?"

סֶ לָ ה

Darash drew Nekoda into the shadow of a wall, slumped to the ground, and hung his head.

I cannot do this! This is too much for me! What was I thinking?

His head began to ache as memories of the day's humiliating defeat flooded him. The mocking, self-confident look in Elias's eyes. He had Nakal's eyes. Not a good quality, in Darash's opinion.

He relived the fight in his mind—fake jabs that, even though recoiled, had made Darash jump back in self-defense, the torrent of blows that had kept him off-center, and then the one he had failed to block. Elias had brought his staff down hard, hitting Darash across the face with force.

Darash saw a burst of light and then darkness as he closed his eyes, grabbed his face, and fell backward. Even when he opened them again, it seemed like he was looking through a sheet of water. Everything had blurred. Even the sounds muted momentarily. But then it all came back in a wave of pain and blood.

Several of the other children and youths had come up to him out of compassion and curiosity. Two offered him a hand. Most let out gasps and oohs and aahs over his misfortune. A few laughed.

Elias reacted differently than Darash had expected. A look of concern immediately crossed his face when he realized his mistake. He did not offer assistance, but neither did he laugh or celebrate his second victory of the day. He simply backed out of Darash's line of sight, which was quickly filled with tunic hems, scuffling feet, and dust.

Easy prey. What if they are right? What if I have taken on another battle I cannot win?

The defeat of this moment mingled with the loss he had felt the night he and his mother were informed of his father's murder. Now, whenever things looked particularly bad, his mind always returned to that night.

He remembered being awakened in the darkest hours of the night by a pounding and then voices. He heard a scream. Throwing back his covers, he stumbled from his bed toward his mother's cries of agony. He had never heard such a sound before or since. It still haunted his dreams.

Revayah crouched over someone who lay on the floor at the feet of three helpless looking Roman soldiers. Darash then recognized the lifeless body of his father. Revayah could not be consoled. Her wails cut the night like a knife.

According to Jewish tradition, they buried him the next day. They hired professional wailers, and friends and neighbors joined the funeral procession. Six men carried the washed and wrapped body of his father, laid out upon his bier. Revayah's parents and brother joined them from Bethlehem, along with other relatives. Tuwr's mother had arrived that same afternoon from Hebron to celebrate Passover only to be greeted with the tragic news. She wailed loudest of all, shaking her fists as they walked, her head covered in ashes.

As the procession wailed and cried through the streets, Revayah's silence was as eerie as her screams had been the night before. Aside from the redness of her eyes and the paleness of her complexion, she was immaculately beautiful. She did not wail nor rend her robes as most widows did—a fact for which she later received no small amount of chiding from her mother-in-law. Revayah walked with grace, one hand extended to rest on the bier, never taking her eyes from him, and saying nothing. This would be the last time she would be with her husband. The last time she would touch him. The last time she would make herself beautiful for the man she loved.

The procession began at their home in the Lower City, walking north past the Temple and through the Beautiful Gate into the Kidron Valley to the east. They wound down the mountainside path into the valley until they arrived in the Valley of Jehoshaphat, the northern stretch of the Kidron.

Darash, like his mother, shed no tears that day. He walked, holding his sister's hand. And when Tsarah began to cry so hard she could no longer walk, he carried her.

Abba is gone, the thought repeated in his head. *How can such a thing be?*

On the western side of the Mount of Olives, lay the family burial cave. It had not been opened in nine years, since the death of Tuwr's father. Earlier that day, some kind neighbors had come early to the tomb to push the large boulder from the entrance. While the stone no longer blocked the entrance, Revayah's older brother entered to remove the bones of Tuwr's father and place them in small, carved, stone ossuary.

Hot tears filled Darash's eyes as he remembered that day. Chaphash had come and walked with him, but he could not remember if any words had passed between them. He just remembered the journey… a journey he still traveled.

Why did you have to die, Abba? Why did you have to leave everything at my feet? You should have known I would fail.

סֶ לָ ה

An hour or so later, Darash finally picked himself up. He knew his mother would still be awake and had no desire to explain either his bruised face or his tears.

Perhaps a short walk will help.

He pulled Nekoda back the way he had come. Rounding a corner to his right, he headed toward the Temple area as the sun cast its last warming rays over the city wall and the sky began yielding itself to the gathering dark. The day had brought an unexpected reprieve from the cold of the coming winter. Now, as he walked through the debris-scattered stone paths, he could feel the city begin to sigh away the tension of the day. Servant girls swept out entryways for the last time, animals ruminated on mouthfuls of straw and allowed themselves to be bedded, robed women stood at their gates and hollered for their children to leave their playmates behind and come home for the night. But though he, too, tried to put aside the day's trials, he found the task impossible.

Darash neared the Temple and took a left, a right, and another left. And he was there. Only a few feet away, in a lonely, filthy, darkened alley, soldiers of the Roman army on night patrol had discovered his father's body lying in a pool of blood. The blood had long since been washed away by rain and the stain buried in layers of dirt, but Darash knew it remained. Blood never disappears. Blood leaves a mark on objects, on people, on hearts. Somewhere someone else knew this—someone stained by this blood—someone who would one day have to answer for it.

For now, the alley revealed nothing more of the truth. Three windows overlooked the narrow pathway. Darash had already questioned all those who lived there and had heard nothing helpful.

And, when all their friends had lost interest, only one man, a rabbi, was still willing to lend Darash an ear and speculate with him about the possibilities.

Darash turned and headed back the way he came but then made a sudden right. It was late, but Rabbi Nathan had never turned him away.

Chapter Fourteen

Truth ~ Pain ~ Hope

"Ah... Darash," Nathan said after straining in the darkness to recognize his guest's features. "This is a surprise. What brings you here at so late an hour?"

"Forgive me, Rabbi," Darash said and shrunk at his imposition on the older gentleman. "It is just that... You see, I.... I was just around the corner at the place where...."

Nathan nodded, stepping back to hold the door open wider. "It is all right, my son. I understand. Please come in."

As Darash entered the darkened room, he realized how late it must be. Only one lamp burned in the corner—the light that was always kept lit. All of Nathan's family had turned in for the night. Nathan's hair lay flat but unkempt against one side of his head. Darash chided himself for his rudeness. How long had he been pacing the street outside before knocking?

"Forgive me," he began, "I should let you return to your rest."

"Darash, Darash," Nathan said in a soothing tone. He gestured toward a low couch. "Please sit. I, too, lie awake at night sometimes thinking of your father, wondering if there was anything I could have done that may have brought about a different—a better—outcome."

"Was tonight one of those nights?"

Nathan gave a short chuckle and shrugged. "No. But it was for you and, as I told you before, you are always welcome here when you need to talk about him."

Darash smiled and relaxed, accepting the seat offered. Nathan added more oil to the small lamp on the table. The flame revitalized and cast a new, soothing light into the darkness of the room.

"Oh, my young friend!" Nathan exclaimed, only now noticing Darash's facial wounds. "You have been in a fight? Who did this to you?"

"Oh, it was nothing, really," Darash said, embarrassed. "I was just stick-fighting and, well... I should have moved faster than I did. I failed to block a blow and, well.... I do not think the other boy intended to hit me in the face."

"Ah, I see.... Still stick-fighting, eh? I suppose there are worse things you could do with your time. But next time... block!" Nathan raised a hand for emphasis, imitating the move.

"I will certainly try," Darash promised.

"Good."

Darash surveyed the room. He had spent many an evening here as a young child and then again after his father's passing. The rabbi, a stout man with black hair and a long, pre-maturely graying beard, joined Darash, sitting an arm's length away on the well-worn couch. Fatigue made him look older, but he and Darash's father had been the same age. Nathan often blamed his gray hairs on his task of being a rabbi.

"Rabbi Nathan, why did so many years pass without you and my father speaking? You were childhood friends, were you not?"

Nathan sighed.

"Yes. Your father and I were childhood friends—like brothers. We grew up together, living side by side since we were but babes. My mother would often watch him for your grandmother, and your grandmother would return the favor and take care of me when my mother had to be away. We remained close all through our years of education at the synagogue House of the Book—sitting next to one another, sharing secrets with one another, and even getting into trouble with one another." He chuckled quietly as he remembered. "He was always more daring than I. He had all the best—and the worst—ideas. He once managed to get us each a newborn lamb for free, through a bet he made with an old shepherd, but he also got us kicked out of the House of the Book for playing games instead of writing out our verses."

"What happened, Rabbi?" Darash asked, determined to not let the rabbi distract him with old stories. "What happened to destroy that friendship?"

Nathan sighed and rubbed a tired hand through his ruffled hair. "Life happened."

Darash grew impatient with Nathan's vagueness, but said nothing, hoping his silence would prompt a further response.

"Your father and I were about your age, I suppose, when the trouble began. He decided to become a merchant, and I a rabbi. Both were good decisions, but they took us in different directions. Over the years, he learned to put his cleverness to use in business, and I gave my heart and my life to the service of Elohim. For a time, he tried to get me to join him in his business, but I could not. Elohim had called me to a different work."

"Is that why you stopped talking?"

"Oh, no. Such a little thing as that was not enough to end our friendship. It did, however, put a little distance between us. We were no longer together every day, as we had been before. Oh, we saw one another quite often, but our lives had taken different paths." Nathan paused, thinking, and then resumed. "Not long afterwards, your father became betrothed to Revayah, and I met my future wife, Ma'yan. After we married and began our families, even more distance grew between us, but I still considered your father my truest and closest friend. I believe he felt the same way about me. Our families got together when we could. I am sure you remember coming here when you were small and having my children at your home as well."

Darash nodded. He also remembered that the rabbi had a rather ugly daughter, and there had been talk of an early betrothal between her and himself which, mercifully, had also ended along with the friendship.

"I also remember those visits suddenly ended," Darash said. "Why?"

Nathan sighed and looked Darash in the eye. Darash swept his hair from his eyes, not willing to miss whatever Nathan was about to say.

"Are you sure you want to know this? Perhaps it is better to remember your father the way you do now. He was a great man, in many ways, Darash. Did I ever tell you about the time he tricked the rabbi into letting us out of class early?"

"Rabbi, please. I need to know. What happened? Please tell me."

"Oh, very well."

The rabbi leaned forward. No trace of drowsiness remained in his face. He eyed Darash as though trying to discern from the young man's countenance exactly how much he was ready to hear.

"I had a cousin who wanted to buy a flock of sheep to give his daughter for her wedding dowry. He asked me who might help him find a good flock at a good price. I, of course, immediately thought of Tuwr, my closest friend, and highly recommended him to my cousin. Two weeks later, my cousin came to me, fists clenched in rage. Tuwr had gotten him a flock of sheep and at a very good price, but by the close of that same day, several of them died from having eaten jimsonweed, a poisonous plant that grew on the outskirts of their former owner's land. Within three days, only a third of them remained, and they were unfit to be sold or eaten. My cousin had gone back to Tuwr and demanded to be repaid. He claimed Tuwr had arranged such a good price with the previous owner because they had already caught the sheep eating the toxic weed and knew they would soon fall ill. But neither Tuwr nor the owner agreed to return my cousin's money or do anything to make it right."

Nathan sat back and sighed. He rubbed his forehead with three fingers before continuing.

"So I went to Tuwr myself. At first, I believed it had all been a terrible misunderstanding. I asked him to make it good again and even offered to help with the financial loss. After all, my recommendation had gotten my cousin into the arrangement, so I felt responsible." Nathan paused, rubbing his chin.

"And d-did my father make it right?" Darash stuttered.

The rabbi sighed. "I am afraid not. He told me he had not realized the man was my cousin, and so apologized for that, but he insisted it was my cousin's fault for not being more diligent to check the flock out for himself before purchasing. I argued, of course, that he would have, had I not recommended your father as an honest businessman. But... well... we both became very angry. It might have even come to blows, but your mother came in at that moment and told me to leave. I did, but not before telling him we were no longer friends." Nathan paused again. "I have regretted saying that many, many times.... He told me never to come back to his home and, as you know, I followed his wishes."

Darash lowered his head into his hand. Shaken, angry, and hurt, he knew not which emotion to examine first.

Could it be true?

He hoped not, but somehow he knew it was. The ache that had crept into his heart as he stood over the place his father had been murdered, now returned, bringing with it a new piercing pain.

"Forgive me, Darash," Nathan whispered. "I did not want to tell you this, but... perhaps it is best you hear it. Perhaps it will help you find the answers you are looking for. You see, your father, in many ways, was a good man. He was a good father, a good husband, a good friend. But, like all men, your father had a weakness. He desired wealth more than he should have. He allowed it to cloud over what he knew to be best. He made a mistake, yes. But so did I. My pride kept me from making amends when I had the chance. I once had a very dear friend in your father. Now I have only my regret."

"I suppose he deserved it after what he did to your cousin."

Nathan breathed out through his nose. "Life is rarely so simple. I have yet to meet a man who is either completely good or completely evil... with the possible exception of one...."

"Of whom do you speak, Rabbi? An evil man?"

"Hmm... Some would say so, yes. But this is not what I have come to believe."

Darash waited for more.

"Perhaps you will find this shocking, but I have been following the events surrounding those who follow the one called Yeshua. Surely, you have heard much of him of late. I used to hear the man teach in the synagogue and even witnessed some of his miracles." Nathan stopped. Darash began to wonder if he intended to continue speaking this near heresy when the rabbi finally said, "But I still have much studying to do on the subject. The Torah and the Prophets have much to teach—even to an old rabbi like me."

"My mother claims Yeshua and my father had an altercation the day before my father was murdered."

"Truly? I had no idea! What kind of altercation?"

"From what I can gather, Yeshua went into the Temple where my father and some other men were serving as moneychangers. He whipped them, overturned their tables, knocked over the cages of pigeons, and sent them from the Temple grounds like common thieves!"

"Ah, yes…. I heard of this incident." Nathan thought on this for a moment. "You feel the man acted unjustly toward your father? Or perhaps, even worse?"

"I do not know what to think… especially after what you have told me about my father. It seems there are some things about him I do not know. But I cannot believe my father deserved to be treated that way."

"Hmm…." Nathan sighed and cupped his chin in his hand, stroking his beard with the ends of his fingers. "Have you considered that, perhaps, what Yeshua did had less to do with your father than it had to do with the People and how we have come to view our duty to Elohim?"

"But certainly my father was serving Elohim by making it easier for people to pay their Temple taxes and purchase animals for sacrifice, was he not?"

"I think Yeshua was more concerned with the People's hearts than their sacrifices…. Your father was a complicated man, Darash. He was not a perfect man, but he was not a bad man, either. It is just that, when it came to money, he had a little trouble saying 'no.'"

"Like when he cheated your cousin."

"Yes."

"So you are saying he was guilty." Darash felt his throat closing and his eyes moistening. "That, because of what he did to your cousin—and perhaps because he did not treat the Temple with enough respect, he probably deserved to be punished the way he was—to die."

"No, no! I would not be so quick to dole out judgment and death! We are all deeply flawed, Darash! We all do things for which we deserve great punishment. I do not know everything that happened at the Temple. In the case of my cousin, Tuwr was right that my cousin should have been more careful. My cousin was right that Tuwr should have dealt fairly. And, I was right that Tuwr should have repaired the damage. But Tuwr and I were both wrong to turn our backs on one another, and to let a small thing like money come between us."

"What happened, Rabbi, to your cousin?"

"I helped him rebuild his daughter's dowry, and she married. But I never spoke to your father again, nor he to me. As the weeks turned to months and then to years, it simply became easier and easier to avoid one another. If I saw him coming my way, I would head the other direction. If he saw me speaking to a merchant, he would wait a long way off until I had left before approaching. It was like a dance we did together—planned out and arranged, but never discussed."

"But I remember you coming to me after my father died. You said you believed he was coming to see you. Why? If you had not spoken in… what? Seven years or more? What made you believe he was coming to you then?"

Nathan sighed. "That is hard to explain. You see, even though our friendship had ended, I always believed in my heart your father still loved me, as I did him. And, I always believed that somehow we would make it right again. But we let the time pass us by and then your father died so unexpectedly, that I...." Nathan trailed off and a long silence followed.

Just as Darash leaned forward to prompt the older man, Nathan resumed. "When I heard of your father's death and the nature of how he had been killed, I began asking questions. I learned it had happened close to my home and after dark. I wondered if he might have found a reason to bridge the gap of our old anger and come see me."

"What would have made him do so after all that time?"

"I asked myself that same question. I decided something must have happened to him that would have made him need me. You see, when we were children, although your father usually led our games and plans, he always came to me whenever he had a problem—whenever he felt frightened or uncertain. Once he thought he had broken his foot after jumping off a wall trying to get away from an irate farmer. I cannot remember what he had done, but he should have gone to his parents or to a physician. No. He came to me. He limped to me, actually."

Nathan chuckled at the memory and continued.

"When Twur was about to be married to your mother, he spent the entire night before his wedding feast worrying to me about whether she would love him. She already did, of course, but he was afraid because she was very beautiful, and your father.... Well, as a rabbi, I must be honest… your father was not the best looking of men. Just be thankful you look like your mother." Nathan chuckled. "Anyway, Tuwr worried and worried, but that was all foolishness because he and Revayah had known one another long before they married. They were already friends, and she already loved and respected him. He had nothing to fear.

"But that night—the night your father died—he most definitely had something to fear—something real, something dangerous, something that caught up with him. When I heard what happened, I wondered if Tuwr had realized the danger he was in. Perhaps something had frightened him again, and he had come seeking me as he had when we were young... but, this time, I was too far away to help."

Chapter Fifteen

In Search of Truth

The next morning, yom revi'i, the fourth day, Darash snuck out of the house early to avoid a confrontation with Revayah. She had not yet seen his bruised face, and he hoped to let it heal as much as possible before she did. However, if his image in the water basin this morning was any indication, he looked worse this morning than he did last night.

As Darash approached the Lower Market, he changed his mind and kept heading north. He knew of a middle-aged couple who made and sold dye in the Upper Market and decided to pay them a visit.

They sat at a colorful booth not far from the shop Darash's father had once shared with Hathal and Nakal. Though the husband spent most of his time finding plants and minerals used in the dye, his pock-marked wife, Millah, and their equally unattractive son worked the booth, draped on all sides with bunches of threads and lengths of cloth dyed to deep hues of blue, green, yellow, and red. The bright colors and elaborately embroidered robes and sashes attracted no small amount of business, but the couple dealt as much in city gossip as they did in fabric. Anyone who had lived long in Jerusalem knew that if one wanted to find out what was going on the city, a visit to the dyers was in order. Pharisees, Roman magistrates, and palace servants often stopped by for a word with the dyer's wife or her husband.

Darash had lately avoided visiting the dyers because of their proximity to his enemies, but he wondered what Millah might have to say about Aphiemi's death.

As he neared the shuk, the sound of the many chickens greeted him with their intense, morning clucking as they searched for breakfast and stretched their wings. Millah kept a flock of them in the room behind the shop, where her family lived, but the feathered beasts rarely stayed there. This morning they filled the shop floor, occupied perches in the window and display counters, and pecked around on the ground at the feet of her first customers. At first, their noises mingled perfectly with the sound of her voice.

Despite the earliness of the morning, several people already stood about outside the dyers' shop, more interested in the recent disturbance than in the colorful cloth, yet Darash could see from the empty places on the walls that Millah had not lost her touch in turning good gossip into good business.

"You would not believe who my husband saw preaching about Yeshua in Bethany just yesterday! Peter and John!" Millah said as Darash joined the others.

"I thought they were in jail," a female customer remarked.

"They were, but they were released the very next day. That was three days ago now."

"Released?" A middle-aged man asked. "So quickly?"

"Yes. They were held for questioning and then released," she repeated, caressing a roll of vibrant red fabric, fingering it thoughtfully with stained hands. "They have been in Bethany since then, but they have not followed the orders of the priests. Is not this fabric just perfectly lovely? And so very soft, too! Like Persian silk! They are still preaching Yeshua as the risen Messiah!"

"Ooo, yes! Lovely! But if they were arrested for preaching about Yeshua and could be arrested again for the same heresy, why were they released at all? Obviously, they were guilty."

"I know, I know," said Millah shaking her head and glancing from person to person, "but surely you noticed the change at the Temple and the synagogues! Many, many people have begun to gather there to pray and worship Elohim. The synagogues have not been this full in decades! Yeshua of Galilee himself taught there, you recall. Many of our synagogues are so full that people must stand in the streets and pass on to one another what is being said inside. Have you seen this embroidery work? Stunning, is it not?"

Millah pushed several samples of embroidered fabric forward and continued, "The priests are afraid to appear too much against these men who have caused such a spiritual revival within their own synagogues. It is quite baffling. They know not what to do. Oh, here! Feel that! Feels like newborn foal, does it not?"

Darash waited and listened until the people began making their final purchases. He finally saw his opportunity.

"Millah, have you heard anything lately about the girl, Aphiemi, who was murdered early last week?"

"Ah," she answered. "I heard a boy was trying to help." She smiled at him. "I am glad someone is trying, at least... but sadly I do not know how I can be of any assistance. ...That poor girl!" She shook her head and clicked her tongue. "Such a terrible thing! ...No. I wish I could tell you more, but all I hear is how upset people are to have something like that happen in Yerushaláyim."

"No one mentioned seeing her with anyone—friends, a man, perhaps?"

"Well, yes. I heard she was often seen with a couple of Hebrew girls. And I know that her father, Barus, though Greek, often does business with Jewish people. He even has some business associates among the Sadducees I believe, though I do not know which ones. Surely they would have known her, too. Perhaps you should ask them."

Darash smiled. "I will. Thank you. One more question, do you know anything of Servius Aurelius, a Roman centurion who mans a watchtower to the south of the Upper City?"

"Ah, yes… the man of secrets…. I am acquainted with his family... what remains of them, anyway."

"What do you mean?"

"He lost his mother when he was very young and his father, also a Roman soldier, died in an uprising several years ago—killed by Bar'abbas, who is now roaming the countryside a free man! This city never ceases to amaze me," she said with an exasperated sigh. "Does your mother prefer blue or red? Oh, I also have yellow fabrics!"

"Why do you call him a man of secrets?"

"Have you heard about the business at the tomb of Yeshua?"

"Yes."

"Very odd, that." Millah paused. "Most of those soldiers are no longer in Yerushaláyim," she said. "Our illustrious governor, Pontius Pilate," here she rolled her eyes, "quickly reassigned them to different Roman outposts or returned them to Rome. But, at least, they were not put to death. Servius, though… He is one of the few who remain. But, of course, he has connections the others did not."

"Such as?"

"He has often been seen with High Priest Caiaphas. And it is rumored he himself descends from royalty, I believe. Distant, but nevertheless…."

"Can you tell me of his family?"

"I know of no brothers or sisters, but he does have an aging great aunt he cares for along with a cousin—a woman who is not yet married or betrothed. Of course, that does not mean she is not spoken for, if you know what I mean." She gave Darash a meaningful look but, apparently, did not elicit the response she hoped for, so hurried on. "They live only a few streets north of the Antonia Fortress. It is the white-washed, two-story edifice with the date trees in front and the large fountain just inside the courtyard. You will know it when you see it. The old woman is a regular customer of mine, but she is no longer steady on her feet, so I go there often."

"Thank you very much," Darash said and turned to go, but thought of something else and turned back around. "Millah, what is his aunt's favorite color?"

סֶ לָ ה

Though Darash would have preferred to spend the day visiting and asking questions, after spending good money at the dyers', he knew if he did not make some sales there would be little for dinner that night. And, of course, there was one house visit he still avoided.

He left the dyer's booth and headed back to the Lower Market. Nib'haz turned toward the youth at his approach, easily distinguishing the sound of his steps from the many others. A few moments later, Darash sat next to his friend, blowing on chilled fingers and discussing his hesitation to return to Barus's home.

"Nib'haz, I still do not know what to do," Darash confessed. "I feel Barus has a right to know about Aphiemi's condition before she died, but perhaps he is better off not knowing."

"Truth or a convenient lie.... Truth or ignorance...." Nib'haz muttered in response. "Difficult.... Difficult... making a decision that should never have been yours to make. Making decisions for others. Decisions that will change their lives...."

"But what choice do I have?" Darash asked. "I am trying to solve his daughter's murder—doing everything I can to find out what happened, but if I succeed, this information may come out anyway. Would it be better if Barus and his family learned it in advance? Her baby was his grandchild, no matter the circumstances. Does he not have a right to know of the child's existence?" Darash shook his head and lifted both his hands in a slight gesture of defeat. "Why must the truth be so painful?"

"That is a good question, young one. One I cannot answer."

Darash sighed, and his mind returned to another difficult truth, what he had learned the previous night about his father.

"It is difficult to be sure," Nib'haz continued. "But I think, no matter what decision you make, you will not be doing wrong. Remember, truth is never the real enemy. Even difficult truth brings its own form of comfort. You must do what is right and wise and good and give the rest to Elohim."

סֶ לָ ה

By that evening, Darash knew what he had to do. He would speak to Barus. He would tell him what Mareh had revealed about Aphiemi's expected baby. He would tell the truth of what he had learned, as he had promised to do from the beginning.

The truth must have its way, for good or for bad. He recalled what Nib'haz had said. *Even difficult truth brings its own form of comfort.*

Still, Darash did not relish the task ahead.

What if Nib'haz was wrong? What comfort can be found in knowing that, before Aphiemi lost her life, she lost her honor? And that, when she died, her child died as well? ...What comfort is there for me in knowing Abba was a betrayer of friends?

Darash sighed.

I will go see Barus. I must see him. Tonight. ...But later. I will visit the magistrate first. Maybe then I will know what to say to Barus.

Darash carried the amulet he had found at the scene of Aphiemi's murder. He drew it from the folds of his belt and fingered it as he walked, willing the small pendant to reveal to him the identity of its owner. He supposed it could have belonged to Aphiemi. He had not yet shown it to Barus or her mother, but he suspected—hoped, in fact—that it belonged to her killer.

A surly slave opened the door at Darash's knock and grunted in displeasure. Before he could slam it shut at the sight of the scrawny youth, Darash stepped forward and braced the door.

"I must see the magistrate," Darash insisted, speaking Greek.

"Look, boy," the slave said with a sneer, "I am doing you a favor. If I allowed you to waste the magistrate's time after all that has been going on in Jerusalem, he will have my head!"

Darash stood bracing the door, resisting the urge to speak sharply to this idolatrous, Roman slave. Despite the streams of heat pulsating through Darash's neck and temples, he realized that doing so would only ensure defeat. Nib'haz had taught him that the difference between success and failure was not measured in immediate satisfaction, but in the long term rewards brought about by the use of one's wits.

Darash slowly released the door, but before the slave could close it, he held out the amulet for the slave to see.

"I have something of value for your master," he said, turning the trinket so that the lamp light caught its rich finish and sent tiny flecks of light dancing along its golden surface. "It would be a shame if the magistrate found you had kept him from obtaining such a costly item."

"I will be sure he gets it," the slave said, reaching for it, but Darash stepped back and whisked it back into his belt.

"I will take it to him myself."

The slave darkened in anger, but he stepped aside and allowed Darash entrance.

"Wait here," the slave barked, giving Darash a full-body sweep with his eyes. He started out of the courtyard, but shot back over his shoulder, "Touch nothing if you value your hands."

Darash waited in the courtyard, a large, tiled area open to the sky. He stood quietly at first, but as more time slipped by, he grew impatient. His stomach growled, and the night air chilled his toes and fingertips. Pulling his cloak tighter about his neck and chest, he began to pace slowly— dragging his broken leather sandal strap across dusty tile. He occupied himself counting the tiles, trying to detect images in the water-stain patterns on the stuccoed walls, and drawing pictures in the dust with his feet, but still no one came and no voices could be detected behind the thick, stone walls.

That careless slave has deliberately failed to alert Magistrate Quintus! He intends to leave me here all night!

Darash walked toward an open door that led into a corridor. He listened for a moment and, upon hearing nothing, peered around it to discover more doors and passages. He stood there for a moment, body on one side of the door and head hanging into the space beyond it, hoping the sour-looking slave would eventually appear out of one of them. He intended to tell the man he would return another day. But a sound behind him made him jump and, when Darash turned around, he immediately caught the disapproving gaze of the magistrate.

The Roman had entered the courtyard from a corridor at the opposite end, and he was not alone. Four Roman soldiers accompanied him who, by their scars, weathered faces, and muscular frames, had seen more than a few battles. Neither Quintus Arrius nor his guests appeared in good spirits. He merely grunted at Darash and then walked the soldiers to the front door.

"What are you doing here, boy?" he demanded a moment later in Latin.

The magistrate had once been good-looking and athletic. He had even, masculine features, somehow having avoided the overstated nose of other Romans. After a long day quelling restless Jews at the Temple, his strong, square jaw had produced a smattering of salt and pepper stubble. Despite broad shoulders and a tall frame, years as a pampered bureaucrat had caused his middle to illustrate the powers of too much wine and rich food. Still, at twice Darash's mass, he formed an imposing figure.

Rumor had it that Quintus Arrius had only three loves—Rome, gold, and women—though not necessarily in that order. He had a wife and children who usually resided in Rome, but he saw little of them, as he kept busy seeing that Rome's interests, and his own, were served in Jerusalem.

The last time Darash came to see him, Darash had been hastily dismissed, though he felt certain he had seen a flicker of recognition in the man's eyes. Darash had dealt with the magistrate briefly last spring, when his father's slain body had been discovered. Even so, whatever sympathy Darash had received as a victim of a crime, which was scarce enough, had long since been forgotten, despite his father's good relationship with the Romans. Darash was now simply a troublesome youth interfering in matters that were none of his concern.

"I came to see you about Aphiemi's murder. I—"

"Who?" Quintus Arrius said, but then his memory returned along with a flood of anger. "I thought I told you to stay out of it," the magistrate barked. "I have enough to worry about without a child interfering in my work! I have my hands full with those followers of the Galilean rebel! They are causing trouble at every opportunity and the Jewish leaders are using this as yet another excuse to rebel against Roman authority! And then you bother me with every idea that pops into your head! Have the gods found some reason to curse me?"

"I found something," Darash said even as his back touched the far wall where he had retreated during the magistrate's tirade. "I found a gold amulet. I think it fell from the gold chain you found where Aphiemi was killed."

The magistrate growled but said, "Give it to me."

Darash held it out in his hand, but when Quintus reached for it, Darash closed his fingers over it. Quintus glared at him.

"I must still show it to Barus to make sure it did not belong to his daughter," he said, but they both knew this to be only part of the reason. It was gold, after all. "Do you recognize it?"

"No. I do not recognize it. No one will recognize it! I do not know what you think you are going to achieve by all this meddling. It did not help when your father was killed, and it will not help now! I am going to give you a warning, Boy. If I catch you in my way again, you will be the one I throw in jail, do you understand?"

Darash's eyes darkened a shade at the threat, but he refused to cower before the much larger man.

"Now, get out of my house, and do not let me see you back here again!"

Chapter Sixteen

Those Who Mourn

Despite Darash's good intentions, going to Barus's home at this late hour did not stand to reason after the long wait at the magistrate's estate—a visit which earned him only the threat of jail. Besides, Darash was now overwrought with hunger, so the truth would have to wait one more day. He headed home, knowing his mother and sister would have retired to bed hours ago.

Once there, Darash prepared a plate of dried meat, day old bread, and three boiled eggs. To that, he added a cup of wine and a bowl of cold porridge with raisins—evidently left over from that evening's meal. Even after eating all of that, he still hungered for more, so he finished off a basket of figs. No doubt his mother would complain in the morning about how little food remained in the house, but despite his thin, spindly frame, a time did not exist when Darash could not eat.

As he chewed, he thought about his disappointing visit with Magistrate Quintus Arrius.

How am I going to find out anything about Aphiemi's death if the magistrate will not let me in the door or, worse, throw me in jail?

He sighed and berated himself for being so foolish. He should have guessed Arrius would be too busy attending to the recent disturbance caused by Peter and John to care about anything else.

Why do these Way followers have to make so much trouble? Yeshua himself was a Jew. He believed in the Torah, did he not? Certainly enough unrest exists between the Greeks, Romans, and the People.

Darash searched the bottom of the basket for another fig, but he had consumed the last one. He ran his tongue around his mouth, dislodging the sweet remaining bits. He remembered another time he had longed for more figs, but his father had told him he could have no more, for they were about the enter the Temple grounds. Darash had been quite young at the time.

As they were about to pass from the Court of the Gentiles and enter the Temple one Shabbat morning, Darash drew to a stop, noticing a sign chiseled into white limestone at the entrance. The Greek and Latin letters had been painted a bright red.

"Why is that there, Abba?" he asked.

"Can you read it, my son?" Tuwr asked.

"I think I can—at least, I think I understand the Greek."

"What does it say?"

"It says, 'No foreigner is to go beyond the balustrade… and the plaza of the temple zone. Whoever is caught doing so will have himself to blame for his death… which will follow.'"

"Very good, Darash. That is correct. Your Greek is quite good."

"But what does it mean? Why would Elohim want to keep people out of His Temple? Are we not taught that He is the Creator of all?"

"Ah, that is a very good question!" Tuwr paused, then put his hand on Darash's back and led him inside. "You are correct when you say Elohim is the Creator of all that is, including people of every nationality. But surely the rabbis have taught you our history as well?"

"Yes, Abba."

"Did they teach you how Adam and Eve sinned and were cast from the garden?"

"Yes."

"And how, later, He told Noah to build an ark and then He destroyed everything that was not on it, because all other hearts had become wicked?"

"Yes."

"And how our forefather Abraham was called out of Haran and set apart unto Elohim to become His chosen People, because all others had begun to follow false gods?"

"Yes."

"And, of course, you know of how we were once enslaved in Egypt and delivered?"

Darash nodded.

"King David also fought many battles to protect our inheritance of faith from the heathen peoples who would destroy it. And then Elohim let David's son, Solomon, build His Temple in this very place. Surely, you remember these things, as well?"

"Yes, Abba."

"And do you know about how the Assyrians and Babylonians also tried to destroy us and scattered us to foreign lands. How they destroyed the city, looted and burned Solomon's Temple, and killed the king's sons. But then we returned with Nehemiah and rebuilt this city and this Temple. You remember this lesson?"

Darash nodded again.

"Then we were overtaken again by Alexander of Macedonia, then the Ptolemies, then the Seleucids, who tried to force us to adopt the idol-worship of the Greeks! And, of course, you know what happened next? Vile Antiochus dedicated Elohim's Temple to the false god, Zeus! He sacrificed a filthy, unclean sow on the altar, destroyed the scrolls, and forbade us to follow Elohim's commandments!"

"That is when Mattathias and his sons rose up against them," Darash said. "His son, Judas the Maccabee, finally retook the Temple. They cleansed it and rededicated to Elohim."

"Very good, my son! You know your history.

"But our freedom did not last."

"No," Tuwr said, shaking his head. "Sadly, it did not. The Romans now march through our streets with their swords and spears."

Darash stood, deep in thought, as the priests began to chant the opening benedictions.

"Abba," he whispered, drawing his father down so he could speak in Tuwr's ear. "So Gentiles cannot enter our Temple because they have no respect for Elohim?"

Tuwr beamed at his son, then spoke in hushed but enthusiastic tones. "Yes, Darash! Yes! They have chosen other gods. And, Elohim has chosen us. In the very early days, we were one people. But, because the world was so evil, Elohim separated out one nation as His own to be an example to the others. But those who follow false idols and hate Elohim also hate us because He chose us. They will always be tempted to destroy those He loves. Again and again they prove this. But, one day, the Messiah will come! He will free us from the Romans and from any who would seek to bring us harm! ...Now, shhh. We are about to begin."

Throughout the lengthy ceremony, Darash found his mind returning to the history of the People, the threat on the Temple gate, and the promise of the Messiah. As he and his family walked back home a few hours later, he asked, "Abba, would the Romans allow the chief priests to actually kill a Gentile for entering this court?"

"Oh, yes! Absolutely!" Tuwr paused. "The Romans have allowed us certain freedoms. We can practice our religion as we see fit, we do not have to serve in their army, and we can pay our yearly tax to the Temple instead of giving it to Caesar."

Revayah, walking just behind them, carrying sleeping, baby Tsarah, spat in disgust. "They only do so to appease us so we will not fight back! They do so to keep us as slaves! They attack us in our homes! Violate our women! Kill our children!" She broke off with a sob, stopped walking, and buried her face in her free hand.

Looking back now, Darash remembered feeling distressed by her extreme, emotional response. Abba had stopped walking, quickly moved to her, and put an arm around her shoulders. "Peace, my wife. Peace. Come," he said. He whispered something in her ear and then said, "We are almost home. You can lie down and rest. The boy will fetch the meal, and I will care for Tsarah."

To this day, Darash had no idea what had so upset his mother, nor had he ever ventured to ask. He learned to avoid talking about the Romans in her presence and, more recently, about Yeshua and his followers.

Perhaps, if Yeshua and his followers had not so adamantly criticized Pharisaical law, this new religious sect might be more welcome.

Even as he thought these things, he knew it was not so simple. The Sadducees cared nothing for the oral traditions of the Mishnah but followed the Torah only. Though the Pharisees controlled the synagogues and everyday religious life, the Sadducees controlled the Sanhedrin, the Temple, and oversaw all Temple ritual. Their claim to these duties and privileges rested in their heritage as descendants of the High Priest, Zadok. But, truth be known, their considerable, cumulative wealth and willingness to associate with their infidel overlords wielded no small say in the matter.

Yeshua had made enemies of them both. He angered the Pharisees by undermining their authority over the People, calling them hypocrites, vipers, and worse. He had also made enemies of the Sadducees by preaching the resurrection of the dead and claiming an authority higher than theirs. When he chased the merchants and money-changers from the Temple, he insulted both sects by insinuating they had allowed Elohim's Temple to be polluted. So, despite their differences, the Pharisees and Sadducees found common ground in their hatred of this self-proclaimed Messiah. Despite their reasons to hate him, Darash had his own.

What really happened that day between Yeshua and Abba?

Darash knew his father had been working for the city as a moneychanger that day, exchanging foreign currency for the silver half-shekel required for payment of the Temple tax by every male Jew over the age of twenty. This they gave in addition to a tenth of their crops. Yeshua showed up, flew into a rage, and chased him and the others out of the Temple grounds with a whip he fashioned from cords. Three days later, Tuwr was found slain in an alley, and no one could account for Yeshua's whereabouts aside from a rumor that he had retired to the Mount of Olives to pray.

Nathan believed Tuwr had been afraid and on his way to seek his old friend's help.

But what would have made Abba so afraid? Had Yeshua or one of his followers threatened him? What motive could they possibly have?

Darash remembered the man, Yeshua. He had even gone to hear him speak once.

"Would you like to come with me to hear the new teacher?" Tuwr had asked Darash one warm morning. They were staying at a Capernaum inn where Tuwr had traveled for business, taking Darash along to 'teach him how to become a shrewd man of business.' "They say he is a prophet."

"Do you not have to meet with the metalworkers today, Abba?" Darash asked.

"Oh, that can wait. Come, put on your sandals."

Darash remembered walking south from the city through beautiful, hilly country that surrounded the lake of Galilee. He was amazed at how many people had come just to hear this man talk. When they arrived at a clearing, a large crowd had already gathered there, and the teacher stood speaking to a woman who carried a small child in her arms. He put a hand on the little boy's head and said something, but Darash and his father were too far away to hear.

As they neared and joined the gathering crowd, some of the prophet's friends went about asking people to take a seat so the teacher could speak to them all at once.

Peter and John must have been there, he now realized, but he could not recall seeing them. Of course, over two years had passed, and Darash had only been twelve years old at the time.

Men, women, and children sat in the hillside meadow, expectantly awaiting a word from this new prophet. Tuwr found a patch of grass, sat down, and pulled Darash down beside him. After a short wait, Yeshua climbed a short distance up the side of a hill so that his voice would project across the crowd below. He looked across the crowds, starting with the back of the crowd and working his way forward until his eyes settled on the faces of his friends, who sat nearby. Yeshua began to teach but, instead of standing with arms raised like a rabbi in a synagogues, this man sat down on a rock and fingered a blade of grass as he spoke.

"Blessed are the poor in spirit," he began, "for theirs is the kingdom of heaven. Blessed are those who mourn, for they will be comforted. Blessed are the meek, for they will inherit the earth. Blessed are those who hunger and thirst for righteousness, for they will be filled. Blessed are the merciful, for they will be shown mercy. Blessed are the pure in heart, for they will see God. Blessed are the peacemakers, for they will be called sons of God. Blessed are those who are persecuted because of righteousness, for theirs is the kingdom of heaven. Blessed are you when people insult you, persecute you and falsely say all kinds of evil against you because of me. Rejoice and be glad, because great is your reward in heaven, for in the same way they persecuted the prophets who were before you."

"I have never heard anyone speak the way he does," Tuwr later said on their way back to the inn. "He said we should love our enemies and pray for those who persecute us. What do you think of that?"

Darash no longer remembered the response he gave his father that day, but he doubted that the man who spoke those words would hunt someone down and murder him in an alley. This man had preached forgiveness and love, not murder and betrayal. And, despite Roman and Jewish fears, his followers had behaved peacefully in the months after their so-called Messiah's death and subsequent mysterious disappearance from his tomb. Despite Jewish and Roman fears that Yeshua's followers planned a revolt, they seemed to prefer to heal people, preach on street corners, and simply make a nuisance of themselves to the Pharisees and chief priests—an easy enough thing to do, considering all the laws and regulations they liked to impose.

Still, Darash could not forgive the man for the unjust treatment of his father so near the time of his death—no matter what others had begun to believe about his true identity as their long-awaited Messiah.

סֶ לֶ ה

The following morning, Revayah noticed the bruises on Darash's face and scolded him all through breakfast. He left the house as soon as she turned her back and headed into the Upper City to Barus's home. Darash needed to speak to Barus as soon as possible. It was already the fifth day of the week, yom khah'mi'shi, and he had gone too long without reporting back his findings. He feared Barus may have given up on him altogether. Besides, Barus needed to know the truth. Darash knocked, and their servant girl admitted him.

"I have come to speak to Barus," he informed her.

"Oh, that is unfortunate," she replied. "He has left town and traveled to Hebron to attend to some business interests there. He will be gone four days."

Just then, Barus's wife entered the room and greeted Darash warmly. He decided against telling her of Aphiemi's pregnancy without her husband there to help weather the bad news.

"I found this at the same place your daughter was discovered," he told her, pulling the amulet from his belt. "Did this belong to Aphiemi?"

The Greek woman reached for the amulet, and Darash laid it in on her palm. She carefully turned it over in her hands, examining it.

"No," she said with certainty. "This was not my daughter's. She had nothing like this."

"Are you certain?"

"Yes," she said, returning it to him. "I know my daughter's belongings well."

"Perhaps she borrowed it from one of her friends."

"No. She could not have borrowed it from any of them. All of Aphiemi's friends were Jewish girls, and, as you can see, this is Roman. Besides, none of them could have afforced such an expensive amulet."

Could I have been wrong? Could the killer be Roman? But how would she meet such a man?

Aphiemi, like her father, seemed to have surrounded herself with Jews rather than other Greeks or Romans. Even as they spoke, he could see into the inner courtyard where a Jewish servant lady swept at a small pile of dust. Beyond her, a teenaged Jewish hired worker cleaned a large clay jug, his body half-way inside the vessel, one foot stretched into the air as he tried to angle himself to reach the jug's base. Darash had only one more question.

"Then you are certain you have never seen it before—not among Aphiemi's friends or your friends or your husband's acquaintances?"

She paused. "I do not think so," she said slowly. "I suppose it is possible, but I cannot recall."

"Thank you very much. But, please, if you do remember having seen it before, would you please let me know? It could be important."

סֶ לְ ה

The following morning, the day before Shabbat, Darash tried a different sales tactic. He left Nekoda partially loaded, filled his arms with bronze and copper dishes, and walked around the shuk and the nearby streets showing them off in the hopes of reaching more customers. It worked fairly well. He sold three dishes by afternoon rest but looked forward to returning home, as the morning had been especially cold. He had not felt his toes since mid-morning and wanted to warm them up by his mother's fire. When Darash returned to fetch Nekoda, he found a tall man standing with his back to him, speaking to Nib'haz. Darash overheard part of their conversation.

"I thought she was, but... for some reason things are now getting worse," the tall man said.

"Children deal with tragedy differently than adults," Nib'haz replied. "It takes them longer... much longer sometimes."

"But she was doing so well and now— Oh! Shalom, Darash. I did not hear you approach." It was Ibnei'ah, the mosaic artist.

"Shalom, Ibnei'ah," Darash answered, feeling awkward to have interrupted what sounded like a personal conversation.

"I actually came to see you," Ibnei'ah told him. "I am supposed to start work on Gabahh's patio after Shabbat and am low on bitumen. I doubt you have a full ephah already, but I thought you might have enough to get me through the day."

"Of course. I will check to see how much I have on hand." Darash turned to his load.

"Good Ibnei'ah here was just telling me about some trouble he is having with his daughter—little Ra'ah, is it?" Nib'haz said.

Ibnei'ah looked away. Darash blushed and wondered if Nib'haz's lack of tact stemmed from his blindness or his age.

But Ibnei'ah answered, "Yes, Ra'ah."

"I think the bitumen you want is right here," Darash said, fumbling with the thick knots securing a medium-sized clay jug to Nekoda's back.

"He says Ra'ah had a nightmare last night," Nib'haz continued, warming to his topic. "Claims to have seen her mother through her window."

Ibnei'ah nodded and gave a sad smile through deep worry lines. "Yes. I was just saying that I thought the nightmares had passed, but now...."

"You say she told you she had a bad dream about her mother?" Darash asked.

"No. Not exactly. She does not seem to think it was a dream at all. That is why this is so bothersome! She claims to have been wide awake, looking out her window and seeing her mother walking around behind our house. But, of course, my wife has been dead these three months. After years of battling, she finally succumbed to her illness. I watched them put her body in the ground myself."

"And your daughter," Darash said. "Has she since been plagued with visions or dreams of her mother?"

"At first, she did have nightmares. She would wake up in the night crying for her mother. I began allowing her to sleep with me, and only a few days ago did she say she was ready to return to her own bed. And now this! But this is different from the nightmares she had. Always before, she knew she was dreaming, and I could comfort her. But this time she insists her mother is alive! When I try to convince her it is not true, she...." Ibnei'ah ended abruptly. "It is at times like this I miss my wife the most."

סֶ לָ ה

As Darash trudged toward home later that same morning with heavily laden Nekoda in tow, cold, stinging rain pricked at his face and arms. Shabbat would come again at sundown, so Darash had hoped to return to the market to sell as much as possible. But with the weather turning sour....

By the time he got home, the cloudburst had morphed into a thunderstorm, and he and his foul-smelling donkey were shivering and soaked through. The only merchants doing business that day would be those who sold the goods necessary to see people through Shabbat from permanent shops, like the one shared by Hathal and Nakal. Darash's jaw tightened at the thought.

Darash presented his mother with two tilapia, as a special treat for Shabbat, as well as a bag of dried fava beans and sack of fresh figs purchased on his way out of the Lower Market. He could already smell the baking challah loaves as he entered the house and knew this Shabbat would be a good one.

Darash ate a quick meal of bread smeared with lentil paste and then spent a little time playing with Tsarah. When Revayah insisted Tsarah get to her chores in preparation for Shabbat, he climbed to the roof and ducked under the lean-to where he kept many of his wares. He might as well make a tally of what items he had on hand. He needed to know what was running low and what he needed to replace immediately. He needed bitumen, of course, and decided to make a trip to Emmaus early in the coming week.

Beyond that, he would like to find some clay lamps and pots, leather satchels, and, if possible, some decorative objects—the more unusual, the better. But, as few coins remained in his belt, Darash worried he might need to sell more items from home. They still had two calves and the donkey foal, but he hoped to at least keep the foal, as Nekoda had grown older and slower.

Noon hovered near as he finished his calculations. He covered his stash of goods with a blanket, but as he did, he noticed a weathered, wooden box of his father's. Darash had often seen his father rummaging through it before leaving on a trip to sell in distant cities. After Tuwr's death, the box had remained forgotten beneath a scrap of oiled cloth. Tuwr had never allowed Darash to handle it before, but Darash had often seen inside it. He knew nothing of interest had been kept in there, just Tuwr's old weights and a few smaller items. But, now that Tuwr was gone, this box was his.

Darash sat cross-legged and pulled the box toward him until it rested squarely in front of his shins. He paused momentarily, remembering his father. Unlike his skinny son, Tuwr had a round belly and broad shoulders. Even standing as straight as he could, he remained a breath shorter than his tall, beautiful wife. Intense but friendly eyes never missed a single detail—whether he surveyed a table of goods or examined a newborn donkey foal. His hands, worn and calloused from a life of travel and loading and unloading goods, moved quickly and deftly at whatever task he put them to. They could be gentle, holding Tsarah or placed on the small of Revayah's back as he led her to their room. And they could be harsh—a swift swat on the buttocks if one of his children got out of line.

How I miss him.

Darash sighed, opened the lid, and peered inside. As expected, only common items lay before him—things any merchant might have. He pulled out a length of string, a small balance, an empty cloth bag, a knife with a wooden handle bound in cording, and the set of weights.

Darash frowned. It felt strange to go through these things as if they belonged to him. Abba's absence felt especially poignant as he did so. This box represented something reserved only for a man. These common objects represented his father's work... and now his own. Darash sighed and began replacing the items.

What more is there to being a man than to work each day and provide for your family?

As he picked up the set of weights, held in their own small box, he noticed something strange. Somehow these weights felt different than the ones he used each day at the market. They were... lighter.

Darash's heart began to beat fiercely within his chest.

False weights? False weights! Is this what Abba had been hiding all these years?

He ripped the round weights from their places and examined them closely, finding that they were indeed lighter than the measurements marked on their sides. Though skillfully painted to look like stone, the weights were in fact made of some other, more porous material. Darash broke one of them in his hands. Unbaked clay!

Hot tears stung his eyes and burned paths down his cheeks.

Is this what it means to be a man, Abba? Did nothing change after your terrible falling out with your best friend? Is this why you were killed?

Darash wiped angry tears from his cheeks with the back of his hand as one hurt-filled question replaced another.

And what of Imah? Does she know of this?

Darash grabbed the box of weights, including the one he had broken. He thudded down the stone stairway and through the front door. Tsarah sat alone on the low couch, mending the hem of a tunic. She looked up as he entered, but said nothing.

"Imah?" he called, unable to restrain the anger in his voice. "Imah!"

"What do you want?" her voice came from her bedroom, her annoyance plain.

He stormed in to find her reclined on her pallet resting. He flung the weights on the ground before her. Two more of them broke and splintered into pieces across the stone floor.

"What is the meaning of this?" he demanded.

Revayah sat up and saw the mess of painted clay, eyebrows scrunched together and mouth open in shock. It took a moment for her to recognize the broken mess for what it was, but then her face relaxed into her usual look of annoyance.

"Did you know Abba used these false weights to cheat his customers?" Darash demanded.

"How do you know he was cheating anyone? How do you know those were even his?"

"I found them in his box!" Darash's rage had not dissipated. "I know they were his! Now all I want to know is if you knew what kind of business he conducted!"

Revayah stood up. Though he had grown a great deal that year, she was a tall woman, and Darash had not yet caught up with her. She moved in close and looked into his eyes with disgust.

"How dare you make demands of me? How dare you slander your father's name so soon after he was taken from me? Your father was not a perfect man, but he was a better man than most! He took care of his family! He took care of you, and this is how you honor his memory?"

Fists still clenched, Darash spun and fled.

"Where do you think you are going?" she demanded. "Shabbat begins soon! Get back here and clean up this mess!"

Chapter Seventeen

A Thief's Legacy

Darash walked, hardly thinking of where he headed, barely noticing the rain. He entered the Lower Market, passed the well and the last shops and kept going. He crossed the Tyropoeon Valley, winding through streets and alleys, dodging people, pack mules, stray dogs, and a company of Roman soldiers marching in unison.

Lies! All lies!

At the escarpment, he left the Lower City behind and wound through the wider streets of the Upper City until he reached the road that, if he stayed on it, would lead him through the New City and out of Jerusalem toward Emmaus.

He sighed.

I need to go there anyway. I can easily make it before sundown.

"Darash! Is that you?"

Darash turned at the voice to see Chaphash approaching, Gabahh's massive home being nearby.

"Chaphash?" Darash moved toward his friend. Misery etched lines in Chaphash's usually jovial countenance. Darash momentarily forgot his own concerns. "Chaphash, are you ill? What happened?"

"I am making one final search, but I fear it is all over," Chaphash responded in a voice that was deep, raw, unnatural. He stopped just out of arm's reach, his sorrow creating the distance.

"What is all over? Search for what?"

"Come with me. I will show you."

Chaphash led him through the arched stone gate of Gabahh's large home to the servant quarter entrance. Light filtered through cracks in the wooden door, and low voices drifted through a small, open window above their heads, an opening designed to allow air to flow in yet keep intruders out. As Chaphash pushed the door open, the voices stopped, and the eyes of three servants turned to them.

Chaphash led Darash through the common servants' quarters and into the smaller room where the servants spread their pallets at night. He placed one hand on the wall to steady himself and covered his face with the other.

"I am finished. I will never escape this prison," Chaphash said. Darash detected tears in his voice. "I will be a slave forever. But the worst part of it is," he said, dropping his hand and glancing up at Darash, "that I will never be able to marry Hacassah." Chaphash nearly choked on her name. "The woman I love and who loves me will be given to another, and there is nothing either one of us can do about it." Sobs wracked his broad frame.

"What happened?" He asked, his heart breaking for his friend.

"The money. The money I saved over the past four years is gone! It has been stolen, Darash!" Chaphash faced him, anger replacing sorrow. "I hid it beneath a statue in the garden—a place I was certain was known to none but myself, but when I arose this morning, it was gone! All of it—gone!" He swiped at angry tears with the back of his hand.

Who could have done this thing? One of the other servants? A stranger who climbed the wall?

"Show me where you hid your money."

Chaphash sighed and shrugged, but agreed. Darash followed him back through the joint living area, down a corridor, and out into the inner courtyard garden. Darash covered his head as they stepped again into the rain, but Chaphash did not bother. He led Darash over to a stone statue of a Roman gladiator that came up to Chaphash's waist—a reminder of Gabahh's regular attendance at the Roman theatre. Chaphash pushed the statue back to reveal a recently excavated hole in the ground beneath.

"This is where I hid it," Chaphash explained. "The hole was smaller, but when I found it empty, I dug around, hoping my bag of coins had been covered by loose dirt. But it is nowhere to be found! It is gone... and with it my future."

Darash's heart sunk a little lower. He felt the weight of his friend's hopelessness, but tried to focus on the problem at hand.

"Was anything else taken?" Darash asked. "I mean, has anyone else lost anything?"

"No. Nothing else was touched."

That is odd. Then it could not have been a stranger. The thief knew what he wanted and knew exactly where to find it.

"And this statue... I suppose it was overturned when you discovered the theft?"

"No. It was standing in its place, just as I left it."

Very strange, indeed.

Darash stood, surveying the courtyard, the outer wall, and the exits. Four doors led from this place. The interior doors led back into the main house and to the servants' quarters from which they had come. The other two passages led to the public street in front and to the stables at the back of the home. The courtyard wall also bordered the outdoors at two locations, but one would have to be an expert climber to scale them or have assistance. Darash sighed.

"I am sorry, Chaphash. This is a terrible thing but, if I can think of any way to help you, I will."

Chaphash smiled sadly and put a hand on Darash's bony shoulder. "Thank you. I know you will... but there is nothing anyone can do."

סֶ לָ ה

The road to Emmaus had become little more than a rivulet of icy mud, but the storm had receded and the rain had slackened by the time Darash neared the small village. Despite the lift in the weather, Darash's mood remained dark and cold. He desperately wanted to get inside and dry himself by a warm fire.

Eltolad, the bitumen supplier he knew, lived on the edge of a rocky ravine in a two-roomed home that overlooked the village.

"What I lack in wealth, I make up for in sons," he often said. He and his wife had seven sons and four daughters. Even so, Darash knew he would be welcome to stay with them over Shabbat, despite the unexpectedness of his visit. But Darash did not relish the idea of sharing a bed with three or four wiggly boys, nor was he in the mood to entertain children.

Perhaps I should not have left home without thinking this through.

But then his anger rose again against his mother, his father, and the lies he had been fed growing up.

Or maybe I should have left a long time ago.

Darash found the seller's home quickly as the noise from their home was always formidable. Children scurried about, played in the mud, and chased chickens and ducks. Eltolad's heavily pregnant wife appeared at the door at his call and welcomed Darash inside as if he were one of the children. She sat him down on a cushion on the dirt floor before a crumb-scattered table and placed a bowl of leben, a yogurt-like substance, before him. A one-year old child with a dirty face and hands climbed into his lap. He waited for Eltolad as the wife went back to busily cleaning, apparently also preparing for Shabbat. Despite her efforts, the unkempt home did not seem to improve.

Seeing the woman's giant belly caused no small amount of discomfort for Darash. He did not know how to react to the distended abdomen, and he feared that their twelfth child might decide to join them at any moment. All of Eltolad's children were younger than Darash, and he doubted any of them would be much help if an emergency arose. He sighed with relief when he heard the creaking of wooden cart wheels across gravel and the children's cries of excitement at seeing their father return home.

"What are you doing with that?" Darash heard Eltolad's voice coming from outside. "Get that out of your mouth, Joshua! And, Sarah, I hope you are not thinking of putting that cricket in your sister's hair. Come, give Abba a hug."

A few moments later, Eltolad entered the house sideways, a laughing child hanging from each arm and a third attached to his right leg. Seeing Darash, he smiled.

"Ah, Darash ben Tuwr! It is good to see you again! I hope you will stay with us for Shabbat."

"Yes, I will. Thank you." Darash stood, still holding onto the small child as he did so.

Eltolad freed himself long enough to greet Darash with the customary kiss of the People.

"Now, come! We will fetch some wood for the fire so that our meal need not be delayed."

סֶ לְ ה

Spending Shabbat with Eltolad's large family proved a new experience for Darash. The meal was sparser, and the ceremonies took longer. Instead of washing their hands in a small basin indoors, Eltolad's wife lined the children up outside, instructed them to stick out their hands, and Eltolad walked down the row, pouring water across their palms. The stories and recitations grew lengthy as Eltolad often stopped to answer questions or ask a wiggly child to be still or quiet. But the blessing of the praiseworthy wife, spoken with heartfelt praise, took on new meaning.

Despite his earlier dark mood and apprehensions, Darash managed to enjoy the evening, finding it an entertaining distraction. Business matters were not discussed, of course, but there would be time for that after Shabbat had passed. In the meantime, Darash tried to push everything else from his mind and enjoy the company of friends.

It is good to be with one of Abba's old friends... at least, this one seems to have liked him....

Darash spent the least restful Shabbat of his life amongst Eltolad's children, but he enjoyed it. The constant noise, energetic games, and the incessant clamoring for attention kept him too busy to worry about his father's betrayal, Barus's search, or Chaphash's troubles—none of which he could do anything about.

He determined to finish up his business with Eltolad first thing in the morning. He had a promise to keep to Ibnei'ah and could no longer put off dealing with his troubles. But Darash, having barely slept, with so many elbows and knees in his back and thighs, woke up later than he had meant to. When he did rise that morning of yom rishon, the first day of the week, he discovered Eltolad had risen early and gone into the village to do some business.

Eltolad's wife gave Darash cold broth and a piece of bread for his breakfast, which he consumed while taking a short walk in the hills nearby. He needed time alone to think. He had hoped to think through what he would say to Barus, as Barus should be home from his trip sometime tomorrow. Instead, Darash's mind kept returning to the vision of his father's false weights lying in pieces at his mother's feet.

Abba was a cheat! A thief! Darash seethed at the thought. *Is this why Yeshua threw him out of the Temple?*

"You have a good memory, a sharp eye, and a quick mind," his father had said. "These are the most important things for any merchant. This whole city is laid out before you. You will go forth and conquer it."

At the time, this had sounded right to Darash. A good memory. A sharp eye. A quick mind. They were all good qualities to have… *but what about honesty?*

That was the same day Abba gave me my own set of weights…. Now I know why. He was trying to hide his falseness.

Darash felt a hot, cutting pain in his chest.

If he had given me his old ones, I would have discovered the truth.

His face flushed with pain and anger as tears filled his eyes.

I thought his gift was special, and he let me think so! But it was just another lie!

Darash stayed in the hills for the better part of that morning. When he mastered his emotions, he headed back to the village, washed his face with cold water from the well, and then returned to Eltolad's house to wait. He did not wait long.

Eltolad returned a little before the noon hour to have his meal and finish their business so Darash could return home. They sat together on a bench outside his home facing the main road, eating bread and fruit while the rest of the family ate inside. Eltolad did not like to conduct business inside the home, preferring the outdoors.

"So tell me, Darash ben Tuwr, how much bitumen do you need?"

"I require at least two ephah. It would be better if I could procure a homer from you, though, as Elohim has blessed me with a new business connection with Ibnei'ah, the mosaic artist."

"Ah! That is good news! I have the bitumen on hand, over there in my cart, but you will not be able to carry a full homer home. That is a load for your donkey. Where is she?"

Darash sighed. "I left Nekoda at home. My journey here was unexpected. I intended to come later this week, but...."

"How soon do you need it?"

"I am not sure. Ibnei'ah has a large project he is working on now."

"I wish I had a donkey I could loan you, Darash. My pair of mules is all I have to get me to the bitumen pits and back each day. However, I will be coming into Yerushálayim sometime this week. I can meet you there with as much bitumen as you need. For now, take what you can carry on your back."

"That brings me to my next problem," Darash said. "I only brought about a denarii and a half."

"That will only get you a seah and a half."

"I fear that, if I do not procure at least two ephah, Ibnei'ah will run out before you get to Yerushálayim. He will have to find someone else to sell it to him, and you and I might lose his business."

"I am sorry, young friend, and I wish I could help you. But I have learned not to give credit until I have worked with someone a long time. ...Listen, take the seah and a half now. In time, if our partnership proves trustworthy, we can be more flexible with one another. Besides, you could not possibly carry more than that."

Darash was disappointed but nodded. It was his own fault for storming out of the house angry and coming all the way to Emmaus without preparing properly.

"Come with me," Eltolad said, gesturing for Darash to follow. They walked over to Eltolad's work cart, which was filled with pitch-black, greasy stones of raw bitumen.

Darash watched Eltolad fill a seah-sized clay jar to the top and cover it with a patch of cloth, which he tied down securely with a leather strap. He filled a second jar half-way and prepared it the same way.

"Wait here," Eltolad said. "I have some lengths of rope in the house we can use to tie to the tops of these jars to make them easier to carry. I will return in a moment."

Darash leaned an elbow on the edge of the cart's bed to wait for Eltolad. His eyes moved to the shiny black stones and then over to his clay jars.

He would never know if I went ahead and filled up that last jar and covered it again.... I bet Abba would have done it.... It would be so easy....

Chapter Eighteen

Ghosts of Deception

Darash bid farewell to Eltolad and his family, grasped the cords holding the clay jars, and took to the road. Eltolad had lashed two jars together and fixed the rope so that they would fit over Darash's shoulders.

I should have left earlier.

He had been reluctant to leave Emmaus, but now that he was on his way, he only wanted to get back. All he wanted to do at this moment was speak to Nib'haz. To tell him about his father… and to confess.

"The LORD abhors dishonest scales, but accurate weights are his delight," Nib'haz had once quoted the words of wise King Solomon. "Remember, an honest merchant will always be blessed more than a dishonest one—perhaps not by men, but by God."

Nib'haz…. I almost made a terrible mistake….

Darash looked down at his feet, wondering what Nib'haz would think of him if he knew what had been in his heart. His broken sandal thong flopped in the dust, leaving a strange pattern in the dirt and flicking up tiny pebbles as he walked.

I should have gotten that fixed before making this trip…. And, I should have brought Nekoda.

Darash glanced back down the road to check if anyone in a cart might be coming along who might deign to give him a lift. And then he remembered.

Nasha, Gabahh's wife should be coming along this road today. …Actually, she should have passed by hours ago, as I sat talking with Eltolad. She would have left early to get back to Yerushaláyim from Lydda by suppertime. She should have passed right by us. …But I did not see her.

Darash's mind returned to the matter of Chaphash's misfortune. Soon Chaphash would have to tell Hadassah's father that he could no longer afford to marry. He might be doing so even now… and Hadassah's beautiful blue eyes would be stained red from tears.

If only I could do something about it!

But Darash could barely afford to keep food on his own table, and his own future starved for security. There was no way he could earn enough gold to pay off Gabahh and free his friend.

Who has done this thing? A friend? A neighbor? One person or more? Is that a lamb kabob I smell?

A cart rolled past. Three children peered out the back, looking at him as they munched fried meat on a stick. Darash's stomach growled.

The thief was no stranger.

That was obvious from what he had witnessed at the crime scene. He thought of Nib'haz and all Nib'haz had taught him about discovering extra information that may escape sight alone. Darash pushed aside the images of Gabahh's home and tried to remember what he had heard and smelled. Though Darash had visited only a few rooms in the house, he had passed several doors along the corridor. He remembered hearing Gabahh's voice coming from behind a closed door, but could not make out what was said. The voice that responded was male and subservient in tone—most likely that of a servant helping his master prepare for bed.

In and of itself, that memory seemed to signify little; however, Darash had also noticed the smell of lye, a mixture of animal tallow and ashes, as he entered the courtyard. The maids had been doing the wash, and a line of clothing hung along the far wall to dry. Strangely, all the clothing on the line had been those of Gabahh or of the servants.

If Nasha had canceled her trip to Lydda, would her clothing not also need to be cleaned? Or is Nasha not at home after all? If she is not home and she was not in Lydda, where could she be?

In this maze of disturbing thoughts, Darash searched for the culprit. At times, he seemed just steps behind an elusive image of this person, but then it would shift and move away. Darkness would descend, and his thoughts returned to the beginning. He followed a mirage... a shadow... a ghost.

Darash came to an abrupt stop. A ghost! One hand flew to his head as thoughts and ideas flooded his mind and began to coalesce. He had it! At least, he thought he did.

Oh, no! If I am right, I must hurry!

סֶ לָ ה

The afternoon had been spent and dinnertime came and went by the time Darash arrived back in Jerusalem. He headed straight to Ibnei'ah's home and banged on the door. Little Ra'ah answered, barefooted and clutching a small doll made of clay and rags.

"Who is there, little one?" Ibnei'ah's voice could be heard from inside. Soon he appeared behind her. "Oh, Darash. It is good to see you, but you did not have to bring the bitumen to me. I would have come for it."

"I am not here about the bitumen, Ibnei'ah, although this is for you." Darash removed the rope from his shoulders and deposited the clay jars just inside Ibnei'ah's door. "I am here about the matter we spoke of at the shuk on yom ha'shi'shi." Ibnei'ah did not seem to be following. "The matter about your daughter and her... and what she saw that night from her window."

"Yes, I remember. But why would that bring you here?"

Darash colored. "Please. I need to see the window in your daughter's room, the window she was looking through when she claimed she saw her mother. Then I will explain."

Ibnei'ah frowned but stood aside. "Very well. Come this way."

Darash followed Ibnei'ah and Ra'ah as he walked and she limped to her room.

"There," she said. "That is where I saw Imah."

The window was high off the ground, far too high for Ra'ah to reach.

"How did you get up high enough to see out?"

Ra'ah pointed to a long-legged table on the other side of the room. It looked foreign in design, perhaps Syrian, but not uncommon.

"Father moved it," Ra'ah explained. "He did not want me looking out at night anymore."

Darash nodded and stepped up toward the window. On tip-toe, he could see directly into Gabahh's stable yard and what he saw made him smile. He stepped back and motioned for Ra'ah to join him. He lifted her up so they could both look from the window together.

"Show me where you saw her."

"She was there," she pointed to a small outbuilding, one that looked quite rundown and no longer in use. "She came from there and went over there."

"And then?"

"Then I jumped down and went to get my father. But when he came she was gone. He did not believe me. He said it was only a dream."

"It is alright, Ra'ah," Darash said and set her down. "I believe you saw someone. But, Ra'ah, the person you saw was not your mother. Do not worry. We will find out who it was. Would you like that?"

Ra'ah nodded. Darash motioned for Ibnei'ah to come look.

"See? That building there. I would like you to accompany me on a brief visit to your neighbors. But you will need to send one of your servants for the magistrate and have him come as quickly as possible. ...I believe we may find your ghost."

סֶ לָ ה

When Magistrate Quintus Arrius arrived, he gave Darash a look of surprise that rapidly transformed into annoyance. Thankfully, Ibnei'ah, being well-known among the elite Romans for his mosaic art, held a little more sway. With him standing nearby, Darash was able to convince the Roman that a crime had been committed. Ibnei'ah then led the way to Gabahh's home. They moved past the servant entrance to the main door. The magistrate knocked loudly. Chaphash answered.

"This is the man whose money was stolen," Darash said, reverting to the common Greek.

"Is this true?" Magistrate Quintus asked, also in Greek. "Your friend says you had four years' worth of your savings go missing?"

"Stolen, I am afraid. And, yes, I have."

"Who are you?"

"My name is Chaphash. I am a bond servant here in the home of Gabahh and his wife, Nasha. I was due to pay off my debt yesterday, but when I went that morning to find the money I had hidden, it was gone."

"Go wake your master and mistress," the magistrate ordered. "I would speak with them."

"I am sorry. My mistress is not here. She has gone to Lydda to visit relatives, but I will fetch my master." Chaphash disappeared through a doorway, and Darash led the small party inside the front room to wait.

Within a few moments, Gabahh joined them with Chaphash following closely.

"Shalom," he said, bowing to his guests, but mostly toward the magistrate.

"Greetings," Magistrate Quintus Arrius replied in a grumble, not one to waste time on pleasantries. "A theft has been reported, and I would like to see where it occurred."

"Yes, my servant informed me on yom ha'shi'shi that he had some money go missing. But it is of little matter to the Roman government, I would think."

"Theft is always of interest to the Roman government as it is our duty to keep the peace in Yerushaláyim. This man is a bond-servant, not a slave, and he has the right to an investigation. Furthermore, I am assured," the magistrate glanced at Darash, "that this matter can be solved quickly. Show me where it occurred."

Gabahh, face blank with his lack of understanding, looked at Darash and then turned back to the Roman official. He reluctantly led the way to the inner courtyard and small garden. Gabahh indicated the statue.

"There. Apparently, my servant hid his money beneath this statue—not a very safe place. As you can see, my property is not impenetrable. Anyone could have scaled these walls during the night."

From the corner of his eye, Darash saw Chaphash sink a little lower at his master's words.

"This theft was not committed by an intruder, though," Darash spoke up. "If a stranger had climbed the wall, he would have needed help. It is too high for one person alone. And, why take only Chaphash's money and touch nothing else? How would they know where to look?"

"Hmm… This looks like no crime scene I have ever witnessed. Thieves are rarely so tidy," the magistrate added, showing genuine interest. He turned to Gabahh. "I would like to speak to your wife. When will she return?"

Gabahh answered quickly, "She has been in Lydda visiting relatives since before Shabbat. I expect her back this very day, before sundown. …Perhaps you can come back later and speak to her then."

"I have just come from Emmaus," Darash said. "If she was journeying back from Lydda, she would have to go straight through there. I was watching the road most of the afternoon. She never came."

Gabahh looked from one to the other. "Th… the… then perhaps she has been delayed… or has gone missing! We should begin looking for her immediately!"

"That is precisely why I am here," the magistrate said. "I have been given some advice about where to start looking—which had better be correct." With a glance at Darash, he followed the young man down a corridor to the stable yard. This section of the property shared its back wall with Ibnei'ah's home and Ra'ah's window.

"Where are you going?" Gabahh demanded following them, robe flying open, with Chaphash on his heels.

The magistrate did not answer. He and Darash moved swiftly into the stable yard and directly to the ramshackle building Ra'ah had pointed out from her window moments ago. Ibnei'ah, holding Ra'ah's hand, followed behind the others, still unsure as to why they had been brought along.

Magistrate Quintus flung the door open, and the small party was greeted with a startled shriek from inside. Gabahh's wife, Nasha, had been found.

"Here is your thief, young man," the magistrate announced to Chaphash through a satisfied grimace. He reached in and grabbed the frightened woman by the arm.

"Who are you? What are you doing?" Nasha yelled. "Take your hands off me!"

Quintus ignored her loud protestations and dragged her into the bright afternoon sunlight. As he did so, Ra'ah gasped.

"That is her, Abba," she whispered

"This is the woman you saw from your window?" Ibnei'ah asked. "Are you certain?"

She nodded and then looked away. Ibnei'ah picked her up, and she buried her face in his shoulder.

"Husband!" Nasha cried. "What have you done? You have ruined us! And look at my tunic! These stains will never come out!"

Gabahh shot his wife a warning look but then recovered quickly with, "Oh, my dear wife! When did you arrive back? We were... all so worried about you!"

"How could you do this to me?" she whined, descending into angry tears. With one hand she tried to cover her mess of hair with a stained length of white linen. "That shack leaks, you know! And there are mice and vermin living in there!"

"Magistrate Arrius," Gabahh said, turning to the unamused Roman. "It is so good you have... found her. Obviously, she is suffering from a troubled mind!"

The magistrate leveled Gabahh with an icy stare, but did not release Nasha's arm. In the commotion, Darash slipped into the shack behind Nasha and, after a bit of rummaging around, emerged again with what he had hoped to find.

"Look," he said, holding a dirty, cloth bag filled with coins.

Chaphash stepped forward, face full of hurt and wonder.

"That is my bag. That is the same bag that held the coins I buried under the statue."

Darash handed the small sack over, and Chaphash opened it to examine the contents. "It is all here," he said. He turned to Darash. "But how... how did you know?"

Darash glanced at Ra'ah. He had to speak loudly to be heard above Nasha's wails, but he explained, "Little Ra'ah claimed that, on the night before last, she saw her mother crossing Gabahh's yard in the night. Of course, it was not her mother, as her mother is no longer among the living. No one believed the girl at first, but when I heard of your thief and realized Nasha and Gabahh had only pretended she had taken a journey, I guessed that Ra'ah's ghost and your thief might be one and the same." He turned back to the group. "She hid herself in this outbuilding, knowing it was unused. She believed she would be safe from discovery. Her husband Gabahh spread word all about town that she would be away in Lydda for a few days. During the night, she slipped out, entered the courtyard and took your money. She returned to the shack and planned to sneak out sometime this evening, pretending to be returning from Lydda."

"But how did she know where to find my money? I had it hidden there for years, and it has never been disturbed before."

"I wondered that, too, at first," Darash admitted, "but then I remembered hearing your master speak of how Ibnei'ah," he indicated the tall man with a nod of the head, "had been contracted to put in a new mural floor in the courtyard. Gabahh was expecting to receive your money in exchange for your freedom, so he began making plans for its use. I suspect that, in preparing the site for the mural, he moved the statue and discovered your money. Once he knew where the money was, he decided to keep the money by making it look like a theft had occurred, and keep you as a bond-servant as well."

"He enlisted his wife," the magistrate added, "to help carry it out."

Chaphash looked from his master, Gabahh, to his ashen-faced mistress and back again. A blank mask of pain and realization replaced his earlier tears. He tugged at the drawstrings of his money bag, opened it, and removed a handful of silver and copper coins—the amount of the bride-price he had promised Hadassah's father. He closed the bag again and turned to Gabahh, now red-faced and dejected. Chaphash held out the bag of coins.

"This is yours. And I am finished here."

Chaphash turned in one swift and determined motion and re-entered the house. By the time the magistrate led Gabahh and Nasha away for questioning by the council, Chaphash and his few meager belongings had disappeared.

Chapter Nineteen

Illusive

Darash walked Ibnei'ah and Ra'ah to their home before returning to his. Evening had come, and he had not yet decided what he would say to Imah when he saw her. Still, he walked with a satisfied smile, reliving his friend's moment of victory and feeling the coins in his pouch which Ibnei'ah had given him for the bitumen plus a few extra for helping his daughter.

Chaphash is finally free! There will be a wedding after all, and little Ra'ah no longer has to wonder what she had seen that night.

Though he felt sorry that Ra'ah's childlike hope of getting her mother back again could not be fulfilled, Ibnei'ah was a good father. He would find a way to comfort her.

At least, the magistrate no longer seems quite so angry with me. Perhaps he will be more willing to listen next time I need him....

Darash's smile widened as he thought of these things, but then it became a grimace when his middle let out a loud complaint. The supper hour had come and gone, and now he felt as if his stomach was trying to digest him from the inside out. He stopped to purchase some food for his family with the money he had made, and treated himself to a marinated lamb-kabob and a cinnamon-braised pear on a stick. They did not last more than two blocks.

Darash's broken sandal finally gave out altogether at the southern end of the Lower Market. Only a few more blocks would see him home, but his feet were already sore from his long walk from Emmaus. He did not favor the idea of going the rest of the way barefooted.

Perhaps I can fix it well enough to last until I get home.

He moved to the side of the street, leaned his back against the wall, and fidgeted with the leather straps. As he worked, he noticed men's voices quite close by. Evidently, two men stood in the alleyway around the corner of the same building, just out of sight.

"We are only in Yerusháláyim for a few days. Then we return to Crete. I was told to come see you about my particular... needs."

"I am glad you did," another man answered. "I think I have what you want. You like them young, right?"

Darash immediately lost interest in his sandal. That second voice sounded very familiar.

"Yes."

"I live not far from here. You can come over and see her for yourself."

That voice! I know it! It is Pertho! That filthy Greek!

The first man paused as though considering the offer.

"If you like her, I can let you spend an hour with her for... ten prutot."

Amah! Sold for the cost of a loaf of bread!

סֶ לָ ה

The following morning, yom shayni, the second day of the week, Darash sat next to Nib'haz watching the old man skillfully mend his broken sandal with a piece of twine. When Darash received it back and tried it on, he smiled at how well it fit.

"I should have asked you to do this a long time ago," he said.

"It fits then?"

"Very well. Thank you."

"Good." Nib'haz nodded.

Darash's mind returned to the previous night and what he had overheard.

"Nib'haz?"

"Mm?"

"Are not all Jews Elohim's chosen People?"

Nib'haz nodded. "Yes, of course."

"Even the poor and those in slavery?"

"Yes. We were all in slavery once, but Elohim delivered us to freedom."

"Then, if Elohim delivered us all from slavery, why do we still tolerate it today?"

"Oooo, Boy!" Valad interjected. "You and your questions! Does this look like the Temple steps to you?" He motioned to the alley. Then he picked up a block of cheese. "Does this look like a scroll of the Torah to you? And, if you think Nib'haz looks like a rabbi, you must be as blind as he is!" He laughed and shook his head.

"That is a good question, young one," Nib'haz answered, ignoring Valad. "I suppose we tolerate it because, despite all our rituals designed to remind us of Elohim's deliverance, we still find it easy to forget. And we do not treat one another as He treated us."

Darash sighed. "Even my father used people, cheated them, stole from them.... Did you know that the first gift he gave me to celebrate my becoming a man was also a deception?" Darash told Nib'haz the story of how Tuwr had used false weights and purchased new ones for Darash. "I thought his gift was special but he meant only to hide his trickery from me!"

Nib'haz was silent for a moment. "Hide his trickery from you? Or protect you from it?"

"I do not understand," Darash said, frustrated. "What do you mean?"

"You thought your father bought you a new set of weights because he loved you. When you discovered his false weights, you imagined his gift was also a lie. You believe he gave them to you—not because he loved you but because he was hiding something from you."

"Yes."

"Could it not be both? That he loved you and he was hiding something from you?"

Darash sighed audibly but did not answer.

"I think he was hiding something from you—the fact that he sometimes dealt falsely with his customers. Would it have been better if he had shared that with you? Expected you to also cheat people?"

"No, but...."

"It would have been better if Tuwr had not cheated at all!" Valad said, supplying precisely what Darash had been thinking.

"True, true," Nib'haz said. "But let us examine Tuwr as he was, not as we would want him to be. And, though we now know he was not always honest, that is no reason to believe he did not love his son. And, Darash, knowing you, it is easy to see that your father—whatever his faults—was a good father to you. He raised you to embrace honesty, did he not? Otherwise, you would not be so upset today. Correct?"

Darash released a breath, letting it filter from his nose in a long exhale.

"Correct."

"Very well, then," Nib'haz picked up a basket and began feeling around its loose edge, as if the matter were settled. "His gift was one of love, after all—perhaps even more so than you thought at first—because with it he also protected you from the worst parts of himself—something many fathers fail to do."

סֶ לָ ה

That evening, as business came to a close, Darash left the shuk and headed across town to the home of Servius Aurelius. The sun descended over the western hills, taking with him the scant warmth he had shared.

Night's approach could be seen as she began spreading her darkened, feathery wings ever closer toward Jerusalem from the eastern horizon.

A stooped, elderly woman greeted Darash at the door. Well-dressed and plump, the woman smiled at him, and her eyes grew bright at the prospect of entertaining company. He guessed this woman to be the great aunt of Servius, of whom Millah, the dyer's wife, had spoken.

"Shalom," Darash bowed. He carried the soft, blue-green sash Millah had sold him. "I bring you a small gift with the hope you might be willing to speak with me for a little while."

Darash handed her the colorful bit of cloth, and she took it in her gnarled hands, turned it over, admired the color, and then rubbed the soft fabric on her sagging cheek. Her grateful smile revealed several missing teeth and her breath smelled of rye and overripe apricots. She placed her right hand on his shoulder and waved him forward with the other. Showing him to a low couch, she handed him a soft pillow and placed a bowl of figs before him. All this she accomplished with hardly a word, but as soon as she sat, she launched into the depths of the many ideas, memories, and whims of an old woman who had her physical needs met but her emotional needs neglected.

"I see you are a stout young lad," she said. "You are so kind to come see an old woman. I am Ana." She patted her chest, now fleshy and sagging with age. "I was born in Rome and lived there as a child. That was many years ago now, but I remember. I do! I remember everything. I remember as if it were only yesterday or last night. I was young once like you, my boy. I was beautiful, too, mind you!" She smiled crookedly, but her eyes glowed with mischief. "If you had seen me then, ooooweeee! Your next stop would be to visit my father to ask for my hand, I vow! Many young men did, you know! Many found me quite a thing to gaze upon, to be sure!"

Darash smiled.

"Do you have a young woman?" she asked. At Darash's hesitation, she laughed. "No, of course you do not! You are but a child! What would you want with a woman at your age? You are barely past piddling on the floor, I imagine. But it was good of you to come. What is age between friends, eh? Oh, the stories I could tell you! I remember one young man so desperately in love with me that he promised my father a thousand head of cattle, can you believe it? He was a wealthy one and so handsome! Ah, I would have married him even without such riches, but it was not to be. My father had the blood of the Caesars in his veins—very little, mind you. But he made that one drop sound like an ocean among his political allies. So he gave me to the son of a diplomat."

Ana paused here for a moment, and Darash detected a hint of sadness in her eyes, but then she continued with a half-smile and a wave of the hand. "Oh, how I cried! I cried until I thought I had no more tears left. But, years later, after I had sons and daughters, I cried no more. What is done is done. I had a family, and my husband did not treat me too badly, and we had good food, a good home, and many friends. It was a good life. Then, of course, there was war. Always war! Always war to come and steal your sons away and break the hearts of your daughters! I lost two sons and a son-in-law in the war and another son to illness. I lost a niece, too, the mother of Servius."

"In the war?" Darash asked his first words since coming inside.

"No, no, no. Women do not go to war!"

But sometimes they die in war.

"You are a funny young thing," she continued with a cackle. "No. My niece was killed by an intruder. And I have lost several grandchildren and other nieces and nephews, too. Disease often claims the young," she sighed. "When you are as old as I, you become a collector of the dead—a collector of memories for the young, who never seem to have time for them. I do not think people were meant to live this long," she wagged her head from side to side with a sorrowful look. "Most memories are bad ones. It is a great burden. I think people should die young—before they are so burdened they can no longer stand up straight anymore. Do you see how my shoulders are bent and sagging?"

Darash was uncertain whether he should admit he had noticed the woman's mild deformity or if he should do the polite thing and protest. Thankfully, she was not the type to allow quiet moments go too long.

She reached back as far as she could and patted her shoulders and upper back. "Do you see? Too much weight. You cannot see it, but it is there. And I think these memories and sorrows cause other ailments as well. My fingers are so very sore," she claimed, holding her crooked hands out beneath his nose and rubbing them vigorously for emphasis. "I cannot do my sewing anymore! I cannot weave or pull cooked flesh from the bone. I can barely even dress myself for all the aches and pains. Still, I insist on doing it myself! I do not want some servant fussing over me like I was a little—"

"Auntie!" a surprised feminine voice came from an inner doorway. "I did not know we had a visitor."

An attractive Roman woman, perhaps ten years his senior, strolled gracefully and confidently into the room. A flowing, white toga with blue and gold edging, belted with embroidered fabric, hung from her perfectly sculpted body. Darash stood upon her entrance. He had never seen someone so beautiful. Despite the wobble in his knees, he managed to bow a greeting.

"Shalom," he squeaked, his voice cracking.

"And whom do we have the pleasure of meeting this evening?" she asked, her eyes taking in every skinny inch of him.

"Shalom," he said again, regaining his voice if not his composure.

"Ah, a young Jew."

"I am Darash. I have come to speak with Servius Aurelius."

"He is my... cousin," the beauty answered with a slight pinkish hue rising in her cheeks. "We both share Ana as a great-aunt and live here together. I am Julia."

Darash swallowed and nodded but could not keep himself from wondering at the nature of Servius's relationship with this young lady. They were relatives, but not especially close. A marriage between them would be favorable, especially if a strain of royal blood could be thus preserved. However, unless granted special permission, Roman centurions were forbidden to marry until they had completed their term of service, usually twenty-five years. Some married anyway, but such unions were not legally recognized. His wife would have no legal claim to an inheritance were he to die in battle. And any children they might have together could never attain Roman citizenship.

Servius did not seem the type to shun convention nor deny his wife and children the security he so longed to attain for himself. So, though Servius and Julia had not yet wed, it seemed plain why he had chosen to keep his beautiful cousin close by. Why else would such a beauty, well past marriageable age, remain unmarried unless she waited for a certain man to be free?

"I hope our great aunt did not steal away too much of your time," the young woman continued. She reached up and played with one of the silky, brown tendrils that danced about her neck. "She has a great gift for catching and keeping prisoner anyone who comes to call."

Darash, though embarrassed for Ana, was captivated by Julia's beauty and poise. Jewish women neither dressed nor behaved in such an open, confident manner around male strangers. Even his mother, quite unreserved in his presence and talkative around friends, always feigned discomfort and modesty around a man she did not know well, particularly if that man boasted wealth or position. Darash was neither wealthy nor well-positioned, he realized, and perhaps not even viewed as a man at all by this woman, yet he felt convinced she had not withheld from him even a drop of her charm.

"I will take you to Servius right away," she said in a voice like sweetened, warm milk. "He is just through here."

She reached toward him and took hold of his hand.

This Gentile woman is touching me! I should not allow this.

Darash did not pull away. He could not help noticing the smoothness of her skin and, though her fingers were cooler than his, her touch created a warm sensation that traveled along his arm to his chest and hollowed out his gut. As she began to lead him from the room, he shot Ana a departing smile before following Julia through a decorative, arched doorway. They found Servius behind the house in a sturdy woodshed, barking at a servant for letting the woodpile get too low. He stood with his back to them.

"My cousin?" the goddess addressed him, and, when he turned and saw her, Servius smiled. Even the relative of this a beautiful creature could not maintain a foul mood in her presence. However, when he saw Darash, his brow and jaw revealed immediate discomfort.

"Thank you… cousin. I will speak to this young man alone," Servius said in a gentle but firm tone. The woman did not question him. She gave Darash one last smile before letting go of his hand. She shot Servius a teasing look before slipping back to the house. Darash was sorry to see her go but liked the way she moved as she walked away. His hand still felt tingly from her touch.

Turing to Servius, Darash tried to force a smile to his lips. It never came. Foul mood quickly returning, Servius gestured to a set of steps that led to an upper room. Darash followed.

Why is it I only talk to this man in high places?

"Now, you listen to me," the muscle-bound Roman turned on Darash as soon as the door to the rooftop chamber closed behind them, "I already told you everything I remember! So let me warn you—I will not allow you to haunt my steps or take food from the mouths of my family! Do you think I will allow a child like you to turn Rome against me? I have given Rome twenty years of my life! I have traveled to foreign lands for her, shed my blood for her, killed for her! I am now a centurion in the Roman army with a hundred men at my command, each of us charged with keeping your city safe from invaders! I am a good soldier and a benefit to this city you call home! How dare you sit in the comfort and safety I provide and then come to me with threats? I have faced much more formidable enemies than you!"

Darash had backed up further and further during Servius's tirade, and now his back pressed against the cold stone wall with Servius's face so close to his, he could feel spittle as the centurion yelled. Evidently, Servius had prepared for this meeting over the last week, and no sign of weakness remained in him. He stood only a pace away, a look of hard determination on his face, and his hand on the hilt of a dagger, once concealed in his belt.

Darash raised a hand in self-defense.

"Please," he managed. "I am not your enemy! I have not come here to blackmail you." Servius gave pause and Darash continued quickly, "I promised you I would not report what I had witnessed! I will keep my promise! I want nothing from you!"

Servius took a step back, but his eyes still stared Darash down with a steely, penetrating gaze.

"...except to speak to you again about that night," Darash amended.

"If you are lying—!"

"I speak the truth! I want only to help the Greek, Barus, avenge his daughter's murder! I pledge you my oath!"

The centurion's knuckles, white from gripping the dagger, now relaxed. He took a few steps back and released his weapon. Darash sucked in a deep breath and swallowed hard. He felt lightheaded for a moment and could hear his heart pounding in his ears, but he willed himself to relax.

"I cannot imagine that there could be anything else I might say that would be of use to you," Servius said. "I saw and heard nothing that night."

"But you also said you were quite certain that you were, forgive me, fully awake."

"Yes."

"Do you not find that strange?"

"Yes, I admit I do... but all the same, I know I was awake that night! I just cannot remember."

"Wait," Darash caught this inconsistency. "You said you had seen nothing and heard nothing, but are you now saying you simply cannot remember anything that happened that night? Nothing at all?"

"I know I was awake. I know a murder occurred that I should have seen or, at least, heard. But I remember nothing about it. I remember coming to the tower that night, ascending the ladder and surveying the darkened hills. I remember looking over the sleeping city...." he trailed off.

"And?"

"And then I remember... I remember seeing a wolf roaming about outside the city wall."

"That is all?"

"No. I remember wondering why my heart would beat so wildly and why I could not seem to take in a breath at the simple sight of a lone wolf. The animal was no different from many I have slain over the years… just sniffing around… no threat to anyone."

Chapter Twenty

Forgotten

Nib'haz sat mumbling as Darash unloaded his merchandise and set up shop the following morning. The blind, old merchant dexterously laid out his stacks of round baskets in neat piles, small to large, in a row before him. Behind those, he arranged the specialty baskets—oval shaped ones, those with handles, and some with attached lids. He kept his brooms and rolls of reed mats at the sides. With the task of laying out his wares completed, Nib'haz set a large utility basket next to his thigh. From it, he pulled a handful of reeds and his tools—bone needles and iron hooks of various sizes rolled in a swatch of leather and tied with a leather thong.

Nib'haz also brought forth a small jug of water and a clay bowl, used to soak and soften the tougher reeds for easier use. With everything prepared, he began fashioning a long, strong reed into a base for a new basket, wrapping it in a tight circular pattern and securing it with a thinner one. He wove the narrow reed in and out with practiced skill. All the while, his unseeing eyes gazed forever before him.

Darash enjoyed watching him work. As the wayward reeds and stringy mess took shape, molded between skilled, patient fingers, a pattern emerged. Something cheap—good only to be thrown beneath animals—became a thing of practical and varied use. Seeing this transformation happen before his eyes comforted Darash. With so much of the good in life wasted and destroyed, even small steps to reclaim unwanted things gave his heart hope.

"There it is... yes... a smoother one perhaps," Nib'haz muttered over his work. "That will need to be trimmed away.... Another over here.... Darash, as long as you are standing there, could you fetch me that bag of figs by your feet?"

"Good morning and shalom, Nib'haz," Darash said with a chuckle and bent to retrieve the figs.

"Good morning, young one." He smiled.

"Can we expect your regal presence the entire day," Valad interjected, "or do you have more pressing matters than mere work?"

"Leave him alone," Nib'haz said, waving a hand of dismissal to his companion. "He has been busy."

"That much is plain! He has been so busy he can barely feed his family. If I was that busy, I would go out of business!"

"He does what he must to keep his business. Perhaps you should pay closer attention to your own."

"Yes, perhaps I should. I am getting tired of watching his things every time he has to run off to do who knows what!" He then turned to Darash, hands gesturing with vigor. "So are you going to stay here today? Or, will you find some excuse to leave us trapped here with all your things?"

"Do not worry. I shall be here today," Darash said, only moderately concerned with Valad's complaints.

"Ah! At last we will be blessed with his presence! I was afraid he had forgotten us! Ah, young lady, some cheese today?" Valad turned to a middle-aged woman who happened by, carrying a basket of fresh bread. "A little cheese to go with your bread? It would make tonight's supper not only more delicious, but also strengthening for your husband and children. I will give you a good price!"

Darash put his back against the wall, brought his knees up, and tucked his tunic between his legs. He rested his forearms on his knees and ignored the rest of Valad's sales attempt.

"I went to see the watchtower guard again," Darash said to Nib'haz. "This time, at his home, and he described the night of the murder a little differently."

"Tell me."

"Before, he kept saying he saw nothing. This time he spoke of it as remembering nothing. Then he described his experience as if part of his memory was missing. Can that even happen?"

"Well, it would certainly happen if he fell asleep."

"He insists he stayed awake that entire night, and the way he described his moment of forgetfulness—if that is what it was—could only have occurred if he had been standing the whole time. When I found him asleep, he was sitting down and slumped over."

"Hmm.... very strange." Nib'haz leaned his head back slightly, his unseeing eyes staring toward a high point on the opposite wall. His hands, which had slowed in their work as Darash spoke, now resumed their task with steady movements. Anyone else might think Nib'haz had given up answering, but Darash knew to simply wait.

A moment later, Nib'haz began to mumble. "Forgotten moments... something seen... something heard... something lost. Pushed out by... fear. ...Fear. Like a child. Like a child...."

Nib'haz went on this way for a little while, but when the mumbling stopped, Darash looked up.

"I knew a man once," Nib'haz began. "When he was ten years old, he went to live with his grandmother. This was strange, because, although his mother had died, his father still lived. Why would a man allow his son to be taken away and never go see him? Anyway, his grandmother lived near me and his father lived in another city. We were friends when we were young, before I lost my eyesight, and I never remember seeing his father. In fact, though I knew the father to be alive somewhere, they almost never spoke of him. So one day I asked my friend, 'Why does your father never come see you?' He shrugged his shoulders and said, 'I do not know. I barely remember him.' At that time, he was eleven and had not been separated from his father for long, so I said, 'What do you mean you do not remember?' He responded, 'I do not remember much of anything before my life here.'" Nib'haz paused for effect, then asked, "Now, do you not think a child of eleven would have a great many memories? Even now I can remember being six years old, seven years old, eight."

Darash nodded. He, too, had a great many memories of his early childhood. "How could he forget so many years of his life?"

"I think I may know why," Nib'haz said slowly, but followed up quickly with, "though I do not truly understand it. Now, I heard from someone else that his father was a very cruel man. He drank much and when he was drunk, his cruelty turned into violence. I know also that when my friend first came to live with his grandmother, he was in very poor health. I think his father was the cause, though the boy himself never claimed such a thing. So now, looking back at it all, I wonder if perhaps his inability to remember the worst years of his life was a good thing."

"What do you mean?"

"I mean, he was a happy child. If he remembered the many beatings and drunken rages and who knows what else, I do not think he would have fully enjoyed the good life his grandmother gave him. He would have been sad, frightened, angry. But, instead, he played, he laughed, he had fun. He even got into little scraps of trouble, but nothing unusual for a boy his age. So, perhaps, his ability to forget the worst times of his life allowed him to preserve the good that was still in him."

"But how does that happen?"

"I cannot say."

"Did your friend ever remember the bad years?"

"I know not. A few years later, they moved to another city. I have not seen him since."

Darash became silent. A few moments later he said, "So you think perhaps Servius Aurelius might have seen something terrible, but then forgot it?"

Nib'haz shrugged. "Maybe. Maybe not."

"But he is a grown man, not a child."

"Perhaps there is something in his childhood, though."

What was it Servius's grandmother said? How many sons had she lost? And a daughter, too? A daughter murdered... murdered by an intruder.

"Darash!" A new voice interrupted Darash's thoughts.

He looked up into the face of Chaphash. It was the first he had seen of him since Chaphash had walked out of Gabahh and Nasha's home. He now stood before Darash, grinning broadly and standing taller than Darash had ever seen him.

"Shalom!" Darash stood to greet his friend, but was surprised when Chaphash enveloped him in an exuberant and compressive hug.

"Darash, you must come to a feast at my family's home tonight! We are celebrating my freedom, and you will be the guest of honor! Because of you I no longer serve those thieves. Hadassah and her family will be there, and you and your family must come as well!"

Darash bowed his head slightly in humble acceptance. "Thank you, Chaphash. I would be honored to celebrate with you."

"Tonight then! At dusk. There will be music and dancing and much food and wine!" Chaphash backed away as he spoke, no doubt hurrying to help with the many preparations, but his smile never faded. "I will see you again soon!"

Darash waved as his friend rounded the corner and disappeared from sight, but then he furrowed his brow and a slight frown replaced his smile. He had planned on visiting Barus that evening. Barus had been due to return from Hebron last night and would no doubt want to know if there had been any progress in tracking his daughter's killer. Darash also wanted to ask about the amulet and, though he knew not how, he intended to tell Barus of Aphiemi's condition. Perhaps he could go now, but that would mean leaving his belongings here again.

Darash glanced over his shoulder at Valad, and their eyes met.

"No, no, no!" Valad said firmly and pointed an accusing finger at him.

Darash sighed.

סֶ לָ ה

"And I want to thank my good friend, Darash," Chaphash said in a loud voice as he held his cup of wine high, "for helping me discover the truth when lies threatened to rob me of my future." Then, glancing to his left at his pretty, smiling Hadassah, he added, "Our future."

Chaphash's left hand moved to his middle, and he removed a small pouch from his belt.

"This is not enough for what you have done," he said, his voice now somber and his eyes steadily on Darash, "but I want you to have it, along with our deepest thanks."

"No, I could not accept it, Chaphash," Darash replied, a hand up, knowing that the pouch must contain a far too generous portion of Chaphash's meager savings. Darash purposely avoided looking in his mother's direction.

"Please, my friend," Chaphash insisted, taking Darash's hand and pushing the sack into Darash's palm. "If it had not been for you, we would have no reason to celebrate."

"Please do take it," Hadassah said, smiling at him, eyes and voice sincere. "By doing so, you will make our joy complete."

Darash nodded and smiled at them. Only then did he glance at Revayah.

She actually looks... proud....

Darash's smile broadened, and he and Chaphash embraced.

Well... now I can afford a proper gift for their wedding.

The night grew late. The meal had been consumed, the music and dancing had ended, and the time had come for those remaining to drink the last of the wine and head for home. Chaphash reclined next to his friend and took another drought of the sweet, red liquid in his cup. Darash had never before drunk so much and began to feel drowsy.

"What have you heard from the magistrate about Gabahh and Nasha?" Darash asked, the words thick on his tongue.

Chaphash's smile turned to a frown.

"They are back home, living comfortably."

"What?" Darash asked, immediately upset.

"The magistrate did what he could, but the Sanhedrin decided to punish them no further. I paid them the debt I owed and my masters had freed me, so why press the matter?"

"Gabahh has many friends within the ruling council." Darash pushed air forcefully through his nose in frustration.

"Yes, but the law is lenient toward thieves once the matter is resolved, and I am only a bond-servant."

"No, you are a free Jewish man with rights!"

"I am now, thanks to you."

Darash sighed in annoyance, but felt Chaphash's reassuring hand on his forearm.

"Do not concern yourself with them any longer, my friend," he said. "I am free, and I will be married soon," he glanced at Hadassah, who blushed her response, "and there is nothing Gabahh or anyone can do to remove Elohim's blessing from us. He used you, you know. Elohim used you to bless us, and we will forever be grateful."

סֶ לָ ה

Darash followed Revayah home. He carried his sister, Tsarah, who slept deeply, and marveled at how heavy she had gotten within the past couple of years. This used to be easy. Now his steps grew shorter and slower with each passing street.

"Did you have a good time, Imah?" he asked, mostly to keep her from leaving him behind and taking the only light, a clay lamp she carried in her right hand.

She slowed a bit and let him catch up. "It was a nice celebration, and the food was good. The wine was cheap, though. It tasted like they watered it down and mixed it with an old leather sandal."

"But you had a good time talking with your friends?" he persisted. "I saw Sapphira there."

"Oh, that woman was there, all right!" He could hear her scowl more than see it in the dim light. "You will not believe what she told me!" She let out a frustrated grunt. "She and her sniveling husband, Ananias, have become followers of that heretic, Yeshua! I could not believe it! They have even begun attending meetings at the home of one of those mystics who claim to be doing Adonai's work! I have never met more weak-minded people in my life! Those two will follow anything that is the slightest bit out of the ordinary. When I asked why she had forsaken the true faith for this new craze, she could not even give me her own reasons. She simply whined that her husband thought these men had appealing things to say! Can you believe that? Why, if I followed every man with appealing things to say, I would be a whore on the streets!"

Darash was taken aback by the intensity and vulgarity of her speech, but could not deny Ananias and Sapphira were known for their fickleness, often promising something and forgetting to follow through, or agreeing to a meeting and never showing up.

"Who was that woman Sapphira was sitting with?"

"Oh! That poor woman! She is the wife of one of Queen Helena's top aides. Sapphira met her a month ago at the home of a mutual friend and has been following her around ever since. She cannot even step out her front gate without Sapphira haunting her steps, nor can the poor woman purchase a new drape without Sapphira buying one to match."

"Is that why she has not come to visit you lately?"

Revayah made face. "I have barely noticed her absence."

A moment of silence passed.

"Perhaps this new sect will be good for them," Darash said, shifting Tsarah's weight to relieve the growing ache in his right arm.

"How can you say that? This is just another flight of fancy. You mark my words! Nothing good will come of this!"

Chapter Twenty-one

The Painful Truth

Darash stumbled from his bed and down the stairs toward the smell of fresh bread frying in oil.

A bit of roasted fish and a handful of olives would make it a perfect breakfast!

He headed toward his mother and the delicious smells rising before her over the fire pot. He frowned, however, to discover the only accompaniment to the bread would be leftover lentil stew, now thickened with age. Even after Revayah heated it up, it maintained its slimy film, mixed in like strips of softened leather. She dished up some for Darash and his sister. It landed in their bowls like mud. Even Tsarah, not generally one to complain, made a face when she peered into the bowl her mother handed her.

"What?" Revayah asked her. "What is that face for? Do not complain about the food Adonai provides," she chided with righteous fervor. "There are many in this land who would be happy for even a taste of what you have been so generously given"

Tsarah nodded and took a spoon from the built-in ledge that lined the back wall of the main room and served as a kitchen. She then reclined at the table next to her brother, still eying the stew suspiciously. Revayah joined them shortly, bringing the bread basket and a small plate of fruit. She set the basket in front of the children but placed the plate of fruit before herself.

"Are you not going to have some?" Darash asked, motioning to the stew and eying her fruit.

"Oh, no, my son. There is not enough for me," she lied. "A mother must make sacrifices for her children from time to time." She sighed. "I will make do with fruit and bread. It is not as filling, but...."

"Well then," Tsarah piped up, "can we have some fruit, too?"

Darash also brightened at the idea.

"What? You would take the best of the food for yourselves and then take my food as well?" She feigned shock and hurt, looking from one to the other. "How can you be such selfish children? Now, eat your food, and I do not want to hear another word about it."

Darash sighed and lifted his spoon, having to use more effort than usual to dislodge it from the goop. Lips pulled back and using only his teeth, he took a bite. Tsarah watched him for signs of danger. He chewed and swallowed, then glanced at her and shrugged. At least it was hot.

"Imah," Darash asked after Tsarah had finished and gone back upstairs, "what do you remember about the days just before Abba's death?"

"Oh, Darash! Why do you insist on bringing up that ugly matter? One should not speak of the dead. The past is gone!"

"But, Imah, I must know if there was anything that he—"

"Darash. Please. Can you not see that speaking of him pains me?"

Darash sighed.

"Imah," he began again, sweeping the hair from his eyes. "Forgive me, please. I know that, when Abba died, that your world crumbled as well... but I need to know more about what happened that night. I cannot—I will not—let this go until I have found out everything I can! ...I believe Abba was involved in something dangerous just before his death. What was it?"

Revayah stared at him blankly for a moment but said, "I do not know, Darash." For a moment Darash thought she would again try to end the conversation but, after a pause, she added in a quiet voice, "But I think you may be right."

"What do you mean?"

She looked down and twiddled a crust of bread between her fingers. "I am telling the truth when I say I do not know what was going on. He did not tell me. But I know he was worried—agitated—in the days, weeks, prior to his death."

"Agitated about what?"

"I told you, I do not know!" Revayah's temper flared, but then she softened. "He acted preoccupied and short-tempered the day of the altercation with the rebel, Yeshua. Every time I asked him about it, he either ignored me or told me to keep my mind on women's work instead of meddling in the affairs of men."

That did not sound like the man Darash remembered. Tuwr often spent long hours discussing business with Revayah, recounting tales of his interactions and sharing his plans and ideas with her. Though their relationship had sometimes been volatile, it had never been secretive. He would not have admitted this to his male friends and associates, but he often relied on his wife's shrewd intelligence and owed a great deal of his success in business to her.

"That annoyed me, of course," Revayah admitted. "I tried to argue with him, but he became angry and.... well, something about the look in his eyes made me stop." Revayah paused, staring at the small pile of bread crumbs she had made. "That was a mistake. When he came to the worst trouble of his life, I left him alone." For a moment, Darash thought he saw tears welling in his mother's eyes, but then she took in a deep breath, swept the crumbs aside in a sudden flurry of motion and added with conviction, "but he was a man, and sometimes men can be incredibly stubborn—to their own ruin! If he was here now, I would let him know exactly how foolish he had been!"

Darash leaned forward and put a hand on one of hers, stilling her. She looked at him.

"Imah… did Abba say anything to you—anything at all to give you an idea of the type of trouble he was in?"

She thought for a moment before answering.

"As I said, he never discussed it with me, but on the night he died, just before leaving the house, perhaps to see Nathan as you suggested, he said in a very determined manner, 'Revayah, my love, there is something I need to find out for myself. I may be back late.' And then he gathered his cloak and a scroll, I believe—I do not know what was on it—and he headed to the door. But then, just before he left, he said, as if to himself, 'A man can only take so much.' And, I think he said something like, 'The truth must be known.' And then he was gone. The next time I saw him, Roman soldiers were carrying him through my door." Revayah removed her hand, stood, and turned away from her son. A hand went to her face. "I promise, Darash. That is all I know about why your father was taken from us. That is all I will ever know."

סֶ לָ ה

"Nib'haz," Darash interrupted the old man's muttering as he fussed over a decorative edge on one of his baskets. It was later in the morning of that same day, yom shli'shi, the third day of the week.

"Uh?"

"Is it possible to live with someone your whole life but never really know them?"

Nib'haz sighed thoughtfully. His fingers stopped moving, and his chin tilted up. "That is a very difficult question, young one….."

Darash waited.

"I do not think your question has an answer," he said at length.

Darash's shoulders slumped. He looked away.

"At least," Nib'haz said, "not a single answer." He paused again. "Some people are quite skilled at hiding parts of themselves from the world. But no one can hide everything. And, Elohim sees all… even the parts we try to hide." He paused again. "Are you thinking of your father?"

"Yes." Darash hung his head. "But not only him. I think also of Aphiemi's killer. And my friend. And my mother."

"Oooo! My young friend! So many?"

"My father hid who he was from me, Nib'haz. How do I know who is genuine and who is false?"

"Darash, did your father love you?"

"What?"

"It is a simple question. Did your father love you?"

Darash inwardly rebelled against the question, but finally mumbled, "Yes."

"Then you knew the most important part of him. As you know, I have been blind for most of my life. Elohim, in His great wisdom, has allowed much of the world to remain hidden from me. But that does not mean I do not know the world." He paused. "Yes, your father had secrets—secrets that were harmful. But those particular secrets did not keep him from loving you or desiring your best. And they did not keep you from knowing him in a very important way—as a son knows a father."

"But should not a son know if his father is a thief and a cheater?" Darash asked, throat tight. "And what of Aphiemi? She trusted the very person who later killed her."

Nib'haz nodded, his shaggy head bobbing up and down with greater intensity than a sighted person might move.

"Mmmm…. What are we most likely to hide, Darash? The evil in us or the good?"

"The evil, of course."

"Yes… and do we all share the same temptations? The same vices?"

"No. The rabbis teach that some of us struggle with the love of money, while others might struggle with the love of wine."

"The rabbis are correct in this. Your father had one vice that he hid from you, while Aphiemi's killer had a different vice that he also kept hidden—his self-love. I believe your father hid his greed to protect you, to keep you from following the wicked path he had chosen. But the killer hid his self-love to protect himself."

Darash thought on this for a moment and then said, "I have a good friend who was recently betrothed."

Nib'haz nodded, waiting for more.

"I have known him since I was quite young—when I first went to the House of the Book."

Darash stopped talking, and finally Nib'haz said, "And you wonder if your friend might be the killer you search for?"

"No! I… I could never think such a thing!"

"So why did you bring him up?"

Darash remained silent, unsure himself.

"If he attended the School of the Book," Nib'haz continued, "he is a Jew and would honor Shabbat…. He was recently betrothed—a good reason not to involve himself with any other young woman. Did he know Barus or Barus's family?"

"I do not know. I have never seen them together."

"Do you know him to be the type to use young women?"

"No, never! He is very much in love with Hadassah—the woman he is marrying."

"Then, I wonder what made you think of him?"

Darash sighed. "I do not know, really… It is just that… I have been thinking of how we thought the killer favored his left hand…. At a celebration I attended recently, my friend did something that reminded me of our school days together. He handed me something."

"What was it?"

"That is not important. What is important is how he did it…. You see, he was the rabbi's favorite student out of all of us. He studied the hardest, learned his lessons the fastest, and never got into mischief. …But one thing made the rabbi scold him. He always tried to write and work sums with his left."

סֶ לָ ה

"I decided not to create the mosaic for Gabahh, after all," Ibnei'ah explained at the shuk later that afternoon. He had come by to apologize to Darash for not being able to purchase quite as much bitumen as originally requested. He stood before Darash and Nib'haz with his back to Valad. "I simply could not stand the thought of working for a man of his character, especially after the trouble he and his wife caused not only your friend, but my daughter as well. Besides, I doubt he could afford to pay me now. But do not worry. I will find another work opportunity soon and will be back for the bitumen. But I do apologize for the delay."

"Give it no thought," Darash said, waving it aside. "I think you made the correct decision. Besides, I did not like the thought of that man—who ought to be in prison—enjoying one of your beautiful works of art."

And Eltolad has yet to deliver more bitumen anyway….

Ibnei'ah smiled.

"How is your daughter Ra'ah doing?" Darash asked.

"She was upset at first," Ibnei'ah admitted, "but I think she will be fine. Yesterday, a neighbor invited her to play at their house. Twin girls live there with their widowed mother and their grandparents," he explained in something of a hurry, but slowed down to say, "I was surprised when Ra'ah actually wanted to go. She has been so shy since her mother's passing, you see. Perhaps this incident has helped her accept her mother's death."

"Is there any more news about the healing at the gate?" Nib'haz asked.

"I have heard little more," Ibnei'ah said. "I know only that Peter and John continue to preach Yeshua as King of the Jews and risen Savior, despite orders to the contrary."

"And what of the cripple?"

"He is gone. He has not been back to his place at the gate since that day. I heard he found Peter and John the day after they were released and followed them. The Followers of the Way are taking care of him."

"Why would they do that?" Valad wanted to know. "The man can walk now. Surely, he can find work!"

"I think he was very poor," Ibnei'ah answered.

"I heard these people share their possessions with one another," Valad said. "One man even sold his best milk cow and gave the money to these men! Can you believe that? Why would he do it? Why should those men get so much of his money?"

"They do not keep the money," Ibnei'ah answered. "They use it to help the poor among them. They all share equally with one another, having all things in common. ...If everyone could do that, this world would be a much better place."

"But not everyone can do that," Valad insisted. "That would require selflessness from everyone, and we all know that will never happen."

"I am afraid I must agree with you there," Ibnei'ah admitted, "but somehow these people are doing it. ...Nib'haz, I need a new basket. Ra'ah wants to use one as a bed for her new doll." He shot a smile at Darash.

"Fifteen prutot for the little one. A sestertius for the middle size and two sestertii for these," he tapped a stack of larger ones to his left.

Darash smiled back at Ibnei'ah, but then turned his attention away. The talk of Peter and John brought to mind the conversation he had with his mother that morning. Imah said Abba had taken a scroll with him the night he was killed. But, though Darash had been asleep when Abba had left the house for the last time, he remembered that night and the following day well. According to Magistrate Quintus Arrius, the magistrate and his men searched the entire area where Abba's body had been discovered, including the body itself. They found his money belt untouched, but they found no scroll with him nor anywhere nearby.

Darash leaned back against the cold stone wall and felt the acrid sting of frustration rising in his throat.

If only I knew what was on that scroll!

Darash closed his eyes and blocked out the noise of the shuk to search his memory. His father often had scrolls lying about—scrolls of business, mostly. A few bore portions of Scripture on them, though they were rarely read. The others contained business contracts, lists of goods, and sales records. Darash had gone through all of these shortly after his father's death in order to prepare himself for taking over the business. He had found nothing out of the ordinary, just the usual items a merchant would have. And Darash had no idea what might be missing.

Perhaps, I should go over them once more. Maybe something will stand out—a name, a date, a number….

"Sleeping on the job?"

The close, teasing voice disrupted his mental reprieve. Darash opened his eyes and his heart sank. It was Hathal.

"How do you expect to compete in business if you sleep when you should be working?"

"I was not sleeping, I was just—"

"Resting your eyes?" Hathal sneered and laughed. "Yes, I have heard that one before. But I have also found that when a merchant rests his eyes, his goods disappear."

Several chuckles arose from those standing about. Nib'haz sat still and tense, listening.

"Ah!" Hathal said, glancing over his shoulder. "Here comes our good friend, Nakal."

Can this get any worse?

"Who have we here?" Nakal asked, approaching with a self-secure saunter, smiling like a snake that just spotted a crippled mouse. "Ah! I see you have found our small friend!"

"Yes! I found him sleeping, in fact."

"Sleeping?" Nakal laughed. "Well, now, that is telling, is it not?"

"I thought so." Hathal leveled his smiling, unkind eyes on Darash.

Darash let his hair hang in his eyes but glared through the black strands.

"I hope you enjoy your rest, boy," Hathal said, and then placed his hands on his knees and leaned forward, speaking to Darash as though to a small child. "You are going to need it. Because you will have to work long and hard for the rest of your life in this little corner just to keep your family fed. So you just go ahead and sleep. You will wake when the food runs out."

Unbeknownst to them, the food had run out. Darash needed to make a sale in order to bring something home for dinner. Otherwise, he would be at the home of Barus right now.

"I do not think he understands you, Hathal," Nakal said. "He is still too groggy."

"Or too young," Hathal replied, returning to an upright position but not taking his eyes from Darash.

"Or too foolish."

"His mother, though, is a smart one. She will find a way to provide for them if he does not," Hathal laughed and Nakal joined him as if in a private joke.

"Yes. She is very intelligent... and beautiful as well." Nakal said. "Surely there is something she could do."

"I know I could think of something," Hathal added, and his friend rewarded him with raucous laughter.

Darash jumped to his feet, jaw and fists clenched.

"Oh, the sleeping child wakes!" Hathal said, almost impressed.

But before Darash could do anything, Valad interceded. "Hathal, I hear you are in the market for some cheese," he said, holding aloft a large block of white cheese.

"No," Hathal answered, barely glancing back.

"Oh, then perhaps it was leben?" Valad persisted.

"No!"

"Milk?"

"No!" Hathal barked, still trying to ignore the obnoxious cheese seller behind him. "I am not in the market for any of those things!"

"Oh! I remember what it was," Valad said, slapping his leg and replacing the cheese on its cloth. "It was sour milk. A little something to match your personality."

Hathal swung around to find Valad rising to his feet behind him. Though Valad was thin, he was quite tall and known for his unpredictable, even reckless, behavior.

"Who do you think you are to speak to me in that manner?" Hathal replied, but took a step back. "You are a nobody and will always be a nobody, squandering your days away in this little cesspool, trying to peddle your moldy cheese! You will never make more than a few prutot your entire life!"

"Ah, yes, it is very sad," Valad said, oozing sarcasm. "I suppose I will have to be content with friends who respect me and do not speak badly of me when my back is turned, unlike you." He shot Nakal a knowing glance.

Hathal swung to stare an accusing question at his friend.

Nakal backed up a pace and stammered, "Wh-what? I do not know what you-what you are speaking of! I-I never—"

Hathal glowered at his friend, but then turned back to Darash, having lost his former pretense at good humor. "Listen, Boy! We came so you could deliver a message to your mother. Her debt is due. And, next time she is late, we will charge interest—to be paid in person!"

Chapter Twenty-two

Midnight Over Jerusalem

Darash could not remember a darker or colder night. The shadows had secured their grasp on the city long before Darash earned his family's supper. After a sparse meal, he headed back through the shuk and toward the home of Barus, amulet in hand. Despite the lateness of the hour, he knew he at least had to try to speak to him before any more time went by.

If the house looks dormant, I will find Barus later and tell him I tried.

When Darash arrived at Barus's home, a bright light spilled from the windows, and he detected movement by the upstairs windows. Darash approached the outer door and knocked. Their servant girl opened the door and ushered him inside the main house.

"Ah! Greetings, young one!" Barus's wife greeted him with a nod and a smile, despite the surprise on her face at seeing him there so late. "My husband has been expecting you to come by any day now, but...."

She turned to glance behind her into the room where he had shared a meal with them. Barus was there, dressed quite formally for it being so late. Then Darash saw the reason. He had company—a man who wore a long tunic with a sash draped about the back of his neck. He stood with his back to Darash. When Barus looked up to see who was at the door, the young man turned as well.

I have seen this man before. He is the soon-to-be son-in-law of Barus's business associate, Jacob. What is his name again?

"Darash!" Barus greeted him warmly as his wife left the room. "Come in! I have been expecting your visit. I am glad you are here."

Darash joined them in room which had been lit with many oil lamps. As Darash approached Barus's visitor, he remembered his name even before Barus said it. Darash also remembered how rude the man had been.

"You remember Ratash, do you not? I introduced you in the Lower Market about a week ago."

"I remember," Darash said and smiled as politely as he could.

"Forgive me," Ratash responded with a look of vague interest, "what was your name again?"

"Darash."

"Oh, yes! You are the boy who promised to find justice for my host's daughter, are you not?"

The way Ratash looked at him made Darash want to shrivel up and disappear.

"And what have you discovered so far?" Ratash prompted.

"I have come to discuss that with Barus," Darash replied.

"You come bearing news?" His brow rose with incredulity, but then he smiled. "Tell me what it is. Perhaps I can help."

"You have discovered something, Darash?" Barus asked, voice full of hope.

"I, uh...." Darash swallowed. He gripped the amulet tighter in his palm. "I have been speaking to people who knew Aphiemi and to the watchtower guard."

"I thought the guard claimed to have seen and heard nothing?" Ratash asked. "Has he now changed his story?"

"No."

"And were there no other witnesses?"

"None."

"And these people who knew Aphiemi, were they able to tell you who she was meeting that night?"

Darash sighed. "Uh... no."

Ratash smirked and shook his head in annoyance. "Barus, please. Do you think this boy is truly capable of helping? I am sure he is trying, but is it fair to you, to your wife, to the memory of your daughter, to keep the tragedy alive in this way?"

"Ratash," Barus said, hands spread before him in a gesture of diplomacy. "I know you would prefer that I drop this matter entirely. Your future father-in-law, and now you, have been good friends to our family through this tough time, and I know you do not want to see us in pain any longer. Still, I must find out what I can. Perhaps, as you say, there is nothing to find. Still, I must try. You would not deny a grieving father that much, would you?"

"Of course not, Barus! I want you to find the killer more than anyone. But is that not the magistrate's job? Surely, it would be better to allow him—a grown man with experience—to look into this matter for you instead of this child."

Barus gave a nod, but placed a hand on Darash's shoulder before responding.

"Ratash, thank you for coming to my home to clarify the business arrangement I made with Jacob, though I think it was hardly necessary to trouble yourself. I am sure he and I can discuss it when I see him in a few days."

Ratash bowed stiffly and turned. As he moved toward the door, his left shoulder slammed into Darash, knocking the amulet from his hand.

Darash quickly bent down to retrieve it. As he raised back up, his eyes met Ratash's. He saw something there—a look of... what? Recognition? Hatred? ...No. Fear.

Darash stepped back and watched Ratash leave. Darash's mind flew back over all he knew of the man.

He is an old friend of Barus's family. He would have known Aphiemi. He is very religious. She would have trusted him... perhaps even loved him. He was recently betrothed to Jacob's daughter—a politically and religiously powerful alliance. And...

Darash thought back to the first time he had met Jacob and Ratash. Jacob handed Ratash something—a book. It had been an awkward exchange. But why? Jacob had handed it to Ratash's right side, and then....

Ratash took it with his left hand!

As soon as the door closed after Ratash, Darash held the amulet out to Barus.

"Do you recognize it?" he asked.

Barus took the amulet, glanced at it briefly, and said, "Yes. I believe this belongs to Ratash. I have seen him wear it from time to time. He must have dropped it just now."

"No, Barus," Darash said. "He did not drop it. ...I did."

"I do not understand. How did you get Ratash's amulet?"

"Do you remember that the magistrate said he found a gold chain next to where your daughter was killed?"

Barus nodded.

"I went there, too. I found this amulet."

"What do you mean? You found this amulet where Aphiemi died?"

"Yes."

"I-I do not understand." Barus's breaths began to come faster.

Darash waited.

"You mean Ratash was there? He was there when Aphiemi was killed?"

Darash nodded.

"Wait.... No...." Barus ran a hand through his thick, black hair. His eyes had widened, but he closed them and hung his head as he tried to order his thoughts. "Darash... are you saying Ratash... that he... killed my daughter?" He looked Darash in the eyes. His voice tightened with grief and anger. "But why? What possible reason could he have for doing such a thing? And why would Aphiemi be out there with him? She would not go to him without good reason!"

"She did have a reason, Barus," Darash said, keeping his voice low and steady. "She was with child."

A cry startled them. Barus's wife stood in the doorway, eyes wide, a hand clamped tight over her mouth and the other clenching the cloth of her robe over her heart. She began to weep. At the sound, Barus moved toward her and put an arm around her shoulders. She leaned into him, racked with emotion.

Darash stepped back to give their grief space. Tears stung his eyes and moistened his cheeks.

"I will kill him," Barus said in a voice unlike the one Darash knew. "I will kill him for what he has done!" Barus released his wife, who crumpled to the low couch in tears. He grabbed his cloak from a peg in the wall, threw it on, and headed toward the door.

Darash stepped in front of him.

"Barus, wait! He knows! Ratash knows we have found him out! He could be waiting for you!"

Barus pushed past.

"We must go to the magistrate first!" Darash hurried to keep up.

Barus paused as he reached the front door. His breath came in angry gasps, but he steadied his gaze on Darash's insistent face. He nodded. "Very well, we will bring him along, but if he does not make this man pay for what he has done, I will!"

Together they left the house and headed into the night. They started toward the house of the magistrate, but again Darash stopped short.

"Wait!" he said.

"What is it now?"

"The magistrate will never believe me. Not without proof."

"You must make him listen. And do not let that churlish slave of his give you any trouble! Knock him over if you have to."

"I cannot. Quintus will have me in chains if I show my face there again. ...But I have an idea. I will go to the home of Servius Aurelius, the man who manned the watchtower that night."

"But you said he saw nothing. How can he help?"

"Because he did see something! I know he did! You go on to the house of the magistrate, and bring him to meet me at Servius's home. You know the place?" Barus nodded. "Tell the magistrate... tell him Servius has new information about the murder."

Barus gave Darash a look of uncertainty.

"Trust me, he will. That should be enough to get the magistrate's attention. Bring him to Servius's home, and then the four of us will go find Ratash together."

סֶ לֶ ה

It has to be close to midnight.

The last comforting voice of a stranger's goodnight to a neighbor disappeared behind the isolating slam of a door. The sound of footsteps echoed and faded to stillness in the distance. Animals ruminated silently in the dark behind closed stall doors.

Darash neared the final street with rapid steps, but when he saw the path ahead, he came to an abrupt stop. A narrow alley lay before him, carved out by tall buildings on either side. He peered into the thickening darkness before him. His chest tightened, and his heart began to pound.

Why are the torches not lit?

The torches set at each street corner had been snuffed out. Whether by the wind or by the act of man, Darash did not know.

Abba, is this how you felt that night? Is this what you saw?

Darash searched the few windows lining the desolate road for any sign of life. Not one glimmered with light or echoed with the comforting sounds of people within. He was wholly alone.

Darash swallowed hard, willing his heart and lungs to be calm.

It is just another street, no different from those I travel every day.

He took three paces forward.

I am too old to be afraid of the dark.

Despite his self-reassurances, Darash knew his fear was deeper than that. He had felt strange the whole way here, as if he was being watched, followed.

What if Ratash waited and watched us leave the house? Did he hear us discussing our plans? Has he dogged my steps all the way here?

Darash had seen no one and heard nothing unusual, but he could not be sure. He only knew he had to make it to the home of Servius. And a nightmare lay in his path.

Darash took slow, deliberate steps forward into the alley. He felt the loneliness of this place—this world of forms and shadows. Somehow, his father felt closer now than he had since that terrible night.

Abba? Where are you now? Can you see me?

In his mind, he could see the body of his slain father lying cold and still in the gathering dark.

I could turn around. Take a different road.

Fear battled against his urgency to reach Servius's home.

If I am being followed, it is already too late to go back. I must go forward.

A squeak to his right startled him so intensely that he jumped three paces from the sound. He could only make out the barest images, but it sounded like two rats fighting at the side of the alley over a discarded morsel, dragged from a rubbish heap. Darash gasped and sucked in air, now trembling in fear. After a few deep breaths, he forced his feet forward across the stone.

Servius's home lay just beyond this alley. I will soon be there. Barus and the magistrate are surely on their way by now.

Darash quickened his pace. Halfway down the passageway, he broke into a run. Once his mind settled on flight, near panic consumed him. Panting hard, his feet pounding into the ground, he imagined his enemy mere paces behind, ready to strike at any moment. He had never run so desperately in his life.

Just as Darash neared the next road, a dark figure stepped into his path.

Darash skidded and changed directions as swiftly as he could, but he was already within a few arm lengths of the man before him. Shadows obscured the stranger's face.

Darash began to back up, unable to look away from the one who had trapped him. The darkened figure followed with deliberate steps. As he came, he drew something from his belt with his left hand. For a moment, the object caught the light of a distant street torch, revealing the blade of a knife.

Can this be happening?

Darash's mind filled with the image of his father, backing away in terror from an enemy in a dark alley, just as Darash backed away now.

Will I die as you did, Abba?

Somehow such an end seemed fitting. Meant to be.

…But something inside him rebelled.

I am not ready, Abba. I am not ready.

Run, my son!

Darash somehow got his legs to move. He turned and raced back the way he had come. Quick, heavy steps followed. Something caught. He felt himself being yanked backward by his cloak. He lost his footing and fell onto his back. His attacker landed on top of him.

The weight of the bigger man crushed Darash's thin frame painfully into the stone beneath. A fist and elbow held him as the man's left hand brought the knife down swiftly. Darash, scrambling to protect himself, managed to block with his right forearm, the blade nearly tearing into his face. As the attacker raised his hand to strike again, Darash grabbed his wrist—this time using both hands—and fought to keep the knife from plunging into his chest. All the while, he kicked and twisted, scrambling to free his lower body. The man could not be shaken off. Despite Darash's grip on his attacker's wrist, the man pushed forward, forcing the blade down.

"No!" Darash cried through clenched teeth. "Please!"

Darash wriggled to his left and, using both his left arm and legs, forced the man's knife and body the other way. A sharp cry erupted in the dark. Feeling his enemy lose control and shift to one side, he wasted no time and tried to scramble away. As he felt himself freed from his enemy's control, he pushed himself up to his knees.

A heavy blow knocked the wind from his lungs and sent pain searing across his ribcage. He fell and rolled over, coughing and gasping, to see the darkened figure standing over him. Darash received another kick in the side and cried out. He rolled away. Only one thought repeated in his mind.

Run! Run! Run!

He struggled to his feet, but found no escape. His enemy stood before him. Sparks flew as a fist landed squarely on Darash's jaw. And then another and another. The man no longer hurried. Instead, he enjoyed expending his wrath on Darash's face and body, relishing the agony he caused.

Darash saw nothing as pain blinded him. He moaned and staggered back, his knees weak. He was given no time to recover. He faltered and began to fall. A hand grabbed the front of his cloak and pinned his body against the cold stone wall of the alley. He struggled, trying to push his enemy away and protect himself from the knife. Again, blinding light shot through his consciousness as his head crashed against the stone wall from behind. Overwhelmed and lost in a sea of pain, he let out a long breath.

Abba, I am coming.

The darkness had grown so thick Darash could see nothing. But he could feel the cold iron of a blade pierce his chest. The knife plunged deep. Too deep.

"You there! Stop! Darash! Are you there?"

A man's alarmed voice echoed down the alley. Darash felt the blade being pulled from his body, ripping flesh as it went. His attacker's grip disappeared. Retreating footsteps reverberated against stone as he crumpled to the ground. The alley rolled on waves of pain and confusion. His head seemed about three times its normal size, and his lower lip felt strange as he fought to breathe. Lungs and ribs burned with each ragged intake of air. He moved a hand to his chest to find a warm, slippery liquid trickling down toward his belly and soaking into his tunic.

I have stained my tunic again. Imah will be angry.

A loud, rhythmic throbbing filled the silence, seeming to come from within his skull. Then, voices filtered into the spaces between the beats.

"Who goes there?"

"Stop!"

"Darash! Are you okay?"

"Steady! Steady!"

The alley, dark and deserted only moments before, now swam with light, voices, and the figures of men. Darash heard the metal scrape of swords being removed from sheaths, angry voices, and the echoing report of hobnailed shoes and sandaled feet against stone. The light moved randomly about the alley at first, but then one came and shone into his eyes, making it again impossible to see.

"Darash! Are you okay? Darash!"

Darash recognized the agonized voice of Barus even before seeing him.

"Please answer me! Darash! No, no! May Elohim save him! Someone! The boy is injured! He is dying! I need help! Quickly!"

The light moved again. More shuffling. Darash felt his tunic being ripped open. The hand of a Roman soldier landed on the wound in his chest, and he found a strength he did not know he had as a cry of agony ripped from his lungs.

He felt wasted, spent, emptied out. Darkness beckoned.

Abba....

The world shifted again. He was being lifted, carried. The light bounced off walls and faces, and then the blackened heavens appeared before him. As Darash stared up into the starless, midnight sky, the lights and sounds began to ebb away, lost in the void above Jerusalem. A warm, delicious drowsiness descended on him. The pain slipped away. He let out a sigh and let the darkness consume him.

Chapter Twenty-three

Morning Breaks

Pain thudded back into existence. It came through the darkness, in the shallow whisperings of thought, with the air that filtered in and out.

Reality dawned for a moment and then disappeared again. But the pain kept bringing it back, seeking him out through the darkness and fog.

Darash became conscious that he was yet in a body. This body did not respond like his old one. He could see nothing. He felt only pain and weight.

A sound nearby attracted his attention. A moan or sigh.

"Darash? Darash!"

A different sound. Familiar, but....

"Imah! Imah, Darash is awake!"

Commotion. Sounds. Too loud.

"Awake, at last? I am coming! Darash! Darash, my son! Imah is here."

Imah. Forgive me, Imah. I have stained my tunic again....

He felt something. Motion. His arm moved. Someone's hands clasped one of his. Soft hands. Stroking. It felt good.

"I love you, my son. Please do not leave me."

Another sound... like weeping.

Before Darash could distinguish voice from thought, darkness again closed the door on pain.

כָּ לֶ ה

Darash. Darash, my son. Please wake.

Abba? Is that you?

"Darash, please. Open your eyes. Wake, my son."

The pain came back in an instant. He drew in a single, agonizing breath and felt it release with force through thick lips, sending darts of pain throughout his body. He did not want to repeat the experience. But this foreign, clumsy body he now inhabited forced another breath.

A whimper.

"Do not move, my son. Just lie still."

I will never move. Not ever again.

Shuffling noises. The motion of a blanket somewhere nearby.

"Is he going to be okay?" This voice was different and further away. A girl's voice. A child.

Tsarah?

"Shall I go to the magistrate now?"

What magistrate?

"Yes. Go."

More commotion. Then silence. The emptiness beckoned again. He moved toward it.

"Open your eyes, Darash. Please, open your eyes."

Imah, why do you sound so frightened?

"Awake, my son. Look at me, please."

Darash tried to focus. With what little energy he had, he focused his efforts on the place he thought his eyes were. He felt a tug, resistance, a flutter. A sliver of light pierced the darkness.

"Yes, my son. Open your eyes."

"Imah?"

A gasp mingled with a sob. "Darash! Darash, I am here!"

She found his hand and squeezed.

Darash discovered he could move his free arm. It felt heavy, unnatural, foreign. Pain accompanied the effort, but he moved his hand to his face, trying to figure out why his eyes refused to open all the way. His fingertips detected more flesh than he expected.

"It is alright, my son," Revayah said. "Your face is bruised and swollen, but it will heal. Are you hungry? Would you like something to eat?"

Darash could not imagine eating. It seemed a strange and disturbing concept.

No.

He groaned.

I must breathe. Sleep.

Darash did not know how much time passed this way. He would awaken, try to focus on the activity around him, but then the pain would consume him again to be replaced with a retreat into unconsciousness. Sometimes he awakened to voices, the sound of weeping, or the sensation of motion—a wet rag across his forehead and eyes, a shifting blanket—but always the comfort of a deep, dark sleep was close at hand.

Before long he realized he was not in his own bed in their upper room, but in his mother's, which was located on the first floor. From time to time, a man came to care for him—a stranger skilled in caring for the sick and injured, but who caused pain when he fidgeted with the bandages on Darash's chest. And there were other voices, some familiar, some he could not place. But Imah was always there. Always.

One morning, Darash found he could open his eyes almost all the way.

"Darash?"

"Shalom, Imah."

She sat at his bedside, leaning close. She smiled and did not bother to wipe the tears from her eyes.

"Imah," Darash whispered.

"Yes, my son?"

"Can I have something to eat?"

סֶ לְ ה

A few days passed. Another Shabbat came and went. Darash continued to occupy his mother's bed while she slept on a pallet on the floor next to him. The magistrate's personal surgeon, a jovial, curly-haired, Greek slave, visited every day—even on Shabbat—to check Darash's wounds and keep infection at bay with honey-based poultices and clean, linen bandages.

"You have done a wonderful job keeping this wound clean," he told Revayah one afternoon, as he replaced the bandage on Darash's chest. "If you continue as you have, your son will be up and helping you with the chores in another few days."

"Oh, no! He must stay in bed until he is completely healed!"

The man chuckled. "You would make an excellent physician," he told her with a smile and wrapped his medical supplies in a piece of leather, which he tied with a cord. "It is truly a miracle this boy is alive. If the blade had gone in even a finger's width to the right.... Well, perhaps, as you say, your El was looking out for him." He walked out of the room with Revayah following. "I will be back in a few days to see how he is faring."

"Are you sure we cannot pay you for your services?" Darash heard her voice from the other room. "We have little money, but I could find something of value to—"

"Oh, no! The magistrate would have my head if I accepted anything from you. Oh, and that reminds me; he said he wanted to stop by for a visit when the boy was well enough for company. I think that time has come."

"Are you certain?"

"Yes, as long as the guests do not stay long."

"Very well. You may tell the magistrate he can come tomorrow evening."

Darash heard the sound of their heavy, wooden door close and the voices cease. Imah must have shown the physician out the front gate as well.

Darash lay on his blankets, staring at the mud-caked ceiling of his mother's bed chamber. For the first time, he felt restless, but the pain of moving—even to prop himself up or turn on his side so Imah could wash him—was a powerful deterrent. His mind returned to that terrible night... to the nightmare.

Fear rose to mingle with the pain in his chest.

Who attacked me? Was it Ratash? Or someone else? Was the man caught? Or will he be coming back to finish what he started?

He tenderly felt the area just below his heart where the knife had gone in. The wound, now buried in thick bandages, was a foreign, unwelcome intruder he could not readily rid himself of. He remembered being beaten and feeling helpless in the hands of his unsurmountable foe. He remembered the feel of the blade entering his body and his inability to stop it. Hot tears rose in his eyes.

Life is not supposed to be this way.

What happened after the stabbing now surfaced as only a shadowy memory. He did not know if he had actually seen the images and faces he remembered. Barus? Had Barus been there? Yes. He was sure of that. But who was the man who had pressed a fist against his wound to stop the bleeding? And who had carried him home?

As the questions rose in his mind, so did his anticipation for the magistrate's visit. Perhaps then he would get some answers.

סֶ לָ ה

"You have visitors," Revayah announced, standing at the top of the stairs and peeking her head in the door of the upper room only long enough for Darash to hear the excitement in her voice. The day before, Darash had insisted he was well enough to make it up the stairs and sleep in his own bed. After much coaxing, she had finally relented. But he still spent much of each day resting quietly or sleeping.

Is that pride in her eyes?

He did not feel he deserved it.

Imah disappeared, and Barus entered, topping the stairs and followed closely by the magistrate, Quintus Arrius. Darash was surprised to see Servius Aurelius come in as well, dressed in full centurion regalia. He carried his red-fringed helmet beneath his arm. He would not have been able to stand up straight in the room otherwise.

Darash suddenly felt self-conscious, lying on his back wearing only a thin tunic in the presence of these important and powerful men. He tried to shift to a sitting position, but the motion sent pain rolling through him like waves in an angry sea.

"For the love of all things holy, do not move!" Barus ordered in Greek, worry in his voice. "Just lie still. You have been through enough already!"

The three gathered around and sat on Tsarah's bed and on the floor near his bed. He felt foolish to have such honored guests sitting in his bare, humble quarters, particularly when Servius had to angle his sword behind him in order to manage it.

"I see my surgeon has treated you well," the magistrate said, also using the common language. "That is good."

"Yes. Thank you for sending him," Darash managed, his chest and lungs aching as he spoke. "But… why did you do it?"

"I could not have the boy who caught a murderer die for lack of care! How would that have made me look?" He chuckled at his own arrogance.

Darash relaxed a bit and smiled. "What happened? All I remember is that a man attacked me in the alley near Servius's house." He glanced at the centurion. "We fought, he stabbed me, and then… then… the rest is a jumble of images and shadows."

"Quintus and I were on our way to the home of Servius when we heard your cries," Barus explained. "We saw two figures struggling in the alley and cried out. When Ratash saw us coming, he ran away—but not before running his knife through your chest."

"So how do you know it was he? I never got a good look at his face."

"We did not at first, either," Quintus said. "My men and I left Barus to tend to you and gave chase. We never would have caught him if it had not been for Servius." He turned to the centurion.

"I heard your cries as well," he said. "My chamber window faces that alley, so I rose from my bed to see what was going on. I arrived at the end of the alley just in time to see a man fleeing. I ran him down and caught him. The magistrate and his men soon joined me and, by their torchlight, I recognized him immediately. And then… seeing him… I remembered everything. …Darash, it was him that night—the night Barus's daughter was killed."

"We further confirmed it," added Quintus, "when we saw the ugly scar around the back of his neck where the chain and amulet had been wrenched off."

Ah…. I only ever saw Ratash with a sash draped about the back of his neck. Now I know why.

"I spoke to Jacob," Barus said. "He is very upset, as is his daughter, as you can imagine. He said they finalized the betrothal between Ratash and his daughter just before Aphiemi was killed—that very afternoon, actually. When they heard of her death, Jacob decided to wait to tell people about the betrothal, not wanting to celebrate in the face of my tragedy. But I wish he had said something. Perhaps it would have helped us discover the truth before Ratash had a chance to hurt yet another." He looked at Darash.

"No good can come of wondering what might have been, Barus," Quintus said. "Take comfort knowing your daughter's killer has been brought to justice, Darash is recuperating, and the man can harm no one else."

Barus nodded.

Darash, remembering something, glanced around the room. "Forgive me. I do not know what happened to the amulet."

"You gave it to me, remember?" Barus said. "I handed it over to Quintus."

"Ratash will not need it anymore." Quintus pulled it from his money belt to show them, but then replaced it and smiled satisfactorily. Once the trial was over, it would fetch a good price.

"So Ratash is in prison?"

"Indeed, he is. We made sure to give him our best cell—mold, rats, everything. The Sanhedrin has set his trial for next week. He will be tried for Aphiemi's murder and for attempting to kill you. "

"What will they do to him if they find him guilty?" Darash asked.

"He will certainly be found guilty," Servius interjected. "We caught him just after the attack, and he has a cut on his hand from his own knife—no doubt acquired in your struggle."

So that is what happened when he cried out in pain.

"He will likely be beheaded with a sword," Quintus answered. "He has too many powerful friends among the Jewish ruling council to be crucified, I would think."

Darash sobered, but the men chatted a few minutes more before Revayah came up the stairs. "I thank you for coming," she said with a gracious smile. "Now my son needs his rest."

Magistrate Quintus Arrius stood up. "I am glad you are healing," he said, "but from now on, try to stay out of trouble. I hope you learned your lesson and will leave the catching of criminals to me."

Darash smiled weakly.

I intend to… except for one.

Barus and Servius also rose to their feet.

"Here," Barus said, pulling a bag from his belt. "This is the reward I promised to whoever solved my daughter's murder. You have earned it." He placed it on the bed next to Darash.

With a nod, Barus followed the magistrate back down the stairs. Servius lingered behind.

"There is something I must ask you," Servius said as the voices of the men began to fade away. "Why were you coming to my home that night?"

"I believed—I hoped—you might remember what you saw the night Aphiemi was killed. It was something your grandmother said, actually, that made me think you might eventually remember."

"What was that?"

"She mentioned she once had a daughter who was killed by an intruder." Darash paused, watching the soldier's face. It grew hard and a bit pale, but Darash pressed on. "Later, while talking with a friend, I realized that woman had been either your aunt or your mother... and you would have been rather young at the time. I thought maybe... perhaps...." Darash paused, not sure how to explain what seemed strange even to him. Servius finished for him.

"You thought I might have seen it happen."

Darash nodded.

"I did." Servius swallowed hard and glanced away. "When I saw Ratash last night, I remembered everything—not only Aphiemi's murder, but other things as well—things that happened long ago. Things I had forgotten. First, I remembered seeing a man going into that alley beneath my tower. I recognized him as Ratash, a young Sadducee I have often seen outside the Temple. Aphiemi was also there, though I had never seen her before. She came alone, and then he joined her. They talked in the shadow of the wall. I could not hear what they said, but I saw Ratash raise his hand over his head. He was holding something. And then he hit her in the side of the head with it." He paused. "She dropped to the ground. He ran from the alley.

"I now remember the death of my mother, also. I was very young when it happened, only five or six years old." He paused. "It was not an intruder, as my grandmother believes."

Servius, who had been staring at the wall as he spoke, now looked squarely into Darash's eyes. "It was my father. He served Rome as a soldier in the army as I do; only he never advanced beyond mere foot soldier. He was a particularly brutal man, especially toward my mother." He glanced away again, looking deep into his newly-recovered memory. "That night my sister and I (she was a mere babe) were in bed with her, sleeping soundly when we were awakened by my father's shouts. He had come home late, and the food she had left out for him was cold. He became enraged! He dragged her from the bed and into the other room. I followed. I saw him hit her again and again. Then he hit her one last time. She fell to the ground and did not move.

"The next day, he told everyone an intruder had broken in during the night while he was gone. He told us the intruder had killed our mother. Everyone felt sorry for him and for us as well. My grandmother came to live with us and took good care of me and my sister. After that, my father was almost never home.

"In time, I believed what everyone said about how my mother had died. I simply lost the memory of what I saw. Perhaps the lie was easier to accept. And then I no longer thought of it at all. I have lived most of my life without that memory. ...But now it is back. I remember everything."

"Where is your father now?"

"He died eight years ago. He was part of a skirmish with some rebels and was killed. I cannot say I was sorry."

"And your grandmother and sister? Have you told them what you know?"

"Not yet," he sighed. "I do not know if I shall ever tell them. I do not think it would do any good."

Darash nodded. No court on earth could bring Servius's father to justice now.

"I want to thank you," Servius said. "I want to thank you for not revealing my... my struggles to Quintus Arrius. And, for helping me remember."

"I am sorry your memories are not better ones."

"So am I, but at least now I have no further fear of them interfering in how I perform my duty." He paused and then said, "Oh, I have brought you a small token of my gratitude."

Servius reached behind him and removed a linen-wrapped, oblong item from his belt and handed it to Darash. Darash fumbled with the twine, finally uncovering a gold-encrusted dagger from beneath the white folds.

Darash's eyes grew wide.

Are those jewels in the hilt?

He tried to mutter a suitable response of thanks, but could not find the words. Servius accepted the boy's nonsensical stammering as thanks enough.

"I took it off a barbarian prince on my first mission as a young soldier. Now it is yours."

Chapter Twenty-four

The Search Continues

Darash remained confined to his bed and then to the house for several weeks. Though glad for the rest, he found his mother's constant fussing nearly unbearable. The only respite he received was when she left to spend some of the money he had received or when he succumbed to the release of slumber, which he did as often as he could. Over the course of those days, his small cuts and bruises disappeared, and the soreness in his muscles melted away. But the knife wound in his chest continued to pain him for some time, and the physician said there would always be a scar.

"Some wounds take a long time to heal," Nib'haz said one day when he and Valad stopped by to visit.

"We are saving your spot for you in the shuk," Valad said.

"What he means," Nib'haz added, "is that he has expanded into your area. Now it stinks even more of cheese."

"Do not concern yourself," Valad explained. "Your place will be there when you return."

"How is Barus doing?" Nih'haz asked. "Your mother tells me he comes quite frequently to see how you are faring."

"He is well, I think," Darash responded. "But, as you said, Nib'haz, some wounds take a long time to heal."

Darash enjoyed receiving other visitors as well. Chaphash came to see him, as did Ibnei'ah and little Ra'ah. Ananias and Sapphira stopped by, leaving Revayah to complain in elevated tones about them as soon as they left.

"Who would purposely want to align himself with anyone from Nazareth?" she railed one afternoon after bidding them goodbye. "Nazareth, of all places! You would think Sapphira would prefer to spend time with me."

Darash felt sorry that his mother's friendship was suffering, but knew better than to comment. And, truly, he did not care where Yeshua had come from. He did not care who decided to follow him and who did not. He only cared whether or not Yeshua had anything to do with his father's death.

Perhaps now I will have time to find out.

סָ לֶ ה

A few days later, Darash felt well enough to take a stroll into town. It was the day after Shabbat, and Darash no longer felt like resting. But, as he walked along, he grew fatigued and regretted his decision to go quite so far. He placed a hand on his aching chest and leaned against a wall to catch his breath.

It is nearing dusk. I should try to get home before dark.

As he breathed deeply and waited to right himself, he noticed Ananias and Sapphira passing by on the opposite side street. A row of tethered donkeys partially hid him from their view.

An air of excitement followed them as they bustled with quick steps. Sapphira primped, tugged, and patted her clothing and hair and jabbered away about something Darash could not understand from his distance. He saw them enter through the outer gate of a modest home. Two of the home's windows faced the street and Darash heard excited but indistinguishable chatter coming from within.

It is a gathering of some sort. A celebration?

A lone man approached the outer door, and a large, bearded Jewish man welcomed him inside with a loud greeting, "Shalom, my brother! I greet you in the name of our Lord, Yeshua, the Messiah!"

A meeting of the Nazarites! So this is where Ananias and Sapphira go to meet with other followers of Yeshua. And could that be the infamous Peter?

Darash watched with renewed interest as several more filtered into the small house. Jews... Greeks... a wealthy woman... a man in rags.... Each was greeted with the same exuberance.

How very odd.

Given the number of people entering the dwelling, there could be little doubt that only standing room remained.

How could so many of such differing backgrounds worship together? And why does this religious meeting inspire such joy? Most of these people are Jews, but this is like no synagogue meeting I have ever attended.

Darash then saw another face he recognized.

Rabbi Nathan!

Nathan and his entire family walked up to the home and entered, greeting the people like old friends.

And then another couple approached.

Barus?

"Darash? What are you doing here?" Barus said, allowing his question to resemble a chastisement. "Should you not be at home resting?"

"I am feeling much better, Barus. But you are right, I should be getting home." Darash pushed off the wall and turned to go.

"Wait," Barus said. "Would you like us to walk with you?"

"No, it is alright. I believe you are expected." Darash nodded toward the house he had been watching. The man he believed to be Peter stood in the door, patiently waiting. Darash eyed Barus thoughtfully.

"You are surprised to see me going to one of these meetings?" Barus smiled. "Truthfully, my wife and I only started coming after Aphiemi was taken from us. We discovered that she had been coming with her friend, Mareh, so now we come, hoping they might help us understand her better... and our own pain."

"Your daughter was a Follower of the Way?"

"We believe so." Barus glanced toward the house. "This is the home of a man named Stephen. He told us she was troubled about something but would not share what it was. We know now, of course, why she was afraid. He told us she had found peace and forgiveness, even though he did not know what her sin had been. He told her that Yeshua came not only to rescue the Jews from their sin, but the whole world. That is still hard for us to believe—or even understand. Still, my wife and I are glad she found some of the joy these people have." He paused. "Why do you not join us? Come to the meeting with us and, when it is finished, we will see that you get home safely."

Darash took a step back.

"Oh, thank you, but no. I, uh... Imah expects me at home. She will worry if I stay out late."

"I understand."

"Darash?" Barus's wife spoke softly. "Before we go, I would like to thank you for telling us the truth about our daughter, even though it was a painful truth. Stephen told us that she and her child are now in paradise. I do not know if I believe it... but I want to. I had lost hope that—" Her voice broke and she stopped.

"We had lost hope," Barus amended. "When we lost our daughter, we lost our hope with her. Now... well, perhaps things are not exactly how we saw them. Perhaps we will get to see her again one day... and meet our grandchild."

Darash remained silent, unsure of how to respond.

Perhaps Nib'haz was right after all. Sometimes even painful truths bring their own form of comfort.

"And, Darash," Barus said. "Thank you for not saying anything about Aphiemi's condition to the magistrate. It may still come out, if Ratash talks...."

Darash nodded.

It would be dark soon. Darash bid farewell to Barus and his wife and watched them enter the home of Stephen. Having recovered from his earlier overexertion, he now headed home. He strolled slowly through the shadows of the city streets. Jerusalem grew quiet after a long day of people scurrying about, trying to raise enough money for their supper, chasing after loose animals or children, and spending the minutes and hours of their days on the minutia of life while trying to forget the more pressing matters they could do nothing about.

Darash passed through the center of the Lower Market. He passed his old spot, now empty.

As the shadows claimed Jerusalem, when all should be at peace, Darash heard a scream.

The sound came from a nearby street. Darash stopped and listened. The scream sounded female—young, frightened—but now no other sound could be detected. He took a few steps in that direction. Rounding a corner, he saw the source of the trouble.

Pertho stood on the side of the road. Amah crouched at his feet, an arm raised above her head. He bent and backhanded her across the forehead, sending her sprawling.

"Let that teach you to hide from me!" Pertho shouted, slurring his words together through thick lips. "You worthless whore!" He took a lumbering, unsteady step toward her.

Pertho's back was to Darash, so he moved forward, unseen.

"Why do I put up with your foolishness and disobedience?" Pertho said, little beads of spittle flying from his mouth as he talked. "I should sell you to that Phoenician you disliked so much! That would teach you!"

"Pardon me," Darash said, still several paces away, making sure to keep out of Pertho's reach.

Pertho swung around, struggling to focus on the new target. His robe hung open at the neck, and the sickly sweet smell of wine emanated from every pore.

"What do you want?" he barked.

"I... I...." Darash stammered, but then blurted, "I overheard that you want to sell your slave. I have silver... and my mother needs a new handmaid."

$$ \text{סֶ לֶ ה} $$

Darash stood in the center of the square, facing off once again with Elias. Elias circled, staff raised at a slight angle, as was his custom at the opening of each new battle. Darash turned with the other boy, keeping an eye on his opponent.

Here I am, ready to make a fool of myself once again.

Darash saw Elias's eyes drop and then sweep back up, taking in the whole of Darash's skinny frame. The bigger boy sneered, confident of yet another swift victory. How many times had they faced off this way? Elias glanced back over his shoulder and caught the eye of his uncle, Nakal. Nakal nodded in support, chin thrust out toward his nephew's easy prey and smiled broadly.

Like Darash, Elias had lost his father. But Elias had Nakal. Darash keenly felt the absence of support. His father had little family, and his mother's family remained in Bethlehem, the place of her birth.

What would Father say to me, if he were here?

"You have found yourself up against a formidable opponent, my son. How will you proceed?"

"I do not know. I am outmatched."

"He is stronger than you?"

"Yes."

"He is faster than you?"

"He is."

"He is more experienced as well?"

"Yes, Abba."

"He is more intelligent?"

"I... I do not know. But what has that to do with this fight? This is not a battle of the mind, but of strength and agility."

"Do not be deceived, my son. Every battle is a battle of the mind."

"Why should I listen to a man who used trickery and deception to swindle others out of their hard earned wages? That is not who I am!"

"Then who are you, Darash?"

"I... I...."

"The battle is on. You must decide who you are."

Elias lunged forward in a fake attack. Darash winced and retreated. The spectators laughed, Nakal loudest of all. Darash colored a deep red.

"Decide! Who are you? Will you use what you have been given and fight? Or will you accept defeat—giving up before the battle has even begun?"

"I am not like you!" Darash moved his staff before him, keeping it securely between himself and his circling enemy. *"...But I am your son."*

"Then, how will you proceed?"

Darash took a deep breath and blew it out slowly. He squared his shoulders and moved his right foot forward.

"I have an idea, Abba. I think I know what to do."

As in many previous battles, Elias moved in with a swift attack. But this time Darash expected it.

"Do it, Darash! Do it now!"

Darash dodged to the right and, in a move Elias did not see coming, took the offensive. He faked a jab toward Elias's right shoulder, drawing the block. In fluid motion, Darash swung the base of his staff low and to the left. He caught Elias in the back of his left leg at the knee. The knee buckled. Darash followed with a hard jab—striking Elias in the chest, forcing his upper torso back, even as his legs struggled to regain balance. Elias, too heavy and over-extended, did not recover. In less than five seconds, Darash had him on his back—this time staring up at the butt of Darash's staff.

"Well done, my son. Well done."

~ The End ~

Sneak Peek!

Book II: The Brazen Altar

Eliana opened her eyes to the sound of moaning and the acrid smell of smoke. She rolled to her side and tried to sit, only to be hit with a wave of nauseating pain emanating from the left side of her skull. Her hand went to the place and brought back a red smear of blood.

"Hazaiah?" she said, finding her voice as the terror returned. "Ikaia?"

A moan.

Eliana turned to see her husband lying next to her groaning weakly through barely parted lips. An ugly patch of blood soaked his tunic over his abdomen.

"Hazaiah! Oh, no! Hazaiah, my husband! What have they done to you?"

She smoothed back his hair from his eyes and tried to revive him, but he did not open his eyes. Eliana's attention turned to her son.

"Ikaia?" she said, looking around. No response. "Ikaiah!"

Eliana fought against the pain and pushed herself to her feet. She took an unsteady step forward and surveyed the devastation. Two servants lay nearby in pools of their own blood. Hazaiah's mules lay slain, still attached to the overturned, smoldering cart.

The cart!

"Ikaia!" she cried again, her voice desperate, haunted.

She raced forward and circled the blackened wreckage. When she saw the place where her little boy once sat and played, she lifted a hand to her mouth and screamed.

סֶ לָ ה

Darash jolted from his sleep, heart beating wildly and fearing to breathe lest he miss the sound again. Something had happened. Something terrible. He searched his fragmented memory, separating dreams from reality to search for the terror that had awakened him.

A scream.

He heard it again. A terrified, helpless sound. Desperate for escape. Desperate for rescue. It sounded like....

Tsarah!

Darash jumped from his bed, ignoring the stabbing pain in his chest from the wound that refused to heal. A quick search told him Tsarah, indeed, was missing from her bed. He ran barefooted from the upper room they shared, along the roofline over the stables, and down the cracked stone steps. A few long strides brought him to the front door.

He heard the cry again, this time closer, clearer. Different.

"Tsarah!" He called.

Darash pushed inside the main room and followed the sound of weeping cries to his mother's bedroom. The sight before him brought him to an abrupt halt at the room's threshold. He caught himself with both hands, one on each side of the entrance. His chest burned in pain.

His mother, Revayah, who he called "Imah," sat on her bed holding a girl in her arms. But the girl was not Tsarah, his eight-year-old sister. Tsarah sat at the foot of the bed, hugging her knees, deep lines of worry crossing her brow.

And Darash remembered.

The girl cradled in his mother's arms, hair askew, wails ripping from her tiny frame was the girl known only as "Amah," female slave. He had purchased her from an evil Greek man named Pertho and brought her home two nights ago. He had appeased Imah by telling her Amah would make a good servant who could replace Imah's beloved maid and cook, Huldah, who left shortly after Abba died because they could no longer support her. But Amah's crippling fear had proved him wrong.

Revayah's eyes met his. They darted to a blanket in the corner of her room, then back to him. He understood.

Darash retrieved the warm, wool blanket, woven with strands of blue against white, and opened it. The girl still wailed.

"Please," Imah whispered, telling him with her eyes to spread it across the girl's back, fearing to release her fragile, unpredictable charge.

Tsarah, eager to finally be able to help, moved from her huddled position to grasp one side of the blanket while Darash pulled the other edge up and around both the girl and his mother.

Revayah snuggled the terrified child like a newborn babe close to her chest as she whispered unintelligible, but soothing sounds into Amah's hair. Darash sunk to his knees, Tsarah returned to her former position, each feeling the stabbing sorrows brought with each cry, each sob, each ragged gasp.

And then Amah began to calm.

As the wailing turned to weeping and the weeping to whimpering, Revayah's voice emerged into the space left behind.

"Be still. All is well. You are safe. Adonai has rescued you. We are with you now. You are with us. You are safe."

סֶ לָ ה

"You look like you slept standing up."

"Shalom, Valad."

Darash tied his donkey, Nekoda, to a post and began fumbling with clumsy fingers to untie a sheaf of hay from her back. He yawned widely, not caring who saw.

"Ah, Darash!" Nib'haz, the blind basket-weaver called to him. "I was beginning to wonder if you would make it today." Then, to Valad, "Move your cheese. Darash is here."

"No, leave it," Darash said. "I am not staying long. I simply came by to speak to Ibnei'ah and find out if he needs any bitumen this week."

Darash dropped a pile of hay before Nekoda, who wasted no time rummaging through it with her round snout.

"Then why did you bring your donkey? And why are you feeding her?" Valad wanted to know.

"I am feeding her because I got up too late to do it at home this morning and she is hungry." He yawned again. "And I brought her because, if Ibnei'ah needs nothing from me this week, I am going to Gophna. There is a metalworker there who—"

"Oh, good!" Valad interrupted. "While you are there, find that no good brother of mine and tell him he still owes me three and a half denarii and, if he does not return it by next week, I am going to come up there and—"

"Peace, Valad," Nib'haz said, one hand in the air. "Be still and let the boy alone. He has no share in your family troubles." He turned toward Darash's general direction and said, "This is your first trip out of town since you sustained your injury, and it is a full day's journey. Is it absolutely necessary? Perhaps someone could go in your place?"

"No, Nib'haz. I appreciate your concern, but if I do not purchase more merchandise soon, I will have nothing left to sell. And Gophnan jewelry and cookery can be had for little and sold to the travelers who come to Jerusalem for a good profit."

"Wait," Valad said. "Why are you in such a hurry? Do you not have that reward money Barus gave you for finding his daughter's killer?"

"Well... I...." Darash hung his head, letting his black hair fall over his eyes, and turned back to Nekoda. He stroked her long ears. She twitched them, preferring not to be disturbed while she ate.

"Oh, no! Do not tell me you spent it all already!"

"No! ...Well, not all of it...."

"Darash!" Valad cried. "I cannot believe this! That was at least a year's wages! Gone in a matter of days? How is this possible?"

Darash turned to Valad, swept his hair from his eyes and said, "I bought Amah."

"Who? You bought a slave girl?"

"No..." Nib'haz said in his low, guttural voice. "He bought the slave girl."

Valad sat starring at Darash as understanding opened his eyes wider. "Ahhhh.... Ah!" He slapped his skinny thigh. "Amah! The Amah! That little mud flower you took such a liking to!" He bellowed a laugh. "Boy, you must be out of your mind!" He laughed again. "I knew you liked her, but—I never imagined this! What are we to do with you, Darash? Ah, ha, ha, ha, ha!"

"My mother needed a servant."

"A servant? A servant! Do you know nothing? Boy, that girl is a prost—"

"I think it was an excellent purchase," Nib'haz interrupted, speaking more loudly than usual. "No amount is too large to free a Jewess from slavery. Do you not agree, Valad?"

Valad was laughing so hard now that tears ran down his cheeks, making tracks in the thin layer of dirt that resided there. "Of course, of course, but... ah, ha, ha, ha!"

"Thank you, Nib'haz," Darash said. "Can I leave Nekoda here while I go look for Ibnei'ah?"

"Yes, my son. Go. Go now."

סֶ לָ ה

Twenty minutes later, Darash led Nekoda through the shuk headed for the Upper City to begin his journey. As he passed the dyer's booth, he heard a loud lament.

"What are you going to do about it, Magistrate?" It was Millah, the dyer's wife. Her voice, normally flowing with choice gossip interspersed with sales attempts, now flowed with complaints interspersed with accusations. "How are we supposed to keep our business running without our son? How could he leave us like this—without even a word! And now his father is ill! He might even die—not that you would care about that! One less Jew to worry about! Then what will become of me? Alone and widowed? You must do something, Magistrate Arrius! You must do something now!"

"What time did he leave?"

Darash recognized Magistrate Quintus Arrius's voice even before he rounded the corner that brought the Roman official into view. The large man stood before the dyer's booth, surrounded by a flock of disinterested chickens and fascinated customers.

"How am I supposed to know?" Millah demanded, her voice rising further. "Sometime in the night, I would guess! We awoke this morning to find his bed had not been slept in and his belongings missing."

"Do you have family in the area? Perhaps he simply went to visit a relative."

"Our closest family is in Gophna, but I do not know why he would want to go there. My sister is such a loud mouth and busybody."

"Would he have reason to want to leave home? ...Perhaps you and he were not getting along."

Millah sucked in her breath and put hands to ample hips. The chickens at her feet, sensing her wrath, instinctively fluttered out of the way.

"What are you suggesting? That I drove him away?"

The magistrate sighed and his eyes landed on Darash.

"Where are you going?" the magistrate asked the boy. "Should you not be at home recuperating?"

"I must take a trip out of town for supplies," Darash answered.

"A trip? Are you sure that is wise? How far are you going?"

"Just out of town."

"But where out of town, Boy?"

Darash swallowed.

"To Gophna."

Character Descriptions

Amah	Pertho's young, beautiful maidservant. Meaning, 'female servant.' (Amah is not her real name.)
Ana	A Roman and the great aunt to both Servius and Julia.
Ananias	Old family friends of Darash's family. Husband of Sapphira.
Aphiemi	The Greek girl who was murdered.
Bar'abbas	A Jewish folk-hero of sorts who violently rebelled against the Romans and was captured, convicted of murder, and scheduled for crucifixion. When Pilate offered to free one of their captives—either Bar'abbas or Jesus, the Jews demanded the release of Bar'abbas, condemning Jesus to the cross.
Barus & his wife	Greek parents whose daughter, Aphiemi, was murdered.
Caiaphas	The Jewish high priest.
Chamal	Shavah's adoptive father.
Chaphash	A Jewish young man and the bondsman of Gabahh & Nasha. Darash's best friend.
Darash	Fifteen-year-old, Jewish boy who recently took over his father's merchant business after his father's murder. He's skinny, with stringy black hair. [Darash: "to tread or frequent, usually to follow (for pursuit or search), to seek or ask, to worship, diligently, inquire, make inquisition, question, require, search, seek for/out, surely."]

Elias	A Jewish, muscular, good-looking youth who is good at stick fighting. Nephew of Nakal. Name is Greek form of Elijah (my God is Jehovah) Skin is a lighter hue—may indicate mixed blood.
Eltolad & Family	Seller of bitumen from Emmaus. Father of eleven children/wife pregnant with their twelfth.
Essene Man	Lives near the site of the murder.
Gabahh	A Hebrew and wealthy Sadducee, and master of Chaphash.
Hadassah	Chaphash's betrothed.
Hathal	Another former business associate of Tuwr.
Huldah	A former house servant who left to find new employment when the money began to run out.
Ibnei'ah	He is a local, Jewish paver—he works with brightly colored stones to decorate the homes/gardens of the wealthy—as well as does regular stone working. He has a six-year-old daughter and his wife recently died.
Jacob	Wealthy & respected Sadducee.
John	Another former disciple of Jesus who is equally hated by the religious leaders.
Julia	Roman cousin of Servius Aurelius.
Malchus	Servant of the High Priest. Peter cut off his ear and Jesus healed it.
Mareh	Aphiemi's Hebrew best friend.
Ma'yan	Rabbi Nathan's wife

Millah	The dyer's wife and the town gossip.
Nakal	Tuwr's former business associate.
Nasha	Gabahh's wife.
Nekoda	Darash's spotted, female donkey. [Nekoda: "Spotted."]
Nib'haz	A Jewish, blind basket seller & friend/mentor to Darash. [Nib'haz: "We shall utter (what) is seen."]
Pertho	A wicked Greek man.
Peter	A former disciple of Jesus. A leader to those who call themselves, "Followers of the Way"--a new spiritual teaching which is highly criticized and feared by the religious leaders of Jerusalem.
Queen Helena of Abiadene	A member of Assyrian royalty who had converted to Judaism and built a palace for herself (and palaces for her two sons) in the City of David portion of Jerusalem.
Quintus Arrius	The Roman magistrate officially in charge of the murder investigation.
Ra'ah	Six-year-old daughter of Ibnei'ah.
Rabbi Nathan	A Jewish rabbi and old family friend. Formerly, Tuwr's best friend.
Ratash	A young Sadducee. Protégé of Jacob.
Revayah	Darash and Tsarah's mother.
Sapphira	Revayah's best friend. Wife of Ananias.

Servius Aurelius	Roman watchtower guard & centurion.
Shavah	A young man who was orphaned as a child but named and raised by Hebrews. He and his wife are expecting their first child.
Stephen	One of the early leaders of the Christian Church.
Teshuah	Wife of Shavah who is pregnant with their first child.
Tsarah	Darash's younger sister, age eight.
Tuwr	Father of Darash. A merchant & moneychanger who was murdered by an unknown assailant.
Valad	Another Jewish, merchant and seller of cheese & goat milk.
Yeshua	Jesus, who eight months earlier, had been crucified, buried, and rumored to have come back from the dead. At this time, His followers are unifying, performing miracles, and boldly preaching Him as the Jewish Messiah.
Zahar	A Jewish priest and former teacher of Darash and Chaphash.

Going Deeper...

Discussion Questions

Chapter One

Read Luke 23:44-46 & John 10:18

Into the Past
"The Sixth Hour" is a reference to Christ's suffering on the cross. At that moment, though it was midday (approximately noon), the whole sky turned black—possibly due to a well-timed solar eclipse. The sky remained dark for three hours. All that time, Jesus hung there, suffering in agony. At the ninth hour, (3pm) He gave up His spirit. Note that Jesus laid his life down. It wasn't taken from Him.

Sometimes in life, our world can become terribly dark. We may believe that hope is lost. I imagine that, at that moment, Satan and His army threw a great celebration, believing they had won. In this book, a young girl loses her life—a tragedy that sends her family into deep despair. But that is not the end of the story. It is only the beginning.

Into the Story
When Darash follows Pertho, the Greek, back to his home to deliver the Egyptian box, how does he react to his surroundings? What are his prejudices? Why does Darash interact with Pertho at all?

Into the Present
Nib'haz, the blind basket-weaver, quotes a passage of Scripture: "Pride goes before destruction." (Proverbs 16:18) What does this verse mean? Are there times in your life when you have been prideful? Have you ever allowed pride to create prejudices in your heart and mind against others? How might you improve in this area?

Chapter Two

Read John 5:1-15

Into the Past
The tradition of the healing quality of the Pool of Bethesda in Jerusalem was a well-known legend at the time of Jesus; however, Scripture does not corroborate the truth of angelic visitations at this place or for this purpose. Note that, unlike the angel of the myth, Jesus did not hide Himself or His purposes. He performed miracles in public places, in the midst of crowds, and for people who could serve as living witnesses to His power and compassion. The fact that we have in our possession manuscripts written within 25 years of these events themselves, is evidence that they are true. It would be impossible to attempt to rewrite history to such a vast degree and so close to the events without drawing a great outcry from those still living who remember.

Into the Story
How does Darash's mother, Revayah, react to Jesus (Yeshua)? What is her opinion of Him, and how does she explain away His miracles? Does she bother to compare Jesus's actions with the prophesies in Scripture regarding the coming Messiah?

Into the Present
Consider the following question: *Did Jesus really perform the miracles credited to Him?* Below is a list of alternative possibilities and a related discussion. Read through them and consider them carefully or discuss them with your group.

A.) Jesus performed miracles because He was Whom He said He was.
If he performed them because He is God, then it is in our best interests to learn all we can about Him and seek a relationship with Him. If you're interested in learning more about the man called "Christ," start by reading the book of John in the Bible. Also, feel free to contact the author of this book with any questions you might have.
(christianwriter.thomas@gmail.com)

B.) He performed them because He is an agent of the Devil.
If He performed them because He is an agent of the devil, there would be some evidence to this fact (of which I can find none), and we would be

admitting a devil exists, which also suggests God exists. And why would the devil go around healing people and trying to get them to develop greater faith in God? So, if the devil exists, God most likely exists, too. And, if God exists, isn't it possible that He might interact with us in this way?

C.) **He managed to pull off some pretty amazing hoaxes.**
If a mere man had tried to pull off these miracles as hoaxes, he would have a very rough go of it. Some of the people Jesus cured were well-known in the community and had been ill or afflicted since long before Jesus was even ministering in the area (and possibly since before Jesus was even born.) It would be very difficult to convince someone to fake a deformity for forty years and to do so ten years before you are born.

D.) **He never performed them at all.**
If Jesus never performed these miracles at all, then He would have had to convince an entire community of people, including His enemies, to keep it quiet. As described earlier, the same stories and letters we have today circulated during the lifetimes of the people who experienced them. But, instead of simply denying the truth of Jesus's abilities (they knew they would not be believed, since they would be trying to convince people not to believe their own eyes and experiences) Jesus's enemies tried to silence those who spread the good news by killing them off.

Chapter Three

Read Acts 5:34-38 & James 1:27

<u>Into the Past</u>
Revayah dismisses Jesus as another false Messiah. She bases her opinion on the fact that several others had come, promising to deliver the Jews from their oppressors, but eventually failed.

Later, Gamaliel would use the same reasoning in his defense of the apostles. Keep in mind that, just because some so-called messiahs were fakes, that does not mean Jesus was a fake. Where others failed, He succeeded. Jesus deserves to be evaluated based on Who He is, not dismissed based on the shortcomings of others.

<u>Into the Story</u>
When Tuwr died, his wife became a widow and his children were considered orphans. At this time in Jerusalem, things had improved slightly for Jewish women. They could create items to sell, inherit property, and handle money. However, it was still incredibly difficult for a woman alone to make enough money to support herself and her children. Families in this state often faced a rapid decline into poverty and the terrors that accompany it. Despite her troubles, we see that Revayah was a very religious woman. But she rejected Christ and the teachings of His disciples. Ironically, what will Jesus's brother write later about people in her position?

<u>Into the Present</u>
We learn that, despite being refused permission to teach at the synagogues (which was every adult, Jewish male's right), the apostles and new followers of Jesus continued to meet there and spread the message of Christ. What does this say about the strength of their convictions? What did this say about their passion for Jesus and the freedom He brought them? What kind of freedom did they find more desirable? Freedom from religious oppression or freedom from their sins? What lessons can we learn from their example?

Chapter Four

Read Exodus 32:29, Leviticus 20:26, & Ezekiel 12:11-16

Into the Past
The Jews have a long history of conflict with idolatrous nations. At the time, the Greeks worshipped many false gods, ate foods the Jews considered "unclean," and engaged in some rather scandalous practices. In the Old Testament, God tells His chosen people, the Jews, that He has "set them apart" among the nations unto Himself to be holy. This means they had certain rules they had to follow as a witness to all others that God had a different and better way for mankind. However, what God intended as a testimony, many used as a way to denigrate one another.

Into the Story
We continue to see Darash struggle with his prejudice against Greeks, despite that Barus's home and lifestyle greatly differs from that of Pertho. Why are Darash's prejudices so strong, and how does he finally justify his presence there?

Into the Present
Nib'haz tells Darash, "Being a seeker of truth is a dangerous business. The truth does not set itself up to please any man. It simply is what it is, whether we would accept it or not, whether it should be or not." Do you agree with him? If true, how should this maxim inform your search for God? Is God a belief—a mere concept? Or is He a Being? Will changing our beliefs about God effect any change in God Himself? How then can we best discover God's identity and character?

Chapter Five

Read Leviticus 21:11, Numbers 19:11, Ephesians 2:1-10, & John 3:16-17

Into the Past

Darash, in his search for Aphiemi's killer, runs up against some difficulty in getting the magistrate's help. The magistrate has his hands full dealing with the growing unrest caused by Jesus's followers. But what was this "unrest?" At this time, the excitement and wonder surrounding Jesus's resurrection was still thick in the air. Hundreds of people witnessed Him alive and well and had seen the empty tomb. Thousands more had come to faith in Him. The Jewish believers, still legally entitled to teaching in the synagogues, continued to do so—only now they loudly proclaimed Jesus as the Christ—their long-awaited Messiah, showing hundreds of very specific Scripture passages that confirmed their belief. But the chief priests, who had sent Jesus to the cross, were desperate to silence them. They knew they had no way to convince the believers they were wrong—far too many were eye-witnesses and Jesus's tomb indeed lay empty—so they bided their time and looked for ways to persecute Jesus's disciples. We see how desperate and unreasonable they had become when, upon witnessing the disciples performing miraculous healings in Jesus's name, the chief priests used minute, legalistic, religious rules to condemn them and throw them in jail. The Romans, unwilling to make a judgment on Jewish religious practice, nevertheless recognized these internal disagreements as potentially dangerous to the peace. They responded by tightening their grip, quickly and brutally quelling uprisings, and playing political games with the Jewish leadership.

Into the Story

What is the Jewish taboo associated with contact with a dead body? How did this particular practice serve Darash's investigation?

Into the Present

The apostle Paul claims that we can live as if we are dead. What kind of death is he talking about? What was God's response to this dreadful condition? Who else had to die and conquer death in order to make true life available to us? How do we acquire this new life?

Chapter Six

Read Matthew 28

Into the Past

Scholars and historians estimate that approximately twenty Roman soldiers guarded Jesus's tomb. We are told that they witnessed the appearance of the angel and became "like dead men." This state could be something like sleep. In Genesis 2:21, God causes Adam to "fall into a deep sleep" and, in Acts 16:16-40, Paul and Silas's jailer, though commanded to guard them carefully, slept through an earthquake that shook the prison so badly that all the cells opened. So it is not without corroborating evidence that God could have simply put them to sleep. But this seems unlikely. They had already witnessed Jesus rising from the dead, so why would God bother to knock them out? It seems more reasonable that they were simply so in shock at what they saw that they couldn't move or speak.

If a Roman soldier was caught sleeping on the job, he would be severely flogged or, if it was a time of war, put to death. Such conduct was so unbecoming of a Roman soldier, the jailer mentioned above actually drew his sword to kill himself. But despite the unlikeliness that all twenty guards fell asleep at the same time, uncaring whether they lived or died or how badly their reputations would be damaged, this was their story. Interestingly, these guards weren't put to death or even flogged. Instead, they were paid off to spread the rumor that Jesus's disciples snuck in amongst them, broke Pilate's seal, rolled that giant stone away from the tomb entrance, carried off the corpse, and did all of this without waking a single one of Rome's finest. (And, of course, if they were asleep, how would they know who stole the body?) From that day forward, they would have had to live with what they had witnessed and what they had done to cover up a miracle so incredible that it laid out twenty Roman soldiers on their backs.

And what would have possessed the chief priests to give these guys a way out? ...Unless they believed the guard's real story and still, in their stubborn, hard hearts, wanted to snuff out the story of a miracle—a miracle that proved how mistaken they had been to crucify their own Messiah.

Into the Story
What is Darash's opinion of the watchtower guard after he discovers him asleep? Remembering that this man was also one of the guards at Jesus's tomb, how does this information affect his willingness to trust the centurion's word?

Into the Present
If you had witnessed a blinding white light, heard the voice of an angel, seen and heard the massive stone being easily moved from the front of a tomb, seen the man you had just watched die (or helped crucify yourself) come out fully alive an restored, experienced all of this with twenty of your closest comrades, and then been paid off to lie about it, what would you believe about the identity of the man who was supposed to be dead? Would you be able to continue your life as usual? Or, would such an experience change your life? What would your opinion be of those who asked you to lie about your experiences?

Chapter Seven

Read Proverbs 31, 146:9, & Deut. 24:17-22

Into the Past
Proverbs 31 was originally learned and recited by men. It was their job to show respect for their wives, honor them, and praise them in this way. How does this contrast to how this passage is viewed by us today? How might modern marriages benefit if the men of today began studying and memorizing this passage and then reciting it as a thanks and a blessing over their wives each week?

Into the Story
Now that Tuwr is gone, Revayah has no one who will recite Proverbs 31 to her each Shabbat. How do you think that makes her feel? What does the Bible have to say about how God views widows and how society should treat them?

Into the Present
The Jewish Shabbat ceremony is both beautiful and meaningful. What did you find most interesting or meaningful? How might you learn from how they honored God on that day and apply it to your life?

Chapter Eight

Read Matthew 6:1-5 & 27:50-54

Into the Past
The Sadducees and Pharisees liked to boast about how spiritual they were. Despite their knowledge of Scripture, history, and prophesy, were so focused on themselves—even in matters that should have pertained to God and His wishes—that they made themselves deaf to His voice. One's relationship with God is intended to be a private thing—an intimacy between two individuals in which neither can deceive the other as to their true beliefs and motivations.

Into the Story
Here we see a description of the Temple Shabbat ceremony. The high priest in this scene, Caiaphas, is the same man who condemned Jesus to a horrible death on the cross. And the Temple had been damaged by a recent earthquake in which the curtain separating the Holy of Holies from the Holy Place had been ripped in two. How did Darash react to this visible reminder of the events surrounding the crucifixion of Jesus? How did these things cause him to doubt his faith?

Into the Present
Sapphira comes and tells Revayah about Peter healing the cripple. How might you react if someone came to tell you a story like this one? What if a great many people—people you knew and trusted—reported seeing the exact same thing? If you had witnessed something like this, could you keep silent about it?

Chapter Nine

Read John 18:10, 25-27, & Luke 22:51, I Corinthians 7:20-23

Into the Past
Jews tended to follow the less restrictive practice of indentured servitude—a condition often willingly entered by the servant in which he works for a limited amount of time to pay off a debt or earn money for his family. It was not a glamorous job, but it was a job, not slavery. These people maintained much of their personal autonomy and retained certain personal rights. However, the Greeks, Romans, and other people groups practiced slavery as we think of it today, and Jews could be taken as slaves—property without rights or hope of escape to be used and disposed of in any way the owner saw fit.

Into the Story
Two servants are featured in this chapter, the girl called Amah and Malchus.

Malchus is the servant of the high priest, Caiaphas. Malchus's ear was chopped off by Peter when they came to arrest Jesus. Jesus then healed his ear. How do you think such an experience might have changed his life? His attitude about Jesus? His attitude about Caiaphas?

Amah is a young Jewess owned by an evil Greek man. Though slavery is never pretty, it was a common practice at the time. Why does seeing her condition bother Darash so much?

Into the Present
Interestingly, Malchus's relative (also a servant of the high priest) later challenged Peter, drawing one of Peter's three denials of Christ. With the concept of slavery in mind, what kinds of things kept Peter as a slave before he fully trusted in Jesus? How did Peter change after Jesus rose from the dead? What kind of "slave" did he become, and how did this impact his ministry and the spread of the gospel? Can you relate to Peter's story? Where are you right now? Are you denying Jesus? Is there anything in your life that is keeping you captive? How might your life change if you exchange your slavery to sin for "slavery" to Christ?

Chapter Ten

Read Exodus 6:6, Ezekiel 16, Titus 2:11-14, John 1:12-13

Into the Past

Darash and his people lived under the promise of Exodus 6:6. But reading further in Ezekiel 16, we see that, despite God's love and rescue, the People often strayed away from God. Ezekiel 16 is an allegory of unfaithful Jerusalem. The first part of this story is one of rescue of an orphan (Verses 4-7a). But later we see that orphan rejecting her rescuer (Verse 15). Still, He continues to be faithful and to pursue her in love (Verse 60). And, He makes a promise, "Then, when I make atonement for you for all you have done.... (Verse 63a).

Into the Story

Chamal tells the story of how he rescued and adopted his son, Shavah. How does this story parallel God's rescue of His children?

Into the Present

How does this story show God's ability and desire to redeem? What offer does God make to us in the Titus passage above? How did Jesus make this offer possible? How might we accept it?

Chapter Eleven

Read Micah 5:2, Matthew 1:18-25, & Luke 2:1-7, 1:46-55

Into the Past
A betrothal is similar to an engagement, except that it is a much more binding arrangement and it is an arrangement between entire families instead of just between the couple. The bride's father arranges a legal transaction, in which his daughter is promised and he receives the payment of the bridewealth. The couple, at this time, are considered, legally, husband and wife, except that they cannot yet live together nor consummate the marriage. When Mary was found to be pregnant with Jesus, she was only betrothed to Joseph; therefore, she could have been stoned. This sheds light on why Joseph did not leave Mary behind when he went to Bethlehem to register for the census. It also made possible the fulfillment of Micah's prophesy that the Messiah would be born in Bethlehem.

Into the Story
Barus quotes Isaiah, saying "He gives strength to the weary and increases the power of the weak." (Isaiah 40:29) How was Barus using this verse for encouragement? What are your thoughts?

Into the Present
Mary suffered a great deal for her willingness to be used of God as the mother the Savior. But, though the trouble itself did not come from God, true to the promise in Isaiah, God gave her weary soul strength and increased her power. How does she bear witness to this fact through her song in Luke 1? How might you react if God asked you to sacrifice your reputation, security, or the future you have planned for yourself in order to bring Him glory? What lessons can we learn from Mary's heart? Her faith? Her suffering? Her joy?

Do you know anyone who has gone through this? What are the fears? The temptations? How might family and friends react? What dangers might the young mother and/or father face? What dangers might the unborn child face? You can be a source of strength, encouragement, and practical help. (For more information about how to help a single girl or a couple experiencing an unplanned pregnancy, find a Care Net pregnancy center near you. Go to http://pregnancydecisionline.org. All services are free.)

Chapter Twelve

Read Acts 3, Luke 19:10, & Galatians 5:1

Into the Past
In Acts 3, Paul recounts the story of a miraculous healing—the healing of the paralytic who had been a cripple for 40 years. According to biblical scholars, this book was written sometime between 63 and 70 AD. Unique among Apostle Paul's writings, he wrote it as a history of the early Church and an expository on both the persecution of early believers as well as the triumph of Christ.

Into the Story
Valad speaks about the miracle performed by Peter and John. How has this event influenced Valad? Do you think his reaction might have been a common one for those living at the time?

Into the Present
What are your reactions to this story? What does it show you about the nature of Jesus Christ? Though Jesus often miraculously healed people from physical ailments—and even raised people from the dead—what kind of ailment did He really come to heal? How did the religious leaders respond to Him? How did the people respond? How should you respond?

Chapter Thirteen

Read Psalm 22, Genesis 28:13-15, Deuteronomy 31:6, & Romans 11:5

Into the Past
The Jews have a long history of going through times when God seemed very, very distant and hope seemed lost. They have faced enemies from every side, famine, disease, war, and even a lengthy slavery in Egypt. Later, Judah was invaded and occupied. The young, strong, royals and wealthy were carried away to Babylon, leaving the aged, incapacitated, and intimidated to remain. At the time of this story, enemies—the Romans—had again occupied Judah (though their methods differed considerably). It is not surprising that the Jewish people and their kings have often gone through periods of great discouragement. But they also have a constant source of hope and strength. They are God's chosen people and He promises to love them preserve them. Again and again, miracle after miracle, God has proven Himself true to His word.

Into the Story
Darash is feeling very discouraged. What has caused him to feel this way? If you could give him some advice, what would it be?

Into the Present
Jesus Himself, when on the cross, cried out, "My God, my God, why have you forsaken me?" (Mark 15:34) In doing so, he repeats David's own words in Psalm 22. What else can you find in that passage that prophesies about what Jesus later endured? This psalm begins with much heartache and intense discouragement, but how does it end? What brings on the change? What kinds of things make you feel discouraged? What can you do in times like these to turn that around? How do you help those around you who are discouraged?

Chapter Fourteen

Read Jeremiah 7:1, Romans, 9:25-33, Mark 11: 15-17, & John 2:13-25

Into the Past
Darash has been raised within a system of strict, religious legality—a system Jesus came to set in order. The Jews believed that following the rules would be enough to get them into Heaven, but the law's purpose is not to make people righteous, but to reveal their sin and their need for God. Jesus cast the merchants from the Temple because they completely missed the point. They had turned the Temple into a marketplace or "a den of thieves," as Jesus called it, indicating that they weren't even dealing honestly. In fact, this event occurred in fulfillment of prophesy. The Jews felt spiritually secure as long as they followed certain rules, but they had no concept of a personal relationship with God. Jesus came to offer them an intimacy with God that went much deeper than anything they had ever known.

Into the Story
Darash is confused as to why Jesus cast the merchants out of the Temple courts. Why is Darash confused, and why did Jesus do what He did?

Into the Present
Sometimes our traditions and the teachings of men get in the way of what the Bible really says. Can you think of any examples of how this has been true in your experience? What is the correct response when dealing with confusion of this sort? What should you do to find the truth?

238 | The Sixth Hour

Chapter Fifteen

Read Matthew 27:13-26 & Act 3-4:22

Into the Past
We know little of this man who, though a killer, gained his freedom while Jesus was condemned to die. We may think of him as the first person Jesus died for. But Bar'abbas was more than just some common murderer. It is believed he was a sort of folk-hero to the Jewish people— a man who lived on the fringes of civilized society but had (unsuccessfully, of course) rebelled against the Romans. He was of little value to the Jewish people—representing yet another false messiah—but he, at least, fought the Romans, whereas Jesus preferred to see the Romans welcomed into salvation and into relationship with God. So, when the Jews freed Bar'abbas instead of Jesus, we see what they truly wanted—military resistance rather than peace purchased through sacrificial love.

Into the Story
Millah, the dyer, forms a formidable branch in the town's gossip vine. With all of our modern technology, we rely less and less on face-to-face conversations, but word-of-mouth news still ranks very high as a means of influence and information sharing. In fact, social media is just a means of making word-of-mouth information more accessible, and look how popular that has become! Think of Millah as the Facebook page of first century Jerusalem. Then, like now, everyone was in everyone else's business. She represents many who would have found news of this new faith and the miracles being performed to be highly newsworthy. Again, we see how difficult it was for the religious leaders to silence the truth and how difficult it would have been to pull off any kind of hoax on a scale as large as this one. The news of Jesus and His followers had gone absolutely viral!

Into the Present
How many "shares" and "retweets" do you think Peter and John have gotten if they had social media back then? How hard would it have been for the religious leaders of the day to get their followers to "block" such news? How does understanding this culture, in light of our own, help us evaluate the reliability of our historical records?

Chapter Sixteen

Read Matthew 5:1-12, Romans 5:12, Revelation 7:17, & Psalm 55:22

Into the Past

The Sermon on the Mount is Jesus's most famous sermon, and it begins with The Beatitudes—a series of blessings and promises. But these blessings each come in response to suffering. We may ask, why does God bless us after we have already suffered? Why doesn't He just remove the suffering to begin with?

We must keep in mind that sin (the original cause of suffering) entered the world through man, not through God. And so, in order to remove the symptom of sin (suffering), He must first remove the cause (sin). The only way to remove sin is to take it on Himself and pay the price for it (death). This He did when He faced death on the cross. But He went further than that. He also conquered death itself by coming back to life! He not only removes our sin, but allows us to come out on the other side of it, alive in Him! All we have to do is accept the payment He made in our place and reap the benefit of His offer of new life. We do this by loving Him, trusting Him, and following Him.

So instead of just wiping away the consequences of sin and leaving the sin (which makes no sense, anyway) and instead of abandoning us to our suffering, God Himself stepped into our mess, suffered alongside us—even to the point of being nailed to a cross, and broke our bonds to sin and suffering once and for all. Sin and suffering create desperate, heart-wrenching questions… Jesus Himself became the Answer.

Into the Story

Tuwr was amazed by Jesus's words when he heard the sermon Jesus gave. Given Tuwr's life as both a Jew and a merchant, what do you think struck him as unusual and insightful about The Beatitudes? How might he have seen himself through them? His family? His clients? How do they impact you?

Into the Present

No one longs for suffering or for occasions to mourn, and Jesus never says we should. But He does promise that those who follow Him will have their tears wiped away. Even during the suffering, He asks us to "cast our cares" on Him. What is His promise if we do this? Are you going through something difficult right now? How can you put in practice what we've learned today?

Chapter Seventeen

Read Luke 24 & I Corinthians 15:3-8, Deuteronomy 17:6, I Timothy 5:19

Into the Past
Luke 24 tells an amazing story which takes place on the Road to Emmaus. Jesus appeared to two of the disciples on the day of His resurrection. While it might be easy to question the authenticity of the accounts of two, Jesus also appeared to a great many others. What does Paul have to say about such appearances in I Corinthians? In that day and culture, two or three witnesses were required to decide anything of great importance. Today, a reporter tries to get at least three corroborating reports that verify the story he/she is reporting on. Eye-witness accounts are highly favored, but other newspaper articles or letter will also do. But, when it came to witnessing the resurrected Messiah, well over 500 people personally saw Jesus *after* He had been crucified and put in the tomb. At the same time! That's a LOT of eyewitness testimony! Note that Paul writes this during the lifetimes of many of the witnesses themselves, so it would have been impossible to spread such a story unless it was true or these people would surely have spoken out to contradict it.

Into the Story
Despite overwhelming evidence that Jesus was who He said He was, Darash still has his doubts. Do his reasons stem from what he knows about Jesus or from his feelings about something else? What is that other thing? What prejudices might Darash be struggling with?

Into the Present
What kinds of prejudices and doubts to people struggle with today when it comes to what they believe about Jesus Christ? What information should we rely on? What kinds of information should not be trusted? Have you taken the time to examine the evidence for yourself? Have you been tempted to adopt the doubts of others?

Chapter Eighteen

Read Proverbs 11:1; Exodus 23:1-9; Romans 3:20-24

Into the Past

The Jewish people benefited from some very specific laws and advice concerning the value of honesty—both in their personal lives among their family, friends, and neighbors, and in their business dealings. Some of these were adaptations from the Code of Hammurabi, an ancient Babylonian set of laws. Others were given directly by God to His people in the form of the Ten Commandments. Both contain excellent advice and principles for how one should treat others and deal justly. But, ultimately, though the law might motivate us to behave, it does not have the power to change our hearts. God is less interested in our outward actions than He is in the condition of our hearts and minds. Why? Because what we do flows directly from what we believe. If we believe correctly, we will behave correctly.

Into the Story

Nib'haz quoted King Solomon. What does this verse mean? Why would it be especially important for a Jewish merchant to know these words and honor them? What kind of witness would they be if they didn't?

Into the Present

How does Darash struggle in these chapters with the new knowledge he gains about his father? How might you struggle if you faced a similar circumstance? What advice would you give him? What advice from Exodus do you find interesting and helpful for your own life choices? Where does true justification come from? From obeying the law? Or, from faith in Jesus?

Chapter Nineteen

Read John 1:1-18, Acts 13:27, & Romans 11:11-24

Into the Past
Though the Romans brought about a peace the Jews hadn't experienced in hundreds of years (the *Pax Romara*) and gave the Jewish people a great deal of freedom of worship, many of the Jews still resented them. More than anything, the Jewish people desired freedom from the control of their idolatrous overlords. They looked forward to the promised Messiah, believing He would free them from Roman control, so when Jesus came, preaching love instead of military rebellion, they did not recognize Him as the Messiah they awaited. Instead, they nailed Him to a cross. But, through Christ's death and resurrection, He ushered in an era of peace that, eventually, gave the Jews precisely what they wanted. The Romans, in time, became converts and spread the message of Christ throughout the empire and beyond. They rid themselves of their idols in favor of new faith in Jesus. Ironically, the Jews still wait for a messiah.

Into the Story
Darash again feels anxiety at the thought of being around Gentiles, only this time it is with Romans. Do we sometimes let our own prejudices stand in the way of forming new friendships or making good decisions?

Into the Present
What did Paul have to say about non-Jews who accept Jesus as their savior? Who are the "branches that have been grafted in?" Do you see this as good news? How did the Roman world change once this invitation became known to them? Has Jesus fulfilled His mission of peace? What still needs to happen?

Chapter Twenty

Read Ruth 1:8-18; Proverbs 17:17, 27:6; Ecclesiastes 4:10

Into the Past

In the story of Ruth and Naomi, we see that Ruth so depends on her mother-in-law that she forsakes her own family, land, and gods in order to remain with Naomi. Despite great poverty, Ruth is determined to stay at her mother-in-law's side, not knowing what the future might hold. We know now that, because if Ruth's dedication and new-found reliance on God, that Naomi was rescued from poverty and Ruth—a Moabite woman—became one of Jesus's ancestors. This story (among many others) shows us that, even during a time when God was calling the Jews out from among the nations as His chosen people, He also always honored genuine faith—regardless of ethnic or economic background. In this case, it was Naomi's friendship with Ruth that became a catalyst for Ruth being greatly blessed and used by God.

Into the Story

Even as Darash gets to celebrate with his good friend, Revayah is struggling with her own friendship with Sapphira. What does Revayah complain about most vehemently? Do you think this is the real reason (or the only reason) she is upset with her friend? What else might be causing her to resent Sapphira?

Into the Present

Do you ever feel betrayed or disappointed by your friends? Have you ever been the one doing the disappointing? What is the best way to deal with situations like those? What does the Bible say about the value of having close friends? In what ways can you maintain and preserve your friendships?

Chapter Twenty-one

Read Deuteronomy 25:15, Proverbs 11:1, 2 Timothy 1:7-18

Into the Past
Honesty would be a particularly important issue for a young merchant in first century Jerusalem. As a Jew, Darash had heard many, many lessons from the "law and the prophets" (the Torah and the accompanying books of the Old Testament which we still have today) about the importance of dealing honestly, as representatives of the chosen people of God.

Into the Story
Darash struggles with knowing who is trustworthy and who is not. He asks, "Is it possible to live with someone your whole life but never really know them?" How would you answer Darash? How can you tell who to trust? What are some of the characteristics of a trustworthy person? Of an untrustworthy person? How can you become a person of integrity?

Into the Present
But Darash also struggled with honesty in character and in life. Often, people will let us down, but there is One who will not. In one of the passages above, Paul writes to Timothy speaking of this Person. Who is He? Why does Paul believe in Him? What circumstances does Paul find himself in? Has his suffering affected his faith in Jesus Christ? If so, how? What lessons might learn from his example?

Chapter Twenty-two

Read John 14:1-14; I Corinthians 15:12-22, 51-58; Romans 8:13-17

Into the Past

Before Jesus came, the Jews had little hope of an afterlife. The Sadducees, in fact, built an entire sect on the belief that no such thing could be possible. For them, the only existence is this existence. But, though indications of God's eternal plan does exist in Old Testament Scripture, Jesus shed new light on that plan. No longer do we have to doubt or wonder about what happens after we die. For those who trust in Jesus, death is just a doorway into a place where sin and disease and decay can no longer touch us. We'll be given new bodies and the whole universe to explore! And all this is possible because, when Jesus rose from the dead, He conquered it once and for all, proving He was who He said He was. So, by that same power, He can raise us up as well. But, remember, this promise is only for those who trust in Him and accept Him as their Savior and Lord.

Into the Story

Darash really struggles with fear in this chapter (and for good reason!) Some of his fear stems from his trauma over losing his father. Later, it stems from what is happening in that moment. At one point, he almost loses hope… but then what does he do?

Into the Present

What things frighten you the most? When we talk about our deepest fears, do they typically center on spiders or heights? Or, is it usually something much more traumatic—like losing a loved one, experiencing a violent attack, or being deeply wounded by someone who is supposed to love and protect us? What about death? Are you afraid of dying? How do you deal with that fear? What does the Bible have to say about fear? About death? What confidence does Jesus offer us in the face of our fears—even death itself?

Chapter Twenty-three

Read John 3:16-21; 16:20-33

Into the Past
Due to the Roman occupation of Judea, Jerusalem operated under rather complicated political, legal, and religious systems. In essence, two very different systems were trying to work together. Sometimes it worked surprisingly well. Other times, not so much. And, when things got complicated, Rome's patience simply wore out and they swooped in and smacked everybody back into line (their line, of course). Because the Jews accepted Roman rule without much of a struggle, they enjoyed a great many freedoms. For example, not only did Rome allow them to choose which god(s) to worship (they chose YHWH, of course), but they allowed the Jews to pay their yearly Temple tax to their own temple instead of to the pagan religious temples of the empire.

Of course, the Jews' freedoms had their limits. They were not allowed to exercise capital punishment, for example. That didn't always keep them from picking up rocks to stone people they thought guilty of adultery or blasphemy, but those killings would not have been legal. The descriptions of Jesus's trial and execution in the gospels provide a fascinating and accurate picture of the legal intricacies of that time and place. They also illustrate the authenticity and reliability of the gospel accounts.

Into the Story
Now that you know the identity of the killer, what were his/her motivations? Did this person have a relationship with God or was this person simply religious? What is the difference? Examine your own life. Where would you fall?

Into the Present
Darash, after reflecting on the evil that nearly cost him his life, thinks, "Life is not supposed to be this way." Have you ever felt like that? What kinds of experiences might cause you or someone else to feel this kind of discouragement? Where can you find hope when the world around you grows dark? What promise does Jesus offer to those who are suffering now but who have put their hope and faith in Him?

Chapter Twenty four

Read Acts 2; Jeremiah 31:31; Isaiah 59:20-21

<u>Into the Past</u>
When this book opens, approximately eight months have passed since the resurrection of Jesus Christ. The giving of the Holy Spirit at Pentecost has already happened, giving birth to the Church (the fellowship of those who have put their faith in Jesus). The Holy Spirit is God who indwells those who have put their faith in Jesus Christ. That doesn't mean that we become gods. Not at all! But it does mean we have access to Him on an individual level no matter where we are or who we're with. It's a deepening of the relationship between mankind and God to a new level of intimacy. Where once we had the law, we now have grace through Jesus Christ.

Interestingly, God chose to give His Holy Spirit on a day already pregnant with meaning. It was the Feast of Weeks or, simply "Weeks" (*Shavuot*, in Hebrew). Originally, it was a festival celebrating God's harvest. Only now, in fulfillment of Jeremiah and Isaiah's prophesies, instead of harvesting grain, God was harvesting souls. On this day, He created a new covenant with His people and all who would recognize Jesus Christ as—not only the Jewish Messiah—but as the Savior of the world.

<u>Into the Story</u>
What strikes Darash about how the Christian meeting differed from that of a typical synagogue gathering?

<u>Into the Present</u>
Have you ever been to a party or a gathering where hardly anyone knew anybody else and then the booze started flowing and, after about fifteen minutes, people started to relax and start talking to one another? Today, we use alcohol to break down our inhibitions and social barriers. We use it to help people loosen up enough to make new friends. But, within a body of healthy Christian believers, the Holy Spirit does this for us. We don't need wine or beer to break down our social barriers—they're already down! We have the unifying bond of the Holy Spirit to remind us who we are in Christ (His deeply loved child), and teach us who everyone else is (also His deeply loved children.) Walking in, we already know we have some very important things in common—forgiveness,

love, understanding, and an unending source of strength and courage. What better reason to get together and celebrate? And what else could possibly matter?

.

Glossary

סֶ לָ ה	Hebrew word "selah," meaning "rest" or "pause" and often used during poetic verse or musical lyrics.
Abba	The transliterated Hebrew word for "father" or "dad."
Agora	The Greek term for market.
Adonai	The Hebrew word for "Lord."
As	A large, bronze or copper coin worth about 1/16 of a denarius.
Ben	This means "son of" in Hebrew. So, "Darash ben Tuwr" means "Darash, son of Tuwr."
Bethany	A small town just east of Jerusalem near the River Jordan. This is where Jesus raised Lazarus from the dead, and it was the home of Mary and Martha.
Bitumen	A natural, black, tar-like substance used in construction as a kind of cement and as a means of water-proofing.
Challot	Challah bread is a kind of braided loaf. "Challot" is the plural form.
Days of the Week	Sunday: yom rishon, the first day. Monday: yom shayni, the second day. Tuesday: yom shli'shi, the third day. Wednesday: yom revi'i, the fourth day. Thursday: yom khah'mi'shi, the fifth day. Friday: yom ha'shi'shi, the sixth day. Saturday: Shabbat, the seventh day.

Denarius	A small silver coin worth about one day's wage for an unskilled laborer or common soldier. "Denarii" is the plural form.
El	"God" in Hebrew.
El Roi	God who sees me.
Elohim	"Elohim" is plural for "El" (or possibly "Eloah"). However, it does not mean "gods," but rather incorporates within it the concept of a triune God—a God consisting of three persons, God the Father, God the Son, and God the Holy Spirit.
Eloheinu	Same as "Elohim" above, except it means "our God."
Emmaus	A town located approximately 7 miles northwest of Jerusalem.
Ephah	One tenth of a homer ($^1/_3$ – ¾ of a bushel or 12-26 liters). The ephah refers to a container which would hold an ephah of produce, such as oil, wheat, flour, etc.
Essene	A Jewish religious sect. They valued an ascetic lifestyle (rejecting all forms of indulgence and practicing strict self-discipline) and lived in organized groups in which they shared all things.
Furlong	One furlong measures 220 yards. The walk Darash and Tsarah took to and from the tower would have been about a mile and a half. Roman soldiers liked to rough up the public when they thought they could get away with it. However, a couple of children would likely have been safer as they offered neither an attractive target (in their unlikeliness to be carrying any money) nor a threat.

Gera — A unit of weight equaling approximately .022 of an ounce.

Gophna — A city approximately 14 miles north of Jerusalem.

Halil — A flute-like instrument.

Hatazotzrot — A variety of trumpet.

Hebron — A city about 18 ½ miles south of Jerusalem, nestled among the Judean Mountains. It was where Abraham settled when he first came to the land of the Canaanites.

Homer — One donkey load and the most common capacity measurement. It equals approximately 3.8 to 7.5 bushels.

Imah — The transliterated Hebrew word for "mom" or "mommy."

Jerusalem — "Yerusháyim" in Hebrew, this city is the capital of Judah and the original site of King Solomon's Temple. It is located on a plateau between the Mediterranean and the Dead Sea.

Leben — A yogurt-like dairy product.

Lepton — A small Greek coin which is the same as the Roman mite. Worth half a prutah. It was the smallest denomination minted by the Hasmonean and Herodian dynasties.

Lydda — A town approximately 15 miles northwest of Jerusalem.

Mishnah — The oral law—a collection of strict, highly legalistic moral teachings, imperatives, and interpretations of Scripture followed and enforced by the Pharisees.

Mitre
A turban-like headdress worn by Jewish priests.

Pharisee
A member of an ancient Jewish religious sect. They observed strict, traditional and written laws, such as those of the Mishnah, and felt it their duty to compel others to live according to highly legalistic requirements. They controlled the synagogues and everyday Jewish life.

Praetorian Guard
Members of the Roman emperor's contingent of bodyguards.

Prutah
A prutah (plural: prutot) is a small, Jewish, copper coin worth about 2 lepta. A loaf of bread was worth about ten prutot.

Quinquessis
A Roman coin worth approximately half a denarius.

Sadducee
A member of an ancient Jewish religious sect. They denied the resurrection of the dead and the existence of angels, demons, or spirits. They also rejected the oral teachings and traditions, believing the written law alone. They controlled the Temple and official religious ceremonies.

Seah
One third of an ephah. One seah of flour might make one bread cake, or one meal.

Shabbat
The Sabbath, the seventh day of the week and the traditional day of rest for the Jews. It begins at sundown on Friday and ends at sundown on Saturday.

Shuk
The Hebrew term for market.

Shekel
A silver or gold coin worth 3 denarii. There was

also a half-shekel coin worth 1.5 denarii. It is also a unit of weight equaling approximately .4 of an ounce.

Sestertius
(Plural: sestertii) A small silver coin issued (rarely) by the Roman Empire worth one quarter of a denarius.

Synagogue
The building where Jewish people met for religious worship and instruction.

Tallit
Either a small undergarment of purplish blue or a large prayer shawl that Jewish men wore over their head and shoulders, particularly as they prayed.

Torah
The first five books of the Bible: Genesis, Exodus, Leviticus, Numbers, and Deuteronomy.

Tyre
An ancient Phoenician city on the banks of the Mediterranean Sea. It was famous for its wealth and commerce as well as its idolatry, and it was the hometown of notorious Queen Jezebel.

Yeshua
"Jesus" in Hebrew.

Yom
"Day" in Hebrew.

Research Bibliography

Adkins, Lesley and Roy A. Adkins. (1994) *Handbook to Life in Ancient Rome*. New York, NY: Facts on File, Inc.

Alexander, Pat, John W. Drane, David Field, and Alan Millard (Eds.). (1987) *The Lion Encyclopedia of the Bible*. Batavia, IL: Lion Publishing.

Anderson, Rebecca J. (1994) "The Sabbath in Ancient and Modern Practice." Retrieved May 2014 from: http://www.rj-anderson.com/docs/sabbath.html

Ariès, Philippe and Georges Duby. (1987) *A History of Private Life*: *From Pagan Rome to Byzantium*. Cambridge, MA: The Belknap Press of Harvard University.

Ayayo, Karelynne, et. al. (2005) *The Archaeological Study Bible: An Illustrated Walk Through Biblical History and Culture, (New International Version)*. Grand Rapids, MI: Zondervan Publishing House.

Baker, Warren, David Kemp, and Tim Rake (Eds.). (1994) *The Complete Word Study Old Testament*. Chattanooga, TN: AMG Publishers.

Backhouse, Robert. (1996) *The Kregel Pictorial Guide to the Temple*. Grand Rapids, MI: Kregel Publications.

Beaumont, Mike. (2006) *Holman Illustrated Guide to the Bible*. Nashville, TN: B & H Publishing Group.

ben Avraham, Yehoshua. (2003) "Hebrew Day and Month Names." YashaNet. Retrieved May 2014 from: http://www.yashanet.com/library/hebrew-days-and-months.html

Berlin, Adele and Marc Zvi Brettler (Eds.). (2004) *The Jewish Study Bible* (Tanakh Translation). New York, NY: Oxford University Press.

BibleHistory.Com. "What did Jesus think when he saw this stone?" Retrieved May 2014 from: http://www.bible-history.com/archaeology/israel/temple-warning.html

Bouquet, A.C. (1954) *Everyday Life in Bible Times*. London: B.T. Batsford Ltd.

Bright, John. (1981) *A History of Israel (3rd ed.)*. Philadelphia, PA: Westminster Press.

Bruce, F.F. (Ed.). (1979) *The International Bible Commentary (Revised Ed.)*. Grand Rapids, MI: Zondervan Publishing House.

Carcopino, Jérôme. (2003) *Daily Life in Ancient Rome (2nd ed.)*. New Haven: Yale University Press.

Chinuch, Merkos L'inyonei (Pub.). (2008) Translation of the Weekday Amidah. *Chabad.org*. From Siddur Tehillat Hashem. Brooklyn, NY: Kehot Publication Society. Retrieved from http://www.chabad.org/library/article_cdo/aid/867674/jewish/Translation.htm

Douglas, J.D. and Merril C. Tenney. (1987) *The New International Dictionary of the Bible*. Grand Rapids, MI: Zondervan Publishing House.

Dowley, Tim. (1999) *The Kregel Pictorial Guide to Everyday Life in Bible Times*. Grand Rapids, MI: Kregel Publications.

Dummelow, J.R. (Ed.). (1970) *The One Volume Bible Commentary*. New York, NY: The Macmillan Company.

Elwell, Walter A. (Ed.). (1989) *Baker Encyclopedia of the Bible* (Vols. 1-2). Grand Rapids, MI: Baker Book House.

Frank, Harry Thomas (Ed.). (2002) *Atlas of the Bible Lands*. Union, NJ: Hammond Incorporated.

Freedman, David Noel (Ed.). (2000) *Eerdman's Dictionary of the Bible*. Grand Rapids, MI: Wm. B. Eerdman's Publishing Co.

Grosvenor, Gilbert, et. al. (1961) *Everyday Life in Ancient Times*. Washington, D.C.: National Geographic Society.

Grosvenor, Giblert, et. al. (1967) *Everyday Life in Bible Times*. Washington, D.C.: National Geographic Society.

Hamilton, Adam. (2009) *24 Hours That Changed the World*. Nashville, TN: Abington Press.

Harrison, Everett F. and Charles R. Pfeiffer. (1968) *The Wycliffe Bible Commentary*. Nashville, TN: The Southwestern Company.

Hart, David Bentley.(2007) *The Story of Christianity*. London: Quercus.

Henry, Mathew. (1964) *Matthew Henry's Commentary on the Whole Bible in One Volume*. Grand Rapids, MI: Zondervan Publishing House.

Howard, Kevin and Marvin Rosenthal. (1997) *The Feasts of the Lord: God's Prophetic Calendar from Calvary to the Kingdom*. Nashville, TN: Thomas Nelson, Inc.

Isserlin, B.S.J. (2001) *The Israelites*. Minneapolis, MN: Fortress Press.

Jackson, J.B. (1957) *A Dictionary of Scripture Proper Names (3rd ed.)*. Neptune, NJ: Loizeaux Brothers.

Jeffers, James S. (1999) *The Greco-Roman World of the New Testament Era: Exploring the Background of Early Christianity*. Downers Grove, IL: InterVarsity Press.

Liles, John. (2014) The Life of Jesus. *The Timeline of the Bible*. Tarzana, CA: Bible Timeline. Retrieved from http://www.bibletimeline.org/webdocs/lifeofjesus.cfm

Lynch, Joseph H. (2010) *Early Christianity: A Brief History*. New York, NY: Oxford University Press.

Packer, J.I. and M.C. Tenney (Ed.). (1980) *Illustrated Manners and Customs of the Bible*. Nashville, TN: Thomas Nelson Publishers.

Rich, Tracey R. (2007) "Shabbat Evening Home Ritual." Judaism 101. Retrieved May 2014 from http://www.jewfaq.org/prayer/shabbat.htm.

Telushkin, Joseph. (2001) *Jewish Literacy: The Most Important Things to Know About the Jewish Religion, Its People, and Its History*. New York, NY: William Morrow and Company, Inc.

Vamosh, Miriam Feinberg. (2004) *Food at the Time of the Bible: From Adam's Apple to the Last Supper*. Nashville, TN: Abingdon Press.

Vamosh, Miriam Feinberg. (2007) *Daily Life at the Time of Jesus*. Herzlia, Israel: Phalpot Ltd.

Viner, J. (Host). (2007). *Lost Treasures of the Ancient World: Jerusalem*. [History Documentary]. United States: Kultur Video. Retrieved April 2014 from: https://www.youtube.com/watch?v=oBR42_UEV5g

Vos, Howard F. (1999) *New Illustrated Bible Manners and Customs*. Nashville, TN: Thomas Nelson Publishers.

Walvoord, John F. and Roy B. Zuck (Eds.). (1984) *The Bible Knowledge Commentary: An Exposition of the Scriptures by Dallas Seminary Faculty (New Testament Ed.)*. Wheaton, IL: Victor Books.

Walvoord, John F. and Roy B. Zuck (Eds.). (1984) *The Bible Knowledge Commentary: An Exposition of the Scriptures by Dallas Seminary Faculty, (Old Testament Ed.)*. Wheaton, IL: Victor Books.

Whiston, Willaim (Trans.). (1987) *The Works of Josephus: Complete and Unabridged (New Updated Ed.)*. Peabody, MA: Hendrickson Publishers, Inc.

Wood, Leon J. (1986) *A Survey of Israel's History (Revised and Enlarged Ed.)*. Grand Rapids, MI: Zondervan Publishing House.

Wright, G. Ernest (Ed.). (1974) *Great People of the Bible and How They Lived*. Pleasantville, NY: The Reader's Digest Association, Inc.

Wright, Paul H. (2002) *Atlas of Bible Lands*. Nashville, TN: Holman Bible Publishers.

Zodhiates, Spiros (Ed.). (1991) *The Complete WordStudy New Testament*. Chattanooga, TN: AMG Publishers.

Other Resources:
Interactive Virtual Tour at the Model of Jerusalem in the Late Second Temple Period, The Israel Museum Jerusalem, http://www.imj.org.il/panavision/model_pre_3eng.html

Holy Land Model of Ancient Jerusalem (66 CE) Holyland Corporation http://www.holylandnetwork.com/temple/model.htm

Wikimedia Commons. Map of First Century Jerusalem. Adaptation of File: Meyers b9 s0200.jpg Retrieved Sept. 2014 from www.wikimedia.org

Wikimedia Commons. Map of First Century Israel. First Century Palestine.gif. Retrieved Sept. 2014 from www.wikimedia.org

More From:

The Dramatic Pen Press

@TDPPress
www.TheDramaticPen.com
Facebook.com/TheDramaticPen

The Holy Land Mysteries Series

Darash's adventures continue with…
Book II: The Brazen Altar

A four-year-old boy disappears when bandits attack a family traveling from Samaria to Jerusalem. Magistrate Quintus Arrius enlists a clever but unlikely helper: a Jewish merchant boy named Darash. When Darash learns of a revival of the ancient cult of Molech, he fears the worst. This notorious cult frequently demands the lives of children as human sacrifices. As sole supporter of his family, Darash has troubles of his own—a demanding mother, a younger sister, and a new servant girl with a past as painful as her midnight cries. Still, the youth finds himself drawn into a race to find the missing child, terrified of what he might discover.

The Scrolls of the Nevi'im Series

The prophets of the Old Testament come alive with…

Book I: Habakkuk's Plea: A Prophet of Elohim

Book II: Habakkuk's Plea: Evil Persists

Book III: Habakkuk's Plea: Elohim Answers

**Interactive Mystery Party Games
for Teens and Adults
S. E. Thomas**

**Who Invited the Stiff to Dinner?
Murder at Surly Gates
Accuracy
Let Them Eat Cake**

A Reason To Celebrate
A Full-Length Christmas Production
S. E. Thomas

For most, Christmas is a time filled with joy. But for many, Christmas can be a difficult season. But let us consider a moment what Scripture tells us of the first Christmas. What really happened? For the first time, God Himself—the Creator of the Universe, the King of Kings, the Everlasting Father—stepped into our world! He stepped in—not to enjoy the wealth or the beauty or the joys—but to experience our suffering, our longings, and our sorrows. From the moment of His birth, He experienced far from ideal circumstances. Yet, we remember His words, "In this world you will have trouble. But take heart! I have overcome the world."

Acting Out Loud
Christian Skits for All Occasions
S. E. Thomas

Whether you are a pastor looking for a skit to help drive home your message, a ministry leader desiring a dramatic reading to speak God's love at a retreat or conference, or a youth group leader hoping to spice up a youth meeting, we have the material you're looking for! Find over thirty skits, short plays, and dramatic readings that cover the following areas: Biblical Tales, Christian Living, Evangelism, Special Events, Holidays.

Lazy Dog
carol fields brown

"The quick brown fox jumps over the lazy dog." This sentence contains every letter of the English alphabet at least one time. The Lazy Dog and the Fox start children on an animal adventure. They can write the sentences, color the pictures, and make up their own sentences. This coloring book provides an opportunity for young learners to explore the intricacies of the English language, practice their handwriting, and explore a variety of animal behaviors in a fun and creative way. Full-color illustrations, matching coloring pages, and lines for handwriting practice are included.

Sourdough Secrets... Revealed!
From Making the Starter to Sourdough Success!
Ray Templeton

Step-by-step instructions that will allow you to make your own starter, make your first loaf, and even learn to make sourdough bread in your bread machine.

Is My Faith My Own?
A Resource for Christian Young People
Leaving Home for the First Time
S. E. Thomas

Everything was going along fine... then you got out on your own and realized it's your responsibility to get the rest of your life right. From here on out, if you're going to follow God, you're going to be doing it on your own. You can no longer coast by on your parents' faith, your pastor's understanding, or your youth leader's morals. Now it's up to you. And you have some questions: Is my faith real? Is it growing? Is it my own?

Complex Simplicity:
How Psychology Suggests Atheists are Wrong about Christianity
Dr. Lucian Gideon Conway III

Lucian Gideon Conway III

In *Complex Simplicity*, prominent psychology researcher Dr. Lucian Gideon Conway III addresses the modern atheist attack on the psychological effectiveness of the Christian religion. As an expert in the science of cognitive complexity, Dr. Conway uses scientific research and personal narratives to argue that Christianity is an effective guide for reconciling the many complexities built into the human psyche. Directly contradicting what many modern atheists believe, he shows that, in approaching human psychology from a complex perspective, Christianity meets our complex needs with complex solutions. To Christian believers, he offers psychological reasons to believe their faith yields positive benefits. To skeptics, he offers a challenge to the growing cultural belief that Christianity is both simple-minded and ineffective. *Complex Simplicity* is important reading for anyone curious about the intersection of Christian teaching and human psychology.

Daily Life in Bible Times
Small Group Study
S. E. Thomas
Workbook & Leader Guide Editions

S. E. Thomas

Come face to face with the people you read about in Scripture by exploring what their daily lives would have looked like. Learn how a young man selected and courted his bride, what occupations they had and how they trained for them, how infants were cared for, and how the ancients mourned and buried their dead. We will also look at the economic and political climate, learn about crime and punishment, and even find out what they ate and how they dressed. And as you come to know the culture of Jesus Christ, you will see Him more clearly, as well. ***This is a 10-week Bible study.***

Please Visit Us Again!

Find fiction and non-fiction books, study guides, plays, skits, mystery party games, fundraising resources, free downloadable templates, writers' resources, and much more at:

www.TheDramaticPen.com

Write To Bless The World